1st April 1949.

A PASSAGE PERILOUS

A PASSAGE PERILOUS

By

NAOMI JACOB

" A Passage perillus makyth
a Port pleasant."

*(Words inscribed on a
harbour wall on Lake Como.)*

THE BOOK CLUB
121 CHARING CROSS ROAD,
LONDON, W.C.2

To

EVE ATCHESON

to remind her of Italy.
With my love and gratitude,
MICKIE.

Dec. 1947.

FASANO,
LAGO DI GARDA.

MADE AND PRINTED IN GREAT BRITAIN BY
MORRISON AND GIBB LTD., LONDON AND EDINBURGH

PROLOGUE

I

OLIVER HALLAM waved his hand at his wife, as Kitty, reaching the little iron gate which led into the meadow with the path running towards the village and the church, turned to wave back to him.

As he heard the distant clang of the gate closing, he lay back in his deck-chair, frowning suddenly.

He thought, ' She's gone; may heaven go with her—that's a quotation, and I'm not sure that I've got it right. In her case, I'd say, " She's gone and heaven goes with her." Gosh, this damned war's going to be hard on women like Kitty. Cliff ready to go, Barbara will go off into something or other, and Clive will never rest until he follows his brother. And me—I shall have to get down to something, forty-four's too young to allow you just to sit back and criticize other blokes' work, and point out their mistakes. That's what we shall do. We did it last time and we shall do it again. Human nature doesn't change much.'

Last time ! It didn't seem to be twenty-one years since the last show ended. We'd all made a pretty average hash of things somehow. This time ? He sat upright in his chair. Why did people still use these awful chairs ? Nothing could be less comfortable, and yet they were stored away in the winter, brought out every summer, and people pretended that they were natural adjuncts to sitting in gardens or watching tennis.

Last time—Oliver's thin, rather craggy face softened a little. He could remember it all so clearly. Going overseas, to Italy, to ' stiffen the Italians ' they had been told. They had joined in the battle which was fought between the Brenta and the Adige. 1916. The worst of the show had been over or as good as over. But that winter of 1916. He shivered suddenly, although his chair was standing in the midst of a bright patch of sunlight.

The miles and miles of snow, Mount Crostis, the long stretch of snow-covered valley looking down from the Freikofel, the Dolomites with their queer jagged peaks, and the long lines of Alpini trudging along, stumbling and falling, scrambling to their feet again, and going on. Poor devils ! They'd been short of pretty well everything. Bad boots, cheap uniforms, food which never seemed to arrive at the proper time, and when it came there was always a little less than there ought to have been. The men were all right. Queer fellows, who'd make their way into the most impossible places, and laugh at the danger ; then, because they got a stomach-ache, they'd hang about like sick dogs, and grow moody and hopeless. They'd got guts all right, though, particularly the Alpini. Danger meant nothing to them so long as they

5

were doing something, getting somewhere. It was inactivity that
killed them, that reduced them to weak, apprehensive creatures.

The officers ! Oliver's rather long sensitive nose wrinkled.
How he'd hated the majority of them. Living behind the lines—
oh, well behind the lines, preferably in hotels in Verona and Padua.
He'd even known them to drive up to the lines in taxi-cabs ! He
remembered how many of them turned up unshaved, with dirty,
wrinkled boots, obviously barely recovering from ' the night before '.
There had been exceptions, of course. That colonel-what-was-
his-name ?—they'd met at an observation post 3000 metres up in
the mountains. He'd looked as if he were just ready to go on
parade. The funny little Major Calloni who had been standing
muffled in a huge fur coat watching the unloading of munitions
over 2000 metres above sea level. He'd chatted to the men, made
them laugh. Oliver remembered how their faces had seemed to
split open when they laughed—mouths like great gashes in their
snow-burnt faces, showing rows of white teeth. Plenty of the
officers had been good fellows—Bellomi, Primo something or other
who played the mandolin, Grecco, Aristilo, and many more.

And best of them all young Antonio Chiot, whom he had met
on the Carso when they rounded up a crowd of Austrian prisoners.
On the whole the Austrians were fine upstanding fellows; most
of them looked sulky, and all of them tired to death. Many of
them seemed too old to be engaged in such hard fighting as that
through which they had come.

Chiot, who had always looked immaculate, very tall and slim,
with a figure which was almost too good, stood watching them.
He turned to Oliver, and said, speaking with scarcely a trace of
an accent, " Poor devils ! It's all a rather silly business, isn't it ? "

Oliver remembered how he had said in reply, " I say, your
English is pretty good."

Chiot answered, " It should be. I was at school in England for
three years." They had grown very attached to each other; Chiot
borrowed such books as Oliver could lend him, they discussed
them at length, and Oliver talked of England and the Thames, the
Broads, and the moors, while Chiot listened, smiling and saying
that one day he must visit England again.

When the King had come to visit the troops at Castelnuovo,
Chiot's father had been with him. A General no less ! Like his
King he was a small man, but while the King was thin and spare,
the General was rotund and paunchy.

Chiot had presented Oliver to his father, saying, " This is my
good friend, *papa*; his name is Hallam."

The General's eyes had almost disappeared in folds of flesh,
when he smiled and said, " Pleze w'affor 'ave you so deeficult
namez ? " then, " Gled to meet you. Nino, tak' 'eem to veesit
h'our 'ouse at Vicenza."

The General had passed on, trotting in the wake of his master
who walked with such surprising energy and swiftness. Nino had
laughed and said that his father was a gallant soldier and an
original.

Oliver had gone to Vicenza for his leave, and Nino had gone with him, though Nino's leave was only for forty-eight hours. The house was a tremendous place, dignified and beautifully built in the style of Palladio. The rooms were immense, hung with splendid silks and brocades, the parquet floors shone with the polish of years. Nino's mother, Contessa Chiot, was very tall, Oliver thought that she must have towered head and shoulders over her diminutive husband; she had masses of snow-white hair piled high above a face which was thin, very white, with immense dark eyes. She spoke very little, and Oliver never saw her smile.

It was obvious that she adored her son, her eyes followed him as he moved about the big rooms, she listened with silent and grave attention to every word he spoke. He called her always, ' Mama mia '. Sometimes when Nino sat near her on one of the wide sofas Oliver would see her hand slide along the cushions so that the tips of her fingers just touched those of her son. When Nino felt that light contact he would turn and smile at her, a smile of such affection and beauty that it seemed almost indecent to watch.

There was a sister of Nino's there, living in the palace with her mother. Her name was Yolanda. Like her brother she was tall and slim, her figure was beautiful, and her skin like a newly ripened peach. Oliver thought that if you could touch her cheek with your finger you would be able to rub off that delicate bloom.

She was to be married, Nino told Oliver, to a Duke. He was with the Army, elderly, distinguished, and—Nino shrugged his shoulders—' a man who has lived twenty-five hours in every day '. She would have a huge house beside the Brenta on the road from Venice to Padua, a palace in Rome, a villa at San Remo, and probably travel backwards and forwards to London. " They say that he might even be Ambassador. Oh, he is clever, brilliant, but dried up, desiccated, bloodless, and quite revoltingly bald."

In three days Oliver was in love with her. She was charming, her laughter entranced him, to see her move across one of the big rooms made him catch his breath. Her English was almost as good as her brother's; she had been educated, she told Oliver, at ' Bournem'ooth '.

They were seated in front of one of the huge log fires, the light was fading, the day had been dark and cold. Oliver glanced out of the window and shivered. Yolanda said, " You're cold ? "

" No, only thinking of the poor chaps out in the mountains."

" Never think of uncomfortable things when you are in comfortable surroundings, my friend," she advised.

" Is that your own rule of life ? "

" I never think of unpleasant things at all. Not "—she laughed —" unless they are pushed r-right under my nose."

He said, rather stiffly, " You must have a remarkably strong will."

" I have ! I can fight—almost all things, believe me."

Oliver stared at her, he felt that the whole scene was unreal, it was as if the spacious room were a stage, and he and she were acting, speaking lines written for them by the author. The whole house was like a theatre; outside was intense cold; in the mountains men were killing each other, suffering, dying; here were great fires, good meals, a small army of servants. It was unreal, fantastic. Here was he, Lieutenant Oliver Hallam, completely absorbed in a girl he had met only three days before, a girl who was young and lovely and who was to marry some old, dissipated Italian duke.

He said, abruptly, " The whole thing is incredible ! "

She showed no surprise, but turned her face towards him, saying, " I had thought so too, my dear."

Startled, he asked, " Thought—what, when ? I don't understand you."

She nodded. " Oh, but you do understand. I said to myself last night, after I went to my room, that the whole thing was impossible, a kind of waking dream. I said, ' Go to bed, Yolanda, in the morning it will have gone with your other dreams.' But in the morning—it was still there to torment me. Of course you understand, you are tormented too—Oliver."

" I don't know—I mean—it can't be true, you're making fun of me."

She shook her head. " No, my dear. It is true."

" It's so difficult to believe—and I want to believe it so very much."

She twisted round, and laid her hands on his shoulders. " Kiss me."

He had gone back to Monfalcone, taking with him memories of her beauty, her sweetness, and the times which they had spent together. The mountains seemed colder and more forbidding than ever by contrast. Oliver hated the snow, the patient plodding of the troops, the acute discomfort, and the general disorganization of transport and provisions for the men. Chiot came to him one morning, Oliver was billeted in a bombed house at Ronchi, next to the villa where the Italian patriot Oberdan had been arrested. Chiot came in smiling, well-groomed and shaved as usual. He said, " My friend, I have some news for you. You must not repeat it, for as yet it is not public property. You are to be sent back—to Vicenza."

" I am ! Back to Vicenza ! But why ? "

Chiot laughed gently. " My dear, what a good thing I came to prepare you ! Otherwise the expression on your face would have —let the cat out of the bag. It was the expression of a man who sees the heavens open ! Shall we say that I am a very bad brother ? If you like ! But I know that you wish to be—shall we say ?—in Vicenza, and a lady for whom I have a great affection wishes you to be there. So ! It is some work connected with transport of stores. It is felt that you have an excellent knowledge of organization—hence, in a few days . . ."

In three days Oliver was ready to leave for Vicenza. Chiot talked to him seriously and kindly the night before he left. They sat huddled over a small, sulky fire in the drab, cold room. The windows were covered with folds of sacking, the wind whistled miserably.

Chiot leaned forward, his hands clasped on his knees.

" Listen to me, Oliver," he said. " I understand everything. I know that my sister loves you. She is to marry Gradisco. I made my protest at the time, my mother was on my side. My mother is a saint. My father is a good soldier, but ambitious. Yolanda was flattered, dazzled at the prospect of being a duchessa. Now, she is wiser, and it is too late. Maybe that I am lacking in morals, maybe that I have no respect for this nasty old man. I don't know—and life is too full at the moment to worry. I only ask that you will not involve my family in any scandal. That is all. Otherwise, my good friend, take what happiness you can find. We may, many of us, not have many more opportunities for happiness. There may be only—extinction. Who knows ! "

Vicenza again, the snow and the white-clad troops left behind; a small flat, where an elderly woman waited on him, and his batman ' scrounged ' enough wood to keep the place warm and comfortable. Oliver had not realized how tired he was, how the monotonous snow-covered landscape had oppressed him, how the intense cold had sapped his vitality. For the first two days he longed only for sleep and warmth; not even his longing to see Yolanda could master those two desires. He managed to go down to the office, to report and meet his superior, a Major Buckley.

Buckley said, " Glad ter see yer. Gad, this place is a one-eyed hole. I say, yer look all in, Hallam. Had a bad time up there ? Look half frozen."

Oliver said, " Thank you, sir. I'm only a little tired. It's been rather heavy going. I shall be all right once I can get warm again."

" Gad, that's what yer want—warmth. Have a tot ? Do yer good. Here—I don't mind if I join yer ! That's better. Take a coupla days' rest. This damned outfit is in such an all-fired mess that a coupla days won't make much difference. I hope ter get off on a spot of leave. I've earned it. Not done much," he roared with laughing and smacked his Bedford-corded knees, " but, God, I've kept the flag flyin'."

Oliver returned to the flat, and again crouched by the fire, while the servant brought him hot clear soup with an egg broken into it. He drank it, it was surprisingly good. He told her so. She beamed at him, told him that it was ' *soupa pavese* ', and built up the fire so that it roared up the wide chimney.

The next morning Yolanda arrived. She came in, wrapped in furs, her eyes dancing. Oliver remembered that she seemed to bring a sense of additional warmth and comfort into the place.

He sprang to his feet, seized her hands and could only stammer out her name. He whispered it again and again, as if he could never hear the sound of it sufficiently often.

She pushed him gently back into his chair, saying, " My dear, sit down. Battista tells me that you are ill."

" Battista ? Who is that ? "

She laughed. " Innocent little soldier ! Do you think that all English officers have a *cordon bleu* to attend to them ? This is Battista, who has known me all my life. She was the cook of my aunt, Contessa Elcano. How do you imagine that all this was arranged ? They had given you a back attic—indeed, yes, an attic in the Piazza. A dreadful place. I have—very carefully—made arrangements. My dear, anything can be done, always provided that one has sufficient determination ! I have sufficient for a whole army. Only—you will not mind if I call and see dear Battista sometimes, she is so attached to me, such an old friend, so good to me when I was little."

" Then I have you to thank for—everything ? "

She pulled a small comical face at him. " Everything ? I should not say—everything. But some things, my Oliver."

He remembered the three months which followed. Remembered how the snows melted, how the yellow celandine began to show in the fields, how the birds began to chirp in the early mornings in the old plane trees, and how the grass in the little squares of the town grew brighter and more brilliantly green every day.

Whatever Battista knew or guessed she made no sign ; she accepted Yolanda's visits, cooked meals for her and for Oliver, meals which they ate together in the long, low-ceilinged room of the flat. Sometimes they heard the roar of aeroplanes overhead, and when Oliver begged Yolanda to come to some place of safety she shook her head.

" No, I shall stay here. It would be a very good solution if a bomb fell on us both together—now. I should not mind, so long as we both died together."

" But if we didn't die, if we were only maimed or desperately hurt ? "

She shrugged her shoulders, " We are going to be—desperately hurt whatever happens," she said calmly.

Again and again Oliver begged her to marry him, she always refused.

" I know nothing of your life in England ; who are you, what are you, where do you live, what kind of life ? I don't want to know. We have our life here now, we are snatching at moments because they will have to last us for the rest of our lives. I am an Italian woman, Oliver my dear, I don't believe that we—transplant very well. What do you do ? Your work, I mean ? "

" My father builds cars—the Hallam cars, and the Markholt. I'm in charge of the works—or I shall be when this is over here—near Shrewsbury."

" You're an engineer then ? And Shr-rowsborry—what a name that is ! I should never be able to ask for a ticket to my own home if I lived at—that place."

" You're treating it all as a joke. I'm serious. I love you, worship you, Yolanda. Marry me. I can keep you, give you all you want. . . ."

She laughed. " How do you know what I want ? "

" I'd make you happy, darling, I swear that I would."

" Make me happy ! Darling, no one can *make* anyone else happy. We can only make ourselves happy—and that rarely enough. No, here we have our own small world, a lovely world, holds only you and me. It won't last, because it's a dream world, and one day we shall have to wake. But while it lasts—oh, it is beautiful."

" And suppose," he said, his face sombre, " suppose—someone discovered—all about us. What then ? "

Yolanda tilted her chin. " I should deny it, and so, of course, would you. No one would question my word ! "

" And this marriage of yours ? You've no scruples about letting me be your lover ? "

He was astonished at the coldness of her voice when she answered.

" Surely that is an ill-bred remark ? " she said. " My marriage is my own affair, my scruples, morals and the rest they also ! I think that it may be that you, Oliver, have developed these—scruples. Well, that is as good an excuse as any other for telling me that—the play is over."

He had been frantic with remorse, he had begged her to forgive him, had assured her that never again would he make such a gross mistake as to ask such questions. He knelt before her, and slowly the coldness left her voice, her eyes met his—soft and kind. She touched his hair with the tips of her fingers.

" Ah, I frightened you, my Oliver. Well, you deserved to be frightened. It was a bad *gaffe* which you made. Listen—do not speculate, do not let us ask each other questions and indulge in probings. Let us say, ' Now, for to-day we are happy—for to-morrow, wait until it comes.' That is the only way to live life when the world is being turned upside down."

There had come a time when she seemed to Oliver to be absorbed, when she had very little time to come to the flat, and when their meetings were restricted and cut short. She explained that her aunt was staying with them, that various cousins were coming to pay visits, that now Spring was here she must visit dressmakers. Once she was away in Rome for five days, and Oliver wandered about the rather sad streets of Vicenza with their tall shabby palaces, their decorative statues, and their old courtyards, lonely and disconsolate.

She returned and his happiness returned with her. Never had she been so entrancing, so gay and so loving. She seemed to snatch by force every moment which it was possible to spend with him; when he had to drive into the country on his Army work she came with him. She took him to visit the farms of old servants of her family, she showed him beautiful places, and gave him stories regarding their history which were never sufficiently long or involved to weary him or lose his attention.

One evening, late in April, she lay on the wide divan with his arms round her. They were silent, content to be together; once she leaned towards him and kissed his cheek. He drew her closer to him. He whispered, " Yolanda, my dearest dear."

She answered, " Will you remember—all this, Oliver ? "

" What a foolish question ! "

" Because this is the last time I shall come here to you, my dear."

He did not speak, he felt as he used to feel in the snow among the mountains, as if not only his whole body but his blood were cold. Yet he had to lick his lips before he could speak, his mouth was so dry. " What do you mean ? " he asked hoarsely.

" Darling, that to-morrow I am leaving for Rome."

" Ah ! " he sighed with the sudden relief. " And you'll come back—when ? "

" I shan't come back. I may come back one day, but I shall not come back as Yolanda Chiot. I am going to be married, Oliver."

Even now, twenty years and more later, he instinctively closed his eyes, and made a movement with his head as if he tried to avoid something which threatened him. He had known that this would come, but he had lived, as Yolanda had advised him, from day to day. The days had stretched into weeks, and the fear and apprehension had receded into the background, had become dim and vague. Now, in that room in Vicenza, they were dragged forward again, and stood face to face with him, sinister, terrible, final.

She had been wonderfully tender, it seemed that with the announcement she had grown older, wiser, more protective. She had held his head in her hands, had talked softly, courageously.

Once when he clenched his hands, and beat them together, crying, " It's the end of everything, can't you understand ? " she had taken them and opened the closed fingers, saying, " My dear one—no. You've so much left in your life. This is only the ending of—the first act."

She left the flat when it was very late, when he fancied that the East was already growing lighter, promising a new day. He walked with her in silence to her home. The great house was dark, only he knew that in her bedroom her old maid, Assunta, would be sleeping in a chair, waiting—but never asking questions.

Yolanda turned to him. " My dear—— "

" Good night," he said, as if he had been bringing her home from a late dance. " Good night."

" Good morning," she smiled at him. She looked terribly tired, almost exhausted. " My dear, dear Oliver."

He walked home, flung himself down dressed on the divan, and fell into a heavy sleep. He woke when Battista brought in coffee and rolls. She only wished him " Good morning," but made no comment upon his having slept there in his clothes. He drank the coffee and pushed the rolls away as if the sight of them disgusted him.

Battista laid a small packet and a letter down on the table beside him.

" This came a few minutes ago, capitano."

He picked it up and held it in his hand. " Thank you."

" And your bath will be ready in twenty minutes, capitano."

Again mechanically he said, " Thank you."
Yolanda's letter was very short.

My dear, it has all been so wonderful. So many laughs, so many happy hours, so much fun. I do thank you, will you try to thank me—just a little ? If you would like to wear this—I shall be glad ; if not—well, I shan't know so I can't be hurt. I send you my love.

There was no signature ; in the small sealed packet lay a heavy old ring, engraved with a coat-of-arms and a crest. That they were not the arms and crest of the Chiots, Oliver knew, and as he looked at it, lying on his palm, he thought, ' I needn't worry, she's far too clever to send me anything that might be recognized.' Then realized that he was thinking of her in a detached kind of fashion. She was no longer someone who belonged to him and to whom he belonged, she was part of a tome that was finished and done with.

He went about his work ; he had always worked hard and now he felt that he must fill every moment of the day. Buckley said, " No need ter kill yerself, old man. Take it easy. You rush about like a scalded cat. Have a quick one, will yer ? Think I'll join yer. Ah, that's better ! "

Once Antonio came to see him. Oliver felt that he couldn't speak to him. He was stiff and constrained, ' shut in ' and abrupt. Chiot watched him, and after a time said, " I am afraid that I didn't give you good advice after all, my friend, eh ? "

Vaguely Oliver answered, " Oh, I don't know—these things happen."

" Sometimes things gather more strength than we believe possible. We think that we are the masters, then circumstances—what you call ' things ' turn and almost destroy us. Is that so ? "

Oliver shook his head as if he were trying to clear away a mist which had gathered, obscuring his vision. He said, " I don't know. I did love her terribly—terribly. It was a shock."

" You wish to hear news of her ? "

" No— please, no ! Only—she is married ? "

Chiot nodded, " She is married."

" One thing more," Oliver said, and held out the ring which Yolanda had sent him, " Do you recognize this ? "

The Italian said, " We spoke of this ring. It was given to you by your friend, Antonio Chiot, a comrade in the war."

Oliver said, " Yes, but——"

Chiot smiled, " Please remember, a present—a *ricordo* from Chiot."

Oliver applied for a posting back to the mountains ; three weeks later Chiot was killed near Lèmerle. Oliver came upon him suddenly at a casualty clearing station, he was barely alive. Oliver bent over him, and the Italian's eyes lit up.

He said in a high whisper, " Bad luck, eh ? Good-bye."

The eyes dimmed, he sighed profoundly, and the orderly made a movement of finality, as if to say, " It is over."

Less than a week later Oliver was wounded in a trench on the Asiago Railway; he was moved to hospital and after ten days' concentrated nursing was sent home to England.

II

He stirred in his chair, then rose and moved it into a patch of sunlight. The sun had left the place where he had been sitting, he felt chilled, wondered if he should not go indoors, then decided against doing so. His mind travelled back again through the years.

The long journey to England, a hospital near Cheltenham, very clean, well scrubbed, situated in an old country house, which now smelt of disinfectant.

He had been too utterly weary to concern himself much with his surroundings. Nurses and doctors came and went, food was given to him, he read and slept, and knew that his wound was healing, and didn't care. People were very kind, solicitous for his well-being—he wasn't interested. He heard that Italy was out of the war, and felt relieved that there would be no more struggling through snow and up incredible mountains for the Alpini. One morning in early June the doctor said, " I think that we might get you out for a little to-day into the sunlight."

Oliver said, " Oh, thanks, yes."

The doctor said quickly, " Don't you want to get out ? "

" Yes, of course, sir."

He was wheeled out on to a wide lawn, where great cedar trees spread wide fan-like branches. The air was pleasant. Oliver sought for a word. Not actually hot—pleasant and—tempered. That was it, tempered. A V.A.D. came bringing him a long drink. He could hear the ice chinking in the glass. She gave the glass a little twist so that it tinkled more loudly.

" Nice sound, isn't it ? " she asked. " Ice against a glass."

He nodded. " Yes, it is a pleasant sound. Thank you."

" Your first day out ? "

" Yes, my first day."

" You've got everything you want ? "

" Yes, thank you."

She nodded and smiled and walked away. He remembered how he had turned his head to watch her, just as he had turned his head to watch her half an hour ago as she went through the iron gate at the end of the garden.

BOOK ONE

CHAPTER I

I

KITTY BLAND had always believed that Marsh Hall was the nicest house in the world, a belief shared by her father, Hugh Bland, to whom it belonged. Mrs. Bland, who had been born and brought up in Nottingham, listened patiently to their eulogies concerning Marsh Hall and, when they turned to her for confirmation, smiled and said, " It's a dear old house, I'm very fond of it."

The kindly tolerance of that statement always vaguely irritated both her husband and her daughter, but because they loved her exceedingly they had schooled themselves to say nothing.

Marsh Hall was a ' dear old house ', one of those small, modest, English manor-houses, making no pretensions to being unique, or possessing characteristics of great interest; a solid, well-built place, filled with a certain dignity and radiating security and stability.

There are hundreds of them scattered up and down England, each with its own small particularity . . . a panelled room, a stretch of wall covered with a faded fresco, a queer old column in the cellar ' we always think that there must have been a chapel here, you know', or even a ' priests hole '—loved and exhibited with pride by the owners. In dozens of such houses, elderly men collect dusty records, neatly docketed and kept in tin boxes; dozens of gently proud wives tell their friends, " My husband is almost ready to begin his history of the house. He has been collecting material for many years. It will be most interesting." The records, the old documents and the like remain in their carefully locked boxes, and it is rarely that the master of the house ever begins to write his book—and if it were written, who would be sufficiently interested to wish to read it ?

Marsh Hall was situated near Northallerton ; it was two-storied, with jutting dormer windows set into a slate roof. " Originally," Hugh Bland told visitors, " the roof was tiled, I have ample proof of that. The slating was done in my grandfather's time. Ugly possibly, but weathertight and lasting. I should have liked to replace the slates with stone—ah, that's the stuff ! Our good, grey stone ! But—times change——" He never added that to re-roof a house like Marsh Hall cost money, and that although he made a comfortable living, there had never been sufficient money for the gratification of what, he told himself, were ' after all only my whims and fancies'.

The rooms were rather narrow, low and dignified, the kitchens were immense, cool in summer and retaining the warmth of the big fires in winter. There had been a considerable amount of land attached, for Hugh's father had been a farmer, though never particularly successful. Hugh had chosen to become a solicitor and his father had consented. The land was rented to Mallison at Burton's End, George Tillett of Low Farm, Hugh retaining only sufficient grazing for a cow and a couple of horses. To Kitty Bland, when as a small girl she stood at the open window of her bedroom and looked out over the garden and the pasture, it seemed that few things could be more delightful than the sight of ' Bruce ' and ' Wallace ' grazing, while ' Sunflower ' cropped busily near them, and the white Leghorn picked and pecked about, looking like pieces of incredibly white paper against the green grass.

She loved the house, and in only a slighter degree loved her father's office in Northallerton, situated as it was in a quiet street, a flat-fronted brick house with a brightly polished plate at the side of the front door, which boasted one of the finest fanlights in the town. The polishing of the plate was the first duty every morning of young Tom Willis; it bore the words Callis, Callis and Bowen. The last name had been obliterated and the name ' Bland ' added. Kitty felt that the two wide black lines drawn through the name of Bowen indicated that the firm was in perpetual and respectful mourning for Mr. Bowen.

She asked old Samuel Baker, her father's clerk, " Who were Callis and Callis, Mr. Baker ? "

Baker took off his glasses and rubbed them on a large white handkerchief, as if by doing so he could see more clearly into the past, before he answered.

" Mr. Callis the elder and his son Mr. Harry Callis the younger," he said impressively. " The elder Mr. Callis was highly respected, it was said that he knew all the secrets of the aristocracy in the district. A trust, as you might say, which reposed in him, a sign of the esteem and regard in which he was held. A very fine gentleman, the elder Mr. Callis."

" Had they all many secrets, Mr. Baker ? "

" That, my dear, I couldn't say, Mr. Callis was as silent as the tomb, as the saying goes. What was confided to his ears in that office where your good father now sits never issued forth from those doors."

" And Mr. Harry, Mr. Baker ? "

" Ah ! Mr. Harry fell serving his country in a most noble manner at Spion Kop. A very fine and splendid young gentleman. Perhaps not quite possessing—what shall I say ?—the strength of character of his esteemed father, but liked by all—by all. His death broke his father's heart, my dear. That was when he took Mr. Bowen into partnership. A very grave error, if I dare say so, very grave. Mr. Bowen—he is no longer alive and so I can speak plainly—was never a gentleman ! "

Kitty, seated on a high stool swinging her long slim legs, would murmur, " Oh dear—that was dreadful, wasn't it ? "

" A catastrophe, my dear. However ' all things work together for good for them that love God', and when Mr. Callis realized that Mr. Bowen was not the type of partner for which he had hoped, the Almighty in His Mercy sent your good father——"

" Was he a gentleman, Mr. Baker ? "

" Your father, my dear, is incapable of being anything but a gentleman in thought, deed, or word. Your father had been working, studying, taking his examinations with Mr. Horace Beamarsh at Darlington. In the year 1896 your grandfather died and your father came to live at Marsh Hall. That was *early* in 1896. In the January of 1897 your father entered into partnership with Mr. Callis, and after the death of Mr. Harry he became like a son to him. But he refused to have the plate changed until 1905. Very tactful, my dear."

" And I was born in 1897 ! It was 1897, wasn't it ? "

Baker beamed at her. " Indeed it was, ten years ago. A bright morning I remember, and your good father coming in about midday, looking as if he was King of Creation. He said, ' Baker, a lovely little girl ! ' And—a lovely little girl she has remained, my dear ! "

All of which was not only interesting but thrilling to Kitty Bland, and the treat which she always asked for on Friday nights was to know if she might go down to the office and talk to Mr. Baker. Should Mr. Baker prove to be busy when she arrived and her father occupied with a client, she sat and talked to ' young Mr. Clarke ' or even to Tom Willis the office boy.

' Young Mr. Clarke ' wasn't really so very young, he must have been thirty-five at that time, but he had entered the firm when he was really young, and the description had stuck. Not very clever, but hard working and reliable, pleasant and well-spoken. Tom Willis was a shock-headed lad of sixteen, like an overgrown puppy, for ever falling over the legs of stools, upsetting the ink and leaving the stopper out of the tin of brass polish which was used for cleaning the plate every morning.

Kitty found life vastly interesting and entertaining. She liked going to school in Northallerton, where, although she never showed any great aptitude for amassing knowledge, she was popular with the girls and, because of her ' nice manners ', liked by the mistresses. She was a pretty child, with fair hair like spun gold, a clear skin and very bright blue eyes, set wide apart. She was well grown, strong, and filled with apparently inexhaustible energy.

Her father and mother worshipped her, and although they both longed for a son to inherit Marsh Hall, they found Kitty so entrancing that slowly the longing died, and Emily Bland confided to her husband, " Hugh dear, perhaps God was wise in not allowing us to have any other children, for none of them could have been so sweet as Kitty."

Hugh invariably replied, " Born on a Sunday they say ' bonnie and happy and good and gay '—well, she only just missed being born on a Sunday, and it certainly applies to her."

She never grew spoilt or self-willed; rather it seemed with all the love which was lavished on her she grew sweeter and more appreciative of whatever was done for her. When she was thirteen she was sent to a boarding-school at Scarborough, and for the first time in her life she learnt what it meant to loathe almost every hour of the day. The girls seemed to her to be artificial, she hated their devotions to various mistresses and their possessive friend-ship with each other; she could work up no enthusiasm over the visiting masters, who seemed to her to be very old and desperately dull, neither did she find the boys from St. Eustace's, who passed the girls from St. Monica's when they were out walking, interest-ing.

"Did you notice him, Kitty?" breathlessly asked Winifred Riston.

"Which was—him?" Kitty asked.

"That tall boy with the fair hair and lovely eyes. I'm certain that he smiled when I passed. You couldn't *not* notice him!"

"I didn't. I thought that most of them looked so scruffy."

Winifred was offended, and told the other girls that Kitty Bland was 'stuck up' and that she gave herself airs.

When her father asked her what she wanted most for Christmas in 1913 she answered immediately, "I only really want one thing, Daddy."

"Unless it's a goldmine or something of that kind, you shall have it."

"Let me leave school. Please, I've been very good, I've stuck it for four years, nearly four. I've hated every minute of it, and I've just longed to get away. May I leave?"

She had grown tall and slim, well-built without the slightest heaviness, her hair still bright as it had been when she was a child; there was the same sense of eagerness in all she said and did. She moved swiftly rather than quickly, her mind was as easily moved as her body. She had never attained any great scholarship, but everyone liked her and many people loved her. Now she stood, her hands clasped lightly, but when she spoke there was a certain urgency in her tone.

Hugh Bland watched her closely. "Have you really hated it, Kitty? You never said so—why didn't you tell us, darling?"

For a brief moment she frowned, then said, "Well, Daddy, I know that St. Monica's is a good school, it's a place where people send their girls when they want to give them the very best that can be found. You and Mummy had always seemed to like to know that I was there—with Lady Mary This and the Hon. Geraldine That. Oh, I don't mean that you're snobs! But it did make you feel that—Kitty Bland was having the best. I'd have hated to spoil your pleasure in it all, even though I did and do and always shall hate it. Can I leave at Whitsuntide?"

Her father smiled. Hugh Bland had a smile which his clients found reassuring and understanding. He might not be the 'smartest' solicitor in the district, but he was certainly the one who held the most secrets in his keeping, the one to whom people

came when they wished not only for legal advice, but friendly
interest and help.

"I don't see why not," he said. "I must, of course, talk to your
mother, but——" his smile widened, "I think that I can promise
that Whitsuntide will find you finished with St. Monica's."

So when Whitsuntide came she was at home at Marsh Hall
'for good', and her relief and pleasure were pleasant to watch.
Hugh felt that with each day her affection for the old place
increased; with each day she discovered something new and
unexpected. The days grew longer, the sun warmer on the old
stone walls, the cuckoo shouted in the woods, and the old-
fashioned flowers bloomed and made the walled garden a blaze of
colour.

Kitty walked with her father in the evening before dinner,
together they paced the trim paths, commented upon the flowers
and the chances for a good fruit harvest. Kitty was filled with a
longing to make jam, jellies, pickles and to bottle fruit.

"You'll have to face your mother," Hugh told her. "She's
been filling her store-room every year since I married her."

She laughed. "You don't know how tactful I am, Daddy."

Slowly the skies darkened, and people talked less and less of
their plans for the holidays, their hopes of a good harvest, and the
prospect of plenty of fruit. Instead they asked questions, and
longed for reassuring answers. Did the death of the Archduke
really affect international politics so gravely? Was it true that the
Germans really longed for war in order to break Britain's power?
What would Sir Edward Grey do, and say? Endless questions, put
because in the anxiety which everyone felt they all longed for
answers which should prove that—after all—this most horrible of
all calamities might not happen.

Hugh read his newspapers in silence, while his wife watched
him, her eyes anxious, and Kitty waited until he folded the paper
and laid it down before asking a little breathlessly, "Yes, Daddy?
Tell us."

The clouds grew heavier, the distant rumbling of thunder came
nearer, the tension increased. Then the storm broke.

Kitty said, "What will it mean—exactly?"

Her mother said, her voice shaking a little, "It means war!"

"I know, darling, but what will it mean to us—all of us?"

Hugh sighed. "I'm afraid the end of many things which we
believed could never end. Changes, differences, untold misery.
The beginning of a new world for people like your mother and
me. Oh, there may well be hardships and dangers, those can be
faced, will be faced, by the British. They're at their best in adver-
sity. It won't only be material things, there will be a change of
outlook, a change in values." He leaned forward and laid his
hand on his wife's. "Not easy for people—like ourselves, Emily."

"Shall I be able to do anything?" Kitty asked.

"Do?" her mother questioned. "What do you mean?"

"That's what I'm wondering—work, be a nurse, go into a
factory—there must be something that I can do, mustn't there?"

Hugh frowned. " Time enough—no need to rush into things, my dear. You're only seventeen. . . ."

II

She stood before her father and mother, her face wreathed in smiles. " I've passed. I was top ! Yes, really. I can't understand it, when I was such a duffer at school, but somehow it all came quite easily. Now, can I go to Balford, please ? "

Her mother said, " Oh Kitty ! Don't you think that you could work here, or at least nearer home. Balford is such a long way off ! "

Gently, but with a quiet insistence which made Hugh Bland imagine that he heard himself speaking to some slightly difficult client, she said, " But Aunt Hilda said that I could go there. It's so large and they're dreadfully short-handed. She would see that I was really learning to be useful. You did say that you'd consider it, Mummy."

Hugh said, " Yes, Miss Impetuosity, that's exactly what we're trying to do. Don't batter us with arguments ! "

Kitty won, she had not ' battered ', she had been quietly insistent, gently reasonable. Her aunt had written asking again that she might come to her at Balford Chase, where there was so much work to be done and where they were so ' short-handed that the situation is deplorable '.

Hugh said, " Kitty, we've talked it over—you've won."

Her mother said, " It's a great sacrifice we're making, Kitty, in letting you go."

" If I'd been a boy, darling, I should have had to go, and to worse places than Balford, shouldn't I ? "

" I suppose so. Oh dear, I hope it won't be all too unpleasant. You are young, you know, to be working in a hospital with wounded men ! "

So Kitty went off to Balford and found herself in the midst of the life of a huge hospital. The place had been a great country house, set in a wide park, among age-old trees and a small stream which hurled itself over stones, working itself into a positive fury of white foam.

Aunt Hilda, immense, kindly, and capable, gave her instructions. " I wanted you, my dear, in spite of difficulties. I shan't see very much of you, and of course you realize that I dare not risk the slightest hint that I showed favouritism—even to my own niece. I wanted you because I like you, I believe you'll be useful. Much better not to be too near home, I feel. You'll have to call me ' Matron ', not that you'll be able to speak to me at all very often. I do hope that you understand, my dear child."

Kitty did understand; she flung herself into her work, and though it was often far too hard, still more often unpleasant and even revolting, she did it very well. She had great energy, she was young and strong, and even though there were times when she threw herself on her bed hardly able to believe that one could be so utterly weary and still survive, she was always able to go on duty in the morning filled with the energy which had flowed back during the night.

Of the progress of the war she, in common with most of the sisters and V.A.D.s, knew very little. Reports of battles, engagements, advances, and retreats filtered through to them, but the majority of them were too busy or too tired to read newspapers with any concentration.

The patients liked her, she looked attractive, her voice was clear and distinct without being oppressively loud, and as she walked through the wards with the sun slanting in through the long windows and catching the few strands of bright hair which showed beneath her cap, the men's eyes followed her with something approaching gratitude in their expression.

She had been at Balford for over six months when John Kahl was admitted. Sisters whispered that he was ' almost famous ', that he was the youngest major in the British Army, and that he was recognised to be a ' coming man '. He didn't look like a coming man when he was brought in. He had been blown up by a mine, his lean young body was badly wounded, and his temper was anything but pleasant. He grumbled at everything, but his constant complaint was that he was ' tied by the leg here ' when he wanted to be back in Flanders. In vain the doctors reminded him that patience would help him towards recovery more rapidly than his continual questions, demands, and grumbles; in vain sisters and nurses tried to assure him that he was really making good progress, Johnnie Kahl continued to sulk and rail against fate.

" Am I getting better or not ? " he demanded of Kitty Bland.

" Of course you're getting better—you're almost better now."

" When can I go out, I bet that any Board would pass me ? "

" That's for the surgeon to say, Major Kahl."

He scowled. " Don't be so prim ! I'm damned bored, that's what's the matter with me. Damned bored ! I think that in all probability I shall go scatty before long."

She looked at him, her eyes dancing with amusement. He was speaking the truth, he was bored and he hated it. She had come to know his type, so long as they were dangerously ill, or in considerable pain, they behaved for the most part like Stoics; it was only when they suffered from nothing except weakness that they began to behave like tiresome children. Johnnie Kahl lay there scowling at her, dark eyes clouded and sullen, his rather full lips pouting like those of a spoilt child. For weeks he had looked far older than his years; when he had first come to Balford she had imagined that he was forty at least. Slowly the deep lines graved by pain had disappeared, some of the youthful curves had returned to his face, now he looked—what indeed he was—twenty-three. He stared up at her, still scowling.

" Aren't you going to say anything ? " he demanded.

" I'm thinking what can be done to avert this catastrophe—we can't possibly allow you to go scatty, can we ? "

" A lot any of you would care ! You're an inhuman, hard-hearted lot ! "

" How little you know us really ! Well, think out some plan to prevent your mind going. I promise you my full co-operation."

The following morning his temper had changed. He was smiling when she entered, made cheerful small-talk concerning the weather, the way in which he had slept, and answered her questions without a trace of his previous sulky boredom.

She said, " You're better this morning. That's because the sun is shining, eh ? "

" Not a bit of it. It's because I've thought of something to end this infernal boredom. It's conventional, but it might work. You did promise to co-operate, didn't you ? "

She nodded, feeling vaguely apprehensive; his eyes were dancing, his lips under the minute moustache were smiling.

" I'm going to fall in love with—my nurse ! That's you ! Lord, you didn't think that I meant that horrible Lifeguardsman of a sister, did you ! Now, how are you going to co-operate ? "

She picked up an empty glass, laughed and said, " By telling you not to talk such rubbish ! "

All day she tried to avoid entering his room, and when at last she was forced to do so Kitty knew that her cheeks were flushed, and that she felt suddenly nervous. He was lying staring out of the wide window, the light was waning, and the whole expanse of the park lay dappled with the last patches of sunlight which came splashing through the leaves of the trees. Johnnie turned his head as she entered, and said cheerfully, " Hello, my sweet."

She said briskly, " Hello, how are you to-night ? "

" Better now that you've come in to see me. You've been avoiding me."

" I've been terribly busy."

" You're looking adorable."

She came a little nearer, and did her best to speak coldly.

" Major Kahl, I don't like you talking in that way. It's—not—well, it's not——"

He said, " I don't know what it's not, neither apparently do you, but it's the sober truth, and you know it. I adore your hair ! "

" Do be quiet ! " Kitty snapped suddenly. She was tired; all day long the thought of this young man had obtruded, the fact had worried her. He was attractive, to flirt with him might be amusing —and there wasn't too much amusement in the hospital. The sandy-haired Scottish surgeon had tried to kiss her, that very stout and elderly colonel had asked her to stay and talk to him, had tried to hold her hand, some of the men had stared and made audible remarks about her looks when she passed, but except that her work was often interesting—life was dull.

He said, " Will you come back and talk to me after dinner ? "

" I can't. It's not possible, and you know that as well as I do."

" Would you like to—if it were possible, Kitty ? "

She knew that she would like to, like to very much indeed. She could imagine all the pleasant, rather foolish, even faintly impertinent things which he would say. He would smile and look younger, hold her hand and murmur what a shame it was that she had so much work to do.

"I—might, but it's not possible."

Before she left him she dropped a light kiss on his forehead. He laughed and said, "That's all right for a beginning! Amateurish, but—oh, well, there's plenty of time, darling Kitty."

That was the beginning. The whole affair began as a kind of game on Kitty's part, because she was young and loved life and amusement, and was beginning to find life rather drab and monotonous. Johnnie—she never actually knew what Johnnie felt. She knew that while other people—surgeon, doctor or sister —were present his behaviour was admirable; it was only when they left, passing through the door that Kitty held open for them, that he would turn and catch her eyes, or even, "Oh, Nurse, would you hand me that book—thank you so much," and as she gave it to him, when he was certain that they were alone, he would whisper urgently, "Quick, kiss me, darling!"

Later he was allowed to walk out in the garden. The first time, she saw a return of his old irritability. He had not known how weak he was, nor realized that moving about in his own room was not the same as trying to walk about outside. Then as he grew stronger, as the restrictions regarding his movements, his hour of going to bed, were relaxed, they would meet in the soft, quiet darkness, and holding her in his arms he would whisper foolish, endearing nonsense to her.

When he was told that he was to go to a convalescent home he declared that he didn't feel sufficiently well; his wounds hurt him, he was sure that his temperature rose every night, his appetite was poor, and other excuses which at first puzzled and then annoyed the staff.

Kitty said, "I believe they're suspicious, Johnnie."

"Mean-minded old devils. When I wanted to go, they wouldn't hear of it; now, when I hate the thought of going, they want to push me off! I say, Kitty, what am I going to do without you, darling? It's unthinkable."

She shrugged her shoulders. "I could say the same."

"You wouldn't mean it, though—I do mean it. Kitty, will you marry me?"

She watched him, thoughtfully, he was so young. He was her senior, but she still felt that she was years older than he. He had done things, seen things, commanded men, risked his life, had astonishing experiences and still he remained—young. He sat now, smiling as he looked at her. Would she marry him? If she said that she would, everything could be arranged; but—she didn't love him, he didn't really love her. They had played their game, they had slipped farther and farther into the parts for which they had cast themselves, there had been times when they had both forgotten that this was all make-believe.

"Will you?" Johnnie repeated.

She shook her head. "You forget that it was all a game, Johnnie."

" It's dead serious now ! "

She laughed. " Not really, you're playing at being serious."

At last he went away to the convalescent home somewhere
on the south coast; she watched him go, leaning out of the
window of the car, waving and smiling. She was conscious of a
sudden sense of relief. When his letters came, short and wildly
affectionate, she read them with a certain amusement. They were
so palpably what he imagined love-letters ought to be. She missed
him, missed his kisses, and his embraces in those dark evenings
when they had walked together, but there was no trace of actual
unhappiness.

Then came a letter saying that the Board had passed him, and
that he was going overseas again; it was the letter of a schoolboy
going home for the holidays. He had ' wangled ' this and contrived
the other; he had said this and that and hadn't he been a very
clever fellow to get what he wanted ? Wasn't she filled with admiration ? Didn't that prove that ' the Army of to-day's all right ! '
and—would she come and spend his last week-end with him in
town ?

She sat with the letter in her hand, staring at it blankly. She
knew that girls did do such things, she had heard some of the
others discussing their experiences with considerable frankness;
their statements had not shocked her particularly, it had merely
seemed impossible that she should ever do such things. Other
people might and did, that was their own affair, but—Kitty Bland,
to go to spend a week-end in a London hotel with a man to whom
she was not married—it was impossible.

She wrote back, treating the matter as a joke, promising that
she would come up to town and have luncheon with him and say
' good-bye ' and wish him ' good luck '. His reply was what in her
heart she had expected. Dear Johnnie, he always took the strictly
conventional line even in unconventional matters. He was hurt,
not only hurt but amazed. He had believed that—' after everything '—she was really fond of him, as he was of her. He hinted
that it might be years before they met again, it was possible that
they might never meet again, ' you know how things are out there '.
He had longed for ' something to remember '—and she denied him
even a ' precious memory '.

Her gravity left her, she began to laugh. She'd go ! After all,
she and Johnnie had disregarded convention sufficiently, what
difference did it make if they did so again—in London instead of
Balford ? Hair-splitting ! She would go. It would be fun to be
with Johnnie again, to laugh, to wear pretty clothes in the evening, to
dance, eat pleasant food, and to listen to him saying charming
things to her. The hospital was going through a slack period, she
asked for week-end leave. Aunt Hilda asked where she was going.
The lies came with surprising ease. An old school friend living
with an aunt in Buckingham Gate, a twenty-first birthday party.
Aunt Hilda beamed and said, " Very nice. You've worked well,
Kitty, you deserve a little relaxation. Go and enjoy yourself."

She packed her bag, she felt happy, light-hearted, expectant.

She didn't really love Johnnie, but then neither did Johnnie really love her. They were young, they wanted amusement, they wanted to find that amusement in each other's company. They would be gay, they would laugh and eat and drink well, they'd dance and take life as it came.

He met her at Paddington, looking brown and well, he had booked a room—a very large and expensive room—at an equally large and expensive hotel. He spent money wildly, and when she expostulated, Johnnie only laughed and said, " Only the best is good enough for you, my sweetest."

She went to Victoria with him, he held her hands in his and whispered, " It's been wonderful—every single minute. When I come back on leave it's all going to happen again—it is, isn't it ? "

Travelling back to Balford, she remembered those two days, and admitted that they had been wonderful. She wondered, if she and Johnnie had really been in love, if those days would not have been clouded by the thought of their coming separation. Well, there had been no cloud, they had been two young people each longing to be happy, to take whatever offered, to be gay. She had no false sentiments concerning ' making the returning soldier happy ', she did not attempt to deceive herself into imagining that she had done anything from altruistic motives. The ' rights ' and ' wrongs ' of the case did not affect her, they had hurt no one— neither she nor Johnnie owed fidelity to anyone.

Possibly all sophistry, none of her thoughts particularly exalted, but at that time they satisfied Kitty Bland, who went back to her hospital conscious that the two days of a completely different life had done her good mentally and physically. She hung up her evening dresses with no sense of regret, the knowledge that a long stretch of intensive hard work lay before her did not bring the slightest sense of dismay. Aunt Hilda said, " I hope that you had a nice time, dear."

She replied, " A lovely time, thank you ; it was great fun."

III

Johnnie wrote a long letter immediately he arrived in France. He wrote of the wonderful time they had had, said how much he longed for his next leave, and added that she was ' the only girl in the world '. Then his letters came less regularly, and conformed even more to type. Kitty felt that they might have been reproduced in some anthology as ' Letters from an average young soldier to a girl with whom he had spent a week-end '. Her own letters were difficult to write, the hospital was filled with new patients, their names or characteristics conveyed nothing to Johnnie ; she told how the garden and the park were looking, wrote small details of her daily life and work, and gnawing the end of her pen, thought what dull reading they must make.

The days were growing shorter and colder ; when bright days came the patients, longing to be out in the fresh air, had to be wrapped in rugs. Matron decreed that they should be given drinks, cool drinks, on the pleasant hot days of St. Luke's summer.

Taking them round one morning, when the sun shone as if the summer had really come round again, she handed a glass to a man who sat staring out completely absorbed in his own thoughts.

She said, " It's really hot enough for a cold drink this morning."

He started and said, " Oh, yes—thank you."

She gave the glass a little twist so that the ice tinkled against the glass and said, " I always think that is such a pleasant sound."

The man said, " It is indeed, very pleasant."

She handed the glass to him and moved on. When she got to the end of the line of deck-chairs, some impulse made her turn to look back. The man had turned his head and was staring after her. He was very thin, almost gaunt, with very dark eyes, and hair which looked soft and smooth. As her eyes met his, he turned away, but a second later looked back. She smiled, and fancied that she saw a little flicker touch his lips.

CHAPTER II

I

HIS name, Kitty discovered, was Oliver Hallam, he had been sent back from the Italian campaign, not only wounded but in a state of complete nervous exhaustion. He was twenty-four, and held the rank of captain.

With studied carelessness she brought his name into a conversation with Nurse Filson while they were having dinner.

" Who's the new man—dark, quiet ? I think his name's Hallam."

Filson said, " Oh, Hallam, yes. He was over in the other wing, but they're moving him to this side, they're terribly full there. He's better, at least better than he was. Silent kind of fellow, reads a lot, never says much. Different from that Major—what was his name ?—Kahl ! Ever hear from him, Bland ? He was rather sweet on you, wasn't he ? "

" Who ? Johnnie ? Not really, just a kind of conventional flirtation with his nurse. I've heard from him once or twice; he's overseas again."

Filson chuckled. " I can't see this Hallam indulging in any flirtations—conventional or otherwise. You'd better cast your eyes over Tommy Carter. Oh, my word ! That's a lad, if you like ! "

Kitty knew a good deal about what a ' lad ' Tommy Carter was, and didn't like either him or his proclivities. Each day she met Hallam, and later when he was moved into A Wing she saw him several times a day and she liked him more. Gradually she found herself looking forward to seeing him, even finding some excuse to see him more frequently than strict duty necessitated; she knew that she was allowing him to occupy her thoughts a great deal, that she indulged in speculations concerning him. Where did he come from ? What was he before the Army claimed him ? Was he married ? Then suddenly she would grow angry with herself, feel her face flush, and give herself the strict reprimand, ' Kitty Bland, don't be such an utter fool ! You're growing as bad as Beatrice Harris, who is always " making up " romances about the patients. Have sense ! '

One afternoon when she went into his room he was sitting near the window, a book lying on the floor beside him.

She said, " Are you bored with that book ? "

Oliver smiled, a very pleasant, rather slow smile. " Candidly, I'm bored with most of the books the library here supplies. Do they imagine that we're all half-wits ? "

She felt shy, terribly young, and she knew that she hesitated a little as she said, " If you'd care to tell me the kind of books you

27

like, I'll see what can be done. You see, they believe that all soldiers are incurably romantic, Captain Hallam."

" Romantic ! Incurably weak-minded I should have thought." Then, " That's a very kind offer and I shall be awfully glad to accept it. I'll set to work on a list right away."

" Mind," Kitty warned him, " I don't promise that I can do very much. I'll try."

She found him some books from the library that had belonged to the Chase, books which were locked away behind glass-fronted doors. She talked to old Mrs. Cartwright, the housekeeper, who had been in the place for nearly forty years, and who had been born in Ayton. That fact had helped to endear Kitty to her. "Afther all," as she said, " Ayton bean't soa far awaay from Northallerton. Ah mean that you cum fra't reit part o' country. Not like these poor Southern folk."

Mrs. Cartwright lived now in a tiny cottage in the grounds, and often asked Kitty to go and have tea with her. The kindly old woman was, as she said herself, ' fair starved fer want o' someone ter have a crack wi'." Kitty liked to listen to her stories of ' the family ', she felt that she knew them all intimately and was able to refer to the various events in their lives with ease. When Mrs. Cartwright embarked on one of her long-winded, elaborately detailed histories, Kitty could interpolate such remarks as, ' That must have been about the time when Master Geoffrey had measles so badly ? ' or ' Was that when Miss Marion went to school in Paris ? ' Such remarks were hailed as proof positive that Kitty's intelligence was of a very high order.

Now she went to Mrs. Cartwright to ask a favour for Oliver Hallam. As she walked through the grounds she realized that it seemed terribly important that she should persuade Mrs. Cartwright to open some of those cases and let her choose books which would give Captain Hallam the mental stimulus for which he wished.

Mrs. Cartwright beamed at her. " Nay, this is nice. Cum yer ways in ! Ah've gotten a nice batch o' parkins. They're just on ready. Noa need ter tell you what parkins are, eh, luv ? Noa—yet sum o' them south country folk 'ud niver knaw if they weer fish nor flesh if you mentioned 'em."

Kitty sat down by the fire, while the old woman bustled about preparing tea, chattering as she did so in her ' comfortable ' old voice. What a pleasant place she had made of this little cottage, where everything was kept so neatly, where the grate shone like black satin, and the copper kettle gleamed like rich gold. There were all the things which went to make up Mrs. Cartwright's history, gifts from her loved ' family ', every one marking some milestone in her life. There was the portrait of Miss Marion at her presentation, there was Master Geoffrey in his first uniform, and various groups of house parties where the women wore what now seemed to Kitty to be unsuitable clothes, and the men looked choked within their high, stiff collars.

Kitty said, " Mrs. Cartwright, I've come to ask a favour. Don't hesitate to refuse if you feel you ought to do so."

" Nay, Miss Bland, Ah can allus refuse if Ah feel like it. What's ter do ? "

She made her request; she told of Oliver Hallam's boredom, she promised to guard the books—if lent—with her very life. Mrs. Cartwright considered. Kitty watched her, feeling that her decision was one of the major pronouncements of the war.

' He must have books,' she thought, and tried to ' will ' the old woman to say ' Yes.'

At last Mrs. Cartwright sighed deeply, smoothed down her apron and in silence poured out a third cup of tea, by this time ' drawn ' to such an extent that it was a dark, rich brown. She stirred it violently.

" Now," she said at last, " Ah'm gannen ter tell thee summat, Miss Bland. Not fur another living soul, except nat'rally one of the Fam'ly, would I soa mooch as consider it. But yer're a Yorkshire woman, same as what Ah am, an' what's mower theer's times when you put me very mooch i' mind o' my Miss Gertrude. That's Miss Gertrude yonder i' that red ploosh frame."

She indicated a tall young woman, wearing a tweed costume with a very long and inelegant coat and a skirt to her ankles; Kitty thought that Miss Gertrude looked like a horse.

She murmured, " Really, do I ? "

" You do, my dear, indeed you do; a finer, mower upstanding and upright young lady nor my Miss Gertrude I never hope ter meet. She weer married in April, 1898, to the Honourable Vincent Marlsham; he has a place at Doncaster. A pleasant gentleman; they've three of the finest children you've ever seen i' all your born days, the eldest—my word, what a fine boy ! But Ah'll tell you about them anuther time—Ah mun get back ter t' subject i' hand—the bukes."

Kitty said, " Oh, thank you, Mrs. Cartwright."

Mrs. Cartwright made a vague gesture in the manner of Queen Victoria brushing away some small compliment from an inferior, and sighed again, tapping her vast bosom with the other hand and saying, " I didn't ought to have had that third cup—but I do enjoy my tea ! Now, I am prepared ter open one of the bukecases—in your presence, but not in the presence of others. You shall select such volooms as you wish, and give me a little list. When those are returned, I shall give you the list back. And so—" she beamed suddenly—" we shall go on ! "

Again Kitty said, " Oh, thank you, Mrs. Cartwright, and be sure that I shall return them and see that every care is taken of them."

" That," replied Mrs. Cartwright majestically, " I very well know, or I'd never have made such an offer."

The next day Kitty was able to take six books from the celebrated library of Balford Chase to Oliver Hallam. She recounted her interview with Mrs. Cartwright, and felt a sense of delight fill her when he threw back his head and laughed.

He stared at her in admiration. " But what a splendid imitation ! How did you come to learn to speak a dialect so well ? "

2

Kitty laughed. " Dialect ! I'll have you know that it's no ' dialect ', it's a language ! And it's my own native language. Don't you know that there is a complete grammar of Yorkshire words, verbs, conjugations, and so on ? Oh, you poor ignorant Southerners ! "

" Then would you call Cockney, for example, or Warwickshire, languages as well ? " He was leaning forward, his face filled with interest.

" Warwickshire—I don't know," she said doubtfully; " after all, it's Shakespeare's county, but Cockney——" She wrinkled her attractive nose. " That's surely only a dialect. It may have certain words—mostly nouns, I imagine—which are really old, old English words, but I am certain that they have no proper grammatical rules as we have."

Oliver listened gravely. Kitty saw that the tension which usually seemed to constrict his figure had decreased, he seemed to have really relaxed, lost that queer rigidity which was part of his nervous illness.

He said, " Nurse, would it be correct to say that you Yorkshire people have a fair amount of—forgive me—conceit ? " His eyes twinkled as he spoke.

" Nay, lad," Kitty said, " conceit—niver, nobbut a proper pride i' oursens ! " Again she heard him laugh, then added, " I must go. I hope that you enjoy the books."

The next day she had a letter from Johnnie, it was short and, she felt, perfunctory. The phrases were stilted and sterotyped. Not that his letters had ever held any great flights of imagination, but this one seemed more sterile than ever. She re-read it, and laid it down with a sense of relief. Johnnie didn't really care, he was not and never had been in love with her; now she was in love with someone else. Not that she had ever felt for Johnnie what she felt now—at this moment—for Oliver Hallam. It didn't matter that Oliver would never love her, that when he was better he would leave the hospital, and except possibly that he might write to her once or twice, he would go out of her life.

That didn't affect the present issue. She must write and tell Johnnie that she had fallen in love, that he must not regard himself as being under any obligation to write to her, and that when he came home on leave there could be no repetition of their week-end in London.

She wrote the letter carefully, weighing every word, but stating simply that she had met a man with whom she was in love, and that while she had no knowledge or even hope that he loved her, her emotions had proved to her that this was something too real, too important, to disregard.

She heard from Johnnie in a fortnight's time. Again she felt that his words were conventional rather than springing from his heart. She knew that his vanity was hurt, and that he had flung himself wholeheartedly into the rôle of ' rejected lover '. He said that her letter had come as a great and terrible shock to him; he added that it was scarcely fair for her to write as she had done at a

time when ' I never know if to-morrow's dawn wil lfind me alive '.
She had let him down, he said, let him down badly. ' I feel that all
my life—if I live through this—I shall be emotionally " halt and
maimed ", for such a love as I felt for you—indeed, still feel for
you—does not come into a life twice.' He hoped that she might be
happy, that her future might be as happy as he had once hoped to
make it.

Kitty could imagine Johnnie reading that letter with a sense of
satisfaction, she could picture him that night in the mess, rather
silent and absorbed. When his brother officers asked, " What's
wrong, Johnnie ? " he would start, as if roused from deep thoughts.

" Wrong ? Nothing really, old man. I've just had rather a nasty
smack in the face. Nothing—I'll be all right."

Men would say, " Poor old Johnnie, I'll bet it's some damned
woman ! " and in two days Johnnie would recover and forget all
about it. There was no need to take Johnnie too seriously.

She replied briefly that she was sorry that she had hurt him,
and repeated that this was something she couldn't fight against,
and had felt it only fair to tell him so. She never heard from him
again.

The weeks passed, Oliver Hallam never attempted to flirt with
her, much less to make love to her. Her efforts to find books for
him had, she felt, meant a great deal. He talked of what he had
read, gave her the names of books which he wanted particularly to
read. He was always charming, and in spite of the fact that he
had never spoken a word to her that all the world could not have
heard, Kitty knew a greater state of contentment than she ever
remembered experiencing before.

Winter came. Hallam was growing rapidly better, and Kitty
watched his recovery with her heart torn between content that he
was growing stronger and dread for the time when he would leave
the hospital

" I suppose they'll send me out soon ? " he asked one day.

" I imagine so—what will you do then ? "

" Go home, I expect. I don't think that the Army will want me
again. For nothing but light duties at all events. My father wants
me to go back to the works—he's the Hallam cars, you know.
My brother, Evelyn, manages the place in Birmingham, I'm in the
other, the Markholt. Of course we've been on war production
and the Guv'nor wants to get back to normal as quickly as
possible."

She said, " You're the Hallam cars ! Fancy that ! "

She wondered why she had never realized that he must be a
wealthy young man, for she had heard him talk of a hard tennis-
court, cars, a bathing pool, and the like as if they were the kind of
thing which one possessed automatically. Her mind went back to
Marsh Hall, that quiet, modest old house, with its one bathroom,
and the garden filled with old-fashioned flowers. She imagined her
mother announcing at breakfast-time, " I'm going to make a little
pastry this morning," saw herself entering the kitchen, coming in
from the courtyard with its worn flagstones, to find her mother,

sleeves rolled up and round, plump arms dusted with flour. There was a tennis-court at Marsh Hall, which her father watered and rolled, where he went looking anxiously for plantains, spud in hand. A nice court, where the grass was old and cared for, tended and admired ; where people came and played games which were never very fast or reached a particularly high standard.

Cars—swimming pools—hard courts—these things seemed incredibly luxurious and expensive to Kitty Bland.

She lay in bed that night thinking of Oliver. He was going; in all probability she would never see him again ; he might remember her as ' a nice little nurse who went to tremendous troub'e to find books for me '—that was all she would mean to him. Lying there, she frowned into the darkness, her thoughts curiously clear and distinct.

It did'nt really matter; the fact that he had never even imagined himself in love with her did not really affect the issue. This was extraneous. What did matter was that for the first time in her life she had fallen sincerely and deeply in love. She had learnt that love was not of necessity a ' snatch and grab ' business; you couldn't grab happiness and hold it. Either it came to you, and remained with you, or it just passed on with scarcely a glance in your direction. That might make you wildly happy or leave you with a sense of loss—though not bitterness. It was something to have known what being in love really meant. She was at least lucky in that.

Two days later she heard that Captain Hallam was going out at the end of the week. She felt that strange sensation of having broken away from her moorings, of suddenly drifting out into an uncharted sea; then she squared her shoulders, and bit her lips to make the colour return to them.

Filson said, " I say, Bland, you don't look awfully fit this morning ! "

Kitty said, " Don't I ? I'm all right. It's my birthday too ! Maybe the excitement is too much for me. I'm twenty to-day. Think of it ! "

Filson beamed at her. " We've got a cake for you, Bland. A magnificent cake. Matron was ever so good about it, candles and everything. And that nice old Mrs. Cartwright of yours came up specially to ice it for us. She thinks the world of you, that old body."

Mechanically Kitty said, " Lovely—how simply lovely ! " While she thought, ' No need for Mrs. Cartwright to open bookcases any more. No need for me to make out little lists—he won't be here, he'll have gone.'

Oliver had been kept indoors for some days, he had caught cold, and his temperature had risen a little. When she went into his room he was sitting in his usual place near the window and he got up when she came in.

" I've got my marching orders—provided this cold clears up. I'm to go out at the end of the week," he said

Kitty nodded. " I know. I heard this morning."

" Oh ! Many happy returns of the day ! How remiss of me
not to have said that the moment you came in ! May it be the best
year you've ever spent."

" Now who told you about my birthday ! I know—Filson.
What an old chatterbox she is ! "

Oliver said gravely, " Ah now, I can't have you saying a word
against Nurse Filson, she's my very good friend and ally. I don't
know what I should have done without her. She's helped me
tremendously."

His voice was grave, but his eyes were dancing, and his mouth,
Kitty thought, looked as if it might break into one of his rare
smiles at any moment.

She said, " How has she helped you ? "

" She helped me to get a birthday present for you. If you'd
come just a little nearer, perhaps you'd let me put it on for you.
That's better."

She felt his careful, slim fingers undoing the strap of her wrist-
watch. She trembled a little, they were so very tender and yet so
exact—those long, fine fingers; never fumbling, moving quickly
and yet without haste. He looked at her. " You're cold ? "

" No—no, but what are you doing, Captain Hallam ? "

" I'm taking off this watch," he said, " I should have thought
that was obvious. As a watch I dislike it, as an alarm clock it may
be admirable. There ! Now quite candidly, don't you think that
looks better ? "

She stared at the watch on her wrist. " But—it's gold ! "

" Ah," he pulled down the corners of his mouth in mock dismay.
" I felt that platinum and diamonds would have been better ! "

" I didn't mean that . . ." Kitty cried, distressed.

" But if you'll wear that—for the time being—you shall have
the more decorative one— later—when we're properly engaged.
Oh, there I go again—what a fool I am this morning, doing everything wrong, saying last and least important things first, and forgetting the really important one ! Kitty darling, you will marry
me, won't you ? "

He had taken her hands in his, held them firmly, kindly and
without undue pressure. She thought that she had never known
such happiness as the warmth of his hands enfolding hers.

" I marry you ?—I mean—are you joking ? I don't understand."

" Sweetness, you're not paying complete attention, which is
paying me a very poor compliment indeed. I am asking you to
marry me, which is believed to be a matter of some importance to
both parties concerned. I'll ask you again—Kitty, darling, will
you marry me ? I've been wanting to ask you for days and days,
I've thought about it for nights and nights. I know that you're all
the things I want and love best. I'll be good to you, my dearest,
I'll take care of you, and work for you and—give you that watch
as soon as ever I can get it."

She heard him laugh softly, and said furiously, " Oh, don't
laugh at me ! " Then drawing her breath so that to Hallam it

sounded almost like a sob, she added, " I'll never wear any other
watch except this as long as I live, never. Oliver, do you really
want to marry me ? Honestly, truthfully ? "

" I believe both honestly and truthfully and—desperately."

" But—why ? I mean—how do you know? You've never
seemed to take any particular interest in me, have you ? "

" Suppose that you come and sit down here," he said. " You
haven't answered my question yet, you know. Have I to ask it
again—for the third time ? "

" Will I marry you ? Darling, it's the one thing I've longed for.
I've been so in love with you for weeks, and you never noticed
anything, you never said anything. I was going to try to forget all
about you—when you went away. Of course I'll marry you ! I
don't know anything about you, except that you make cars, and
have a hard tennis-court and a swimming pool——"

" I haven't," Oliver corrected, " they belong to my father."

" And you don't know anything about me ! And——"

He drew her to the chair in which he had been sitting when she
entered, and knelt beside her holding her hand in his. " I've been
learning about you for weeks," he said. " I've learnt that you are
kind and tender, that you never ' fuss ' or get flurried, that you have
the most charming voice in the world. Yesterday I learnt that you
are twenty years old to-day, that you are having a magnificent
birthday cake—of which I shall want a large and satisfying slice,
remember. I went through all the things I had learnt about you
last night in the small hours, and thought—' It is quite obvious
that I have not learned nearly enough about her, there's nothing
left for me except to ask her to marry me ! ' Which I did as soon as
possible. Now, all that I need is time to continue my studies."

Kitty stared at his pleasant, lean face, with its good eyes and
well-cut lips, lifted a little at the corners as he watched her.

" What a birthday ! " she whispered.

" Forgive me, but all the usual formalities are not yet complete
—it is usual——" He leaned forward, put his arms round her
and kissed her lips.

II

Aunt Hilda could not have been more gracious to Oliver Hallam ;
the thought that her niece was going to marry this exceedingly
eligible young man, that they had met in her hospital, and had
both behaved with the utmost correctness, delighted and charmed
her.

That night she wrote a long letter to Kitty's parents, seated in
her trim sitting-room, erect even when she wrote. Aunt Hilda
presented a picture of herself as a kind of all-powerful being who
arranged these satisfactory marriages. The words ' Hallam motors '
and ' Markholt cars ' figured largely in what to all intents and
purposes was a kind of saga of Balford Chase.

Oliver wrote carefully, modestly, and stated his position to
Hugh Bland ; he was not really wealthy, he explained, but he

hoped to be one day. His father believed in his ability, his father was generous, and the whole family would welcome Kitty as a wonderful and charming addition to the family.

Kitty's letter was almost incomprehensible, so filled was it with happiness and admiration for Oliver. She tried to paint a verbal picture of him and failed completely; indeed when her mother read the letter she passed it to her husband, saying, " He really sounds too dreadful, like one of those men in advertisements for hair cream, or a film star ! Do you really think he is like that, Hugh ? "

" Probably an ugly devil," Hugh returned, " with what you women like to call charm ! "

Kitty had never known such happiness, had never felt so secure, so utterly content. Oliver loved her, and she in return gave him an affection which was passionate in its devotion. Again and again she had to remind herself that she must not allow everyone to know what a stupendous and immense thing her love for Oliver was; she could not tell him, for when she said sometimes, " Oliver— I didn't know that it was possible to love anyone as I love you. It's—it's frightening," he looked at her smiling, and yet with gravity in his eyes and said, " But you mustn't be frightened, and you mustn't love me so much, sweetheart. It's giving me too much responsibility. Suppose that I disappointed you ? "

" You couldn't."

" Suppose that you found out that I'd not been such a very nice person."

" You mean that you'd loved other women before me ? " He nodded. " Well, suppose that you had ? You didn't know me then; you didn't even know that I was in the world. You couldn't be held responsible for what happened when you didn't even dream you'd meet me, could you ? "

" Perhaps not, but my behaviour then—in those dark ages when I didn't know you—might be a kind of ' pointer ' to my probable future deeds or misdeeds, eh ? "

" Listen," she said, and twisting round on the sofa so that she faced him, she laid her hands on his shoulders, " can you tell me that there is no one in the world to whom you owe a duty, a duty which would make it wrong—yes, wrong, for you to marry me ? "

He considered for a moment, looking into her eyes, and said, " I can— there is no one to whom I owe a duty of that kind."

Kitty nodded. " I can say the same to you, that is all there is to be said about it. All we have to do is to go on being happy."

She had wondered if she ought to tell him about Johnnie, she had searched her heart to find a decision which was right and honest, and had come to the conclusion that, as she had told Oliver, she had not known that he even existed. Oliver, for his part, had remembered Yolanda, and had been surprised, and even shocked, to find how dim her memory had grown. He could no longer recall the sound of her voice clearly, he could not visualize her walking through the old narrow streets of Vicenza—she had become vague and indistinct.

When Kitty said, " I can say the same to you," he felt faintly amused, this serious, blue-eyed girl of twenty assuring him that she had no one to whom she ' owed a duty '. She had entered Balford when she left school, and he knew that Aunt Hilda was reported to be a dragon among matrons. He loved her gravity when she talked to him, her serious interest in his work and plans; each day Oliver Hallam told himself how fortunate he had been in finding such a girl as Kitty Bland.

He left the hospital and returned to his father's immense and admittedly vulgar, if essentially comfortable, house near Birmingham. Jabez Hallam was a self-made man and took no pains to disguise the fact; he had made a success of life, a success which was due to hard work, a certain imagination, and complete honesty. His one recreation was reading history, and he devoured heavy, ponderous books on this subject with real and complete enjoyment. He had named his eldest son Evelyn, after the diarist, for whom he had an admiration; his daughter was named Victoria because, after reading the many volumes of ' Letters ' by the Queen of that name, he felt that she was ' all reit—not mooch nonsense aboot 'er '. Oliver, the youngest, was called after the Protector whose portrait—plain, blunt, and slightly ferocious—hung over Jabez Hallam's library mantelpiece.

His wife was short and stout, she described herself as a ' homely body ' and privately longed to be allowed to ' slip into the kitchen and show that stuck-up piece how a Lancashire hot-pot *ought* to be made '. The huge over-furnished house oppressed her, as did the jewellery which her husband showered upon her, and the number of dresses which he liked her to buy. Alice Hallam was a kind-hearted soul, and Oliver's news that he was going to marry Kitty Bland filled her with romantic delight. Oliver was her favourite child, Evelyn was cold, she felt, and Victoria had been educated at the most expensive schools which could be found, emerging from them with an accent which was fantastic in its refinement.

" Tell us," she said confidingly to Oliver when they were alone, " what is she like, darling ? "

" Lovely, Mummy, lovely. Twenty and looks it, fair hair like spun gold, eyes like forget-me-nots, and a laugh like a chime of silver bells."

She smiled and dabbed her eyes, which were overflowing with happy emotion.

" Luverly," she said, " joost luverly. D'you think she'll think that I'm all reit, Oliver luv ? Like—she'll not turn 'er nose up at me, will she ? "

" If she could even imagine doing such a preposterous and outrageous thing," he said, " she'd not be the girl I know her to be ! She'll love you as you'll love her."

When Kitty, released from the hospital on the plea of an immediate marriage, and a statement from the doctor that she needed a rest, came to visit the Hallams at Martingly Park, Alice, in her own phrase, ' was all of a-twitter '. Jabez had declared that they must give a ' round o' parties an' entertainments; can't 'ave the young lady thinkin' uz dull ', but Oliver refused to allow him to do so.

" She wants to get to know you and Mummy, Guv'nor," he protested, " not to have to make polite conversation with a lot of people she's never met. No, have one ' family ' dinner if you like, and let it go at that. Anyway, it's not considered good form to entertain too lavishly in wartime."

Jabez laid his thick capable hand with its short stubby fingers on his son's arm, and patted it gently, " Nay, I'm reit glad ter 'ave you back, Nollie lad. Evelyn's all reit, but 'e won't be *bothered* ter tell me things like yon—like what's good form, an' what's bad, like what you do. Nay then, we'll leave entertaining alone this time, eh ? "

He fell in love with Kitty, as did his wife; they talked of her as they dressed for dinner, a rite which they both piously performed every evening, believing that in doing so they were proving that they had attained to ' county rank '.

" Luverly, Muther, eh ? Our Nollie's picked a beauty—and in saying a beauty I am thinking not ondly of form, but of character."

" Would they be well-to-do, Jabez ? I mean her family."

Jabez paused in the struggle which always took place when he tried to make his stud enter the proper place in his stiff collar; he left it dangling round his neck, and addressed his wife.

" Well off, no. Comfortable, yes. Like many of the smaller gentry of England, they probably supported the King in the struggle between King and Parliament. These people, in their convinced and unalterable loyalty, gave not only their lives, their land, but their all. Silver was poured into the coffers of the King, to be melted down to obtain sufficient coin to continue the war, and many of the smaller gentry, as well as their more important Royalist friends, were faced with complete ruin when the King was finally defeated." He broke off and spoke again in his ordinary voice, abandoning the slightly ' sing-song ' tone which he had been using. " Soa," he said, " that's 'ow it is with our Oliver's young lady's fam'ly. That's, as I see it, their position to-day." His wife stared at him, admiration in her eyes; the fact that she had no idea of the significance of what her husband had said in no way decreased her respect for his knowledge.

" Well, luke at that ! Conservatives, I suppose, her fam'ly ? "

Jabez, his lecture over, was again wrestling with his collar-stud; he replied in a muffled voice, " Something like that, Muther."

" Well, there's nothing to their disgrace i' that," she answered with spirit. " I don't hold with Socialists, as you know. Anyroad, what does matter is that she's a lovely girl, I can see with half an eye that she loves our Oliver, and he doates on her."

The stud slipped into its proper place, Jabez sighed gustily. " I'm very well satisfied," he said.

CHAPTER III

I

THEY were married in the little old church where Kitty had been
christened and where several Blands were buried, their characters
and attributes fully described on large flat stones let into the wall
of the church, expressed in florid Georgian terms. Oliver's family,
except Evelyn, came up to Yorkshire for the wedding, and both
Jabez and his wife fell in love with Marsh Hall. Jabez, walking
briskly in the garden filled with pale winter sunlight, Hugh Bland
at his side, stared back at the house and puffed out his lips.

"This," he said, "is 'ist'ry. Part of England, Mr. Bland." His
voice changed, became slightly artificial and studiously correct.
"These manor 'ouses, built of good English stone, standing there
meeting all the four winds of 'eaven, are monuments. They
represent the attainment of the yeoman families of England,
holding tenaciously to their beloved acres, their possessions, and
their roof-trees. That's the sober truth," he added. "I'm proud
to be a visitor in such a house, Mr. Bland, I am indeed."

Hugh Bland, faintly amused but deeply touched, said, "It's
not a bad little place. I've an affection for it—so has Kitty."

Mrs. Hallam begged to be shown everything, and the kitchens
roused her to both envy and admiration. Her aspirates were flung
to the winds, she stood with clasped hands and shining eyes noting
everything.

"My word, that's what I call a table, that is. Milk white.
Mine's got a marble top, nice fer pastry, but—cold, ovver cold
ter my mind. Eh, and what a grate ! My word, I never saw one
better shone. My servants turn up theer noses at a bit of good old
Nixey's ; they want patent rubbish put on wi' a brush like paint !
And that larder o' your'n, perfect, better than all them patent
'frigerators and the like. Luverly slabs o' slate ! I've got it in me
'eart to envy you, Mrs Bland, that's the trewth."

But they liked each other, the fundamental sincerity which
lay in the hearts and minds of them both bridged the gap, and
made them immediately recognize how much they had in common.

Kitty was entranced at the opportunity to show Oliver her
beloved home, to watch his appreciation of old wood, the sheen
of china, and the view from the house where the green fields
stretched away until they seemed to melt into the soft dull purple
of the moors, and the moors themselves became absorbed into the
gentle slopes of the hills.

He watched it gravely, his face peaceful and gentle as Kitty
loved it best, then turning to her he smiled. "I don't wonder
that such country breeds people like you, darling. It's wide fine
country, fit for wide fine people, nothing mean or cramped here,"

and he touched her cheek softly with the tip of his finger, " or there," and with a sweep of his hand he indicated the prospect before them.

For a moment Kitty experienced a sense of panic. Was she deceiving him; ought she to tell him about Johnnie; would he really understand or would the knowledge shatter this complete beauty and love which existed between them ? She caught her breath, and felt her heart beat more quickly, then Oliver was speaking again, talking of their own home in Warwickshire, and the moment for speaking seemed to have passed.

That night when she lay in bed, Kitty thought, ' If ever again I have the impulse to tell him—I'll speak. If it never comes, then I shall know that I'm not " meant " to tell him.'

She had no sense of dishonesty, the whole thing had ended, and even while it lasted had made so little mark on her. Love, as she knew it now, for Oliver, was something which had played no part in her relationship with Johnnie Kahl. She was going to marry Oliver; her real life was going to begin.

They were married on a cold clear day in January. Oliver had been released from the Army, Kitty had finished with her nursing. Oliver was still suffering from the nervous breakdown which had been the real cause of his illness after the Italian campaign. Kitty was, as Aunt Hilda admitted, tired to death, though she could have continued to do her work had not her marriage automatically released her.

Jabez Hallam had bought them a house near the Markholt works in the village of Coltsby. A pleasant place, which, although it was within twenty minutes' train journey from Birmingham, had still retained its completely country atmosphere.

On the first day that Kitty and Oliver entered the house as their home she took him out into the cold wintry garden, and together they looked back at the place which was to be their home.

Kitty said, " I like it. It's a kind house, it doesn't look fierce as so many houses do when you ' take possession ', as if they resented your coming there at all. It's pleased to welcome us, that was why all the fires were burning so brightly. If they'd been sulky fires, I should have known that the house wasn't really glad to see us."

He slipped his arm through hers. " Fanciful child you are," he said. " I feel sometimes that I've snatched you from your nursery and toys."

She glanced up at him, smiling. " I'm a wise child, Oliver, make no mistake about that. I'm going to grow up here in this house, I'm going to make it a home for us both—and for our children. I promise that."

" You want children ? You're only twenty. Don't you want to just enjoy yourself, to be free to go where you like, do what you like for a few years ? "

She pulled herself away from his restraining arm, and stared at him in genuine astonishment. " But I want children," she protested. " I want them while I'm young and not full of set ideas, and while I've lots of energy. Oh no, Oliver, I don't want to just run about to tennis parties, and go week-end motor trips, and rush over to Paris to buy clothes. There's lots of time for that when the children are growing up, when they can be left or when they're at school."

" But," he persisted gently, " you are so young, we're both beginning a new kind of life from the one we've had to live during the war. We're—well," she saw his lips curve into the smile which she loved, " we're so very content, at least I am, and believe that you are."

" I know, I know "—eagerly; " we're terribly happy, that's the time to have children, so that they grow up with a father and mother who are still—in love. Later, oh, we shall still love each other, but you may become more absorbed in your business, I may become absorbed in the house, ordering meals, a hundred things. This is the time when we can give children some of the— glory and the gold of our lives. Don't you see ? "

He returned, slipping his arm through hers again. " I see that you're a wonderful person, and I flatter myself that I was a brilliantly clever fellow to find you, and—catch hold of you. I shall never let you go, remember that."

Their first son was born in the December, they named him Clifford to please Jabez, who was at that time immersed in the history of Baron Clifford who was deprived of his estates in 1461. In 1921, twins were born to them, who nearly cost Kitty Hallam her life. A boy named Clive, a girl called Barbara—both names chosen again by their grandfather for reasons of historic interest.

When she was so ill that her life was almost despaired of, Kitty's one injunction to the doctors was that they must not allow her to die, for she could not bear to leave Oliver.

The specialist who had been called in stood before the dining-room fire, sipping Oliver's excellent brandy, and talked to the local doctor.

" Strange young woman. Appears to have no fear for herself, apparently the one thing that frightens her is the idea of leaving her husband. Not her children, mark you—her husband. There she was, her lips blue, her pulse practically non-existent, whisper-ing, ' I must get better. We've only been married for three years. You must make me better.' Very devoted, are they ? "

The local doctor shook his head. " I suppose so. I've never really thought about it. They seem to be very happy. Nice young people."

Kitty won, and slowly, as the winter gave place to spring, she began to be able to come downstairs and to sit in the big window-space which looked over the garden. She loved her children: Clifford, who was so sturdy, so pink and gold, who knew exactly what he wanted—and contrived to get his own way whenever humanly possible; the twins, small and exquisite, strangely unalike—for she had believed that automatically twin children were ' as like as two peas '. Lying there, watching the birds flocking down to pick up the crumbs which were scattered for them on a special wooden tray every day, laughing at the energy of the blue-tits picking, quarrelling, and swinging on the coconut which Oliver had brought for them and hung where she could see it easily, Kitty reviewed her life, her present and future.

She was twenty-three, the gold was returning to her hair, which during her illness had looked dull and lifeless, now it had begun to shine again like gold. The light was coming back to her eyes, the colour to her cheeks, every day she was conscious of increasing strength. The specialist had told her that she would have no more children, smiling as he added, "After all, Mrs. Hallam, you've done quite well, and three children isn't such a very small family."

"And I shall be quite strong again?" she had asked anxiously.

"I see not the slightest reason why you should not be perfectly strong."

"Able to go about, travel, take long journeys . . . ?"

"Are you planning to go on voyages discovering the South Pole?"

"No, only I do want to be able to go about with my husband."

"Again I see not the slightest reason why you should not be able to do so."

Three years spent with Oliver Hallam had found her more deeply in love with him than ever. She could not have said exactly what she found so completely satisfactory in him, or why he exercised such a fascination over her. He was good to look at, even if he were not, strictly speaking, handsome. He was clever at his work, Jabez had told her that. He liked work, had ideas and ambitions, and after three years Kitty knew that financially he was far better off than when they had first married. He was not particularly talkative, his laughter came slowly, and his smiles were infrequent.

Lying on the broad sofa, Kitty shrugged her shoulders.

'I don't know,' she decided, 'I can't say why he's so attractive to me, why he completely absorbs me. I love the children, but I know that I love them more because they are his and mine. Something that we have achieved—together. They're part of not Oliver, not me, but—us. I love him far more than when we were first married. I don't know why, I can only think that it's because he is—Oliver.'

So their life together continued, sunlit with the light of complete affection and understanding, filled with the interests which they had in common. The children, Oliver's work, the hundred and one things which go to make up happy, busy, essentially normal lives.

The children grew, were sent to school, returned for the holidays to change the quiet house into a bear-garden for the duration of the time they spent there. Old Jabez adored them all. "Nay, theer niver was such youngsters, niver sick nor sorry, allus bright as buttons." His wife believed them to be the most splendid creatures in the world, and spent her time marvelling at their intellect and intelligence.

"Jabez, their 'eads is crammed wi' knowledge like a egg's crammed full o' meat. I niver mak' out wheer they gather it all. Talk about birds, beasts, fishes—it mak's no matter, they've got all the answers ready." Hugh Bland and his wife, if less insistent in their praise, were proud of Kitty's children; Hugh would watch them with a smile of satisfaction, and Alice spent her time making cakes and sweets for which they showed their complete approval.

Clifford was clever, he wished to study history, to Jabez's intense delight; Clive and Barbara, though less intellectual, were intelligent and charming. The twins were devoted to each other and, although they were completely different in their looks, they shared the same type of mentality. Both were impetuous, intolerant of anything which seemed to them to be unworthy, passionate in their love of the country things, they spent the greater part of their holidays ranging round the countryside or rowing on the small slow-moving river which ran so calmly at the edge of the paddock.

II

Kitty Hallam walked out of the house and, crossing the lawn, stopped for a moment beside the deck-chair where her husband lay reading. He lifted his eyes, laid down his paper and smiled.

" Isn't it too hot to go out, Kitty ? "

" I must go, there's a meeting at the Rectory to make plans." She shivered and Oliver impulsively stretched out his hand and caught hers.

" Don't get too worried darling."

" How can I help it ? " Her eyes were wide, and her voice higher than usual. " How can I help it. My children are too old and my husband is too young for me to be able to avoid worry. Anxiety— one would feel that in any case, but added to that is the sense of personal fear—desperate, awful, terrible fear." She laid her hand over her heart as she spoke. Oliver thought that she looked drawn, years older than she had done a few months ago. This cursed war, these clouds which had gathered and been dispelled only to gather darker and more menacing than ever !

He said, " My dear, we've got to face it. No use trying to wish and hope and ' pretend '. It's here—or practically here; it's got to be faced as well and as bravely as we can. We can only hope that— we all come through."

She nodded, he could see the muscles of her throat contracting as she fought down her emotion.

" I know," she said, " only Clifford would go—isn't he training already ? Clive and Bar would go too, and," her voice sank to a whisper, " they'd take you, Oliver, they'd take you. Or perhaps they wouldn't take you, your work might be of national importance —oh, I know that your plans are all made at Markholt, that you're all ready for the ' change over '. You've told me nothing, but I know just the same."

" My dearest, I didn't want to talk to you about it, I didn't want to distress you."

She turned her wide, clear eyes on him, watching him as if she were so much older and wiser than he was.

" I know," she said gently, " I know; I understand that. But a woman does not love a man as I've loved you, Norry, for over twenty years without gaining an extra sense. I don't have to be told about what concerns you, and you should realize that, darling."

Oliver smiled and shrugged his shoulders as if he deprecated her knowledge.

" Perhaps I ought to have told you—it was only that I wanted——"

" I know, I do understand, but it's *no use* ! That's one of the penalties of being so—close to anyone as I am to you. There ! I must go, or be late for the meeting at the Rectory." She turned away, then came back to him. " Norry, do you think that there is anything—between Bar and young Cardingly ? "

Oliver sat suddenly upright. " Bar and that young fellow—the curate ? Good lord, Kitty ! D'you think that there is ? I've not noticed anything."

" That's nothing, my blind-bat husband," she retorted. " You see very little that isn't pushed firmly under your nose. He's always coming here. I don't say that he actually ' fishes ' for invitations to dinner, but he does contrive to get asked here quite a lot. I don't mind, he's a very pleasant young man, but—I wondered what you thought."

" But, confound it, Beamarsh's curate ! He couldn't keep Bar ! Oh, I can be practical, Kitty, remember that, won't you ? I'm not prepared to allow Bar to marry any feller who can't keep her decently ! "

She shook her head, smiling. " Incredible creature," she said, " assuming the rôle of stern parent without knowing a thing about it all. He may be Stanley Beamarsh's curate, but he is also his nephew, and Stanley Beamarsh is—distinctly county ! Cardingly's father is Sir John of that ilk, and they are all remarkably well provided with this world's goods. It's not a question of being able to keep Bar, it's a matter as to whether Bar would like being a clergyman's wife."

Oliver ran his fingers through his dark hair, hair which was only touched with silver at the temples, but otherwise was as dark and thick as it had been twenty years ago.

" Oh, *gosh* ! " he said, " these children are a complication. I can't see Bar married to a parson somehow, however pleasant he was. Bar wouldn't really *conform* readily, d'you think ? "

" I refuse to think about it at the moment," Kitty said. " I asked for your opinion, and you haven't really got one. There, I must fly." At the little gate which led to the field path, which in its turn led to the village, Kitty turned for a moment to wave to him. He watched her figure grow smaller in the distance, then turned back to his paper. The sound of a car coming up the drive made him turn to see who was coming. He saw a small and very disreputable Austin, badly battered but still pulling gallantly; it stopped and his elder son scrambled out. Oliver called, " Clifford —come over here ! " and the tall young man in uniform came

towards him across the cropped turf. A good-looking young
man with bright fair hair like Kitty's, with the same bright, clear
blue eyes, well built, moving easily with the movements of a man
who is perfectly trained and physically fit.

" Hello, Daddy, how's things ? " He flung himself down, and
lit a cigarette.

Oliver asked, " Any news ? " No need to ask what news,
everyone knew.

Clifford blew out the match which he had used and carefully
pushed it down into the ground, then he nodded. " The kick-off
will be announced in the morning."

" Definite ? "

" Umph, umph, certain. Everything's set. I'll be going over
there almost at once—that is, our lot will."

Oliver pulled out his handkerchief and wiped his forehead. He
had been expecting this, and yet now that it had come—this news—
the shock was greater than he had imagined. War—Clifford
going overseas—Clive would go, he might possibly remain in
England for training for months, but eventually ' war ' would
catch and claim him too. Bar—if he knew anything of his daughter's
character, she would fling herself into some immediate work. He
might offer to take her on at the works, or send her to the larger
Hallam works at Birmingham. That might be a solution—not
that Bar was easy to influence. Bar had a mind of her own.

And he—what would he do ? He was fourty-four, he might be
thin but he was whipcord and wire, he had scarcely had a day's
illness in his life—at least, for the past twenty years. The works
would be all right—there was Fearnley, they'd never take Fearnley,
he was turned fifty. There was Bulstrode, the works manager,
capable, reliable, clever, but he limped badly as the result of a
accident that happened when he was an apprentice. No, the
works would be all right, with Fearnley, Bulstrode, the various
Heads of Departments—a grand bunch of men : Watson, Harris,
Hartley, Mandres, and Wilton. He realized that he and his son
were sitting in dead silence, both absorbed in their own thoughts,
and Oliver thought, slanting a glance at his son's grave face, ' By
the look of it, Cliff's are no more pleasant than mine ! '

He said, " How do you feel about it, my boy ? "

Cliff shrugged his shoulders. " Oh, there isn't anything much
to think or feel. It's not going to be a picnic, that's certain. 'Fraid
that Mummy's going to take it hard, eh ? Clive 'll go, probably
Bar—I fancy that they'll send you kids from London, evacuees,
to billet them here. It won't be too pleasant for you both."

Oliver said slowly, " No, not too pleasant ; still, if it's got to be
done, that's all there is to it. Incidently, I don't suppose that I
shall be here, Cliff."

Clifford Hallam twisted round to stare at his father. " Eh ? "

" I said that I didn't suppose that I should be here either."

" You'd be over at Markholt ? "

" If possible I shall be over—wherever they send me. I have no
particularly high ideals, Cliff, I don't believe that war is a real

solution to any problem, not a real and lasting solution. But I have a kind of elementary decency, and if my sons are going to fight—to defend something in which I believe and they believe, then so long as the authorities will take me, I've got to go too. I shan't like it, I didn't enjoy the last time. . . ."

He let his voice drift away into silence, and sat, his hands hanging loosely, staring out into vacancy. Clifford was too absorbed in his own thoughts to notice that his father had stopped speaking. He had his own preoccupations. Would he be able to see Irene again, dare he ask her to wait for him, was it fair to ask such a promise ? Did she really like him or was it just that she found him pleasant to dance with because their steps suited, and because they liked the same kind of music ?

Oliver saw nothing of the garden, of the herbaceous border which was Kitty's pride and upon which she had lavished so much care, the gently sloping fields beyond his own paddock were blotted out, he was back in the long low room of an apartment in Vicenza, Yolanda was telling him that she was going to Rome. That she was going to marry the Duke of Gradisco, that—everything must end between them. Yolanda—she must be waiting, as he was, to hear that the world was once more plunged into chaos. Somewhere, perhaps, she was sitting in a garden where oleanders bloomed, where magnolia blossoms filled the air with their heavy scent, where perhaps a little fountain played, scattering sunlit drops of water into a wide stone basin. How long it was since he had even vaguely remembered her, and yet—he had never known such despair as had filled him on that night when he left her at the doorway of her father's old palace in that narrow street in Vicenza.

Had she changed ; had she children like his own who would be caught in the whirlpool of this tragedy ? Was she thinking now of her sons, her daughters, wondering how long they would survive, trying to fight down fear and make hope strong and unshakable ? Did she look the same ? She must be a year or two older than himself—forty-six or forty-seven. Was her skin still pale with a faint bloom on the cheeks, were her eyes still large and dark and beautiful, did her lips still curve into that adorable smile which he could remember ?

He felt no love for her, that had died years ago, had never really existed after he met Kitty, but a sense of tenderness lingered. Together they had listened to the roar of fighter 'planes, together they had watched men come back from the front line, together they had talked of the hardships which the men suffered on the Adiege and as they climbed those terrible slopes of the Dolomites.

He made a violent effort, fought his way back from the distances of time and space, back to the quiet of his own garden, back to his son who sat silent at his side.

" And now it's all happening again," Oliver said.

Clifford said, " Yes, you've been through it once. It's a damned shame ! "

Oliver stretched out his hand and laid it on his son's arm. " Come

on, let's go in. We're getting filled with self-pity, maudlin—what
we both want is a drink, never mind if it is too early."

His son said gloomily, " They say that whisky's going to be
frightfully short, and going to cost the earth ! "

Oliver said, " It did last time, but we managed somehow."

III

Barbara Hallam flung down her racket and sank into a wicker
chair. The young man beside her watched her intently, then
lowered himself to the grass at her side. A good-looking young
man, tall and well-built if slightly too narrow in the shoulders,
his dark hair already inclined to recede a little from his high, wide
forehead; his eyes were good and well-set, his nose rather too
long and faintly melancholy, his chin firm and jutting forward.
Altogether a good-looking fellow without the slightest claims to
actual masculine beauty.

He said, " That was pretty good, eh ? "

She nodded.   " I'm playing better this season.   Not exactly
' centre court ' form, but distinctly better."   Then abruptly, " What
would you do—no, it's too late to ask that—what *will* you do ? "

He pulled up a little blade of grass and rolled it in his fingers.
" You mean, if this . . . ? "

" I mean," Barbara answered, " what will you do *when* this
war begins ? "

" It hasn't begun yet, Barbara."

" Oh, don't talk that rubbish. It's going to, and we all know it.
Do try to answer my question, Michael."

He sat up, his hands clasped round his knees, and looked at
her. She was worth looking at as she sat there, her face a little
flushed, her eyes very bright and eager, her brown hair, with its
red lights, catching the sun which came slanting through the
leaves of the old elms. Strictly speaking and judging by conventional standards of actual beauty, Barbara Hallam could not
be called lovely. Her nose was short and faintly tilted, her mouth
was generous and too large, but her colouring, her air of loving
life, of finding interest in everything and everywhere made people
speak of her as ' that lovely Hallam girl '.

He considered, then said slowly, " I hope that I should do what
I believed to be my duty."

She stared at him, her expression a mixture of disgust and
astonishment. She liked Michael Cardingly; there had been
moments when she wondered if she did not like him sufficiently
well to consider him as a possible husband. There were times
when he amused her, when she liked his outlook, his good manners,
and his kindness, when his ability to be a clergyman and yet enjoy
amusements, dancing, laughter, and the like seemed to argue that
he was really a very pleasant and human young man, untrammelled
by his profession or the exigencies of his calling. Only at intervals
did he make remarks like that which he had just uttered, making

her feel that there must always be moments when he seemed to set himself aloof from the other young men of his own age by virtue of his cloth.

She said, " Good lord, what do you mean by that pompous pronouncement ? "

He flushed and answered rather stiffly, " Exactly what I said."

" You mean that you might be able to convince yourself that you had a right to stay—out of it all ; to let other men go and do the dirty work for you ? Is that right, is that what you really mean ? "

" Shall we leave it ? " Michael asked. " War is not declared yet ; who knows that it may be avoided at the last moment."

" How can it be, unless we let Hitler have another chunk of someone else's land ? Be yourself ! And how can you—*leave* a matter like this ? There can't be two opinions, no one likes war, no one with any sense believes in war, but you can't hide behind other people. I can tell you one thing—when this comes, I'm going. Oh, indeed I am ! " seeing his gesture of protest, " and not to nurse or roll bandages, but into one of the Services. Not because I'm bursting with patriotic fervour, but because I want to retain my own self-respect." She was growing angry, a thing not unusual to Barbara Hallam when she flung herself into an argument, " I'm going home ; tell Mrs. Cotton that I had a lovely time, if you see her, please. I don't know where she is at the moment."

He sprang to his feet and stood beside her, " Barbara, let me walk back with you, please."

Her eyes were cold, that full, generous mouth set tightly. " You'd be much wiser not to ! "

" Perhaps I am not very wise where you are concerned," Michael said.

They walked in silence to the gates of ' Woodstock ', and meeting Mrs. George Cotton assured her that they had spent a wonderful afternoon. She beamed impartially upon them both, for Elsie Cotton, like the rest of the village, had long ago gathered that Michael Cardingly was, to say the least of it, ' attracted ' to Oliver Hallam's daughter.

The silence remained unbroken until they reached the little footpath which led through the fields to Oliver Hallam's house, then Michael said tentatively, " Barbara, your good opinion does matter tremendously to me, you know that, don't you ? "

She retorted, " It's quite easy to earn it ! "

" But don't you realize that I can't allow even you—even you—to force me to take a course of action in which I do not believe. It would be like paying a kind of spiritual blackmail ! "

" You don't believe ! " she flashed back at him. " You're not a conscientious objector or a pacifist, are you ? "

" No, but I am a clergyman. This is a very large and very scattered parish, my uncle is not strong, his heart has never been right since he had rheumatic fever ten years ago. He may not be able to do all that he would wish to do—it may be my duty to stay here, to do what I can. You see," he spoke gently, " I am—under orders, Barbara."

" Oh, I *know*." Her tone was irritable. " I know that you can justify what you do—or don't do. All that I know is that, to me, it sounds perilously like sophistry. You're right, Michael, don't let's discuss it. Surely your uncle can dig out some superannuated old parson to come and help him. There must be dozens of them."

" But a superannuated old parson wouldn't be any use, it needs someone young, active, strong. Bar.dear, do be reasonable."

She stopped abruptly at the little iron gate which led to their garden.

" All right—maybe you'll get this straight. I only hope that you manage to do so soon. Are you preaching to-morrow night ? "

His face brightened. " Yes, will you come and hear me ? Do—please."

" What's your text ? "

" Saint Mark—twelve, verse seventeen—you know: Render unto Caesar . . ."

She frowned. " Not easy to preach on that text at the moment and get away with it. Good night, Michael. . . ."

" Oh, Bar, don't go, do let us try to get this straight."

" Better not; you see, I have got it straight. Good night."

She found her father and mother, with her two brothers, in the drawing-room. She greeted them, then frowned as she looked intently at her mother's face.

" Mummy darling, what's the matter ? Daddy, what is it ? "

Kitty answered her. " Only that I am greeted with the news that Cliff will be going overseas, that Clive wishes to join the Air Force immediately, your father is determined—in spite of the fact that he is over age—to join the Army in some capacity if possible—added to which I have been warned that my home may be invaded by hordes of evacuee children and their mothers in the near future. It only needs you, Bar, to tell me that you are going to rush into uniform, and my cup of happiness will overflow ! " She looked at them all, the people she loved best in the world, her bright eyes angry and hostile. For a moment no one spoke, then Clive rose and came over to sit at her side.

He was fair as she was, and had that particularly well-washed appearance which some people do not achieve but which clings to them in all circumstances. He was reputed to be brilliantly clever, the authorities in his schools and during his first term at the University assured him that a splendid career lay before him. Learning came easily to Clive Hallam, and he always wondered a little if he earned the praise which was showered upon him. It was all dead easy, anyone with reasonable intelligence could learn, and, anyway, learning was pleasant and often amusing.

Now he took his mother's hand and spoke lightly. " Darling, aren't you losing your sense of humour ? Allowing yourself to dramatize it all a little, seeing yourself as Rachel bereft of her children ! I'm sorry about the evacuees, because I know that except for your own delightful and utterly charming brood you have no great love for other folks' brats. Clifford will probably—if I know my brother—dig himself into some very cushy job and remain there for the duration, I shall run about on some airfield and watch the 'planes go up while I remain with both feet firmly planted on the ground. Bar will spend laborious days in washing up filthy plates, scrubbing floors, and the like, and Daddy—well, darling, come, come. They'll take one look at his adorable but ' wintry pow ' and wave him away to ' take people's particulars ', and there he'll sit in a stinking office and do nothing in particular, ' and do it very well '. Bless you, they don't want old gentlemen, however charming."

Kitty turned on him. " And even in fun—and it's very poor fun, let me tell you—don't speak like that about your father. I won't have it."

Clive rose, winked at his father, and said, " Darling, to think that you had to remind me so pointedly. I beg your pardon, Mummy darling, what *will* you have—Martini, Pink Gin—say the word."

She smiled suddenly. Oliver thought that her smile was like the sun breaking out after a sudden storm, and said, " Impertinent crowd you are, all of you. Give me a Martini, and make it dry."

CHAPTER IV

I

KITTY HALLAM stared at her reflection in the mirror which stood on her dressing-table. She leaned forward, narrowing her eyes as if to see more clearly. She decided that she looked older, there were tiny lines at the corners of her eyes, she fancied that her mouth sagged a little at the corners. She shrugged her shoulders. What did it matter ? If she looked a hag, who was there to comment on her appearance ?

Clifford was in France, he wrote grumbling that the Americans were right, that it was a ' phoney war ', nothing much to do except put up with the mud and the cold. " Never believe people who tell you that the South of France is warmer than England," he wrote. " It may be on the coast of the Mediterranean, it certainly is not inland."

Clive was training in a camp outside Edinburgh, he wrote that the place was a " dreary desert, but the actual work is amusing. I shall shortly be an Air Vice-Marshal, if everything goes according to real merit, which of course it doesn't."

Barbara had enlisted in the W.A.A.F., had been told that she would be ' sent for ', and for three weeks had heard nothing. She wandered about, bored, lonely, and acutely depressed. Kitty watched her and wondered what were her real feelings concerning Michael Cardingly. At times they seemed excellent friends, at others the mere mention of his name was sufficient to make Barbara's face assume an expression of distaste and even disgust. And Oliver—he had gone too. When he told her that the Army had accepted him, that he had passed his medical examination success-fully, she had felt that someone—something—had cut away the ground before her and that she stood on the edge of a precipice, at the very end of the world. For over twenty years they had scarcely been parted, and even when business had taken him away for a few days his return had been hailed as a kind of festival. How many times had she gone about her household duties, conscious that she smiled involuntarily, that it was almost too easy to laugh, that everything was ' new ' and exciting, because her heart sang, ' Oliver is coming home to-day '? That was how she had felt after his absence for a few days, a week, or at most a month. Now he wrote every day, brief, affectionate letters from a place called Safton in North Devon, and said how he longed for the leave which might be due to him in another five months. Kitty knew for the first time in her life what loneliness meant. For years she and Oliver had discussed everything that affected either of them—that was one of the charming things about him, he never protested that things were ' scarcely his business ' or that ' I'm afraid you'll have to settle that yourself '. Whatever she wished to talk over with him—-whether it was the new housemaid, the butcher, the matter of ordering new covers for the drawing-room chairs, Oliver had always thrown himself wholeheartedly into everything; she had felt that he liked nothing better than to take all her difficulties as if they had been a skein of tangled wool, and slowly, carefully, and with completely full attention, Oliver had unravelled them and handed the neat, compact ball back to her.

In addition to everything else, a woman, wearing a repulsive uniform of dark brown with dull red facings, had called to see her. Her hands had been full of papers, forms, and sheets of instructions. She was tall, filled with energy, and possessed a large mouth which appeared to overflow with teeth. Her name was Miss Eunice Malten. She was standing near the window when Kitty entered the drawing-room, and turned, flashing a complete set of bright porcelain teeth; her eyes sparkled, and it was obvious that she was determined to be bright and desperately cheerful. She advanced with outstretched hands covered in thick doeskin gloves.

" Mrs. Hallett, I don't want you to hate me. Everyone does, y'know. They all think that I am trying to work off a personal spite. Nothing could be less true, of course. I am the billeting officer. I have to find homes—I prefer the word ' homes ' to ' quarters '—for these poor children from the East End. Your name has been given to me, Mrs. Hallett."

Kitty said, " Incorrectly, I'm afraid; it's Hallam."

" Really. *How amusing.* Now, how many of these bairns can you take, do you think ? "

Kitty considered. " I have at the moment three maids, two will leave immediately they hear the children are coming. I don't blame them. I should leave myself if I were in their place. Cook, I imagine, will stay. That will leave Cook and me. I might be able to get Mrs. Parkiss from the village. How many children, Miss Malten ? "

Miss Malten waved a sheaf of papers wildly, and after dropping several and retrieving them again, said, " Help—that is, household help—need not worry you. There will be two mothers coming with the children."

That was when Kitty sat down and said, " Good lord ! Mothers ! "

" I have you down for five children and two mothers, Mrs. Hallett—I beg your pardon, Hallam, Mrs. Hallam. Two families. The Carters, number seventeen Hollywood Street, East Ham, with Sidney, Edith, and Alice, and Mrs. Perry, of number six Cotswold Street, Bow, with Henry and Susie. Mrs. Carter and Mrs. Perry will, of course, help with the housework and the cooking of their children's meals."

" I don't think that Cookie will like that," Kitty said doubtfully. " She's very much the autocrat in her own kitchen ! "

Miss Malten nodded brightly. " I know, I know, but ' times change ', the country is at war, and," she laughed, her teeth flashing, " we must all be prepared for invasion, even cooks in their kitchens ! "

" I thought that we were to be prepared to repulse invasions," Kitty said.

" My joke, Mrs. Hallett, my joke. I always say, ' with a joke all loads are lightened '. It's so true. Then will that be all right ? Five children and two mothers. I don't think that I need inspect the rooms, I'm sure that they will be completely satisfactory. Here are the forms." She immediately dropped a sheaf of them to the floor, again retrieved them and pressed them into Kitty's hands. " They're all quite simple, you'll receive certain rations and certain allowances. But you can read them through at your leisure. I mustn't keep you, must I ? "

" But when are they arriving ? " Kitty felt lost, submerged, she longed insanely for Oliver to read these forms, to make out lists, and generally stand by her in this minor crisis.

" Ah, that I can't say exactly. It depends on a certain gentleman. If his 'planes become tiresome that will speed up the evacuation. But shall we say in about a week's time."

She shook hands firmly, repeated that she hoped that Kitty did not hate her, which by that time Kitty did completely and fully, and drove away in a small but very smart coupé. Kitty watched it disappear round the curve in the drive, and turned back into the house.

She made her way to the kitchen, where Cook, Martha, the elderly house-parlourmaid, and Clarice, the pretty young house-maid, were all engaged in partaking of ' elevenses ', consisting of rock cakes and cups of strong tea.

Kitty said, " No, don't get up. I want to talk to you all. Yes, give me a cup of tea, Cookie, not too strong. Now you've all got to make your decision, and remember that you have a perfect right to do what you wish. I am told that I am to have five children from London to live here—with their mothers."

Cook said coldly, " 'Ow many mothers 'ud that be, m'um ? "

" Two—three children belong to one, two to the other."

Cook set down her teacup and breathed the word, " Gawd ! " piously.

Martha said, " Did you ever hear of such a thing, and this a free country ! Why, your house isn't your own any longer. That's a thing, that is, if you like ! Interfering with the liberty of the subject."

Kitty looked from one to the other. Clarice didn't really matter, she was certain to go, but suddenly Kitty was conscious of an intense wish that these two elderly women, both of whom she had known for so many years, might decide to stay with her. She said, " Well, Clarice . . . ? "

Clarice flushed, and made crumbs of her rock cake as she answered that she had been on the point of coming to speak to her mistress.

" I'm goin' to join the A.T.S., m'um," she said, " me and Mrs. Cotton's Agnes decided it larst night. She's twenty and I'm twenty-one, and they'd want us to do war work, any road, if you see what I mean, m'um ? "

Kitty said, " I quite understand, Clarice. Now, Cookie, what about you ? "

Cook—her real name was Sarah Ann Scott—laid her hand on her broad bosom and breathed loudly. " Onless you see fit to discharge me, madam, which I should be sorry ter see you do after neerly thirteen yeeres' service, I shall stay w'ere I am. I've no fancy fer a crowd o' East Enders straveging about in my kitchen. I'm fifty-two next year an' I've no intention of getting myself dressed up in uniform and brass buttons like a penny monkey, not to please Mr. Chamberlain nor 'Itler nor none of them ! That's my unification, madam. We've 'eard a lot of this one an' that one handing out unifications lately—well, that's Sarah Ann Scott's."

Kitty laid her hand for a moment on the broad, print-covered shoulder, and said, " That's good hearing, Cookie." Then, " And you, Martha ? "

Martha said primly, " As we're tellin' ages, m'um, I'm the same age as the master; we've often laughed about it, often." Kitty wondered why the fact that Martha and Oliver were the same age should be amusing, but she contented herself with smiling. " They won't want me, and if they did," she added darkly, " they'd not get me. I know my 'istr'y, and what I say is what was Magna Charter for, and what about the Habeas Corpus Act ? Some of them are losing sight of them things, m'um. Rights are rights, and wrongs are no man's right. If five children come here, they'll learn to behave themselves here, or my name isn't Martha Brown."

Suddenly Kitty saw two faces—Cook's broad and highly coloured, Martha's thin and leathery, swim before her eyes, she saw them through a mist of tears which came unbidden. She stared from one to the other, then sat down on the hard kitchen chair, laid her head on her arms and began to cry. They seemed all that were left to her, these two women she had known for so long, they were the only solid, permanent things in her life, everything else had been taken from her. Cook and Martha were going to stay with her, to remind her of all the things that had once seemed lasting and enduring.

She heard Cook saying, " Now look at that, prop'ly over-done, she is. It's a shame, a damned shame. Now, m'um, now, this won't do. I'm 'ere, an' Martha's 'ere. 'Ere, drink your tea, it 'ul put heart into you."

And Martha's thinner, dryer voice admonishing her gently. " Now, m'um, this isn't like you, this isn't. It's goin' to be all right, we'll soon settle everything between us. Don't let Clarice going upset you, she'd have to go, anyway, it's not because she'd not like to stay, is it, Clarrie, my girl ? "

Kitty lifted her head and dabbed her eyes; she looked at them, and Cook thought, ' Even wi' all this bother, she wears well, does the missus, looks downright young sometimes. Like a lost child she looks.' Kitty said, " I'm sorry, only this morning everything seemed to get on top of me, everything seemed too heavy. Of course, I know that Clarice must go, but I was so afraid that you and Martha might want to go too, and "—her voice shook— " I felt that I couldn't face it all. Please forgive me, I am sorry. You've not often seen me do that in thirteen years, have you, Cookie ? Now, Martha, come and let us decide where these people are going to sleep. They'd better have a sitting-room too, I think."

Martha sniffed. " People ! I call them hordes, that's what I call them."

II

Barbara was smiling as she came in to tea. She said, " It's all right, they hadn't forgotten me. I'm to report at Nottingham on Monday morning. I'm awfully glad that's settled. Mummy, please don't hate my going so badly."

Kitty said, " I will try not to, Bar. Only it is going to be pretty damnable, alone here with crowds of children and mothers, and you all away. Scattered ! I never thought that it could happen."

" We shall all be drifting back for leave, you know."

" I suppose so, darling. I shall get used to it. There, let me give you more tea. I believe that tea in the Services is simply terrible. Make the most of it while you're here."

Barbara sipped her tea, watching her mother as she did so. She was glad to be going, not glad to leave home, certainly not glad to leave Mummy—poor Mummy, who'd loved having them all with her, who had always wanted to give them the best possible times, and had succeeded. But she longed to feel that she was actively joining in the same effort in which Clive was working, to feel that, even though they might be divided, they still shared a common cause. He was R.A.F., she was to be W.A.A.F.—the same service, and the idea thrilled her. They'd even wear the same coloured uniform !

She set down her cup and said, as if she had suddenly remembered what she wanted to say, " Oh, Mummy dear, Michael Cardingly wants me to be engaged to him. Do you think that it's a good idea ? "

" Doesn't that depend upon whether you love him or not, Bar ? "

" Yes, I suppose so. That's where it's all so difficult. There are times when I think that I like him better than any man in the world —except Clive, of course—and then he says or does something which infuriates me, makes me feel that he's sanctimonious, and pompous, and—oh, other things as well. It's very puzzling. What would you do, Mummy ? "

" Nothing until I was quite certain—one way or the other, Bar."

" He wants me to be engaged to him before I join the W.A.A.F.——"

" What is he going to do ? "

Barbara's face flushed scarlet, Kitty saw her eyes harden, grow bright and cold. "That's one of the things I don't understand. He hasn't made up his mind. Oh, it's not exactly 'scruples' about fighting, but he thinks that he's needed—in the parish. I told him that his uncle could easily find some old 'dug-out' to help in the parish; after all, that's what they're doing in offices and banks and works, even in the Army. Then he gets offended and looks hurt——"

"Which in itself is not surprising, Bar dear. You're scarcely tactful, darling, are you?"

Bar got up and looked down at her mother, frowning. "I know —it's awful. I know that I hurt Michael, but then remember that Michael hurts me. I do like him, but I don't like watching him hide behind that dog-collar he wears. Oh yes, Mummy, that's what it looks like to me! Just plain *hiding*. His mother is coming to see him. I'm glad that I shall be gone. Mummy, don't you think that I'm right. Daddy didn't hide behind his age—did he?"

Her mother sighed. Kitty Hallam wasn't clever and she knew it. Every one of her children outstripped her so far as brains and intellect were concerned. Oliver had often told her that she was 'intuitive', and although she never understood precisely what he meant, she felt that it was a good thing to be. She knew that her own feelings were that every man ought to go and fight, but she also knew that this sentiment was not engendered by a spirit of patriotism, but because she felt that with her own men all ready to defend their country, it was unfair that every other able-bodied man should not do the same. Her own common sense and instinctive fairness told her that had Oliver decided to remain at the works she would have felt more kindly towards George Cotton and even Oliver's own brother Evelyn. Oliver had decided to go into the Army, and Kitty knew that she felt angry and intolerant towards all men who were not imbued with the same impulse.

She said, "Bar darling, I don't know. I can't advise you. I feel that I'm unfair to many people—really only because your father has gone. I don't see why young Cardingly should stay at home, when my two sons have gone. I could work myself into a perfect passion about the injustice of it all. I should be wrong—oh, yes, I should! Look, here we are, you and I, within half a yard of each other; look at that tea-tray there. If we were given pencils and paper and told to make a drawing of it—not that I've ever been able to draw a line in my life—although we're so close together, although we should be drawing the same tea-tray, covered with the same pieces of china—our two drawings would be quite different. More than that, we should probably *see* everything differently. That cup might be the centre of my drawing, to you the teapot might be the really important thing. That's what I feel we're all doing to-day. Looking at the same thing and seeing it quite differently according to the exact inch on which we stand. Michael may move, so that he sees everything as you do—you may move so that——"

Her daughter interrupted, "I shan't move an inch, Mummy. Not an inch!"

Kitty said, " Darling, if you love him, then everything is all right, or will be all right. If you love people they come to understand you, and you understand them. If you don't—then keep out of an engagement until you are certain, quite certain, of your own mind. You're going away for training, when you come back on leave, everything may have changed. My father—your grandfather—always says, ' Don't rush your fences '. It's good advice, darling."

III

Barbara went off to Nottingham and by the afternoon train the evacuees arrived. They were driven up in the two cabs from the ' Wagon and Horses '; their goods were piled on the roofs, the children were hanging out of the windows wildly excited and yelling at everything they saw which was new and strange. The cabs drew up at the door and Martha, who was waiting, motioned the drivers to go round to the back. That done, she announced to Kitty, " They've come, m'um. Round at the back door. I'll have something to say to that Percy Wright, bringing these people to the front door ! What next ! "

By the time Kitty reached the kitchen Martha was already giving Percy Wright her opinion of his conduct. " An Englishman's home is his castle," she announced. " That doesn't mean Kenilworth Castle on a free day. Just bear that in mind, if you please."

Percy Wright said, " All right, all right, no need to create ! Now, missus, let's git this pram off the roof. Walter, give me a hand wi' this, then I'll come and see ter your little lot. Easy does it."

Two small groups stood huddled near the kitchen door, one a small, pale-faced woman, who kept sighing rather than saying at intervals to two small, pale children, " Now see as you be'ave, both of you. You 'ear me, 'Enry, d'you 'ear, Susie ? "

To which they both replied in small, pale voices, " Yes, Mum, yes."

The other group was slightly larger, presided over by a tall, stout woman with an immense bust and hips; she held a birdcage in her hand in which a canary hopped feverishly from perch to perch. A small boy with red hair and a heavy powdering of freckles was fighting with a girl rather taller than himself, while another child, also a girl, watched dispassionately, saying from time to time, " It 'er, Sid," or " Give 'im one, Edie."

As Percy and Walter worked, a collection of bags, boxes and brown paper parcels gathered round the group. Kitty surveyed them.

" Ah, you've arrived." Then, seeing the perambulator, she exclaimed, " Oh, is there a baby too ? "

The stout woman, administering a swift and accurate cuff on the ear of her son, replied, " Biby ? No, thank 'eaven. It's fer the shopping, thet is! Siddie—be'ave will yer, or I'll knock yer 'ead clean off of yer neck!'"

They were transported into the kitchen, where they stood and stared in a slightly hostile manner at Cook; her face was impassive.

Mrs. Carter, the stout woman, demanded, " Is this w'ere we eat in the kitching?"

Cook returned, " It is not; it's arranged that you and your friend an' the children eat in the back kitchen—there it is. Nice and bright, plenty of room, and I don't hold with children eating with their elders, no more does my friend Martha here."

Surprisingly enough, it was Mrs. Perry who raised objections. Mrs. Carter looked at the back kitchen and pronounced it " Nice bright room, thet is. Bit diff'rent to my kitching in London." Mrs. Perry sniffed and rubbed the back of her hand over her nose.

" Scarcely nice, is it, ter shove uz in the beck kitching?" she asked.

Mrs. Carter returned, " Oh, dry up, Lucy, s'long as the grub's theer what the 'ell does it matter."

It was Mrs. Perry who grumbled at everything, in that pale, small voice which held a singularly carrying quality; she could be heard from morning to night objecting to one thing after another. Mrs. Carter regarded the whole thing as a kind of grim joke. She cuffed her children heartily but without actual malice, she offered to ' lend a 'and ' in the kitchen, though Cook told Martha that ' the poor creature makes more mess nor what she's worth '. Mrs. Perry barely consented to clean her own room, and even then did it so badly that Martha protested that it was easier to do it herself ' first as last '.

The children were badly behaved and desperately untidy. Their dirty fingermarks were to be found in the most unexpected places, and both women seemed incapable of keeping them in order. Mrs. Perry wailed at them, Mrs. Carter administered cuffs generously; neither had the slightest effect. Martha watched, coldly disapproving.

Kitty held her breath. What would happen if Martha decided to leave, if she protested that the children were too much for her? She said tentatively one evening, after they had been in the house for three days, " Martha, I hope those children aren't too much for you and Cook."

Martha answered, " I've been allowing them to have their heads, as the saying goes, just while they settle down. Then—I'm going to do a bit of settling on my own account. They're nothing but a lot of savage Hottametots, those children. But—there's a change coming, m'um."

The change came. Martha, quiet and speaking as one with authority, ordered the lives of the London children, and Kitty listened with something like awe to her speaking to them in the hall one morning.

" I thought I told you never to let me find you in this 'all?"

Sidney answered, " We gotter come dahnsteers, ain't we?"

" You have, *and* to come down quietly, *and* to make your way as fast as ever your legs will carry you to the back kitchen where your breakfast's waiting."

His elder sister added, " I 'ate this plice ! I 'ate you worst of all ! "

" Nothing to what I feel for you," Martha answered; " and while I am talking to you, understand this, the next time I have to speak to you—or any of you—there's the finest tanning you've ever had. Mind that."

Sidney retorted, " I'd like ter see yer do it, thet's all ! Old cow ! "

Judging from the sounds which reached her, Martha made good her promise. Sidney's howls filled the hall, Edie cried in sympathy and Alice screamed, " I'll tell my Mum, thet I will ! "

Kitty drew a deep breath, this would mean quarrels with Mrs. Carter, arguments, and in all probability Martha would pack her boxes and leave. She walked out into the hall, where the ' tanning ' was apparently just over. She watched Martha dust her hands, as if the contact with Sidney Carter had soiled them, heard her say, " Now get on, the lot of you ! And walk quietly ! " And saw the three children make their way down the long passage to the kitchen.

She said, " Martha, did you beat that child ? "

" Indeed I did, m'um, and shall again if he can't behave himself."

" But do you think that—well, that you ought to ? "

Unmoved, Martha replied, " I do, m'um. His mother told me that she can do nothing with them—I promised that I'd show her that I could. Don't worry, m'um, we had nine in family, eight younger than what I was. I taught them manners, there isn't one of my sisters and brothers that doesn't worship the very ground I tread on."

In the kitchen Mrs. Carter demanded, " Whatcher 'owling fer, Sidie ? "

" Martha lammed 'im, Mum," Edie supplied the information. " Give 'im a proper 'iding, she did."

Alice said, " Our Sidie didn't 'arf cry, Mum ! "

As Martha entered, Mrs. Carter demanded, " Did you give my kid a 'iding ? "

Imperturbably Martha replied, " I did, Mrs. Carter, and will again, if he gives me any of his nasty lip.".

Mrs. Carter nodded majestically. " Ah, nasty lip 'e 'anded art, did 'e ? Na, I'll tell yer what, all on yer. Martha, I give you full permission ter tan the 'ide off of any of 'em as 'ands out lip. Let alone nasty lip. 'Ere you are," she continued, addressing her off-spring, " me givin' you a charnce ter live in a loverly 'ouse, ter mix wi' gentry, an' yer too damned thick-'eaded ter take advan-tage of it. I've a blasted good mind ter give yer all another 'iding—the three of yer ! "

Later the village school was reopened and the children went there. Mrs. Carter gave instructions that her children were to be ' made ter be'ave at whatever cost '. Mrs. Perry announced that if either of hers was so much as touched, ' someone 'ul 'ear abart it '.

Cook discovered that Mrs. Carter had one passion, and that to scrub anything which was scrubbable. She was useless at preparing vegetables, Cook said, ' Willing but handless '. But when given a brush and hot water would, as she put it herself, ' knock 'ell and the dirt outer anything at the same time '. Mrs. Perry continued to do nothing except embroider traycloths with a stitch which she told them was called ' the lazy daisy stitch '.

Mrs. Carter would shout at the top of her voice, " 'Ere, wheer's ole Lazy Daisy got 'erself to ? Blimy ! niver gits off of 'er backside except ter come dahn ter meals wot other folks 'ave got ready."

Martha had been right, the three small Carters adored her, and each Saturday morning they might be found busily cleaning brass, polishing knives, or making Martha's cycle look like a new machine.

Kitty said, " Do they enjoy doing it, Martha ? "

" Love it, m'um, an' Mrs. Carter—she's all right, rough but ready, as the saying goes—is delighted to see them occupied. They get a penny each, and think the world of it."

" And the Perry children ? "

" Little rats," Martha said viciously. " Children like them want putting down by law. Nasty, 'orrid creatures. Them and their mother, sitting in that small sitting-room, doing *fancy work*, while the children make a mess of everything with crayons. Crayons ! I'd crayon them both."

Oliver came home on his first leave, to find his home filled with strangers, not that he really minded, he was far too content to worry about what appeared to him to be trifles. He saw a small red-headed boy busily cleaning his shoes with tremendous application and earnestness, he saw two small girls polishing brass candlesticks, and a huge, ungainly woman on her knees scrubbing the kitchen floor. She looked up as he entered, grinned and said, " 'Ow are yer ? Glad ter be back, I'll bet ! "

Cook wiped her floury hands on her apron and said, " This is nice, to see you home, sir. This is Mrs. Carter of East 'Am, she's kindly givin' me a hand."

" That's remarkably good of her, but you've got another woman and her children down here, haven't you ? "

Mrs. Carter opened her mouth and roared, " 'Ave we ? I'll sai we 'ave ! Ole Lazy Daisy an' 'er kids. They keep theerselves ter theerselves, don't they, Cook ? Bit superior to uz—Lazy Daisy, Duchess of Bow, an' 'er brats Lord 'Enery an' the Honourable Susan ! "

Oliver told Kitty later, " Most astonishing. An immense woman, scrubbing the kitchen floor and bawling offensive epithets about her co-evacuee. It was most of it Greek to me. She seemed happy enough, and some ginger-haired children, working like beavers."

To Kitty it was as if for the brief seven days for which Oliver was home her world had righted itself. He looked so well, he was tanned and had an air of well-being; he was still the same, still gentle and sweet and the centre of her world.

She talked of the two boys, of Bar still in Nottingham and, in spite of all the hardships, declaring that she loved her work. She talked of the Carters and the Perrys, of Oliver's father and mother, of his sister Victoria who was driving a car for the Ministry of Information, she talked of every subject—except one. That question which she longed to ask she dare not speak. " When are you going out ? "

Oliver told her, " No need to worry, darling, I shan't be going out for months. Not until the New Year at all events. There is just a remote chance—not a big one, so don't be disappointed—that I might get home for Christmas. This leave is a pure piece of luck because I had to go and see my father on business. I've never seen the Old Man so happy and so busy. He looks years younger ! "

She didn't care about Jabez Hallam, much though she loved him. As Oliver talked her heart was singing ' He's safe until the spring—he isn't going out yet ! ' She looked younger, felt younger, her laughter came easily, and nothing seemed to matter. The fact that Clifford had written that the weather was damnable in France, and that he hoped to become engaged when he came home on leave, sunk into insignificance, only Oliver's safety mattered. Her children, and how she loved them all three, were precious. Oliver was—her life.

CHAPTER V

I

OLIVER had gone back to Devon; Kitty was alone again. His visit had helped her, she felt that having come home once, she could believe that he would come again and not be snatched from her and sent overseas without another glimpse of him.

In vain that he had assured her, " Darling, before we do go— and if we go—I shall have embarkation leave," she had read that in his letters dozens of times, had shrugged her shoulders and felt that this was only ' Oliver trying to soothe me, it's not really true '. Now he had been home, she had heard him singing—a little out of tune—in his bath, she had heard his voice as he talked to Cook and Martha, she had seen his brushes lying on the dressing-table again. What had happened once might conceivably happen again. She was serene if not actually happy.

Clive had come home before Christmas, talking a strange jargon which was incomprehensible to his mother. Sidney Carter was entranced at the idea of a ' reel airman ' living in the same house as himself; he cleaned Clive's shoes several times a day, he polished buttons and ran errands. His eyes were filled with dog-like devotion when they followed his hero. Clive was tolerant, con-descending and Jove-like in his attitude towards the small boy. Martha and Cook vied with each other to gratify his lightest wish.

" Mummy," he asked one evening as he and Kitty sat together by the bright fire, " what about Bar and Michael? Anything doing?"

" I don't know. She doesn't mention him in her letters. She thinks that he ought to join the Army—as a chaplain, I suppose."

Clive frowned. " We have one," he said in much the tone that he might have admitted that they kept a dog; " he's all right. The Catholics have one as well, queer feller, not like a parson at all. I shouldn't worry about Bar, Mummy. She'll make up her mind for herself."

" Michael looks acutely miserable; he comes here sometimes to see me."

" Oh, he'll get over it too. Either it will work out all right or it won't, no use worrying about it. Honestly, I'm not really keen on having a parson in the family."

She loved having him at home, and tried to understand his queer slang, and follow his explanations as to why they did this or that At the sound of a 'plane he would rush out, stare up into the sky, and point to some speck, announcing its make and type.

" How do you know what they are, Clive ? " Kitty asked.

" When they're as high as that by the sound mostly," he told her; " they've all got individual sounds. You can tell that, can't you ? "

3

To Kitty they all sounded exactly alike, dull roaring monsters, flying to deliver death; terrible machines in which young men risked their lives, facing horrible things, laughing at danger.

" You don't fly, Clive, do you ? "

" No—oh no, I've not been at it long enough. I should *like* to fly."

" Oh, Clive darling, *don't*," she begged.

" Mummy darling, everyone wants to fly. Honestly, it's almost as dangerous on the ground. We had three chaps killed last week —all on the ground. I swear that's true."

She experienced that strange sick feeling which she had come to know every time she thought of Clive being allowed to fly; now it appeared that the ground was dangerous too.

" What pleasant surprises you all give me ! " she said. " And I imagined that you were perfectly safe."

He returned, " Well, in the main it's pretty well *all* safe, you know. Nothing to worry about—actually nothing."

He went back, and she fought down her longing to beg him not to learn to fly, knowing that to have done so might have made him feel resentful, repressed, limited. The whole thing—the war— the part which her husband and children were destined to play in it, all seemed so fantastic, so incredible, that Kitty realized that it was all completely out of her sphere. They were not really ' hers ' any longer, they had become absorbed into this strange new life of which she knew nothing, of which she comprehended nothing. All that she could hope for was that they would return home from time to time, uttering their strange unfamiliar words and phrases, chattering about this unknown life which they all lived, growing excited over matters which seemed to her completely trivial, and treating as if of no account things which she felt were grave and important.

' Seven days ', she thought, ' seven days here and there, snatches of seeing them all, listening to them, and then—they disappear. That's all that I can hope for, those blessed, agonizing ' seven days '.

II

Michael Cardingly had brought his mother to call. Kitty met a tall, handsome woman with cold, grey eyes and elaborately dressed grey hair. Michael said, " Mrs. Hallam has been most awfully good to me, Mother. We had great fun here when all the family were at home, didn't we, Mrs. Hallam ? "

Kitty said, " Yes, although it seems so long ago I've almost forgotten about it all. Does the war seem to have been going on for years to you too, Lady Cardingly ? "

The other woman answered in a voice which Kitty felt was as cold as her eyes. " I am always so busy, I have so many responsibilities, you see. My husband has recently left England, and there was so much to arrange. We have turned our house into a small hospital for officers. That is why I am here with Michael. I want to take a house here until the war is over. I don't see enough of my son."

"Are you staying here, Michael?"

She saw the look of distress and indecision on his pleasant face; he was about to make some reply when his mother spoke.

"My son is going, I am glad to say, to do what he feels to be his duty. My brother is growing old, he is a delicate man, and the parish he assures me is large and difficult. Until such a time as Michael feels that he has some definite ' call ' to alter his way of living—the work which he is doing—he will remain to do the work which lies to his hand."

Kitty said nervously, for this austere woman, with her talk about ' calls ', made her feel diffident and uncomfortable, " Yes, everyone must do what they feel to be right—for them, of course."

"Exactly. Michael is too strong a character to be open to out-side influence."

Mechanically Kitty answered, " Oh, yes—of course—much too strong," and thought immediately afterwards that the very state-ment had been made to strengthen Michael's character. Did this mother of his know about his affection for Barbara, and did she disapprove? Kitty knew that instinctively she felt angry. That any woman should disapprove of her son's wish to marry Barbara! Unthinkable, preposterous!

Suddenly she longed to fling courtesy and even civility to the winds, to say frankly that when her two sons and her husband and daughter were all doing their duty it behoved everyone to give them their full meed of admiration and approbation.

Lady Cardingly glanced at the watch which she wore on her wrist.

" I'm afraid that we must be making a move. Michael wishes to introduce me to several of his parishioners."

Her tone unusually tart, Kitty returned, " They're still Mr. Beamarsh's parishioners—actually, that is."

"Quite," the tone was gracious but held a hint of patronism, " but my son is doing so much, he is to all intents and purposes my poor brother's deputy. Are you—er—interested in the various organizations for war work in the village, Mrs. Hallam?"

" I go down to the sewing meeting," Kitty felt suddenly like a naughty child trying hard to make excuses. " I'm afraid that I don't do a great deal. You see, I have five children and their mothers in the house. My cook and my housemaid are very good, but there is a good deal of work to be done, and I like to write very often to my husband and the children. The days really scarcely seem sufficiently long——"

" But," coldly and reprovingly, " don't the—er—mothers work in the house? Surely they should do so—to release your servants for national work?"

The pleasant room which she liked and which Oliver always said was ' restful ' seemed charged with a new atmosphere. Kitty Hallam felt that she was ' disapproved of ', that she was being accused of doing less than her duty. Her face flushed a little, and she felt that her muscles tightened instinctively.

" My maids are both past the age for the Services," she said, and added, " or naturally they would have gone long ago. Neither of the women from London can do housework—one scrubs splendidly, but that is the extent of her knowledge, it appears; the other does nothing at all ! I have my husband and my children coming home on leave—at intervals. I want them to have a home to come back to which is at least comfortable."

Again she thought, ' What am I doing ? Why should I explain to this hard-faced, cold-eyed woman ? What has it all got to do with her ? I'm mistress in my own house, I am not answerable to her. I wish that Michael had never brought her ! '

Lady Cardingly smiled, a chill smile that held nothing of either amusement or warmth. " Naturally, everyone must make their own decisions. I realize that——"

Kitty said, " Of course—like Michael ! "

" Exactly. But when I remember the last war—how we all *flung*, that is the word—*flung* ourselves into work of national importance, it does seem to me that this time there is less enthusiasm, less fundamental patriotism, perhaps, than there was then. I may be wrong, I hope that I am wrong."

Michael stood turning his eyes from his mother to Kitty Hallam. He realized that the voices of the two women were losing all friendliness. They were both on the defensive, both waiting to be able to—what was the phrase ?—' plant barbs ' in each other. His mother was splendid, of course, her work had been wonderful; already she had begun to organize all kinds of new ' efforts ' in the village; her energy was wonderful. But Mrs. Hallam was doing more than his mother knew, more probably than even Mrs. Hallam knew herself. Wherever he went, women, standing at their cottage doors, spoke of her with smiles and admiration. Only that morning Mrs. Hibberts, who grumbled at everything and everybody, had said, " S'no use, sir, I've no time ter goa ter meetin's and cookin' classes, an' what's mower I don't give a damn 'ow you mak' a flowerpot out'er a old salmon tin ! My 'ands is full enough, an' my 'ead, wi'out trying ter cram a lot o' rubbish inter it. I sed as mooch ter Mrs. 'Allam w'en she was 'ere yesterday. She laffed ! I just love ter' ear 'er laff, does yer 'eart a power o' good. ' Nay,' she says, ' you're like wot I am, Mrs. Hibberts, you an' me is just a pair o' Marthas ! I bin turning sheets,' she says, ' sides ter middle, an' say what you like,' she says, ' I 'old wi' doin' it *be hand*. It's never t'same if you use a machine, say what you like ! ' Nay, she and me 'ave given plenty ter t'war, we're doin' our bit, an' when ours come back home we're goin' ter see as they 'ave a *home* ter cum to, not a piggery."

Everywhere it was the same. Some old man assured him that " T'broth wot Mrs. 'Allam sent me did me a power o' good." Or an old woman busy knitting with fingers which were swollen and stiffened by rheumatism nodded and said, " I niver th'out as I could do nothink wi' my poor 'ands. Mrs. 'Allam brou't me this wool an' sat 'ere showin' me a easy pattern. It's a comforter fer some pore chap on t' North Sea, this is. Ay, she fetched t'wool an' all. That's wot I call a—laady, that is."

He heard Kitty's voice speaking and wrenched himself back from the comments he had heard in the village. No one had said a word against his mother—no one could do so—but it was this little fair-haired woman who was Barbara's mother of whom they all talked, whom they all praised.

Kitty was saying, her voice pitched higher than usual, " You are wrong, Lady Cardingly. There is just as much energy and patriot-ism and sense of service to-day as there was in the last war. More, possibly. The boys and girls of to-day *know* what they're going to have to face. I don't suppose that my daughter likes having to do the things that are part of her duty. But she knew all about what lay before her when she joined the W.A.A.F. My boys—one up to his knees in mud, chilled to the bone, sitting wondering when this ' phoney war ' will end and the—real fighting begin; my other son in Scotland, wooden huts, not much heat, out at all hours, working with hands that are half frozen—but he knew something of what he might expect when he joined. My husband "—Michael heard her voice shake for a moment—" who served all through the last war, he's *training*—and he'll go out again ! Go out to some-thing that he knows—only something which will be far more hateful than anything he knew last time. I was a V.A.D.—it was hard work, but it was no harder than the work which I am doing now and—there wasn't the same sense of anxiety. You've no son, as I have——"

Lady Cardingly said in her cool social voice, " Really, you were a nurse in the last war? How interesting. I had many friends who were nursing. You weren't at Colmore by any chance, were you ? "

" No, Balford. My aunt was the Matron there."

" Really ! Balford. You weren't married then, of course ? "

" No, I was hardly twenty . . ."

Lady Cardingly pinched her lower lip between her finger and thumb, then said, " Wait a moment, surely I knew someone who was at Balford ? A Miss—Miss Filson. Nurse Filson. Did you ever meet her ? "

Kitty's annoyance had vanished, she smiled again and looked, Michael thought, years younger; even her hair, he thought, looked brighter.

" Filson ! Why, of course. I knew her very well. A darling, but what a chatterer ! If you ever see her do give her my love—Kitty Bland's love. How I should like to see Filson again ! "

" Oh, I can't say that we actually correspond. I just remem-bered that she mentioned Balford to me. Michael, my dear boy, we must go. Good-bye, Mrs. Hallam. I wish that I could persuade you to join our knitting circle. We're adopting the crews of two minesweepers. Surely——"

Kitty said, " My knitting is abominable. I've too much to do to learn to improve. Good-bye, Lady Cardingly. Good-bye, Michael."

Later, when Martha came in to carry away the tea-tray, she found her mistress lying back in her chair, her eyes closed.

Kitty opened her eyes. " Hello, Martha ! I'm tired, I think."

" I'd not be surprised if you were, m'um. Surprising to me how people that's that busy organizing work fer other people ter do finds time to go calling of a afternoon ! 'Specially close 'and on Christmas. Would you come down and give a stir ter the pudding —fer luck, Cook says ? "

Cook was standing like a presiding goddess at a great brown bowl, the small Carters were gathered round, and in the background hovered the two pale children of Mrs. Perry. Mrs. Perry was seated near the fire when Kitty entered, Mrs. Carter was scrubbing the table which stood by the window.

Cook said gloomily, " I tuk' the liberty o' asking you to step down; they say as it's lucky ter stir the Christmas pudding. I don't know. It doesn't seem ter me that luck's so busy flingin' itself about i' great chunks at the moment. Theer you are, m'um, give it a good stir, and wish. My mother used ter say, ' Stir the pudden deep, deep, deep, An' quiet in your bed you'll sleep '. All I can add ter that is—'Appy Dreams, I'm sure. Mrs. Perry was wishing ter 'ave a word wi' you, m'um. Now, Mrs. Perry—come on."

Mrs. Perry did not rise, she sat in the rocking-chair by the fire and stared at Kitty with her pale, milky blue eyes. Kitty said with what brightness she could muster, " Yes, Mrs. Perry ? "

She sensed rather than actually heard that the scrubbing of the table had ceased, caught sight of Martha with her thin arms folded, her face set into an expressionless mask, while Cook continued to stir the pudding with grave intentness.

Mrs. Perry said in a voice tinged with truculence, " It's like this 'ere. I was led ter b'livve as if my 'usband 'ad time off at Christmas time, it was 'is *jew*—an' mine—an' the kids—that 'e should come dahn 'ere fer 'is 'ollider. You've sed nothink abart it, soa I'm speaking up, as it weer. My children think a lot o' theer father, I think a lot o' my 'usband, an' if so be as yore goin' ter raise objections I may as well sai—first as larst—as I shall tike the matter further."

A hoarse voice from the window said, " There's some of uz as 'ud be lukin' forward ter a lot merrier Christmas if you'd take yerself further."

Kitty said to Cook, " I didn't know about this. But of course, Mrs. Perry, your husband must come down. You've got your own sitting-room, that will make it possible for you to sit quietly and have long talks. Yes, of course. When would Mr. Perry be here ? "

" Carn't git off before Christmas Eve. Theer that pressed, as I wrote 'im 'e mite as well be in the Army. Proper slavery it is, 'e says. With a bitter luck 'e mite be 'ere Christmas Eve, an' 'e'll 'ave ter be back ter start on the mornin' after Boxing Dai. That 'ul mean leaving Boxin' Dai arternoon. Nice thing ! As you mite sai—prack-i-kly speakin' no Christmas 'ollider, an' 'im working like wot a slave does ! "

Martha asked heavily, " Then with your permission, m'um, Mrs. Perry's 'usband will be 'ere for Christmas ? "

Mrs. Perry answered, " Thet's right, you 'eard wot she said."

Martha disregarded the speaker and continued with immense dignity, " And if you could spare a minute to speak to Mrs. Carter, m'um ? "

Mrs. Carter came forward, her vast bosom gathered under her folded arms. Her scarlet face was wreathed in smiles, her small twinkling black eyes shone, she beamed at Kitty. Kitty instinctively returned the smile .

" It's this road," Mrs. Carter boomed. " 'Ere am I, an' my three gawdfers, it's a bit of a packet, thet is. Mind yer, missus, I'd never 'ave thought as my kids 'ud 'ave come on like wot they 'ave. Sidie, if you shuffle abart like thet whiles I'm speakin' ter the lidy, I'll bash yer 'ead clean off ! My ole pot an' pan, 'e's a decent ole lad, carpenter bi trade. Nacherly 'e'd like ter see the kids—I dunno so much abart seein' 'is bit o' trouble an' strife ! Bin married fourteen ruddy ycres ! Tikes a bit o' livin' dahn thet does ! I wrote ter 'im, nice letter it was too, I sed ' Dcre Joe, if the lidy wot lives 'ere can do with you fer Christmas, an' I've not arsked 'er as yet, mind yer, yer come dahn 'ere ter do a job o' work.' I said. ' Fetch yer tools, theer's a coupler cheers wants repairin', ter sai nothink of a gate i' the garding. It mite be as you'd find a few other odds and bobs ter git crackin' on ter.' Thet's wot I sed, an' thet's 'ow it is. Joe'll earn 'is keep while 'e's 'ere, if you can do with 'im, thet is. Sai the word, ducks, I'll understand ! Nah, let's 'ave the fair truth outer yer, queen ! I carn't sai no fairer, can I ? "

Kitty looked from one face to the other, Martha grim and expressionless, Cook still intent upon stirring her pudding, and Mrs. Perry with her pale eyes staring at the fire, her lips prim and tight.

She said, " Well, Mrs. Carter, ot course he must come, only I don't want him to come here to work—surely Mr. Carter will want a rest——"

Mrs. Carter said, " Mr. Carter—nothink, call 'im ' Joe ', dear."

It was arranged. Cook and Martha seemed almost excited at the idea.

Mr. Perry arrived, slightly the worse for wear, and he and his wife departed to the sitting-room to consume the contents of various bottles which he had brought with him. The children, after wild and hysterical shrieks of, " It's me Dad," and " 'Eer's 'ar Dad, o-er, he's tiddly ! " subsided and quarrelled gently.

Joe Carter came by a later train, a short, massive man with shoulders like a bullock; his red hair stood up like a brush on his bullet head, his hands were like scarlet hams. He carried a large bag of carpenter's tools and various packages of food, most of which were damp and sticky.

Mrs. Carter brought him up for Kitty's inspection, and to present her with the parcel which he had brought for her.

He stood before her, his eyes shifting restlessly round the room. Joe Carter had never been in such a house in his life, the cleanliness the soft carpet, and the bright covers on the chairs seemed to him to be something which belonged to a world of luxury.

Mrs. Carter said, " Wi'out wishin' ter intrude, missus, I've brought me ole man. Speak up, me ole cock-sparrer, sai yer piece ! "

Thus encouraged, Joe cleared his throat audibly, shuffled his feet, and said, " Ai brought yer a small present from me and me missus, missus. Nothink much, but goodwill in every claw, as yer sai. It's a nice crab. Many thenks alser for many kindnesses ter me missus an' the gawdfers. Happy Christmas, an' a Gled Noo Year."

Once the door had closed behind them, he whispered hoarsely to his wife, " Blimy, so thet's 'ow the ruddy rich live, eh ? Wot a gime, s'welp me ! "

Kitty never saw Joe Carter again until the morning when he left, and came cap in hand to thank her for the ' grendest 'ollider I ever 'ad or 'ope ter 'ave '. He was never in the kitchen when she passed through it; somewhere she heard the sound of a handsaw, the sound of sandpaper on wood, the sound of a hammer on nail-heads. Added to that a shrill and piercing whistling which appeared to indicate the fact that ' Joe ' was not only working but content.

Mr. Perry she saw once on the stairs, when he seemed to be swaying from side to side, the remainder of the time he spent in bed, and Mrs. Carter confided to Cook that it was ' better ter leave 'im be, let Lazy Daisy 'ave the bother of 'im, we don't want 'im dahn 'ere. Nice party we're makin' dahn 'ere bi ourselves.'

Cook replied graciously that she had rarely experienced a more pleasant one, adding, " Proper handy that husband of yours. I dunno when I've seen a man who can turn his hand to anything like what he can."

Martha added, " And something of a caution, I'd say."

" Proper caution ! Life an' soul of any party is our Joe," his wife assured them.

III

Barbara came home on Christmas Eve, Clive arrived in the early hours of Christmas morning, and Oliver drove up in a car half an hour after his son's arrival. Kitty beamed on them all; nothing tired her; all that she longed to do was to make their time at home as full of happiness as was humanly possible. They looked well, they were all in good spirits, and to them she seemed to be younger, prettier, and more charming than ever.

Oliver held her at arms' length and said, " Let me look at you. Gosh, Kitty mine, you're lovely ! Far prettier than when I married you. If I met you now, and at the same time met the girl I married —I know which one I should choose."

On Christmas Day, when they sat at dinner, she looked at them all, feeling that this was something too wonderful to be true—if only Cliff were here, if only the end of the war was in sight, if only that fear of Oliver being sent overseas did not obtrude like some dark shadow falling across the brightness of the hour. Oliver had said nothing, he merely talked of his work, of the men with whom he spent his time. He was unchanged, still to Kitty Hallam the one man in the world who was perfectly and completely satisfactory.

They had been to church on Christmas morning. Oliver had warned Clive that, in spite of his being tired, " Your mother would like it. Oh, she won't ask you to go, she won't say anything if you don't go, but I happen to realize that it will please her—and so "— with that particularly pleasant slow smile—" I think that we shall all turn up, eh ? "

Clive, yawning hideously, said, " I never somehow thought that Mummy was religious, Dad."

Oliver continued to smile. " I don't think that it is completely a matter of religion, my boy. A great deal of it lies in the fact that your mother is the proud possessor of a pretty daughter, a reasonably good-looking son, and an incredibly handsome husband. She is imbued with the highly Christian wish to make all other wives and mothers jealous of her. Who are we to deny her that small pleasure ? "

She was proud of them. She felt that, although there were other people in the church that morning wearing uniforms of various kinds, her own family far outshone any other individuals. To have them round her, to be able to watch Oliver finding the hymns for her, to feel the momentary touch of his fingers as he handed her the book, to meet his eyes watching her, filled Kitty's heart with gratitude to the God she had come to worship. A somewhat nebulous God, perhaps, a God who alternated between dispensing strict and impartial justice and who yet might, if approached properly, tilt the scales so that the balance swung over a little in favour of Kitty Hallam and her wishes. She had prayed so hard and with complete faith that some of her family might be home for the Christmas festival, and now—with three of them at home —she knew that her heart filled with profound gratitude to the God who had not only listened to her prayers, but granted them.

When the Rector entered the pulpit and began his sermon she saw no reason why, leaning a little against Oliver's arm, she should not allow her thoughts to wander. How pleasant the church was ; she liked the queer, almost metallic, smell of the evergreens, the flowers in their tall vases on the altar, she liked the church itself. A safe place, where wars and talks of war did not enter. Michael Cardingly was watching Barbara ; she wondered if Barbara had come to any decision regarding him. A nice fellow, and obviously in love with Bar. Why didn't he make up his mind to go as a chaplain ? Surely Stanley Beamarsh could find someone older to take his place ? Probably his mother didn't want him to go. Hateful woman !

Kitty mentally rebuked herself. She mustn't allow herself to feel like that about anyone on Christmas morning, particularly when God had been so nice, so generous about allowing three of

her family to be home on leave. Probably Lady Cardingly was
really very nice, but she had—an unfortunate manner. Kitty felt
that her conscience was soothed by that concession—not hateful,
but the possessor of an unfortunate manner.

They walked home, Kitty sensible that she was at peace with
all the world. Oliver giving that quiet smile of his to all and
sundry whether he actually knew them or not. Clive hurried on
ahead of them; he was determined, he said, to prepare suitable
cocktails for their consumption.

Kitty, her fingers resting lightly on Oliver's arm, said softly,
" Think of it, that baby mixing cocktails ! It's almost pathetic."

Oliver answered vaguely, " Oh, I don't know . . ."

As they entered the house Cook met them in the hall. Kitty
realized that never before had she seen Cook outside her own
kitchens. She looked strangely out of place. Her face was scarlet,
her eyes shining.

Kitty said, " Well, Cookie, what is it ? "

Cook replied grimly that it was ' them Perrys '.

" Are they ill ? " Dreadful if Christmas Day was to be upset
by ' them Perrys' !

Cook snorted with considerable force. " They're gorne ! Went
this mornin' after me and Mrs. Carter give them a piece of our
minds. Martha was upstairs doin' the bedrooms, when they came
down. Neether of them what you might call—theirselves. The
two kids was grizzling an' goin' on. Well, one word led to another
—an' they've gorne ! "

Oliver asked, " Gone—where ? "

" To the ' Red Lion '," naming the inferior of the two inns
which the village possessed. " The kind of place to which, sir,
they belong."

" And the Carters ? " Barbara said.

" The Carters is all right, Miss Bar. I've nothink ter say against
the Carters. I can do with the Carters an' so can Martha. Then,
that's all, I think, m'um. Luncheon's just on ready, just a light
luncheon, as I'm savin' meself, as you might say, fer the evening
meal, sir."

Oliver nodded. " We'll do the same, Cook."

Kitty looked back on that Christmas Day as a thing to remember.
They did nothing particularly exciting, they sat and talked and
for a short time Oliver closed his eyes and slept. Kitty watched
him. How good it was to see him back in his own home, quiet
and tranquil, as if he were not going away back to this strange
new life almost immediately. That was what they were all learning
to do—to live life day by day, because no one knew what to-morrow
might bring. The days for planning for months ahead were gone,
no use now discussing where the holidays should be spent, no use
hoping that next year you might go to Switzerland for the winter
sports, no good doing more than take one step forward at a time
and to be thankful that the ground was still firm beneath your feet.

' Everything is changed,' Kitty thought, and then as her eyes
rested again on Oliver's calm, sleeping face, she smiled. ' Not you,

my darling. You're just what you've always been, the dearest person in the whole world.'

As if he had sensed her thoughts through his dreams, Oliver opened his eyes and gave her back her smile. That was one of the things she loved about him, his ability to wake immediately and to be fully conscious without any stretching, yawning, and rubbing of eyes.

He said, " This is very pleasant, you know, my Kitty."

She nodded. " I was thinking in church this morning, that God had been very kind to let me have three of you at home for Christmas. I'm very grateful."

Oliver narrowed his eyes a little, as he always did when he was trying to understand anything that was new to him, then he said, " Does religion mean a great deal to you ? "

" I don't know—I don't believe that it did, before the war. Then, honestly, I felt rather ashamed of myself. I've always *asked* for things, and I suppose believed, provided they were good for me, that I should get them. I mean I always asked God for things. Yes, right back to the days when I was a V.A.D. and met you, and wanted you to like me. I asked for that ! When the children were ill—when Cliff had diphtheria, when Clive and Bar had measles so badly—do you remember ? Then when the war came, I asked for all kinds of things—and was given them. But all my life I've been asking and asking and expecting to be listened to, but until now I've never bothered a great deal about either saying, ' Thank you ' or even thinking a great deal about—religion."

He was leaning forward, his thin, fine hands clasped, watching her intently. He said softly, " Yes, go on, Kitty—go on."

" That's really all, darling. Only I do feel that when things are given to you, you ought in common decency to say ' Thank you '. You ought, perhaps, to give something in exchange—well, that's what I feel. I've said that it doesn't matter what happens to me, so long as you and the children are safe, and—come through it all. The children because they're young, and they've a right to have years of happiness and work and play before them; and you— because the world without you would be such a dreary place." She laughed nervously.

He rose and came over to her, taking her hands in his, and looking down at her very tenderly.

" My dear, what do you imagine the world would hold for me —without you ? Nothing much, nothing that really mattered. Darling, don't make bargains with your God. Accept it that if He is ready to give, you do your part in saying that you are grateful. You do say it—in your whole life, in every hour that passes. Don't—try to pay back, Kitty. You do and always will— pay your debts, no matter to whom you owe them."

He left the next morning; when Kitty asked him if he had any idea how long he would remain in Devon, he shook his head and told her not to ' build bridges to meet troubles '.

" It may be years—months at least, I swear that is all that I can tell you. Try to make the best of that, won't you ? "

Clive and Barbara were leaving the next morning. They spent hours together. Kitty could see them pacing up and down the gravelled path which led to the gate, talking earnestly and intently. Then Barbara left him, and went off, her mother suspected, to meet Michael Cardingly, and Clive came into the drawing-room.

He said, " Bar's gone off. I thought I'd come and have a talk with you, Mummy. I've really got a whole lot to say. I've been telling Bar some of it, only I've not got all the ' gen ' yet, and I have to go slow. Mummy, would you mind awfully, and would Dad mind, if I said that I'm thinking of becoming a Catholic ? "

Kitty stared at him. He was her son, a child, standing there in his blue uniform, looking so grave, and speaking with so much sincerity in his young voice. Clive—thinking about his religion, and debating as to whether he should change it or not—the idea seemed incredible.

She said, " I don't know, darling. I don't suppose so, if it would make you happy. Tell me about it."

Clive sat down, and laid his sun-browned, weathered hands on his knees.

" I told you, didn't I, that we have chaplains ? We keep several. One's a Catholic padre. I don't quite know how, but he and I got talking. Now, believe this, the last thing he talked about was—religion. In fact one day when I said that I'd like to know something about it he was almost offhanded over it." Clive laughed. " You see, I was sufficiently conceited to imagine that he'd really go to town on my saying that ! He just said, ' Oh, it's quite easy to find out anything you want to know, no difficulty there '. However, I went on thinking, and I managed to get hold of a couple of books in a second-hand bookshop in Edinburgh. I read them and went to this padre. Mind you, he still wasn't all over me ! D'you know, I really rather liked that. There was nothing of the feeling that they wanted to grab me, that I was doing them a favour—not on your life ! It was the other way round. I've been talking to Bar about it, she seems doubtful— d'you think it's because of Cardingly ? I mean because he belongs to the—opposition ? "

" I don't know, Clive dear. It's all rather surprising and a little disturbing. I don't know anything about Catholics. I've always thought that their churches were quite pretty, but—well, I don't understand it all. You won't do anything rash, will you ? I mean you'll think it over well. Don't be hasty."

Again he laughed. " Mummy, they take jolly good care that you're not allowed to be hasty. It means study and sticking to it like anything. Only you don't mind, do you ? "

" No—I don't mind." Her tone was dubious. " I shouldn't like them to make you believe that your father and I were going to everlasting hell or anything of that kind. It would seem so— well, so unkind."

He stood up and eased the knees of his trousers. " Don't you worry. I'll keep you well posted and report progress. It 'll take ages anyway ! "

CHAPTER VI

I

KITTY HALLAM frowned as she darned one of Oliver's socks; it had been an upsetting and difficult day. First Clive talking of changing his religion, and talking in such an odd way, as if it were all completely matter of fact. Kitty had no very clear idea as to how she expected people to speak about religion, she rarely discussed her own, and the conversation she had with Oliver was the longest she could ever remember indulging in on that particular subject. Not that she had anything against Catholics—she had not known many of them, but they had been very pleasant people. Their religion had always seemed to her something which was traditional, something which they ' kept to themselves ', not something which might stretch out and be embraced by people who were members of a totally different Church.

Clive hadn't said that he felt he had ' seen the light ', or that he had ' found the truth ', he had talked in his ordinary fashion. He had not even protested that the Catholic padre was particularly interesting, that he was a ' fine fellow ' or even a ' true Christian '. He had only stated that, when he explained that he was curious to know more, the chaplain had been ' almost offhanded about it '. Surely that wasn't the way to treat people who wished to become converted ! Particularly Clive, who was admitted to have an intelligence above the ordinary. If Clive were really interested, she wondered if she might write to this priest and explain that Clive was very clever, that his brain was of a first-rate quality; carefully and tactfully she might hint that to convert Clive Hallam would be something of a feather in the cap of not only the chaplain but of the Church itself.

She sighed, rolled up the sock neatly, and decided that she would wait until she heard from Clive. She wondered what Oliver would say. Oliver was so tolerant, he believed that people should do what made them happy. She had heard him say that so often. Yes, better to wait to hear what Clive said.

Then there was Bar. Bar who had come into her bedroom while she was changing last night and had asked, " Can I talk to you, Mummy ? "

" Why, of course, darling. What is it ? "

Bar, seated on the stool covered with the embroidery which Kitty had worked, swinging her neatly brown-shod foot, hesitated. How pretty she looked, so well too—this training seemed to agree with her. Her hair had never looked brighter, her skin more clear.

The silence lasted for some time; Kitty did not attempt to break it, and at last Barbara said, " Life's a hell of a mess, isn't it ? "

Mildly Kitty expostulated, " Darling, do you have to swear ? "

" Nothing else seems to really fill the bill," Barbara replied gloomily. " I mean, everything used to be plain sailing; you knew where you were; now it's all different. Clive was telling me that he wanted—or thought he wanted—to be a Catholic ! That's not like Clive, is it ? Then there's Michael—he wants me to be engaged to him. Oh, it's all tedious, and very difficult."

" I should leave Clive to settle his own difficulties——"

" Yes, I know, in theory that's all right, but we've always done things together. Now if he's a Catholic he'll have to go all pi and strait-laced, and say prayers at odd hours and believe all kinds of astonishing things. For two pins I believe I'd look into it, just to see if I couldn't make out what it all means. I might even join myself if it was all right. Then there's Michael. I like Michael, but I don't like his hanging round here, going to have tea with old ladies, and preaching to the Sunday-school kids. He's planning a herbaceous border for the garden of the new house he and his mother are taking. Honestly, Mummy ! "

Kitty finished powdering her face, laid down the powder-puff in its bowl and turned to her daughter; she laid one hand on the blue-clad arm.

" Bar, what matters is—are you in love with Michael ? "

" That's what I'm damned—sorry, Mummy—if I know. There are times when I think that I am, others when he nearly drives me scatty—when I get so cheesed off with him that I can't bear him another minute."

Her mother said mildly, " ' Cheesed off '—is that the same as being ' browned off ' ? "

" Umph, just the same."

" Then, my dear, until the times when you feel that you love him outweigh the times when you feel that you don't—wait to come to a decision. That's my advice, Bar dear."

" He was pestering me to-day to let him take me to see his mother. Have you met her, Mummy ? "

" Yes, once."

For the first time Barbara laughed. " Like that, eh ? I see. She sounds awful. Anyway—it's all left in the air. He wanted me to promise not to marry anyone else. I said, ' I don't want to marry anyone. I want to get on with my job.' Then he was hurt and asked if I didn't think he was getting on with his. I said, ' Yes, the herbaceous border ! ' Then he was more hurt. Oh," she kicked her feet backwards and forwards vigorously, " what the devil ! I'm fed-up ! "

Now Barbara had gone, and the house seemed deserted and rather lonely. The Perrys had returned, somewhat chastened, to collect various forms and papers; they were returning to London.

Kitty, braving Cook's scowls and Mrs. Carter's grunts of protest, had said to them, " Now do you really think that it is wise, Mrs. Perry ? Is it quite fair to take the children into danger ? Bow is a very congested area, isn't it ? "

Mrs. Perry replied, " Wot I sai is, better the devil wotcher know than the devil wotcher don't know. Oh, I'm not sai'in' as you've not been kind an' all thet, but I've alwais bin partickler 'oo I mixed with, alwais ! "

Mrs. Carter turned round heavily, her scarlet face purple. " If thet's a 'int at me an' mine, fer tuppence I'll knock yer 'ead off ! "

" If the cap fits, weer it," Mrs. Perry replied.

Cook, who was obviously enjoying the exchange of remarks, said, " Now, now, thet's enough ! My mistress ain't uster listen ter vulgar abuse from you, Mrs. Perry. If you'll kindly let me 'ave the papers, m'um, I'll see these people off of the premises."

That was the last any of them ever saw or heard of the Perrys.

II

Kitty sat there, thinking and wondering, going over Clive's ideas, Barbara's worries over Michael Cardingly, only Oliver seemed untouched by the new circumstances under which they all lived. Change seemed everywhere—except that there was no sign of change in Oliver Hallam. He had made the small Carters laugh, they regarded him as something scarcely removed from a god; Cook had beamed at him, declaring that it was pleasant to have a gentleman at home again who really appreciated food which was cooked as it should be, and Martha fussed about him, smiling and ready to giggle at his lightest joke.

" If I was at home for long," Oliver said, " Martha would make me believe that I was a first-rate comedian. I should find myself forced to get a release and to join ENSA."

No, Oliver didn't change, perhaps because he had grown ' set ' as regards his character; the children were pathetically young, poor little souls. Their characters were in the melting-pot of the war.

Martha entered, holding a salver on which lay a visiting-card.

" Lady Cardingly, m'um. Asked if you could possibly spare her a few minutes ? " Stooping lower and dropping her voice, she added, " I'm afraid she saw you through the window, m'um. She said, ' I see Mrs. Hallam is at home '. I didn't think that was very nice manners, peerin'. through windows, I must say. Will you see Lady Cardingly, m'um ? "

Kitty nodded. " And bring tea, Martha, will you ? I want a cup of tea very badly."

Lady Cardingly entered the room as Martha, stern and disapproving, stood back against the opened door. Kitty felt again that sudden sense of dislike for this tall, slim woman with the beautifully dressed hair and the cold blue eyes.

" Mrs. Hallam, I do hope that you will forgive the informality of this call. . . ."

" Of course, and in the country we are never very formal, you know. Have you had a pleasant Christmas ? "

The other seated herself very gracefully and easily. " Tolerably, thank you. A time of very hard work for my son, of course. He was tired out. He takes his work so seriously—rightly too, of course."

" Yes, I'm sure that he does." Kitty tried to talk lightly of having her son and daughter and Oliver home for Christmas. She touched on the episode of the Perrys, trying to make it sound amusing. Lady Cardingly's face did not change, there was no sign of an answering smile.

" All these people are ungrateful," she said coolly. " I feel that this billeting of them upon people—like ourselves—will only serve to make them envious, jealous, and finally—Socialistic."

" The Carters, on the other hand, are delightful ! They're from the East End. Mrs. Carter is a great worker, her passion is scrubbing ! Her husband came down for Christmas. I have never seen a man fling himself into work as he did—I doubt if he ever entered the house except for meals. He's a carpenter, Mr. Carter, he mended—— Oh, thank you, Martha. Milk and sugar, Lady Cardingly ? As I was saying . . ."

She thought, ' What is the matter with me, babbling like this ? She doesn't want to hear about Joe Carter, she isn't interested. I'm nervous, why should I be ? Barbara's done nothing wrong; if she doesn't love Michael I certainly shall not try to persuade her to.' She said, " I hope that tea is as you like it ? And a cake ? They're Cook's speciality. We can still manage to have a few. I love hot cakes at tea-time ! Very childish and rather greedy, I suppose. Still—they are nice." Again Kitty felt a wave of nervousness sweep over her, again she was conscious that she was being vapid and silly, that her voice was pitched a little too high, that she was speaking far faster than usual.

Lady Cardingly sipped her tea and set down the cup.

" Mrs. Hallam, I came to talk to you about my son and your daughter."

" Oh yes ? They've known each other for quite a long time. We like Michael to come here in the summer for tennis, and of course the children were all at home. . . ."

" Quite. Is your daughter attached to my son ? "

Kitty laughed. " I might ask—is your son attached to my daughter ? "

" I am afraid so, Mrs. Hallam. He told me that he was devoted to her."

" Oh, poor Michael, because, you see, Barbara is very young, and though she admitted to me that there are times when she does like Michael very very much, she is—well, she's undecided. This new life she's leading, I believe that they are kept very busy, occupied all the time, and they can't have very much time for reflection. She's only eighteen; that's not a great age, is it ? "

" No." The other woman's voice sounded deeper, there was something ominous in its tone. " No—but you must use your influence to end this—indecision, Mrs. Hallam. I beg that you will do everything in your power—everything."

Kitty knew that she flushed. This woman was intolerable. ' You must use your influence ', ' do everything in your power '.

Let Michael Cardingly fight his own battles; if Bar didn't want
to marry him, then no one in the world had any right to coerce
her.

"Lady Cardingly," she said, and heard her voice shake a little
with the annoyance she felt, "my daughter must make her own
decisions. If she wishes to marry your son, if she loves him, and
he loves her—then her father and I shall be satisfied. On the
other hand, I should never attempt to influence her in any way.
She is young, I know, but I think that she is sufficiently old to
know her own mind, and to know where her affections lie. I am
sorry, but—no, I can't and won't influence her."

"Ah!" A long-drawn sigh. Lady Cardingly leaned forward a
little as she spoke. "I am afraid that I have not made myself
perfectly clear. I am sorry. I wished to spare you any pain. I
tried to be as—er—diplomatic as possible. I do not wish you to
persuade your daughter to marry my son. I wish you to make
it quite clear to her—in whatever way you think best—that she
cannot, must not, marry Michael."

The words and the tone in which they were spoken brought
Kitty to her feet. She was being ordered to prevent her daughter
from marrying this woman's son. Did she imagine for one
moment that Oliver Hallam's daughter was not of sufficiently
good social standing? Did she think that her son was too important a person to marry the daughter of a man who designed
motor-cars, and made a success of so doing?

Her voice had lost all trace of nervousness when she spoke.
"Really, Lady Cardingly, I am a tolerant woman, but those
remarks seem to me to verge on distinct impertinence! My
daughter—in common with her father and her two brothers—
has entered the service of her country. She might easily have
waited until she was 'sent for'; she didn't, she volunteered; so
did the rest of my family. If anything would count against your
son in my daughter's estimation it would be the fact that he is
remaining in complete safety—to—plant herbaceous borders.
I think that there is no more to be said. May I wish you 'Good
afternoon'?"

The cold face with its expression of aloof austerity did not
show the slightest embarrassment. Lady Cardingly spoke calmly
and evenly.

"Mrs. Hallam, you are being very foolish. Please sit down.
You force me to say things which I should have preferred to leave
unsaid. I repeat that your daughter cannot marry my son."

"And I repeat that it is exceedingly unlikely that my daughter
would wish to marry your son."

"Please let me explain. . . ."

"I am waiting for you to do so."

"Your name before you were married was Bland, I believe?"

"Yes."

"You were a V.A.D. at Balford Chase?"

"Yes—what has this to do with——"

Lady Cardingly held up her hand. "Let me finish, if you

please. Do you remember a patient called Major Kahl? John
Kahl?"

Kitty frowned. "Johnnie Kahl? Yes, I remember him quite
well. Why?"

"He went back to France, he did very brilliantly, he changed
his name by Deed Poll to Cardingly—he felt that Kahl sounded
too much like a foreign name. He married me and Michael is
our only son. Now is everything becoming clearer, Mrs. Hallam?"

Kitty experienced a sudden sense of panic. Where was all
this leading? What had it to do with her? Whatever had existed
between her and Johnnie was over long before he met this cold-
voiced woman and married her. She struggled with her feeling
of oppression, battled against the thought that some disaster was
awaiting her.

"I'm afraid that I still cannot see why, because you married
John Kahl, it should affect me in any way."

"Before my husband——"

"Before he was your husband, you mean?"

The other continued as if she had not heard. "Before my
husband went back to France, after he left the hospital, you spent
a week-end with him in London. Do you deny it?"

"I neither deny nor agree. I want to know why anything that
you imagined happened to me should be any business of yours.
You admit——"

"My husband kept some of your letters. He probably forgot
all about them, he is a very busy man indeed. I found them—
letters from you, promising to come to London to meet him, other
letters containing references to—the week-end which you spent
together."

A flash of Kitty Hallam's old temper showed. "Sentimental
fool! Johnnie always was!"

"Then you admit it all?"

"Listen, we were both very young. Johnnie was bored with the
hospital. I suppose that I was bored too. He was going away,
he wrote asking me to go to London with him. I remember how
I longed to wear nice clothes again. No, don't sneer—I'd been
nursing for a long time—and neither of us was in the least hurt.
It wasn't a question of being deeply and sincerely in love, it was
just——"

"Lust. I understand."

"Lust! Don't talk such sanctimonious rubbish. Two young
people, both wanting to dance, to eat nice food, to have a good
time. I don't say that it was commendable, but I do say that it
was understandable."

"But surely you see that my son must give up all idea of your
daughter, and that she must most certainly have no thought of a
possible marriage with him. It—it is—unthinkable!" For the
first time Kitty heard that icy voice change a little, it was filled
with indignation, and a hint of horror.

"If my daughter decides that she loves your son, if he still
wants to marry her—which frankly I hope neither of them will—

then I see no reason why they should not do so. I don't suppose that Michael knows anything of this. . . ."

"I would rather die than let him know that his father had ever——"

Kitty made a little gesture of dismissal. "I know, I know—he knows nothing about this; my daughter, of course, does not. Only you and I know; you have these silly letters written by a rather silly girl, and which, if Johnnie hadn't been the thoughtless fool he always was, would have been burnt years ago. Well, burn them now. I suppose that it does not occur to you that it was Johnnie's duty to destroy them? It was, you know."

"I wish that you would not refer to Sir John as 'Johnnie', Mrs. Hallam. I should not dream of burning those letters. They are my one weapon to protect my son. Can't you see that it is terrible, abominable, to imagine that my son might marry the daughter of—his father's one-time mistress?"

Kitty threw back her head and laughed, it held very little amusement, but it held all the defiance and fury of which she was capable.

"His mistress! I never had any present of value from him, he never bought clothes for me, he never paid the rent of a flat for me, all he did was to spend three nights with me at a London hotel. Mistress! You don't know what you're talking about. Johnnie was never my 'keeper'. I never wanted him to spend money on me—he never did, except on that one week-end."

"For the last time, will you co-operate with me? I don't care what you think or feel, to me you were, in the eyes of God, my husband's mistress. Your daughter cannot and shall not marry my son. I believe that to allow it would be not only to commit, but to connive at, a deadly sin. For the last time, may I count on your co-operation?"

They were standing, facing each other; the one cold and austere, the other hot with anger, her cheeks flushed a little, her bright blue eyes shining.

"No. You come here talking of sins and crimes, but do you realize what you are trying to do? To blackmail me! Yes, blackmail! I won't be made a victim of that. My answer is—no, and no, and no again."

"Very well. I advise you to think well, Mrs. Hallam. I believe that I am protecting my son. He admitted to me that he loved your daughter, that he is prepared to wait for her, to work with all his might to win her for his wife. If you will not help me, then I must use such weapons as I have elsewhere."

"And that means?" Kitty demanded.

"That I shall tell your husband this story."

For a second Kitty was shaken, then she recovered herself, and knew that a wave of indignation caught her; she had doubted Oliver. Only for a brief second, but she had doubted him. She stared at Lady Cardingly, her face calm and smiling again.

"For one moment," she said, "I was fool enough to imagine that—it would affect my husband. It won't. We have discussed these things, we discussed them years ago. It won't make any

difference to Oliver. But it will make a difference to you, **Lady
Cardingly.** Whatever level you like, in your splendid righteousness,
to believe that I sank to, you will be falling far, far lower. I hope
that you will get a great deal of satisfaction out of your blackmailing activities ! Good-bye."

" Mrs. Hallam, for the last time———"

" For the last time," Kitty said evenly, " good-bye."

III

She heard the front door close, and the steps of her visitor die
away, then Kitty dropped into her chair, and realized that she
was shaking. Her heart was hammering against her ribs, her
hands and feet were cold, she felt physically ill.

After so many years that foolish piece of folly—for she refused
to regard it as anything more serious—had returned to roost.
What would happen if Barbara discovered that she loved Michael
sufficiently to marry him ? Would that horrible woman tell her
the story, would she tell her son ? How would Barbara look at
it all ?

' It's so unfair ', Kitty thought. ' Not a word of blame for
Johnnie. No question of telling Michael that he must put Barbara
out of his heart because his father spent a week-end with her
mother. All the blame is loaded upon me. So like Johnnie, the
sentimental fool, to keep letters, and leave them for all and sundry
to read. I remember now, the first time she came here, she asked
about Balford—trying to ferret everything out then, and marshal
her facts. How loathsome it all is ! '

Then her thoughts turned to Oliver, and the possibility that
Lady Cardingly might make good her promise to tell the story to
him. She remembered how for one moment she had been afraid
of what Oliver might think or do ; then she recalled that conversation which they had had together so long ago. They had
agreed that, what either of them had done, whatever love affairs
they might have experienced before they met each other, should
never be discussed, never alluded to. What Oliver had said then,
he would feel still. Again she experienced that queer sense of
having been disloyal to him in even allowing a passing doubt
of his sincerity and understanding to cross her mind.

One thing she knew, she did not want Oliver to have to listen
to the whole story told to him by that cold-eyed, grim-faced
woman. Oliver must hear it from his wife, not from the lips of a
completely unknown woman, lacking in both pity and understanding. To-morrow she would go down to Devon.

She felt better, more certain of herself, and reaching forward
poured herself out another cup of tea. It was not very hot, and
Kitty grimaced a little as she sipped it.

" I was longing for my tea," she grumbled softly, and then
smiled. What an unpleasant scene, what a disgusting woman,
daring to come and blackmail her in her own house. Vaguely she

wondered why Johnnie had married her, she could never have been pretty, obviously never possessed any great charm. Johnnie had been so impressionable where women's looks were concerned. What did he look like now? she wondered. Apparently he had made a success of his profession. Why had he been knighted, and when? She'd never wanted Oliver to get a title, though his father had a distinct longing to see both of his sons with handles to their names.

Johnnie Kahl—the smile still lingered round Kitty's lips—how many years since she had even thought of him? Certainly not once in the last twenty, probably not since she and Oliver had had that talk about their experiences before they met. That proved how little impression that whole foolish business had made upon her. She could not, even now, bring herself to regard it as anything actually wicked. True, she hoped that Barbara would never do anything of the kind, and yet she could not quite understand why the very idea that Barbara might was unpleasant. The boys—did Clifford go away with the girl he wanted to marry —what was her name?—Irene Woodstock? Again that sense of mentally adding, " I hope not."

She herself seemed a different proposition. She could never remember that she had suffered from any sense of guilt, and even now the most harsh word that she could bring herself to apply to the incident of Johnnie Kahl was ' silly '.

However, all these speculations, Kitty reflected, got you nowhere; they were profitless. To-morrow she would go down to Devon, talk to Oliver, and he could write to Lady Cardingly and tell her to mind her own business. Rather viciously, Kitty hoped that Barbara made up her mind not to marry Michael. Barbara would never tolerate his mother, of that Kitty was perfectly certain.

When Martha came in for the tea-tray, Kitty said, " Martha, I'm going to take a little holiday."

" Not a very good time of year for a holiday, m'um, is it ? "

" I'm going to Devon to see the conditions that your master lives under." She laughed. " I'm quite excited about it. I shall send him a telegram on my way to the station."

" You must wrap up well, them trains can be treacherous, m'um."

Back in the kitchen, Martha confided to Cook and Mrs. Carter. " The missus is off to Devon in the morning. Smiling and laughin' like a girl going to meet her sweetheart. Bless her heart."

Mrs. Carter nodded. " W'en 'e was 'ere I could see as 'ow they was still fond of each other. Proper pair of love-birds, I sed ter my Joe."

Cook nodded in unison. " Married fer yeres too." Why, 'ow old 'ul Mister Cliff be, Martha ? Twenty-one, ain't 'e ?

" That's right. His birthday's in December—the twenty-second. Poor lad, 'e spent it in France this year. It's 'ard, mind, not ter be home on 'is birthday. The missus always made a big fuss on all their birthdays. Sometimes I see her face go quite white when a telegram comes. As if she was always afraid somethink had happened to Master Cliff."

Kitty telegraphed to Oliver on her way to the station; he had always laughed at her proclivity for sending tremendously long and expensive telegrams, and now she wrote more fully than usual, and hoped that he would laugh at it.

Coming to see you shall go to best hotel in Talerton can you get away to see me not ill only wanted to see you and talk to you no need to worry long to see you fondest love Kitty.

The journey was long and, as Martha had predicted, cold. It was a relief to arrive at the market town of Talerton and to discover that the hotel was, as she had been assured, ' right up tew the mark ', A pleasant-looking place, with an air of homely comfort, cleanliness and cheerful fires. Kitty smiled at everyone, she knew that she was actually excited to be going to see Oliver again. He had only left her two days—no, three days—ago, and she felt that they had been separated for months. The actual reason for her visit was almost forgotten, all that mattered was that at any moment Oliver might come in, take her in his arms, and say, " Kitty, my dearest, this is a wonderful surprise ! "

Down again to the little private sitting-room, with its old colour-prints and horsehair-covered chairs; a centre table on which were placed at equal distances books which looked as if they had never been opened, and lace curtains carefully looped by crocheted bands of a bright blue.

She wrinkled her nose in amused disgust, thinking, ' You funny little room. I wonder how many people have waited here—as I'm waiting now.'

The door opened. Oliver came in, caught her in his arms, and said, " Kitty, darling Kitty—what a marvellous surprise ! I've been so homesick since I got back. I was actually planning to desert and come back to you."

" You got my telegram ? "

" Angel, be reasonable. If I hadn't got it, should I have come here to meet you ? Even your wonderfully brilliant husband can't divine things, you know."

" I've ordered some claret for dinner. You love good claret, don't you ? "

" How do you know that it is good claret ? "

" Because the proprietor assured me that you said so, last time you dined here. And with whom did you dine, please ? "

" A lovely blonde, a contortionist who was here with an ENSA concert party. We dined in this very room, alone. A wonderful evening, I shall probably join her when she is playing near Bristol."

" A lovely blonde," Kitty mocked, " one of those bottleblondes. Oh, darling, what fun it is to be with you again."

He slipped his arm round her, and rubbed his cheek against hers.

" Then you're not jealous of my blonde ? "

" I should be if she existed—which she doesn't."

" Wise woman. Now sit down and talk to me. I'm going to have a whisky-and-soda. What about you ? No, don't say, ' I'll just have a sip of yours, Oliver,' because the answer is that I want all mine for myself. Yes ? "

She nodded. " I'll have one all to myself then. I've ordered the most lovely dinner. A pair of ducks—because you always say, ' A duck is a silly bird, too much for one and not enough for two '; peas—they won't be fresh peas, of course; an orange salad—I brought some oranges with me to eat in the train, and mercifully didn't eat them. Oliver, do go and make them hurry up with those drinks. My poor lamb, I felt certain that they didn't look after you properly."

He came back, bringing the whiskies with him, and together they sat by the bright fire, content and serene. Oliver asked questions about Clive and Barbara as if he had not seen them for weeks. Kitty told him about Clive's talk with her about the Catholic Church. Oliver listened, shrugged his shoulders, and said that the boy must do what would make him happy, adding " Though if Bar takes it into her precious head to marry young Cardingly, he'll probably try to use his powers of dissuasion on Clive."

Kitty exclaimed, " Oh, Nollie, I've just remembered why I came down to see you in such a hurry—how stupid ! "

" Oh, there was a definite reason then ? I imagined that you had come simply for the sake of my bright eyes. Another illusion gone."

" Well, I did partly come for that—but there was something else. It's all very stupid, even annoying. That Lady Cardingly came to see me. What an unpleasant woman she is, how I dislike her—and I don't usually dislike people, do I ? She wants to stop Bar marrying Cardingly."

" I say, that's pretty cool. If our daughter isn't as good as Cardingly's son I'll eat my hat. Of all the silly asses, John Cardingly is the silliest. He may have done brilliantly in the last war, they say that he did; there's precious little brilliance left now."

" Do you know him ? "

" Darling, he was here when I first joined. Tallish chap, with ginger yellow hair—what there is left of it—and a very ' haw haw ' manner. He's gone now, got some big staff job."

Kitty said eagerly, " Oliver, don't interrupt me, I want to get this over. It wasn't a question of Bar not being good enough, it was— oh, it's so *silly*—it's me ! I'm the stumbling-block. Do you remember Balford, the hospital where you were in the last war ? "

" Of course ! Didn't I meet you there ? I should say I do remember it."

" Well, before you came there, Johnnie Kahl was a patient there."

Oliver said, with assumed, overdone patience, " Darling, could you possibly stick to the point ? First, we're talking about Bar; now we've arrived by way of old Cardingly and Balford to someone called Carl."

" No, it was spelt K-a-h-l, that's why he changed it to Cardingly, because it sounded like a foreign name. It's the same person. He was a patient there, and I nursed him. He was terribly bored, and it all began as a kind of joke—he pretended to fall in love with me.

I never was in love with him, Oliver dear. I liked him; he was amusing in those days and quite good-looking. He was going back to France—this was after he'd left Balford for a convalescent home —and he wrote and asked if I'd spend the last week-end in London with him."

" Damned impertinence ! And you told him what you thought about him, and the blighter's never forgiven you—that's the story, eh ? "

" No, darling, it isn't quite that. I went."

He stared at her, and repeated, " You *went*—to spend a week-end with Cardingly ? Kitty, do you know what you're saying ? "

" Yes, darling, I do. We stayed at an hotel, and then on the Monday morning he went back to France. I've never seen him since. Then—no, Oliver, *listen*—then I met you and fell in love with you. The moment that happened I realized that, even if Johnnie came back, I never wanted to see him, he just didn't matter —and you did, you were the only person who did matter, who has ever mattered."

" Good God ! " Oliver muttered. " Good God ! "

" I wrote and told him that I had fallen in love really. Oh, I never pretended that I'd been in love with Johnnie. . . ."

Oliver frowned. " I wish you wouldn't keep repeating that damned silly name ! "

" Then he wrote back, and I answered. But it appears that he had kept some of my letters and Lady Cardingly found them. She wanted me to persuade Bar to give up any idea of marrying Michael; said that unless I promised to do so she would bring the letters to you. I told her that she could do exactly as she pleased, that I should not attempt to influence Bar, and that I should tell you myself."

" What did she say to that ? "

" Oh, she tried to argue. I told her that she was blackmailing me, and I refused to allow it. You remember, just before we were married we talked about what had happened in our lives before we met. Do you remember ? And you said that whatever had happened before we met each other—well, just didn't matter. Because we hadn't known one another then. I forget if you said that or I did, but I know we agreed, and when this damnable woman was talking to me yesterday I kept saying to myself, ' Oliver will understand, because we discussed all this years and years ago.' "

He nodded. " Yes—yes, I see." Then abruptly, " Did you see Cardingly again ? "

" Never—the last time I saw him was at Victoria Station on——"

Oliver said, " Yes, I understand. And you never saw him again ? "

" Darling, I've told you that, I didn't."

He nodded, and replied mechanically, " Yes, I remember— you did."

She came over to where he sat and slipped her arm round his neck, saying, " Darling, you do understand, don't you ? We did talk all this over."

Oliver answered almost petulantly, " I wonder why you didn't tell me before—when we were talking about such things ? Why didn't you ? "

She moved away from him, astonished and terribly hurt. It couldn't be possible that Oliver was going to go back on what he had said with such conviction.

" Darling, because you said that what happened before we met each other didn't matter. You said that—well, virtually the world was a different place and we were different people—before we met. Oliver, you do remember—oh, you must remember. It was when we were at home—my home, at Marsh Hall."

He stood up, finished his drink, and stood staring at her, frowning a little.

" Frankly, Kitty, it's been something of a shock. I didn't think that anything like this could ever have happened to you. I ought to have known that it was possible. You were very young, it must have been a tedious business nursing people. You were—and are still—terribly attractive. It was—I didn't think that——Oh, well, let's leave it all. I'll deal with this damnable woman, and to some tune, believe me. Only," he caught her in his arms, and kissed her violently " only, Kitty, swear to me that you've told me everything."

" But, of course." She knew that her eyes had filled with tears, and added with a certain pathos which did not reach her husband, " there wasn't a great deal to tell you, Nollie."

" No—no." He was holding her face in his hands, the hands which she loved and admired so much. " Let's forget it, Kitty dear. It's all over and done with, isn't it ? "

" Over and done with, my dear, long before I promised to marry you."

CHAPTER VII

I

SHE sat in the corner of the railway carriage, staring blankly at the passing landscape. She felt lonely, cold, like a child who has been forcibly pushed from a warm room where it has gone expecting friendship and kindness. Again and again she laid her fingers over her eyes, and thought, ' It's not true—it cannot have happened to me—I'm having some stupid dream. I shall wake up presently —I must wake!' But the miles flew past and the dream still continued, until she began to understand that she was not dreaming but experiencing reality.

Last night, sitting in that queer, ugly little room, she had talked to Oliver, had told him about Johnnie Kahl, and he had listened, quite calmly, except that once or twice when he asked her a question his voice had a new sharp note which was unfamiliar.

She had said, " You do understand, Oliver, don't you? It was all before I met you, and——"

He interrupted, " Yes, I understand, of course. Only I wish that you'd told me before, that's all."

" But we talked about things—like this—and you said——"

Then he had snarled suddenly, unexpectedly, " Oh, for God's sake don't go on talking about it! Leave it!"

She felt that it would have hurt her less if he had slapped her on the face. Oliver—her beloved Oliver—to speak in that new and hard voice to her. She had felt her eyes fill with tears, and held out her hands, saying, " Nollie, Nollie, don't speak to me like that, dear!"

He had changed, had become kind and very tender; with his arms round her he had whispered, " Poor little Kitty, what a shame. Don't worry, I do understand, I swear that I do. Let's forget all about it."

They had eaten the dinner which she had ordered, they had laughed and Oliver had teased her very gently and made her smile at his remarks. The whole world had righted itself; she had no fears of anyone or anything. Only a great sense of happiness that now, at last, no secrets existed between her and Oliver.

They had walked together in the cold clear air, with the stars twinkling down at them, she had felt that the stars were actually smiling because she and Oliver were so happy to be together— really together again.

She had slept with his arms round her, in that huge old-fashioned bed, with a tester over them and curtains. She had said, " If we pulled them we should be shut away in a world where there was only us."

He had laughed, and said, " My sweet, but a stuffy world!"

In the morning he had to go back to duty, and she was returning home. She lay in bed, watching him dress, thinking how easily and swiftly he moved, how he never ' fumbled '; how studs, buttons, all seemed to slip into their proper places at the merest touch of his fingers.

He hadn't talked much, and when his eyes met hers they were grave, with no laughter in them."

" Have you got a headache ? " she asked.

He frowned, a swift frown which came and went immediately. " No—no, I haven't got a headache."

" I thought that you looked—well, as if you might have."

" No, I'm all right." Then he had stood at the foot of the bed, his hands resting on the high end, while he stared at her intently.

" What is it, Oliver ? "

He drew a deep breath, then said slowly, " Tell me one thing, then we'll never refer to this damnable business again, Kitty— is Clifford my son or not ? "

She had flung back the clothes, sat upright, and actually laughed because it seemed quite impossible that Oliver could have asked such a question seriously.

" Oliver—be sensible ! "

He nodded. " That's what I'm trying to be. I want to *know*."

" But you do know, I've told you. I met you late in the year, we were married in the January, and Clifford was born in the December. Oliver, do be sensible. You don't realize what asking such a question implies."

Oliver answered, " You swear to me that you never saw Cardingly after that time in London, you swear it ? "

Then she had lost her head, because she felt that the whole world was crumbling before her eyes. She had said all this last night, now he was going over it again, asking the same questions, wanting fresh assurances. She sprang out of bed and went to where he stood, seizing his hands in hers, holding them tightly.

" I've told you ! " she said, " I told you last night. You didn't have any doubts then—did you ? Last night you were glad to take me in your arms. Now, this morning, you want me to give you promises and swear oaths, and even then you'll doubt me. I've been wrong, I believed that, of all people in the world, I could trust you to understand. No matter what I say, no matter if I swore by all the oaths in the Bible, if I went down on my knees, you'd still doubt me. I know that from now on this is always going to happen at intervals; do you think that I shan't *see* ? I shall find you watching me, frowning, see you staring at Clifford, wrinkling your brows as if you were trying to find something which eluded you. Only for my own sense of satisfaction I shall say it again. . . ."

He pulled his hands away, covered his face with them, and said, " Kitty, don't, don't, my dear. I was wrong. I ought to have never spoken of it again. I *know* you, darling. I don't want you to say anything."

She said, " But I want to say this, and you will listen. I never saw him again after that morning at Victoria. I only wrote to him twice. I married you in the New Year, and our son was born in the December. During that year we were never separated for a single night. Now that is all I have to say."

She turned, caught up her dressing-gown and flung it round her. Oliver was shaking, his face was very pale. When he spoke his voice was colourless, dead.

" I know," he said. " I do ask your pardon, Kitty. It was despicable of me. Try to forgive me, darling, try if you can."

" I do forgive you."

" Don't go home to-day, stay until to-morrow," he urged.

" No, darling. This would only recur, or else we should both be so desperately anxious to prevent it doing so—we shouldn't be real people at all. *This* would always be waiting to lift its head, to leer, to whisper, and we should both try to pretend that we didn't know that it was there. No, I shall go home."

" But you forgive me ? "

She felt almost too tired to speak, she thought that her whole body ached with weariness. She pulled her dressing-gown more tightly round her, and said, " Yes, yes, I forgive you. I've said so."

There was a hint of reproach in his voice when he spoke. " But don't say it like that, darling. You make it sound so mechanical."

Kitty stared at him. She thought, ' What a baby he is ! Having said what he has done, when he has destroyed something which was so precious, so wonderful, he can go on saying, " Forgive me ", and actually feel hurt because I don't reply in a tone which is reassuring.'

She said, " I feel rather—mechanical, Oliver."

He turned away and began to buckle on his belt. That done, he came back to where she stood leaning against the bed. He took her in his arms, and spoke very gently.

" Darling, I am ashamed of myself. Really ashamed. I'll prove to you that the whole thing is finished, dismissed completely. Neither of us will ever think of it again. I love you so dearly, I believe that you love me. Make allowances for my stupidity."

Now, alone, Kitty wondered if her response to his pleading had not been something of habit asserting itself. The pain of his doubts concerning her truthfulness, the horrible doubt which had made him ask that question concerning Clifford, had been like wounds inflicted upon her. Only when she listened to his voice, the voice which she had loved, had found the most beautiful music in the world for so many years, it had been impossible not to assure him that he was forgiven completely. Yet the sense of pain persisted. She had been so certain that Oliver would understand, that what he had said before they were married would still be his firm convictions, and he had listened, frowning, hurt, and doubtful.

She experienced, too, a peculiar sense of fear, as if she were entering a strange, unknown land. They had never quarrelled, they had never questioned what the other said; now—it was changed. There had been a breach, and though it might have been repaired, repaired so that the original damage did not even show, yet the place was there and they both knew it. Imagine if tidal waves of doubt should wash away the place where the damage had been done, so that the great yawning gap existed again.

Martha met her, looked at her intently, then said, " Not worth it, rushing up and down the country in this cold. You look properly tired out, m'um. Better have a hot bath, go to bed, and Cook 'ul send you up somethink nice on a tray."

Almost to her own surprise, Kitty answered, " Do you know, Martha, I believe that I will. I am tired."

Oliver wrote to her, the letters were as they had always been, tender and affectionate, only his reiterated, " Tell me that you really have forgiven me " worried her. Why must he refer to all that horror ? Why not let it die, bury it for ever ? He was keeping it all alive ! Each time she read his letters, whenever he gave her some assurance of his love, or made some new plea for complete forgiveness, she read, thinking, ' He hasn't forgotten, he still thinks of that dreadful morning. If only he would never mention it again.'

Then came his letters telling her that he had seen a solicitor, and ' giving him a hypothetical case, got his advice as to how best to deal with that unspeakable woman Cardingly '. He was writing to her immediately. Again another letter, enclosing a copy of the one which he had sent to her, commenting upon his words, and advising Kitty to refuse to see Lady Cardingly if she tried to obtain entrance to the house.

Later came an enclosure of a brief cold note from Lady Cardingly, a note which Oliver stigmatized as ' vaguely unsatisfactory '.

Kitty, reading all these letters, felt that this thing was looming large in both their lives, that it was pushing forward demanding that they should not forget the existence of this fragment of her girlhood. ' It's not growing less present,' she thought; ' on the contrary it is occupying more and more of both Oliver's thoughts and mine. It's growing to be a huge monster. I'm afraid of it.'

She did not see Lady Cardingly, by silent agreement they avoided each other. Michael came to see her and asked her if she thought that Barbara had changed her mind.

" Do you think that there is a chance for me, Mrs. Hallam ? " he asked. " I am devoted to Barbara, I'd do everything in my power to make her happy. Do tell me if you think she will marry me ? "

Kitty watched his pleasant, serious face, noted his steady eyes filled with an expression which was appealing in its intensity.

She said, " Michael, I don't know. Can't you wait until her next leave ? She'll be home quite soon now. I can't possibly tell you if you've got a chance with her."

He sighed. " No, I suppose not. I want her to meet my mother so much. She's such a wonderful woman, and I am certain that when Barbara came to know her they'd get on awfully well. I wish that you knew my mother better, Mrs. Hallam, I'm sure you'd like her, and she you."

Kitty experienced a mental shrinking, as if he had touched an open sore. She thought that here ' it ' was coming closer again, she felt that the old story was filling the whole room, tingeing the atmosphere.

Feeling almost giddy, speaking half unconsciously, she asked, "Where is you father now?" and having spoken wondered instantly why she had uttered the words. She didn't care where Johnnie was, she wouldn't recognize him if they met, but the thought that he might one day appear in this little village seemed to threaten her.

Michael said, "He's in London, at the War House at the moment. I believe they have a big job for him later. He's got a flat in town. He might come down here for a few days now my mother has the house all in order." He laughed. "I'm afraid that my father is something of a sybarite—he likes comfort. That's why he hasn't been down before—the idea of painters and plumbers in a house horrifies him."

Mechanically, Kitty said, "Oh, really."

II

Oliver was coming home, he wrote that he had managed to get a 'spot of leave', and that he must have 'this wretched woman settled for good and all'. Kitty, he wrote, was not to worry, he would attend to everything, he had taken advice—good advice, and everything should be straightened out. His letter was affectionate, he could not have written more tenderly, but again Kitty had that sense of oppression, of some cloud which was gathering preparatory to bursting upon them and their lives.

He came, and when she saw him Kitty knew that her heart beat as it had always done with the pleasure of being with him again. He held her hands in his, said that she looked charming, but complained that she was thinner. He looked round the familiar room, sighed contentedly, and told her that it was good to be home.

"Particularly when that home contains you, my sweet."

She would not open the subject of Lady Cardingly; with that old sense of apprehension, she longed to delay the discussion as long as possible. Oliver was home, her own Oliver, sitting opposite to her, talking in the voice she loved—she hoped passionately that he might make no reference to what he planned to do.

'To-morrow', she thought, 'I shall have grown used to seeing him here again. I want this evening to be like our old evenings, not spoilt and tarnished. God, please don't let him discuss all that to-night.' With every hour her content grew, and when the morning came she woke feeling that she had been granted her hours of respite, and that now she must listen to Oliver and face whatever he planned with equanimity.

After breakfast, he said, "Now, darling, shall we get this business over? Come into the study, we shall have quiet there. I lit the gas-stove when I came down to breakfast."

She went with him, though she hated the idea of discussing anything in his small, rather gloomy study, which held an air of officialdom. He sat down at his desk and opened his brief-case. She watched him, thinking that he looked absorbed, formal, and judicial.

' I feel that I'm a culprit, and that Oliver is going to deliver judgement,' she thought, and then silently rebuked herself for being unkind to him. He looked up from his papers and smiled.

" Now, darling. Let's get it all over."

She pulled up her chair close to his, and said in rather a small voice, " Will it worry you if I sit near you ? I'm being rather silly about all this—it's frightened me, Nollie."

Again he smiled. " Not when I'm with you. You've never been frightened when you're with me, never in your life. Now, as you know, I wrote to that unpleasant lady, her reply was cold and rather offensive. I saw this solictor bloke—in fact, I've seen a couple in consultation as it were. The result was that we all agreed that—well, to put it plainly, that what was sauce for the goose was also sauce for the gander, and—I wrote to tell her, politely, to go to the devil ! No, don't frown, Kitty dear, the thing is here and we've got to face it. If she talks to my daughter, then I shall most certainly talk to her son. I've told her so too."

" Nollie, I don't want Barbara to know. Nollie, please ! I couldn't face it."

She watched his smile die, saw his lips tighten.

" My dear, if I know, if I understand, can't you trust your daughter to do the same ? I don't believe that the question will arise. I believe that this woman, with all her sanctimonious outlook, her essentially severe family upbringing, will cave in. She won't want her son to know, she won't let him know if it's possible to avoid doing so. Believe me, I have given this a great deal of thought, a great deal. It's worried me a lot, I promise you."

Kitty sat there watching him, trying to believe that this was not some fantastic trick of her imagination. Oliver's words, ' It's worried me a lot, I promise you ', seemed to convey in reality, ' Thanks to you, I have been worried a lot '. He was being kind, he was longing to be helpful, but she felt that he was ' dealing with her case ', not behaving as the man who loved her, but as someone who was wiser, more balanced than she could hope to be, and who ' had the whole matter in hand '.

For the first time, she thought wildly, desperately, ' Dear God, why did I ever do this stupid, idiotic thing ! And having done it, why did I not tell Oliver everything despite his protests ! What a crass fool I've been.'

He was speaking again, and his words came to her tangled with her own thoughts; she could hear him speaking, see the pale sunlight slanting in through the window, touching his dark hair, catching the signet ring that he wore, lighting up the dark leather of the fittings of his desk. She had bought them for him as a Christmas present years ago, he had smiled and shown his delight, had admitted, " Something that I've always longed for, but how extravagant, darling."

" To come here this morning. . . ." He was talking now surely of Lady Cardingly; panic caught her again, she didn't want to have to listen to that icy-voiced woman. " I'll see her alone. The woman is a despicable creature : you were right when you told her that she was to all intents and purposes a blackmailer. I don't want you to be mixed up in it at all, Kitty dear." But she didn't want Oliver to be talking about her with this strange woman while she waited in another room.

She said, " I think that I'd rather stay here, Oliver."

" No, no, darling. Much better not. It might distress you, annoy you. Leave it all to me."

" Very well." She was beaten and she knew it. Oliver had come to a decision, and she felt that she had not sufficient strength to try to change it.

He patted her hand as it lay on the desk near his own. " Don't worry, it's going to be all right. I'll—I'll "—he laughed, screwing up his eyes at the corners in amusement—" twist her tail for her, old cat ! "

Kitty experienced a sudden sense of revulsion. How disgusting it all was ! Blackmail, ' tail-twisting ', arguments—and all because years ago a rather silly girl had spent three nights with a very selfish young man who was going out to fight in France.

Martha opened the door. " Excuse me, sir, here's Lady Cardingly to see you. I've put her into the drawing-room. Will you see her here, sir—or where ? "

Oliver sprang up briskly, he looked almost excited. Kitty remembered that he loved pitting his wits against those of other people. Only, surely, this was different.

He said, " One moment, Martha, and then show Lady Cardingly in here." The door closed, he laid his hand on Kitty's shoulder, and said, " Now, my sweet, let's get it all over and done with, once and for all, shall we ? "

She went out into the morning-room, and heard his steps moving quickly across the hall. She sat down and covered her face with her hands, she knew that she felt soiled, ' grubby '—yes, that was the word—' grubby '.

The door opened, again Martha stood there, watching her narrowly.

" Have you got a headache, m'um ? Let me fetch you a nice cup o' tea. Me and Cook's just having one. Eh ? "

" I'd like one, thank you. Yes, I have got a headache."

" That's right, an' the post's just this minute come. He gets later every day, I tell him. He says, ' No cure fer that, I get older and slower every day '. That's it—cup o' tea, bit of Cook's nice buttered toast, and the letters. You'll feel better in no time."

As she waited Kitty wondered if Martha realized that ' something was wrong ' ? She couldn't know precisely what, but when anyone had lived in the same house with you for so many years they developed a kind of sixth sense about you. Tea, buttered toast, and the letters. They were going to effect a cure. Shakily she laughed.

" There you are, m'um. Everythink nice as nip. Drink your tea and eat your toast ; you didn't eat much at breakfast, I mentioned it to Cook. There's your letters. Look ! "—as she might have spoken to a child—" look, isn't that nice ? A letter from Mr. Cliff and another from Miss Barbara. There, now you read 'em in peace."

Tea and toast. Why did they act as tonics? Such simple, ordinary things. But the tea was hot and fairly strong, exactly as she liked it, the toast was crisp, and the feeling of Clifford's letter in her fingers was comforting. He was still safe, still able to write. Dear Cliff!

Dearest Mummy,
Here I am still cooling my heels and getting so bored just waiting for leave to come through. It won't be long now and I shall be back home again for a blessed respite from this tedious business. I want you to let me bring Irene to see you. She has promised to marry me. She is a darling and terribly attractive. You will like her, I'm sure. . . .

She dropped the letter into her lap and sat very still, thinking. Cliff was going to be married. Her first baby, how excited she had been about his coming. How marvellous it had seemed to have a baby which belonged to you and Oliver. Then she shivered—and only a short time ago Oliver had asked if Cliff were really his son! Violently she tried to push the recollection from her, quickly sipping her tea, nibbling the toast, refilling the cup, doing anything to attempt to drive away the picture which remained in her mind of Oliver standing at the foot of the old-fashioned bed in the country hotel, saying, " Kitty, is Clifford my son or not?"
She mustn't allow herself to remember, she must forget. Oliver had been foolish, had allowed his anxiety to run away with his good taste. But what right had he to be anxious? she argued with herself.
' Never mind about right or wrong—he *was* anxious.'
' Yes, but surely he ought to have known that——'
' Oh, be quiet. I want to read Barbara's letter.'
Barbara's writing always seemed to bring a feeling of stability with it, she wrote so clearly, evenly, it seemed that nothing could ever shake her.

Mummy darling,
Sit back and take a deep breath. Something's happened. First, I shall be home on leave in about ten days, I'll wire you the exact date, and please may I bring a man with me? His name is Lenman Temple—he's a ' flying type ' and he wants to ask if you and Daddy will let me marry him. He's all right and he wants to get it all laid on for us to be married. He's really Canadian, and—oh, when I remember that I actually imagined that I even liked that frightful binder Cardingly, I could laugh. Mummy, I swear that you'll just adore Lenman. I'm only afraid that when he sees you he'll give me the air and make passes at you. I promise you, darling, it's the realest thing that ever happened. . . .

Again Kitty laid down the letter, and sat staring before her, seeing nothing. Barbara had decided! At this moment Oliver was in his study talking to Lady Cardingly, and here was the solution to every-

4

thing. Barbara was going to marry a Canadian called Lenman Temple, and wondered how she could have ' imagined that I even liked that frightful binder '—what was a ' binder ' ?—' Cardingly '. Her nervousness had vanished, she finished her cup of tea, then rose and, going to the mirror—Oliver had bought it for her in Bath once when they spent a week-end there, she remembered—touched her hair, brought out her compact and powdered her face, applied lipstick with care and discretion, then, picking up Clifford's and Barbara's letters, she walked out of the room and, crossing the hall, entered Oliver's study.

III

Lady Cardingly was sitting very upright on one of Oliver's Chippendale chairs, Oliver stood near his desk, fidgeting with an ivory paper-knife. He turned as Kitty entered, frowned, and said rather sharply, " Did you want me ? "

She smiled, it was easy to smile again. " I couldn't wait to tell you. I'm sorry to interrupt, Lady Cardingly, but something rather important has happened. I've had a letter from Clifford—he's my eldest son—I mean *elder*, don't I, Oliver ? He's coming home on leave, and he wants to bring the girl to whom he is engaged to see us. He says that she's charming. Isn't that nice, Oliver ? "

His face was still clouded, her tone was so light, so confident, that he was puzzled, even disturbed. Here he was, trying to straighten out a very difficult—and unpleasant—tangle, caused through no fault of his own, and Kitty had to come in with news of Clifford.

Mechanically, he said, " Delightful ! Good for him ! Now, darling, if——"

She continued to smile, easily, charmingly. " But wait—that's not nearly all. Oh, Oliver, what is a—binder ? "

" A binder ? It's an R.A.F. expression. A bore—that's a binder."

" Really ! The slang these children contrive to pick up. I've had a letter from Barbara—she's coming on leave quite soon. Dear child, she's so happy. She's engaged to a ' flying type ', whatever that means, called Lenman Temple. She's bringing him here to see us. Aren't you pleased, Oliver ? Think of it, two of our children writing to say they're going to be married—and both so obviously wildly happy about it. Bless them ! "

There was complete silence. Kitty looked from Oliver's astonished face to Lady Cardingly's cold one, she smiled impartially at them both. Lady Cardingly made a small involuntary movement with her hands, the bag and a heavily sealed letter slipped from her grasp and fell to the floor. Oliver made a movement to retrieve them, but Kitty was quicker than he was. She stooped, picked up the bag and the letter; the former she returned to its owner, saying, " I hope, if there is a mirror in it, that it's not broken. Are you superstitious ? I am, and seven years' bad luck is such a terribly long time. And this," she turned the letter over in her fingers, " this is mine, I think. Thank you."

For the first time Millicent Cardingly spoke. " On the contrary, that letter is mine, Mrs. Hallam. Kindly return it to me at once."

Kitty continued to twist the thick envelope in her fingers, she was completely composed, there was even a faint hint of amusement on her lips. Oliver spoke nervously. " Kitty, please give that back to Lady Cardingly. We were in the middle of a conversation when you came in."

" I know, darling. I know all about it. After all I told you, didn't I ? Only now, you see, the whole matter is at an end. Bar doesn't want in the least to marry Michael, she's very happy with her Canadian. I believe that there are *supposed* "—the stress on the word was very slight—" to be letters of mine in this ? " She held up the envelope as she spoke.

Oliver said urgently, " Kitty, please leave us to finish this most unpleasant discussion. I beg you."

" Oliver dear, if my letters are in here, I'm going to have them and end all this nonsense. Lady Cardingly had scruples about allowing her son to marry Barbara. Well, Barbara doesn't in the least wish to marry him. Don't let us go on and on repeating the same thing again and again. No. Oliver, don't interfere ! Lady Cardingly, if I indulged in blackmail I should keep these, your husband might value them. They might even interest your son." She wrinkled her nose in disgust. " Pah, they say that evil communications corrupt good manners. I couldn't have even imagined that kind of thing—a few months ago. You were very clever—nearly as clever as you believed yourself to be. You thought that I should be afraid of my husband discovering these silly letters written by a very stupid young girl. I wasn't afraid. But I'm putting an end to it now."

Rapidly and exactly she tore the envelope and its contents into shreds, while Millicent Cardingly watched her fixedly, breathing heavily. Carefully she laid them in the big, bronze ash-tray which stood on Oliver's desk, then turning to him, smiling again, she said, " Is your lighter working this morning ? Please give it to me." Silently he gave it to her, she lit it, applied the light to the papers, and stood back to watch them burn. When they were completely consumed, Kitty dusted her hands together lightly, as if she wished to brush away some dirt which lingered on them. She handed the lighter back to Oliver, saying, " Thank you, for once it worked."

Lady Cardingly said, " Those letters were my husband's property —I hope you realize that you have done an unpardonable thing."

" How did they come to be in your possession ? " Kitty demanded, her voice interested and coolly conversational.

" That is beside the point."

" I suggest that you write to Sir John and tell him the whole story. I am quite convinced that he will forgive me for what I've done." Then changing her tone, she turned to Oliver. " Now, my dear, will you show this lady out ? Make it quite clear to her that if she attempts to come here again my servants will not admit her. All this has been most distasteful. At once, please, Oliver. I want to tell you all about Cliff and Barbara."

" Please, Lady Cardingly." Oliver stood at the door.

" I am not certain yet," she returned, " as to the steps which I shall take. I am exceedingly angry about what you have, illegally, done, Mrs. Hallam."

Kitty was reading Barbara's letter, her face intent and calm.

Millicent Cardingly raised her voice a little. " Did you hear that I was speaking to you, Mrs. Hallam ? "

Without raising her eyes, Kitty said, " Yes—oh, do please go. I do dislike your being in my house ! "

Oliver returned a few moments later, she greeted him with a smile, saying, " Isn't it wonderful news, Oliver ? Darling children! "

He answered gloomily. " I'm not sure that I approve of what you did."

" Nonsense, Nollie ! The whole silly business was getting completely out of hand. It was getting on the top of us, making us far too serious. Lawyers, solicitors, discussions about something which happened years ago, and was over and done with before Clifford— who is old enough to be married—was born."

He still continued to watch her gravely, heavily, she thought. She held out her hands, and trying to dispel his seriousness, said, " Now, Nollie dear. Don't you want to read the letters from the children ? "

He sat down at his desk, noticed the ash-tray filled with charred paper, and pushed it away irritably.

" Can't we have that damned thing taken away ? " he asked. " I don't want that to remind me."

" I'll take it away." She moved it to another table, then came back and sat down near him. " Listen," she said, " I was right when I said that we were allowing this to get out of proportion. Nothing can ' remind ' you unless you allow yourself to be *reminded*. A few pieces of charred paper. I'm the same person that I was when I came to Devon to tell you about this. . . ."

" But perhaps not the same person that I had always imagined you to be."

" You mean that ? "

" Isn't it natural ? I'm only human."

" Human ! " she repeated. " Human to disregard all the evidence of twenty years and more ! If this is—being human, then no wonder the world is upside down at this moment. Oliver, how can you think such things, much less say them, and to me ? "

" I don't know," and she saw that his face was haggard. " You seem to take it all so lightly. You told me that you didn't care for Cardingly, that you knew nothing about him, and didn't wish to. Now—his wife tells me that you were asking Michael about him the other day, that you wanted to know where he was, if he was coming here——"

" I was ? I was asking about Johnnie ? "

Oliver sprang to his feet, his face was distorted with fury, she saw that his hands were clenched. "Haven't I asked you before not to go on referring to him by that damned silly name? That's how you've thought of him, is it, for all these years? You're always prating about him—as Johnnie! Why did you want to ask Michael about him? What does it matter to you where he is, or whether he comes here or not? Then you expect me to believe that you've never given him a thought since you met me! Kitty, be reasonable, don't expect impossibilities from me for God's sake."

"And what did I ask Michael? Have you discovered that?"

"You know where he is—that he may be going abroad in some big job—they *would* choose that 'wet' to do the big spectacular jobs! That he might come down here soon, that—— Oh, why go on? You can't deny that you know all these things, can you?"

"No."

"And that you heard them from young Cardingly?"

"He volunteered all that information. I didn't ask for it."

"Do you mean to tell me that you didn't ask one single question about his damned father?" His voice was filled with suppressed fury, she had never seen him like this, he seemed a stranger to her—this couldn't be the Oliver she knew.

"I believe that my only question was—these may not be the exact words—'Where is your father at the moment?'" Kitty said.

"There! You admit it! What the devil does it matter to you where he is? How can his movements affect you? Answer me, damn it, can't you?"

She picked up the letters which she had longed to read over with him, and said, speaking slowly and quietly, "No, my dear, I can't answer you anything. I've finished with answering questions —to you or anyone else. You say that I am not the person you believed me to be—I say that you, as you are now, are a stranger to me. A stranger, Oliver, whom I don't even like very much. You've allowed that wicked, degraded, filthy-minded old woman to come and gossip to you about me. You—or you as I thought I knew you—would have turned her out of the house. You didn't really approve of my burning those letters. Can't you see that I wanted to finish it all? Now—so far as I am concerned, it is finished."

He asked hoarsely, "What do you mean?"

"I mean that—for a time at any rate—I am going home. I've never run to my parents when I was worried—to be quite truthful I never have been worried until now! I'm not used to it. Oh, I shall come back, when I've reorientated"—she laughed shakily— "what an important word that sounds—myself. I can't and won't stay here now. Good-bye, Oliver."

"I shouldn't do that, Kitty," he said; "stay and let's get everything straight; sit down and talk it over——"

"That's what we've been doing for months, either talking or writing. No, the only chance is for me to get away. You mustn't try to stop me."

"I'm going back to-night," he said.

"Then I'll wait until you've gone."

CHAPTER VIII

I

LUNCHEON was a difficult meal, Oliver ate in silence, staring gloomily at the food which lay on his plate. Kitty could eat nothing. Martha frowned and clucked about her, asking if her headache persisted, or if it ' mightn't be a good idea to send for Dr. Blaydon ? '

" The Missus hasn't reely been herself for a time now," Martha said, addressing herself to Oliver. " Kept putting a bright face on everythink, but it didn't deceive me, neether did it Cook."

He looked up and watched Kitty's face narrowly, his anxiety was obvious, and she felt that old sense of security come rushing back. Oliver did care, cared more for her than anyone and anything in the world. This difficult time would pass, only—and she was surprised at her own ability to make a decision—she and Oliver must give themselves a chance to forget. In a new set of surroundings that might be achieved, here in the house which had been their home for so long, where every room, every piece of furniture, held memories, to forget would be impossible. Once she could get back to Yorkshire, back to the country which she had never ceased to love, everything would slip into its proper place, take on its right proportions.

Martha said, " The telephone, m'um," and returned a moment later to say that Oliver's father was calling. Kitty rose and said to Oliver that she would take the call. The expression of gloomy detachment had returned to his face and he merely nodded.

Old Jabez bawled happily into the telephone as he always did.

" 'Ello, Kitty, my love, 'ow are you ? Oliver 'ome ! Noa ! Noo, I s'all be ovver this arternoon. Can you wait in while I come ? Noa, it's nothink desprit as you might say, but important. That's all—barring the fact as muther sends her love. About three ? Right. Love to Oliver."

When she returned Oliver raised his heavy eyes and asked " Anything important ? "

With determined cheerfulness, Kitty answered, " Your father wants to come over this afternoon. He'll be here about three. He says nothing—desperate, but something important. Bless him, he loves a little mystery ! "

Oliver nodded. " I wonder what it's all about." Those were the words he spoke, but Kitty felt that he experienced no active wonder at all, the whole thing left him unmoved, disinterested.

They drank coffee, they went into the drawing-room; Oliver said that he must leave at four o'clock. Kitty returned brightly that he would have time to see his father for a few moments.

Oliver replied, " I mustn't be late in leaving. It's a long run."

At five minutes to three Jabez Hallam's large Daimler drew up before the house. Kitty started up and said, " Here he is."

Oliver, who had been lying back in his chair with his eyes closed, opened them and said, " The Guv'nor's always on time."

Jabez Hallam entered like a whirlwind, his hands outstretched to grasp Kitty's, he embraced her, nodded—smiling—to his son, and then rubbed his fat capable hands together.

Kitty said, " This is a pleasant surprise, and how lucky that Oliver was home ! He's off again at four o'clock."

Jabez, continuing to rub his hands, said, " Lukeing well, Oliver. Army life seems to agree with you. Well, I can say all as I have to say in ten minutes. Joost give me your attention, and keep oppen minds. Noa, Kitty love, dean't offer me coffee, it gives me indigestion suthink shocking. Got a wisky-and-soda, Oliver ? That's my mark. Go get it, theer's a good lad." As Oliver went out, his father calmly appropriated his chair, stretched his short legs out before him, and beamed at Kitty.

" Nice to see you again, Kitty. Muther sends her love, she's well, but a bit worried. It were her suggestion that I came here to-day. She said, ' Nay, Jabez, goa and have a talk wi' Kitty. Kitty's got a headpiece on her ! ' Soa, get that headpiece o' yourn ready, my dear. Thanks," as Oliver returned with the whisky-and-soda, " that's the style. Now, boath on you listen to me."

Kitty, watching him as he sipped his drink, thought what a nice little man he was, so thoroughly decent, trustworthy, and—sane. Yes, that word expressed him—sane. He was extremely successful, he was acknowledged to be one of the finest motor mechanics and inventors in the world, he couldn't speak the King's English, but there wasn't a business man in England or America who would not take his word as being as good as twenty contracts from other men. Queer to think that Oliver was his son—Oliver, who was so slim, elegant, who had such an air of polish, whose beautifully modulated voice enunciated the English language so delightfully. Yet, and she caught at this thought gratefully, there was a likeness. They both had the same uprightness, the same integrity of purpose. Oliver might be being difficult, insensitive, even cruel at this moment, but—mentally she squared her shoulders—that would pass.

Jabez said, " Ah, that was good. I wanted that ! Anuther ? " in answer to Oliver's raised eyebrows. " Why, Oliver, I don't know as it's not a good idea. Have you got enough ? I've still a few cases left at Martingly if you're short. Just let me know. Now, Kitty, this is the position. How many bedrooms have you got here ? "

" Bedrooms, Father ? Eight—in the house and three over the garage."

His small bright eyes twinkled. " When I were a lad eight an' three made eleven. Not that I ever was at school mooch, Kitty. Mostly the schoolmaster were abroad when I went to the school." She had heard him make that joke a hundred times, but she always contrived to laugh, and was repaid by the increasing twinkle in his eyes. " Now—thank you, Oliver. The Gover'ment want to tak' over Martingly for a hospital. Evelyn's got officers billeted on him, and muther's dis-trac-ted ! That was when she said, ' Goa and talk to Kitty '. Now, your bairns, bless them, are all away, our Viccy's got herself a job with the Ministry of Information, she's got a car—it's her own car, but seemly she's loaned it to them— she's dashing about the country—though between ourselves, what she's doing I'd not know ! That leaves muther and me. There's ondly you at home, Kitty, if you think they'll let you keep this place to yourself, you're wrong. They'll not. Got an idea what I'm driving at, Kitty ? "

She glanced at Oliver, he was listening intently, with that look of despondency still on his face; she smiled at him and nodded, then began to speak very rapidly.

" Father dear, it's quite incredible. This morning Oliver and I were talking of what I believe is in your mind. We were—wondering how long you'd be allowed to keep Martingly. I'm going to be quite frank. I've got a sudden longing to go back to Yorkshire. The children can come there for leaves quite easily, my father and mother are not very young any more, they'll love to have me. Oliver can come there too. Marsh Hall may be—is indeed—very small when compared with Martingly, but there is plenty of room. Cook and Martha are both past ' calling up ' age—they must have the opportunity to come with me, if they wish to do so.

" Then," her smile widened, " there is my Mrs. Carter and Sid and Edie and little Alice. They're fixtures, Father. They ' go with the house '. Mrs. Carter will scrub the whole place for you ten times a week if you give her the chance. Now—have I guessed right ? "

Jabez raised both his hands and smote his knees with them. " Oliver, did I always say that you'd married a—wonder ? That's what she is—a proper wonder ! *Ondly*," suddenly very grave, " ondly, be it onderstood, as muther and me didn't want to turn you out, Kitty—doan't imagine for one——"

" No, no ! I promise you I was going—to turn out. That's true, isn't it, Oliver ? "

" Yes, Father, that's quite true."

" Well ! " He leaned back in his chair. " Well, it's like a mirrackle ! Muther was that disturbed, the idea of going into some hotel, or furnished rooms or this or that prop'ly upset her. But you swear to me—I want a sacred oath, mind, that we're not turning you out. I'd not do that for all the tea in China, Kitty. You know that, doan't you ? "

" On my sacred oath, Father," she said, and wondered what a ' sacred oath ' was on which she seemed to place so much importance.

Jabez sighed deeply with obvious relief, then held out his glass to his son. " That's somethink off of my mind, that is. Oliver, I can do with anuther. Better have one yourself, you're looking a bit dowly ! Nothink wrong with him, is there, Kitty ? I'll bet he doesn't care about being soa far from home. Now, when do you want to go, love ? I believe that I can fix transport for you. No call to take trains and the like. You'll have a bit of luggage I don't doubt."

" Lovely ! What a kind person you are ! I shall leave Augustus, you'll take care of him, won't you ? He's a dignified old gentleman, and I don't think that he'd stand transporting very well. He's the kitchen tabby."

Jabez beamed. " Muther'll love to have him. Anyone else ? "

" Three ferrets which belong to Cliff, and a breeding cage filled with canaries. Is that too much ? "

" If it were the damned zoo as you wanted to leave, I'd say it was all right. Kitty, we'd have liked you to have stayed, dear, muther and me think mor'n of you than you know; but maybe it's as well, for old folks don't always mix that well wi' young ones. But—we shall always remember this is *your* home, come what may." He took his glass from Oliver and nodded his thanks. " This having to leave Martingly has cut muther up a lot. For years she's grumbled and said as it was over big, but now—well, it's a wrench. To come to this house—your house, 'ul soften the blow in a manner of speaking. They've given me ten days to get out. That over-quick for you, Kitty ? "

" I shall be ready to go—if you can arrange transport—the day after to-morrow, Father. I've only got to go and talk to Cook and Martha. You'll be nice to my dear Mrs. Carter, won't you ? and allow Joe—that's her husband—to come down at Bank Holidays ? "

" Whatever you say—it's done ! " he replied.

As the door closed behind her, he pulled out an immense white linen handkerchief and openly wiped his eyes. He cleared his throat and then addressed himself to his son.

" The Hand of God is in this here," he said. " I can see that, though I'm not actually a religious man. Oliver, what's wrong with you, lad ? Standing listening there and not a word—scarcely to fling at a dog. Summat gone wrong, bother, trouble in your work ? Speak up, my lad. Let's hear from you ! "

Oliver blinked his eyes as if to dispel a mist. " Nothing wrong, Father. As you say—it's all worked out wonderfully well. I'm very glad. There's only one thing I want to say." He was speaking very quietly and rapidly, his eyes turning again and again towards the door. " Don't repeat this to Kitty—swear that you won't ! I will not have a woman who lives here, a Lady Cardingly, to come into my house. I don't care upon what pretext, she is not to come over that doorstep. I know the woman, she's an unscrupulous mischief-maker. Is that quite clear, Father ? That's the only stipulation I make—must make."

His father nodded. " Ay, Oliver, I've always bin able to see as far through a brick wall as most folks. I'll lay that she's some scandalizing old geezer—I'll lay more'n that, she's jealous of that canny wife of your'n. Have I hit it, Oliver ? "

Grimly Oliver answered. " Near enough, Father. But—under no pretext does she come into this house, remember. You might give my mother a hint, will you ? "

" If I tell your muther she's had anythink to say against our Kitty," Jabez said, " half a hint—half a hint, mind you—'ul send her round after this old baggage with a butcher's chopper in her hand ! And you know what a gentle creature your muther is ! Now, throw it off of your mind, lad. Kitty 'ul hold her own again all the old cats i' Christendom. I'm glad you spoke out. I could see as somethink were on your mind."

II

In the big sunny kitchen, Martha, Cook, and Mrs. Carter were drinking tea.

Kitty said, " Yes, give me a cup," and sat down at the white-scrubbed table. Martha bustled about, Cook murmured that she'd have had some fresh cakes, " If I'd a' known." Mrs. Carter folded her arms on her more than ample bosom and beamed at Kitty.

Carefully she told them of her decision to return to Yorkshire, and they listened silently, attentively. When her story was ended, Kitty explained that if they wished they could remain with her father- and mother-in-law, if not she was prepared to take them with her.

Martha enquired, " How many kept, m'um ? "

" Two—though I believe that the cook was going, she's just a young woman. That would leave only the house-parlourmaid. It's not a very large house, you see. There is a very nice woman who comes to do the washing every week, I remember."

Martha said, " I shall come with you, m'um."

Cook stirred her tea violently, took a large and noisy ' gulp ' and set down her cup firmly.

" I've allus wanted ter see what this Yorkshire was like, m'um. I allus had a fancy ter travel—here's my opperchunity. I pesoome that we shall return 'ere arfter the juration, as you mite say ? "

" Of course, this is only for the time that Martingly is——"

A sudden loud roar from Mrs. Carter interrupted her. That lady, her always scarlet face now a deep purple, demanded, " An' what abart me ? "

" Mrs. Carter, I want you to stay here."

" Wot ! Wi'out you, wi'out Cook and Martha ? My pore damn' kids 'ul break their 'earts ! When I tell my Joe as 'e can't come 'ere no mower fer 'is 'olliders, Gawd knows wot 'e will sai ! Tike ter drink or suthink ! "

Kitty sought about for some adequate reason which she could give Mrs. Carter for insisting that she stayed in the house; Cook was making clicking noises with her tongue, Martha was murmuring, " Pore soul ! " Mrs. Carter looked on the point of angry tears.

Kitty said, " Mrs. Carter, don't think that I don't want to take you, but I *must* leave someone here. The maids that Mrs. Hallam will bring are such nice women—not young girls—they don't know where anything is, I was hoping that you'd show them. You know how I like everything kept, that's why you've been such a help to us—eh, Cook ? Eh, Martha ? "

" Great an' reel assistance, m'um," Cook said.

Martha added, " Different from that Lazy Daisy an' 'er brats."
" Then there is Augustus—you do understand him, Mrs. Carter."
" Like wot my own Siddie is to me—that cat, like a child. I love
that animal ! " There was emotion in Mrs. Carter's voice.
Kitty followed up her advantage. " And Mr. Clifford's
ferrets——"
" Oh, them's my Siddie's job, them is, m'um. Give me the
canaries."
" That's just what I am doing ! " Kitty cried in triumph.
" Augustus and the canaries for you to take care of and the ferrets
for Siddie ! "
" Edie an' little Alice can give a 'and with the canaries, cleanin'
art and sich like, and Siddie with them ferrets—well ! A proper
damn marvel ! 'Arken 'ere, m'um, leave them all ter me. If—I say
if, fer it's not likely ter 'appen—one o' those gawdfers o' mine
neglects so much as a 'air of the ferrets, or a feather o' the canaries
—I'll break their damned necks for them as sure as my name is
wot it is ! "
Kitty pushed away her cup and rose. " Oh, what a relief, Mrs.
Carter ! I wonder if any woman ever had three friends like—you
are to me ! "
Cook answered, placid and without emotion. " It might interest
you tew know, m'um, that sim'ler remarks 'as bin parsed regardin'
you in this very kitchin, Martha, Mrs. Carter—is thet right or is
thet right ? 'Ow often 'ave we said, ' Go w'eer you will, north,
south, east, *or* west, you'll never find a missus like our Mrs. 'Allam.'
Not once, m'um, but a 'undered times."
Mrs. Carter breathed, " 'Undered ! Faversand times ! "
Kitty returned to the drawing-room. Jabez was standing before
the fireplace and announced that he was ready to go, adding that
time waited for no man and that time was money and various
other aphorisms of a like kind. When they were left alone together
Oliver laid his hand on Kitty's arm and drew her to him.
" I've been a fool," he said quietly, " and I know it, which
doesn't make anything easier. I've behaved badly, and I know
that too. I love you just as I have always done, completely,
desperately. No man in the world ever had a wife who was more
dear, more sweet. I wish that you weren't going away. But I do
see that you have a right to go. May I come and see you when I
get leave again ? "
" But my dear—you don't have to ask that ! Only," very
gravely, " everything that we've loved and believed in is—
threatened. You must work to save it—we must both work."
He bent and kissed her. " I will, darling, I swear that I will."

III

She turned to wave for the last time to the weeping Mrs. Carter
and the three small Carters, who were all alternately wiping their
eyes and waving their handkerchiefs, then settled down for the

long drive back to Yorkshire. Cook and Martha were in the second car, surrounded by bags and more packages than it seemed possible for two women to gather together.

Cook said, " Mind, in a way, glad as I am of having the opper-chunity to travel, it's sad."

" Almost like the breakin' up of a 'ome," Martha agreed.

" Nothink to what that 'Itler 'ud do if he got his hands on good ole England, mark my words."

Every turning each new view over the soft mellow country, brought back some memory to Kitty Hallam. Here they had picnicked on the twins' tenth birthday; at this turn of the road Clifford had fallen off his new bicycle and been brought home with a sprained ankle. Here she and Oliver had narrowly escaped being flung into the ditch when a tyre burst; and here at this twist in the road you could obtain your last glimpse of their house.

A beautiful, peaceful country, where the vast factories and furnaces were hidden by the low hills, and only the beauty remained. Yet she had no deep regret at leaving it; to her, Yorkshire had always been ' home ' and not even more than twenty years in the Midlands had erased that feeling. She had loved the gentle springs, had rejoiced at the sight of the early primroses, violets, and bright celandine; she had loved the rich summers when the grass grew tall, and where every hedgerow held the scent of meadowsweet and honeysuckle; the autumns with their changing colours, their harvests and ripe fruits hanging everywhere; even the cold winters had been pleasant with their contrast of cold winds and hard frozen lanes and the bright fires which greeted you on entering the house.

The house too had been a ' kind house ' as she had once told Oliver; from the first it had welcomed them and been friendly. Kitty had always loved to endow inanimate objects with life and intelligence, and often when they had planned some improvement to the house or garden she had felt a sense of satisfaction as if the house gave its approval, and the garden smiled back its pleasure at the care which she had bestowed upon it.

Well, Marsh Hall, too, had a garden, a garden which was far older than the one which she had left; where tiny box hedges had grown thick and sturdy with years of clipping, where the grass was smooth and even, and where old-fashioned flowers bloomed in profusion. There were the red rose trees—lacking the little wooden tags which proclaimed their ' pedigree ' names, their names were forgotten, they had just become ' the red rose tree ' or the ' white scented tree '. There was one which climbed over the back of the house, with tiny flowers which pushed in through open windows, and in the early morning, when the little breezes of dawn ruffled them, tapped gently against the panes. There was her mother's little, neat herb garden, where you might walk and pluck a leaf here and there at random, then crushing it between your fingers the scent would reach you—sweet, aromatic, pungent, or exquisitely fragrant.

She had always loved to look out of the bedroom window,

over the garden to the wide, green field, where a stolid cow grazed
and where the hens fluttered like pieces of white paper, down to
the little pond where the ducks waddled in single file—charming
and comical.

The country was changing, they passed through grim, busy
towns, where trams clanged their way, and the sound of clogs
echoed on the pavements. She spoke to the driver, " Can you make
York in time for luncheon ? "

" Oh yes, madam. Might be a rather late luncheon, but we can
make it."

" That's nice, thank you."

She was glad to be leaving her old house, the last months had
filled it with something which had filtered through into everything, the peace and content were lost—and that last terrible
morning with Oliver and Lady Cardingly had finally driven out
all the sense of safety and tranquillity, the unpretentious happiness
which had been one of the characteristics of their lives there.

Now kindly old Jabez and his gentle wife, Alice, had taken
possession. Kitty smiled, for if two people existed who could
restore the atmosphere which she had loved—Jabez and his wife
were they. To be suspicious, cruel, or unjust were things which
neither of them had understood, or ever could understand. Jabez
might be brilliant in his business, but his outlook was completely
simple, and his mentality free from any taint or hint of unkindness.
It was recorded of him that he had spoken to his workmen more
than once, invariably using the same words.

" Nay, it's nobbut right as you s'ould 'ave Unions. Them's
necessary to yew. Ter pertect yew against bad measters, and God
knaws theer's a main on 'em knocking aboot. Boot—I like ter
'ope and b'lieve as yew don't need no pertection against this
partic'lar measter—that's Jabez Hallam. Boot—we mun all stick
tergether, an' fer yon reason if fer noa other, Union rewles will
be respected i' my works, not ondly by yew, boot by me ! "

Jabez and Alice Hallam might restore the old house, might
wipe out those dreadful memories of doubt and estrangement
which had come between her and Oliver. She was content to leave
it in their care, they should ' minister ' to the old house, and heal
its scars.

The chauffeur said, " Here's York, madam. It's only a quarter
past one."

" Very good going, Hawkins. Ah, there's the Minster."

There were the beautiful towers, and round them the ancient
walls of the city. Immovable, lasting, real. She stared at the
beauty of the old cathedral which, so long as she could remember,
had never failed to move her.

Cook and Martha, with a slight hint of self-righteousness,
refused to come into the hotel to eat. Cook said with dignity,
" We've everythink as we want, m'um, and sufficient fer the
drivers an' all. We saw to that before we lef'. No, thank you,
m'um, we shall do very well, an' in these days it be'oves us all not
to be wasteful."

Kitty said, " Oh, Cook, do you think I'm being wasteful ? "

Martha answered. " Excuse me, m'um, you're different. I'd not kere to see you eating sangwiches in a car for everyone to stare at, no more'd Cook."

How the place had changed ! She had been brought here as a small girl as a treat and reward after a visit to the dentist, she had always liked the quiet of the place, the big windows looking over the gardens, with a view of the Minster dominating everything. Now, everywhere she saw uniforms, men hurrying in and out, men lunching, talking, laughing. Some of the waiters were new too, but one elderly man waited upon her, and she caught his puzzled frown as he handed her the menu.

" Excuse me—madam," he said. " It's—Miss Bland that was, surely ? "

" It is indeed. I'm on my way to Northallerton—to my home."

" Not living in London, are you, madam ? "

" No, in the Midlands."

" Ah ! " His expression implied that his opinion of the Midlands was of the lowest. " Nothing to beat Yorkshire, madam. We don't change much in Yorkshire."

Kitty glanced round the big dining-room, looked at the uniforms, heard the preponderance of male voices and said, " Not fundamentally, but the war has made changes."

Again the elderly waiter bowed his assent. " Ex-actly, madam."

When they left, taking the road which led to Ripon at her request, Kitty knew that her heart was filled with a certain excitement. Here were the roads which she knew; as they passed through Boroughbridge she longed to stop again so that she might visit the old inns, see again the sporting prints which she remembered her father showing her when she was a little girl; she craned her neck hoping to catch a glimpse of the Devil's Arrows, while memory told her that she had done that every time she had passed through the town—and never succeeded. On towards Darlington, and at last they were on the outskirts of Northallerton. There was her father's office, with the worn, brass plate ; that office where she had loved to go and talk to old Samuel Baker. Poor old man, he had died four years ago and ' young ' Mr. Clarke reigned in his stead. Tom Willis was in the Army, her father had written. Through the busy little town—and here, too, were uniforms everywhere—out on to the country road again, and Kitty sat upright, her blue eyes very eager, anxious as she always was to get the first glimpse possible of Marsh Hall.

There it stood, with its good, grey roof, its mellowed stone, and its well-kept though modest drive.

" There it is, Hawkins," she said, and in her own ears her voice sounded young and excited.

Hawkins answered, " That's right, madam. The master has visited here, I b'lieve. Spoke very highly of the place to me, madam."

" He loves it almost as much as I do, I think, Hawkins."

" I can b'lieve it, madam, from the road he spoke."

Kitty clasped her hands tightly, she was at home again, home with people who knew nothing of the cloud which had descended upon her and Oliver, people who were kind and loving, devoid of suspicions and incapable of doubting her and the truth of anything she said.

The big old door was open, and over the opening hung the curtain of cream linen with the wide, dull red stripes which she remembered was brought out at the first hint of sun, and religiously washed and laid away on the last day of September as a sign that summer was really over.

The curtain was drawn aside and she saw her mother, standing with outstretched hands; her darling mother—it was over a year since Kitty had seen her! Plump and still pretty, though she must be—how old was Mother?—she must be sixty-four this year; and Daddy was five years older. Sixty-four and sixty-nine. For a brief instant the sun seemed less bright. Old—both of them, how dreadful that everyone must grow old!

She called, " Mother—we're here, darling."

Then she saw her father, watched him coming down the wide steps to greet her. He didn't change, he was still as brisk and alert as she had always known him.

" Kitty, my dear, this is delightful! How happy you've made us. Your mother has been making my life unbearable ever since your telegram came. Never has this house suffered such an intensive cleaning! Poor old Mrs. Lynes from the village was pressed into service, bringing her daughter and grand-daughter! My life has been a misery! "

" Yet you say that I've made you happy! "

" Except for the thought of your arrival, I should not have survived."

Her mother joined them, and Kitty, listening to them both talking to Cook and Martha, thought how charming they were, how clear were their voices, and how friendly was their tone. She could hear her mother talking confidentially to Martha.

" . . . a really nice woman . . . not young but certainly not old . . . with me for nearly seven years. I'm sure that you and Cook will like her . . . and she you . . . happy and comfortable . . . tea first . . . I insist."

Kitty called, " Cook . . . Martha . . . do you like my home ? "

Martha replied, " It seems to be a very well-built house, m'um."

The maids and the drivers disappeared into the house, bearing bags and boxes, and she was walking after them, between her father and mother. In the hall, where the old oak gleamed with years of honest polishing, she stopped and sniffed.

" I should know that smell if I were blindfold," she said. " It's one of the first things I can remember—the smell of Marsh Hall."

Her mother smiled. " Beeswax and turpentine and plenty of elbow grease."

" And I've heard you say that ever since I was a small child! "

The drawing-room with its white painted panelling, its rather

faded but beautifully laundered chintz covers, the water-colours
in their gilt frames, the china cabinet, which gave an additional
touch of brightness to the room as the sun caught the gold, blue,
and lovely red of the Crown Derby. The big tea-tray which carried
the old silver teapot which she knew so well, the little spirit kettle
which her father had given his wife on their silver wedding-day,
everything was familiar, homelike, and good.

Her eyes filled with tears as she stood looking at all the things
which had been in her life as long as she could remember. Her
mother patted her arm gently. " You're tired, Kitty—come, my
dear, a cup of tea will do you all the good in the world."

Kitty blinked away her tears, just as she had done when she
was a little girl. " I'm a sentimental idiot," she said, " and—yes,
perhaps I am tired, and I certainly want my tea ! "

BOOK TWO

CHAPTER I

I

HOW easy it had been to settle down at home again. Kitty had been at Marsh Hall for three weeks, and to-day Barbara was coming and bringing Lenman Temple with her.

She stood at the window of her big bedroom and let her eyes wander over the scene that lay before her. No, nothing changed very much here in Yorkshire! There lay the hills, rolling gently away in the background, and before them the wide expanse of moorland, tinged with that purple which later in the year would glow in such royal splendour. There were the white hens fluttering about in the field, they couldn't be the same hens as those she remembered, but they looked exactly the same! And two stout, slow-moving cows, cropping away at the grass steadily, methodically. Nearer to the house was the wall of the kitchen garden, brick built and mellowed to a deep, warm rose colour with its lovely pattern of espaliered fruit trees—how often had her father said to her when she was a child, " These old walls are warm, you see, and they were built to catch every bit of sun that God saw fit to send. As a matter of fact he is very generous to that old wall, my apricots are the envy of the North Riding."

She wondered if she had caught that trick of thinking of God very personally from her father. Hugh Bland was not particularly religious, he was certainly broadminded and fond of good living, but he had admitted to his daughter very frequently that 'I could never get along at all, my dear, if I had not a real and profound— yes, and personal affection for the Almighty. I've always asked Him for anything and everything that I wanted. He's almost invariably given me what I asked for; therefore I feel that it's only reasonably well-mannered and decent to go and say " Thank you " once a week.'

Perhaps it was due to this attitude of his that going to church had never seemed tedious and unnecessary to her, she had grown accustomed to say ' Thank you '. And even as a child that fact had robbed Sunday of the tedium which it appeared to have for many people.

Her eyes went back to the garden; there was old Harris plodding along with his basket of vegetables for the kitchen. There was the ginger garden cat—always known as ' Thomas Cat ' even when the one of any given period produced multitudinous litters of ginger kittens.

" Why are our cats always ginger ? " she had asked the cook—

not the present cook, but the big, stout woman who had later married Mr. Harrison of the ' Brewer's Arms '.

Cook had heaved a deep sigh, produced from a vast bosom. " Miss Kitty, it's that ginger cat down at Tillet's at Low Farm."

" But that is not our Thomas Cat, Cook," she had objected.

" That I very well know," Cook answered, " but it's Tillet's cat as is t' villain of the piece, as the sayin' goas."

However, the ' villain of the piece ' must have been gathered to his fathers years ago, but the cats at Marsh Hall still remained invariably ginger.

She could hear Cook's voice, pitched rather higher than the Yorkshire folks', demanding some extra gooseberries from Harris. How well Cook and Martha had settled down ! True they were faintly patronizing concerning the North country and its people. Martha never walked into the village without returning to state that she ' only understood one word of every five they utter ! ' Cook eyed all the vegetables with slight contempt, and Kitty heard her telling Harris one morning that his peas were ' nothink like as good as what ours are at Croxton '.

Harris nodded and growled. " 'Appen they are, 'appen they're not, they suit ma measter and missus, an' Ah'll lay they'll 'ave ter suit thee, Croxton or noa Croxton ! "

Jane, the elderly house-parlourmaid, gave it as her opinion that both Cook and Martha were ' a lot different nor what Ah 'tout they'd be; foreigners dean't gennerly settle down like the road they've done. An' clean they are, they might 'ave been born noa further away nor Leeds. Not that I think all t'folks i' Leeds is what they might be.'

She turned from the open window and picked up the photograph of Oliver which stood on the dressing-table. He had had it taken when he first went to Devon, saying that it behoved every good wife to carry about her husband's photograph taken in uniform. She looked intently at the lean, intelligent face, with its well-cut features and good eyes. In the picture he was smiling a little, the corners of his mouth lifted slightly. Kitty sighed, he hadn't smiled when he left her at Croxton. He had held her hands tightly, and whispered, " Kitty—darling Kitty, I promise you that everything is all right. Try to forgive me."

He wrote to her very often, his letters were as they had always been, kind, amusing, and deeply affectionate. There were times when she read them and felt that all the horror was passed and done with, yet some trace remained. It was as if a rough, heavy finger had brushed away the bloom of their relationship. She knew that she loved Oliver as fully and completely as she had always done, knew that she longed to see him, be with him, to feel his arms holding her, and yet when he wrote that with the extension of the fighting it was probable that he would be sent abroad, and that before he went he would have ten days' leave, she experienced a vague sinking of the heart.

She could not face those dreadful scenes again; the memory of Oliver's set, coldly furious face, of his voice questioning and accusing her, filled her with terror. Yet the longing to see him remained as strong as ever.

She put down the photograph, saying softly, " My darling Oliver, it will all come right—it must—it shall."

Downstairs the house seemed filled with flowers, her mother had been up early and was filled with excitement and expectation at Barbara's arrival.

" Your father will go to the station to meet them, from the office," she announced. " He'll drive them back here. They should get in at Northallerton about half-past two—unless the train is late. It never *used* to be late, your father always said that he could put his watch right by the half-past from York."

" I remember, and in the next breath he would boast that his watch never needed putting right ! "

Her mother babbled on happily, expressing her delight that the good weather looked like ' holding ', adding, " Your father says that the glass is as steady as a rock." How everything that happened, great or small, in her life was bound up with what her husband said and did ! It was charming, Kitty thought, to listen to her. She might utter nothing but trivialities, but her voice was so gay and so pleasant that they sounded delightful.

Impulsively she said, " Darling mother, I am being so happy here ! "

Ellen Bland laid down the paper she was holding and glanced at her daughter. Kitty looked happy, and so young too, it was impossible to remember that she was forty-five ! Her skin was so clear, so completely unlined, her hair and eyes still bright as ever, her figure as neat and shapely as it had always been.

Ellen said, " That's pleasant to hear, but—weren't you always happy at Croxton ? "

Kitty's eyes met hers, good frank eyes which clouded for a moment before she spoke.

Ellen thought, ' I'm right ! Leaving Croxton meant more than just that the Hallams wanted to live there ! '

Kitty said, " Yes, darling, of course. You know that."

" Always ? "

" Mummy, what a tenacious creature you are ! Why should you imagine that I wasn't happy ? Naturally it was a difficult time when Oliver and the children joined the Services; naturally I worry about Clifford—but—of course I was happy."

Ellen Bland picked up her paper again; if Kitty didn't wish to admit anything she would not probe and delve. The great thing was that Kitty was here and that here she was happy.

II

The train from York was late, and the time was nearly four when Hugh Bland drove his granddaughter and Lenman Temple up to Marsh Hall. Over tea, which Ellen Bland insisted on serving as a ' proper meal ' because they must be hungry, Kitty listened to

Barbara's chatter and watched the tall, lean Canadian who wished to marry her daughter.

She liked him instinctively. He spoke slowly, drawling a little, and with an accent which sounded strange to her ears; but his eyes were kind and steady, his chin was firm and strong, and his hands looked capable and were well shaped and kept.

Again and again Kitty saw him turn to Barbara and watched the little half-secret smile which they exchanged. She thought, ' My darling Bar is in love with him and he with her—how charming ! Oh, how I hope they'll be happy ! '

Later Barbara followed Kitty into her bedroom and asked immediately, " Mummy, do you like him ? Oh, say that you do ! He's not handsome, but who wants a handsome man ! I don't. They think a great deal of him, you know. He's going a long way everyone says. He is nice, isn't he ? "

" He's delightful, angel."

Barbara chuckled. " To think that I once believed that I could fall in love with that frightful stiff Cardingly ! Does he know about Lenny ? "

Cardingly ! How it all came rushing back, Michael calling with his mother, Lady Cardingly coming to see her alone, trying to make her promise to prevent Michael marrying Barbara ! The journey to Devon, Oliver—Oliver's visit home, Lady Cardingly again—horrors, arguments, and almost disintegration.

Kitty went over to her daughter and laid her hands on her shoulders. " Barbara, promise me one thing. If you really love Lenman Temple, and he loves you—as I am sure he does—don't have any secrets from each other. Never mind what he's done before he knew you, or you have done before you met him—be frank about everything, both of you. Promise me that, darling. Promise me."

" Why, Mummy, how serious you are ! Do you mean that I ought to tell Lenny about Michael ? Of course I will, but there isn't really anything to tell. He was sloppy, and I was ready to get almost as sloppy until he infuriated me by staying out of the Army to make herbaceous borders ! I know all about Lenny. He's never cared a great deal for women, he's terribly shy. He once fell in love with a girl in Canada called Eleonora Something or other, he met her at a parish tea or a bun-worry or something like that. However, it never came to anything, and she married a friend of his called Hector. I don't believe that he's ever slept with a woman in his life ! "

In spite of herself Kitty exclaimed, " Barbara, my dear—really ! "

" You're not shocked, Mummy, are you ? Lots of types do, you know. But Lenny just isn't—well, he's not that kind."

" Barbara—you "—how difficult it was to put into words—" you have never had a serious affair, have you ? "

" You mean gone to bed with anyone ? No, darling, honestly. I don't quite know why, because there were several blokes who were ready to have a crush on me when I first joined—and I knew the kind of types they were, and what they'd have been out for.

Maybe I was, unconsciously, waiting for Lenny. You don't imagine that I ever had a brisk roll in the hay with Michael, do you ? "

Kitty shivered, then said, " Barbara, do you have to be quite so coarse ? Is that the way all you girls in the W.A.A.F. talk ? "

" Mummy, darling, don't be prudish ! You brought it up, and I was trying to set your mind at rest, and to carry it all off with a light touch."

" A distinctly grubby touch," Kitty assured her. " Never mind, Bar, only you won't forget what I asked you, will you ? I really, honestly meant it, every word."

The girl sprang to her feet and caught her mother in her arms. How strong and firm they felt, how strange to think that this was her daughter, serving in the Forces, wearing a uniform, and preparing to marry a man who would carry her off to Canada. Kitty laid her cheek against Barbara's and sighed.

" Nothing wrong, Mummy ? "

" Nothing, angel, only I wish you weren't all growing up so very quickly It's breathtaking."

That evening Lenman Temple spoke to her, saying, " M'am, I'd take it as a great favour if you'd show me that garden I can see from my window. It looks really good to me, and I'm something of a gardener myself when I'm home."

As they walked along the neat, bordered paths, Kitty noticed how his eyes seemed to observe everything, his comments were intelligent, and his interest sincere. When they reached the old brick wall he saw the seat which stood there.

" Now if it's not too cold or too late, m'am, this might be a first-rate place for me to sit and tell you something about myself. I find that I can talk a lot easier in the open air than in a room—even in such a charming room as your mother's drawing-room. What a lovely old lady she is, and your father ! That's a real type of English gentleman, I'd say. I don't believe that I could have found a lovelier girl or one with a grander family than Barbara."

Kitty laughed. " Mr. Temple, if you go on saying those pretty things you'll warp my judgement, and I shan't be able to keep an open mind about you."

" Why, then, it looks as if I'd better keep on saying those pretty things, which all the same are perfectly true. No, I'll come clean, Mrs. Hallam. I'm twenty-three, I've never had a day's sickness in my life. My dad's in the timber trade, and he's mighty successful. I suppose you might with justice call him a rich man I'm the only son, my sister's married to a man in Chicago. I lost my mother when I was eighteen, I've never really gotten over that. I thought the whole world of her. That's my history, m'am, and my future— well, I want to make that as good as possible by marrying your daughter, if you'll allow me to do so."

She turned and smiled at him. Lenman Temple was a simple young man, and the sight of her bright blue eyes seemed to him one of the most beautiful things he had ever seen. There was warmth in her smile too, that made his throat contract as he remembered the mother who had died four years ago.

He said, " One thing I'd like to say, I'd do my very best to make
Barbara a real good husband, and I'd like to be a good son to you."

" I'm sure that you'll succeed in being both," she said.   " I think
that you must write to my husband, Mr. Temple, and then——"

" You couldn't make it just—Lenny, could you, Mrs. Hallam?"

" I think that I could, Lenny. I'll write to my husband to-
night."

" That's a great relief," he said.   " I've been getting cold feet
about this interview."

As they walked back to the house Kitty told him that she had
talked to Barbara that afternoon, and repeated the words she had
said to her, and the promise which she had made her give. Temple
looked down at her, his grey eyes shining.

" Why, m'am, I don't know that I've got such a lot to tell Barbara.
I've never run after girls, maybe I've been too shy, too backward.
When I met Barbara, I kind of shook hands with myself that I'd
been that way. I'm not all that good, or religious, but I can show
a clean bill as regards—well, running wild and making love to any
girl who'd let me."

They all liked him, and when they returned to duty even Hugh
Bland said how much he missed them.

" I'm a funny old fellow, Kitty," he told her.   " I don't really
like strangers in my house, however nice they are; but that young
fellow's such a pleasant, modest chap. Never intruding, and yet
always there when he's wanted. Only one thing I wish—that he
wasn't a flying man."

" I know, I've thought about that, so has he. That's why he
wants them to get married as soon as possible. He told me that he
wanted to cram as much happiness into his life—while the going
was good. Oh, don't imagine that he's melancholy or unduly
apprehensive, but I suppose they must all realize what might
happen. Poor children."

" You'd like them to be married? Married soon?"

" I think so, Daddy. If everything—is all right, as I hope and
pray that it will be—why not? And suppose anything did happen
to the poor boy—no one can take away from Barbara the happiness
that she'd had."

On May the tenth Hugh was rubbing his hands because Churchill
was Prime Minister, now he said Britain would show the world!
The first days of that ministry were not auspicious. The Dutch
surrendered, the Belgians were on their knees, France was crashing.
Kitty read the news, her eyes wide with horror. Where was Clifford,
what was going to happen? The story of Dunkirk drove her half
frantic with anxiety, with every announcement the hope of saving
the British fighting men seemed to grow more faint. On June the
third Clifford telegraphed that he was in London, and coming North
the following day. Might Irene join him later?

He came, and Kitty stared at him blankly. Was this gaunt,
hollow-cheeked man in a stained and shabby uniform her son?
Could it be possible that he was only twenty-one? He looked
thirty or more.

She held him in her arms, and he laid his head on her shoulder; she could hear the long difficult sobs which shook his whole body.

"Darling, it's all right," she whispered, "Mummy's got you"; exactly as she had spoken when he was a little boy and woke in the night, crying because some evil dream had frightened him. "Mummy's got you."

He raised his head, and wiped away the tears with the back of his hand, as he had always done when he was a child.

"Sorry, Mummy, I'm afraid I'm a bit overtired. I'll be all right in a day or two. It's not been really amusing, that evacuation."

"I know, I know, but it's over, it's all behind you. Don't think of it more than you can help. Don't think that you need tell us about it, that can wait until you're stronger, less tired—or wait for ever if you like."

That night, again and again, Kitty went on tiptoe to his room, to hear him shouting and muttering in his sleep; each time she laid her hand on his shoulder and whispered, "It's all right, darling, Mummy's got you. Go to sleep . . . there, there." Each time at her touch his voice ceased, and he slept soundly and peacefully. But for many nights she had to go to him, to soothe his restlessness, to drive away the nightmares which attacked him.

She said to her father, "I never want to hear stories of Dunkirk. I've heard too much. My poor Clifford! He talks of it every night, he's back there in his dreams. I have to drag him back—literally—from those awful memories."

Slowly he seemed to come back to normality. When he talked of Dunkirk it was to tell stories which were amusing, the story of the two Guards officers, the story of the Yorkshireman who recounted the evacuation to his friend, stories of men who waded to the boats with scarcely a stitch of clothing on their bodies, stories of men arriving in London and being rebuked by a policeman and warned, "If it was a Military Policeman as saw you now, you would be in bother. Go home and get yourself dressed properly."

Kitty asked, "What did the soldier say?"

"That, my dear, is something quite unfitted for your ears."

He had been home for nearly ten days when Irene Woodstock arrived. She was tall, elegant, and almost beautiful; her sophistication was evident, and Kitty suspected that in a few days her boredom would be extreme. Her conversation was chiefly concerning films and film stars, theatres and theatrical people—she appeared to have an intimate and extensive knowledge of all scandals concerning them. She refused to mention the war, or to listen to the B.B.C. announcements.

When they heard that the French and German armistice had been signed at Compiègne Kitty heard Clifford groan.

"Pretty awful," he said, "but after what Churchill said—I suppose we can't really be surprised. Think of it—signed at Compiègne in the same railway coach as—last time. That's twisting the knife a bit, eh?"

Irene Woodstock said calmly, "Well, the more people who

come out of the wretched war the sooner it will be over ! I can't imagine why Italy was such a fool as to rush into it ! "

Clifford watched her, his eyes cold. Kitty thought, ' This won't last, he'll grow to hate her.'

He said, " I imagine that a good many Italians are asking the same question, Irene."

She answered almost pettishly, " Oh, what does it matter ? I get so *bored* with all this talk of war, don't you, Mrs. Hallam ? "

She stayed at Marsh Hall for a week, and then carried Clifford off to London with her; he returned after a fortnight, he was going out again.

" Where, Clifford ? " his grandfather asked.

Clifford winked. " Destination not disclosed, probably we shall know at a later *date*. Clever fellow I'm getting, eh ? I imagine that I shall be able to make sand castles if I get any leave."

That evening he told his mother that his engagement with Irene Woodstock was broken off.

" She gave me the air," he said. " Found me too stogey, I fancy. Oh, she was really awfully nice about it, and curiously enough it didn't hurt much, I'd have married her like a shot before I went to France, but I don't believe that we should have made a go of it somehow. Pretty girl, though. Perhaps I'll find some lovely desert rose on my travels."

" And you're not desperately hurt, Clifford ? "

" Honestly, no. Oh, for the first twenty-four hours after she told me I felt a bit sick, then I began to see that it was all for the best. Not just sour grapes, Mummy, honestly. She is lovely, but she's damned extravagant, and somehow, after being out there, the things that once seemed frightfully important—strike you as being a bit trivial. Oh, don't think that I don't like a good time, I do. I hope I always shall, but—damn it, life can't be *all* dancing and dining, seeing flicks, staying at topnotch hotels, and getting new clothes. There is a bit more to it than that. Anyway, Irene likes something a bit more important than a ruddy captain ! "

" Had you known her for a long time ? "

He looked at her, giving her what she had always called ' Clifford's sideway look ', then said, " Before I went out, darling."

" Did you meet her people ? "

" Her father's in the States. I met her mother. Can't say that I exactly fell for the lady, or that she precisely regarded me as the ' blue-eyed boy '. I believe her mother divorced her father. She lives with some rich old fellow who—from the look of him and his conversation—keeps a bucket-shop or runs a bookie's business. What's the sudden interest in Irene, Mummy ? " Again that ' sideway look '.

Kitty said, " I wondered just how well you knew Miss Woodstock ? "

He grinned suddenly. " Oh, you did, did you ? You're a wicked old lady, Mrs. Hallam ! I won't be drawn, angel, even by you."

" My dear, you've answered me. I wasn't going to be intrusive, or unpleasant, or even shocked."

Something in her tone startled him. He was a very ordinary young man. In his heart he believed in ' taking his fun where he found it '. He had no particularly high ideals but he had a deep and sincere love for this pretty mother of his, and to hear her speaking to him in a tone which was so quiet, which held a note which was almost childlike, shook him. What was at the back of it all ? She certainly wasn't shocked, wasn't going to ' talk to him seriously ', in fact at that moment he felt himself to be her elder. It couldn't be that his father had—he pushed the thought from him—no, that was unthinkable, incredible.

He sat down and laid his hands on his knees, staring up at her.

" Mummy, what's worrying you ? " he asked. " There's something at the back of all this. Come on, let's thrash it out."

She met his eyes very steadily, he thought how blue hers were, how young and fresh she looked. Like a garden newly washed with rain. She said, " I don't know, Clifford. I'm puzzled. Perhaps I've always lived—at least since I married your father—a life in which these things didn't—oh, they *existed* no doubt, but somehow we didn't admit of their existence. Have people changed ? Do such words as chastity, honour, fidelity seem very old-fashioned to you ? Do you set any store by those qualities ? Or "—she spoke more slowly—" don't you mind that some woman with whom you fall in love has had—experiences, affairs, and all the rest of it ? Are you, you young people, content to marry women who know all that there is to know of love, or do you still want ' your wife ' to be immaculate ? I'm like ' Rosa Dartle '—asking for information. I suppose that it's queer to ask these things of my own son, but you're—yes, you're different, Clifford. Grown up, matured. I feel sometimes far younger than you are."

His face was very grave, again she felt that although he might only be twenty-one in actual years, in reality he was far older.

He said, " Sit down, darling. Now listen. Don't think that I'm making the blasted war an excuse for everything, I'm not. Only when it came we were all chucked into a completely new world, a world with different values, with very few—I'm being frank now—ideals, except how to turn out a workable, well-trained fighting force.

" Values changed. We didn't know what was in front of us, we heard of our pals ' going for a Burton ', chaps who two days before had been playing cards with us, laughing, swopping stories —mostly improper—and life began to show itself as an uncertain kind of business. That filtered through even to the camps in U.K. A fellow looked a bit green about the gills. ' What's the matter with old So and So ? ' The answer would be that he had heard that his brother had gone—shot down, sunk at sea, killed some old way or the other. He'd be all right in a couple of days, but he got, and you got, a sense of impermanence. We were all young, we were going out to sock Jerry, or Jerry might sock us. You had the feeling, ' I don't want to miss anything ! I'm young and I'm not going to be cheated of all the fun that's going.'

" Then when I went to London on leave I met—the person of

whom we've been talking, and I fell, hook, line, and sinker. She was lovely, she was exquisite, scented, beautifully dressed. All the things that young chaps dream about and don't find in a camp ! She promised to marry me—oh, she was frank enough about herself, or rather she just expected me to accept everything. I don't see why not either. After all—she was older than I was, and whatever had happened—well, it had happened before she knew that there was such a person as Clifford Hallam in the world." He stopped abruptly. " Mummy, you're not ill, are you ? I'm not making you feel disgusted or horrified, am I ? "

Kitty shook her head. " No, darling, no. Cliff, you really meant that ? You'd have married her and—not minded ? Truly, honestly ? "

" Why yes, surely that's only fair and logical. She never pretended to be an innocent young girl—she was a good deal older than I am, you know. I think for a short time she really did love me a whole lot. Well, there it was. I knew that overseas loomed ahead, I didn't know what I should find there, didn't even know if I should come back. The fact that I did—with tremendous good luck—didn't affect what I felt then obviously. It *was* grand to walk into the Savoy or the Berkeley or the Ivy with a swell-looking girl, and you and Daddy were always so darned generous to me that I could do it. I had a grand time, and lots of fun, and I was tremendously in love ; she was the be-all and end-all of everything. I'd got it all planned, what I'd do when this show was over. Heaven only knows when that will be. It looks like lasting for ever.

" Then I went overseas. She was very good to me, sent me all kinds of marvellous parcels and luxuries and what-nots. Then, after it stopped being a ' phoney ' war and got going, and there were roads crowded with wretched people, all being machine-gunned, lying in ditches and lots of them being left there ; then the beaches and sheer horror and terror. Frightened, cold, wet, hungry—every damned unpleasant thing you can imagine and a whole lot that I hope you can't even imagine. I was lucky, I got back and got to London, and did my best to tidy myself up as well as I could, which wasn't a terrific success, by the way. I met her, and everything was grand. She was lovelier than ever, she was charming to me, and I was as happy as kings are reputed to be and most probably never are. Slowly, after the first couple of days, I knew that we didn't speak the same language. I'd been sucked into the war, I'd gone in right up to my neck ; she'd shut the war out, with determination and resolution. It wasn't my fault, it certainly wasn't hers.

" I don't want to sound self-important, or to make mountains out of molehills. I'm a captain in the infantry, a blasted foot-slogger, but I'm young, and I suppose, impressionable. War's a nasty business, ugly, fierce, cruel. It brands you. At the same time it blunts you, I think. Horrible wounds, people—men, women, and children—mutilated, death, and not nice peaceful, clean quiet death, either—they lose their importance. Here, before the war, when, for instance, old Augustus got a thorn in his foot, that really *mattered*. I suffered about it. When I heard that Walter Bains—if you remember, a chap I was pally with at school, had died of pneumonia, it upset me for days. That's over. As I said, it's just, ' Poor old Billie—gone for a Burton, too bad '. So when she said that I'd changed, and that we didn't get on as we had done before, I knew that she was right. I had changed, things that mattered to her didn't matter a damn to me, and t'other way round.

" It did hurt for a little time—a very little time—then I knew that I wasn't *going* to be hurt. Plenty of hurts waiting for me over there. Oh, I shall fall in love again—lots of times probably. Other girls will give me the air, and I shall adapt that verse of Rupert Brooke to myself and say that I shall find some girl perhaps.

" ' And a better one than you—and I dare say she will do.' One day I shall settle down and get married and have some charming children as you and Daddy have done." He smiled at her. " And until then—well, what life offers I'm going to take. I don't want to develop into some nasty, lecherous brute, but I'm not going to deny myself anything that will make me happy and won't hurt anyone else. There, Mummy, I've done. Tell me that you're shocked and that you don't like me a lot."

She said resolutely, " I'm not shocked, and I adore you—as I adore all three of you. But when you meet this *final* girl, and want to marry her, are you going to mind a great deal if she has—has lived more or less as you will have done ? "

He wrinkled his forehead, considered, then said, " Look, Mummy, if I can go into some frightfully exclusive shop with a whole wad of lovely, clean, Bank of England notes, fresh and marvellous, then I shall want something which is—like the shop—exclusive. If, on the other hand, I've only some rather dingy, shabby notes and not a great many of them, then I must make the best of it. So must she. She won't be getting a ruddy little Sir Galahad, but she'll be getting a chap who is prepared to play the game dead straight once he's married. I haven't got *any right* to expect her to give me what I can't give her. After all," he laughed softly, " tradition gives the man the right to ask a woman to marry him, and I needn't ask a girl if I don't want to, need I ? The day I get engaged I shall run straight, I shall expect her to do the same, if she loves me. Our lives, as they concern each other, *begin* from that day. After all, darling, men and women are very much alike really. The day when people believed them to be so different is surely over."

Kitty shook her head. " It sounds reasonable," she admitted, " but somehow, I don't like it very much."

Clifford laughed again, and patted her hand. " I didn't say that I actually liked it—or anything else—very much ; I accept these things. There's a devil of a lot of accepting to be done in these days, my dear."

CHAPTER II

I

OLIVER came to the North; he looked tired, Kitty thought, and more silent. He was going, so far as he knew, so far as anyone seemed to know anything, to Cairo; after that—he shrugged his shoulders, no one could say.

He was very affectionate, and not until the morning he was leaving did he begin to talk of what Kitty knew had been in his mind since he first arrived. There had been a sense of strain, although they had both tried to behave as if they were not avoiding any particular topic. Again and again Kitty had felt that they were walking down a long road with danger signals at intervals, each one of which must be carefully negotiated.

Croxton, that was a moderately safe subject, until Kitty would ask if Oliver had heard how old Butterworth the sidesman was. That was a danger signal which she ought to have avoided, for Butterworth was connected with the church, the church meant touching on Michael Cardingly. Even Barbara's engagement to Lenman Temple was not completely safe, because that was tinged with memories of young Cardingly; if they talked of the war she always felt a certain nervousness lest someone should mention Sir John Cardingly and his work. She disliked asking about Oliver's work at the camp, because that reminded her of the little inn where they had stayed together.

Then, on his last morning at Marsh Hall, Oliver asked her to go for a walk with him. He looked drawn and apprehensive, and she felt her heart fill with pity. Oliver must have sensed that strain which existed as she did, and although he had done everything in his power to show his delight at being with her again, the shadow still lay over even their happiest hours.

Together they walked over the fields, towards Low Farm, speaking very little, that strange nervousness oppressing them both.

At last Oliver said, " Let's sit down here, the view's lovely. I've always liked this particular place."

He took off his tunic and spread it for her to sit on, then lay down on the grass at her side, not speaking, but pulling up bits of grass and nibbling them reflectively as she had seen him do so often.

Gently, Kitty laid her hand on his arm, and said, " Talk to me, Nollie."

He sighed. " It's been difficult to talk, hasn't it ? And yet everything's all right between us, Kitty, isn't it ? "

" Yes, my dear, I think we're both rather trying too hard. I think too that we're both nervous because we did have a very bad fright."

" I know. I might have smashed everything; I know what a fool I was."

She laughed rather shakily. " Oliver, my dear one, don't pile too much blame on yourself, I can't bear it. Let's look on it, if we must look at it at all, as one of those dreadful nightmares which Clifford used to have when he first came back from Dunkirk. They passed, he sleeps now as soundly as ever he did. Just know that I shall miss you while you're away as much as I have always missed you when you were not with me. You know how much that is, don't you ? "

He sat stiffly upright, his hands clasped round his knees.

" Kitty, I don't know how long I shall be away, I might not come back at all. War's a sticky kind of business at the best of times. If I don't—I don't want you to live alone. Get married again—be happy with someone, you're young and—you're the kind of woman who is at her best with a home and a husband. Please remember that, if anything did happen to me."

She looked at him, a faint smile touching her lips. Dear Oliver, he was miserable, perhaps a little afraid, and he was determinedly doing his best to make himself even more depressed and unhappy. There was something of self-pity in his tone, and this in any other person would have made Kitty feel nothing but irritation. Oliver was different, at that moment he had almost ceased to be her husband and had become another of her sons.

She said, " Oliver, what rubbish ! In the first place, nothing is going to happen. The casualties in this war—so Colonel Magerson was assuring Daddy last week, will be incomparably smaller than they were in the last war. And if anything did—and God knows how I pray for you all, that you may come back safely—I'm coward enough to wish that you'd all, you and Clifford and Clive and that nice Lenny Temple, get some kind of wound which might not be too dangerous but which would keep you all safe in hospital until the war's over. But—to go back, I rather got that remark into a tangle, didn't I ? If anything did, don't try to extract even a half-promise from me to fling myself into the arms of some man, because you think that the marriage state is good for my character." She laughed, but he turned and stared at her moodily.

" I'm glad that you can laugh about it," he said.

" I laugh, dearest, because it's all so silly. You're allowing yourself to get depressed and downhearted; once you let that mood catch you, you sink lower and lower into an awful slough of despond. As Clifford would say, snap out of it ! "

" I don't see why it should be so silly," he said. " I may be away for a very long time; suppose that during that time you met someone you found you loved, really loved. Would you write and tell me frankly ? "

She made a little movement of irritation. " This is a new line of argument," she said. " First, I was to marry again immediately if you were killed, now I am to be prepared to fall crazily in love with some man the moment your back is turned. Really, Oliver, you are being childish. I don't like this conversation, and please change it immediately."

His voice told her that she had annoyed him, he spoke coldly and crisply.

" As you wish, I was only trying to . . ." She frowned, and he stopped abruptly. " Very well, I won't try to explain if it annoys you. I had no wish to be childish about anything, I assure you. Everything is in order, my father has all my papers—and—don't let this make you angry—my will. I'm sorry that I seem so depressed, perhaps I hate the idea of going overseas more than you understand. After all, in the near future England may not be such a pleasant or such a safe place as it is now. We are *not* as well prepared as some fatuous fools would like us to believe. I can promise you that. I shall worry about you."

" Invasion ? " she asked rather breathlessly.

" In some form or another—sea or air."

" But here—in the country—you needn't be afraid, darling."

He turned to throw his arms round her; at that moment she felt that the old Oliver had come back, that he had flung his depression and self-pity behind him, and all that remained was his anxiety for her. " Kitty, I shall go crazy with worry if they begin attacking England. It won't only be London and the big towns, it may be everywhere. Swear that you'll not run risks. Swear that you'll obey any orders which are given by the authorities. Don't run into danger. I played with the idea of trying to get a job which would keep me in England, but I couldn't bring myself to do it when it came to the point. I love all the children dearly, but they don't count when I think about you."

It seemed that she had Clifford with her again, Clifford crying and whimpering in his sleep, where only the touch of her hand could soothe and tranquillize him. She spoke softly, tenderly, as she might have talked to a child. Slowly, she felt the tenseness of his body relax a little, the clutch of his hands loosen, and his breathing become regular and normal.

He said, " Sorry, Kitty. I'm all right now. That worry has been gnawing away at me for weeks. Only you will take precautions, swear it to me." For the hours that remained he was like his old self, he laughed and joked in his quiet, humorous fashion with Cook and Martha. He seemed to be younger, as if the prospect of going overseas were almost exciting to him. Kitty was content. She told herself that she could bear to see him go, so long as he went with a smile; his unhappiness was something she could not face. His going abroad was inevitable, something outside of her power to avert, but his depression, his fears, and his obvious worries were things which she had always been able to fight and dispel.

Looking back, she remembered how he had always been the one to worry over illnesses, to exaggerate small difficulties into apparent disasters, it had always been her work to reassure him, to laugh at his fears, and to re-establish him. How often, when one of the children had been ill, had she watched Oliver's face growing whiter and more strained, had she heard that note of fear in his voice when he answered the telephone when his father boomed enquiries.

His mother had said to Kitty more than once, " Nay, Oliver's a good boy, but he'd have the bairns all dead an' buried i' five minutes if they had no mor'n a cold. Proper faint-hearted is Oliver."

Then again, he had a strange inability to speak what was uppermost in his mind. That morning, he had talked of his own death, of her remarriage, of a dozen things before he could bring himself to speak of the thing which was of the greatest importance to him. It was as if he refused to put into words his most pressing worry, and tried to deny its existence by talking widly about other matters, which might conceivably be concerning him but which were not of paramount imprtance.

It never occurred to Kitty Hallam that she understood her husband far better than he had ever understood her; unconsciously she had made his character her constant study ever since they were married. She had studied him with all the love and comprehension of which she was capable, and only once—she shuddered when she remembered it again—had he failed to act in the way which she had believed to be inevitable, and in keeping with the man she loved and considered in everything.

Now he had gone, she had watched him drive away, having refused to go with him to the station, because that old ghost had seemed to rise and might remind Oliver that once, long ago, she had seen another man leave a station at the beginning of his journey overseas.

" You're sure that you won't come to the station ? Oliver asked.

She shook her head. " No, darling, I hate railway stations, hate saying ' good-bye ', unless it's to someone who doesn't matter a bit to me. You matter a great deal."

She wondered if she had seen that faint shadow touch his eyes, wondered if he remembered too how she had gone to Victoria to see Johnnie begin his journey to France.

His voice had not changed when he spoke. " All right, I do understand. God bless you, and take care of you—and don't leave all the ' taking care ' to Him. Do some of it yourself, won't you ? "

II

To Kitty Hallam it seemed that Marsh Hall slept the months away peacefully, that they were out of the world, and were only wrenched back to it by the newspapers and the B.B.C. announcements. The old house was very quiet, untouched and undisturbed. From time to time Clive came on leave, or Barbara—stationed in the North of Scotland—arrived with a new collection of her strange slang phrases and unfamiliar words; twice Lenny Temple came and Kitty found him restful and strengthening.

Clifford in Libya, Oliver in Cairo, were, Kitty thought, inhabitants of another planet. From time to time Oliver sent presents, hideous leather bags, slippers which could not be worn except by suffering the greatest discomfort, once or twice silk stockings which were rapidly becoming unobtainable in England. She thought a great deal of Oliver, of that strange restraint which he had shown, and of his apparent inability to throw off the effects of the Cardingly affair. Not that he had not tried, it was evident that he had tried with all his might, and that to some extent he had succeeded, but she felt that in making the effort he had used too much determination and strength of will, that it had left him queerly changed.

It was to Clive that she talked once when he was on leave. Clive who was ready to be received into the Catholic Church at any time, his instruction was over, and he told her that he was ' just settling one or two minor points in my own mind '. " But," he added eagerly, " it's all right, I'm certain about it all. It's so—logical, Mummy."

She said, " But isn't it difficult to believe, Clive ? So many things which are new and perhaps surprising, can you really accept them completely ? "

He considered gravely, he had grown much older, she felt that he was reliant, and that his opinions on many things were more mature than those of his elder brother. Clifford wanted material things—good times, laughter, love, when he could find it, he wanted the brightly coloured things of life. Clive was more ready to stand and ' look on ', to think and argue out problems.

Now he stretched out his long legs, and gravely stared at the toes of his boots. Finally he said, " You see, Mummy, I'm lucky. I've got a capacity for belief. It's not a thing which I have cultivated, it's just a quality with which I was, I suppose, born. Like some people can use either hand equally well, or possesses a naturally correct ear for music. When the Padre told me that this and this and the other was true, it wasn't difficult for me to accept them, more than that—to completely satisfy myself that it was dead true. Mind, in most cases everything is completely logical, completely understandable, but there are certain things which you must take on trust. Mysteries—which cannot be made clear yet to us, because they are infinite and we are, while we're on this earth—finite."

" And you found that you could accept them ? "

He frowned, wrinkling his smooth young forehead, considered, then said, " Look, Mummy, if you were to tell me something completely astonishing, something which I could not possibly *comprehend*, if you said that your statement was the sober truth, then—because I believe in you, in your honesty, and sense of honour, I must take your word for it. More than that, I should feel that although I could not argue the truth of what you had told me, it was logical and right to accept your statement. I'd argue it out this way. I've known you all my life, all my life I've known you to be a grand, honourable, truthful person. Then it's illogical to assume that, because you say something which you state to be the truth, and I can't completely understand it all, that I should imagine that you have changed. You've been someone I've believed in all my life—someone I've trusted always, and someone who has never let me down. It would be not only mean but darned silly to suddenly begin to suspect you of lying, eh ? "

Her mind flew to Oliver. Oliver had not believed her, yet she had never lied to him ; Oliver had been beset with doubts as to her complete truthfulness, and here was her son putting just such a case—even though it applied not to temporal but to spiritual matters.

" All people don't find that belief is so easy, Clive, do they ? "

" No, of course not," he answered eagerly. " I told you, it's a kind of natural gift. Chaps have talked to me and said, ' But you *can't* believe that such and such a thing is possible.' The only answer I can give is, ' But I can, and I do, and I don't find the least difficulty in doing so.' You remember Saint Thomas, well, I don't doubt for a moment that he was just as devoted and filled with faith as the other disciples—Saint Peter, for example. But he just couldn't bring himself to believe something which seemed to go dead against all that he *knew*—or thought that he knew—of either his Master or humanity. He wanted *proofs*, he wanted something that he could see and touch and handle. Not that he wanted to imply that his comrades were liars, but just because he had not the gift of faith as highly developed as they had. I'm afraid I'm not making all this clear as I should like—I'm just fumbling about."

She made a little impulsive movement, denying what he said. " No, no, go on, Clive. Tell me something else. Do you honestly believe that this lack of ability to believe can be applied to other and more mundane things as well as to religious faith ? "

" Why not ? " He smiled. " The greater includes the less, doesn't it ? There might be people who are ' doubting Thomases ' over dozens of things. Might not be able to clear their minds of doubt even with the people they loved and trusted most. Particularly, I suppose, if they happened to be folks with no great imagination. I mean, if I came to you and told you that I'd been getting hopelessly binged every night for a week, but that I'd chucked it for good and all—*you'd* believe me. You might be grieved at what I'd done, but you'd believe what I told you. Someone else might want to believe me, but they'd find it terribly difficult. They'd watch me, they'd sniff my breath when they came near me, they'd wonder where I'd been if I was ten minutes late, and so on. Yet they might be awfully fond of me, might even love me dearly."

Kitty nodded. " Yes I see what you mean. Thank you, darling." She thought that night of what he had said, and remembered Oliver's distress, his suspicions, his doubts, his apparent inability to forget and believe in her completely as he had once done.

Then she asked herself, ' Had Oliver come to me and told me the same kind of story, if he had assured me that it was all over and done with—should I have believed ? ' She went over what Clive had said, she remembered that Oliver had never lied, had never been anything but truthful and honourable—Clive was right, it would be illogical to doubt.

'Perhaps,' she thought, 'I'm like Clive. I have the gift of ability to believe. My poor Oliver!'

III

The war dragged on, hopes rose and fell, certainly fluctuated, and there were times when Kitty almost believed that never again would she have her husband and children with her, or live in her own home, a normal tranquil life. Her father, she knew, worried more than he ever admitted, and there were days when the cloud of depression appeared to descend upon him, colouring his whole outlook, changing him from the cheerful, optimistic man she had known to someone who lived, it seemed, only for the daily papers and the radio announcements.

Her mother refused to read the papers, and contented herself with 'hearing the six o'clock news'. She explained to Kitty that she had never been able to 'find my way about *The Times*, or understand half of what they printed'. She was always busy, always immersed in some scheme in the town for the help of war victims, for encouraging people to save, or to learn new ways of bottling fruit and vegetables, or making the best use of the substitutes which were already appearing in the rations.

In May of 1941, Barbara and Lenny Temple were married; she was going to Scotland again, and he was being moved south. Barbara grumbled at the rules and regulations which prohibited her—as a non-commissioned officer—living in the same station as her husband, declaring that 'after this war I shall be a rank Socialist!'

Clive was sent to Canada to enter a flying school, and Clifford was sent back to England after a bad dose of jaundice. He was in hospital in Berkshire, and Kitty visiting him there found him thin, with yellow-stained eyes and a grudge against the whole world. Oliver wrote that he 'might not spend the rest of my life in Cairo. I shall be thankful to get away. The gaiety, and the additional comforts, don't atone for the sense of inaction and frustration.'

Kitty felt that sense too, and in the December, when Barbara returned home to Marsh Hall because her baby was expected early in the following year, Kitty enrolled at the big aeroplane factory which had opened about a mile away.

Her father expostulated. "My dear, is it necessary? You've a husband and two sons fighting, a son-in-law, and your daughter is going to have a child. Haven't you done enough? Your mother isn't as strong as she used to be, I'm growing old and crotchety."

"I'm sorry, Daddy, I haven't enough to do here. We've three women to look after us. Barbara is here to help if she's needed, and—I'm growing stale and lazy. It's not sufficient for me to go down to the Institute, to pack parcels, to knit stockings, and write letters to my family. I'm getting rusty."

Martha and Cook disapproved wholeheartedly.

"Of course, m'um, if it's your patriotic juty, well, it's fer you to decide, but I have grave doubts as to what the Master 'ul say," Martha told her. "It's not as if you was reelly young. You may look a lot younger nor most, but I've heard that theer's no surer way ter loose your lukes than by entering one of them aeroplane factories."

Cook said, "Theer's suthink they uses fer putting on the wings or the tails, I b'lieve, that smells 'orrible. Gives folks some kind of narsty stummick trouble. It may not be trew, but that's wot I've heard, m'um."

Kitty refused to be persuaded, and by Christmas she was a charge hand, working as she had never worked in her life before. The hours were long, and at first she used to come home completely exhausted; slowly that phase passed and she was able to do her work more efficiently; but with less expenditure of actual effort. It was as if her muscles and brain worked in greater harmony, and by the time Barbara's baby was born, in April of the new year, she knew that she had never felt better in her life. She was popular in the factory, her girls liked her, and worked well for her. They even took a pride in the fact that ' she 'is a laady is our charge 'and, Mrs. 'Allam. Ah'd a lot rather work fer 'er than fer some common cat. Be'aves proper pleasantly, does Mrs. 'Allam.'

Samson Leigh, making one of his official tours of the works, said to Gilbert Carter, one of the foremen, "That's a capable woman, that fair-haired charge hand, isn't she?"

Carter said in reply, "Dean't you knaw 'er, Mr. Leigh? She's Mr. Bland's daughter, Bland the solictor i't' High Street."

Samson said, "Bland of Marsh Hall?"

"The saame. My word, wo'th her weight i' gold is Mrs. 'Allam."

"Attractive woman," Leigh said, and they moved on to another department.

Three weeks later Kitty was sent for to the manager's office, where a meeting was in progress. She knew most of the foremen, and nodded to them as she entered. Samson Leigh sat at the head of the long table, and signalled to Wilson, the secretary, to give her a chair.

"Sit down, Mrs. Hallam," he said briskly. "Now, we're considering moving you. Giving you a special job. It's new, it's important, and it's a dead secret. So secret, in fact, that only three people in the works at this moment fully understand it and its potentialities. Roughly, this is the idea. The piece of mechanism —it's remarkably delicate—can be made in one of the shops— minus the one small piece which gives the thing its tremendous value. That can be added by one person, who must have skilful fingers, intelligence, and who won't chatter. I have discussed the matter with several of the heads of departments, and particularly with Mr. Carter, and they were all agreed that you were the ideal person. We should ask you to swear on your honour not to discuss the invention with anyone—not even your nearest and dearest."

Carter leaned forward, his arms folded on the table. "Sitha,

Mrs. 'Allam, Ah'd be a good bit easier i' my mind if you were to tak' it on. It 'ul not be soa hard as t'job you're on now, I'll promise that."

Kitty laughed, and Samson Leigh thought that it was pleasant to hear light laughter in that oppressive room, pleasant, too, to see a woman sitting among these heavy-faced, absorbed men, to watch the light on her fair hair, to notice with pleasure how bright her eyes were.

She said, " I don't like the insinuation, Mr. Carter. When have I ever complained that I was over-worked ? "

" Nay, nay," he protested. " Nay, you've got me took up all wrong. I niver said nout o't sort, Mrs. 'Allam. I weer joost tryin'——"

" To make the idea as attractive as possible." She smiled at him.

" Then will you consider it, Mrs. Hallam ? " Leigh asked.

" I have considered, Mr. Leigh. If you think that I'm capable of doing the work, then I'm very much flattered at the confidence you have in me. I say," she sent that attractive smile flying round the table again, " Thank you all, very much."

" Then if you'd be so good as to wait for five minutes, we shall have finished and I'll take you round to the little workshop which we've fitted up. Thank you, Mrs. Hallam."

He joined her a few minutes later, and walked to the small workshop which had been constructed during the last week. It was well lit, with sufficient bench room, and lockers fitted with keys.

" Everything must be locked, except the mechanism on which you are actually working," Leigh told her. " When you go to the canteen, or if you go out to speak to Carter—if only for five minutes, everything must be locked. I have a set of duplicate keys, these of yours must be given to the cashier to put in the safe every night when you leave."

" You make me feel terribly important," Kitty said.

" It's one of the most important things evolved in this war," he said gravely. " One of those things which are so essentially simple that one can scarcely understand why it has not been discovered long ago." Very simply, he began to explain the device to her, leaning over the wide bench and making diagrams on an envelope which he pulled out of his pocket. Kitty watched the firm, exact lines, the ease with which he made his explanations. His voice was deep and full without being loud. He was a tall, rather heavily built man of about fifty; she had the impression that despite his heaviness he was in good condition, that he was ' hard ' and took a pride in being so. His face, as he bent over his drawing, was grave and intent, closely shaven, and slightly florid. But he seemed to exude a sense of perfect physical and mental fitness. His words came easily, he never halted or sought for phrases. Kitty thought that he was like some of the machines in the works, precise, and efficient.

" Now, there," Leigh said, indicating a point on the diagram, " is where your work begins. That is where you will insert a minute piece of this highly valuable product, the name doesn't matter, its nature is of no consequence—except to our enemies. For that reason it is better that you merely accept it for what it is—the very heart of the contrivance. You will put—the heart into this invention."

For the first time he smiled at her, and she thought, ' How much younger he looks when he smiles.'

" Then you'll begin work here in the morning. Carter will have everything ready for you, and will give you your first lesson. There's the buzzer ! Can I drive you home, I go near Marsh Hall."

" That's very kind, I'll be at the gates in five minutes."

Hugh Bland, when he heard that Samson Leigh had driven her home, said, " I know him slightly. Good fellow, I believe. His old father, Gladstock Leigh, made several fortunes, I imagine, out of Leigh's agricultural implements. Rolling in money."

Barbara listened, giving it as her opinion that she had a pretty accurate idea as to the nature of the invention.

" Lenny told me that something was cooking, and I suppose Leighs have got the contract. I imagine that it's——"

Kitty said, " No use telling me, Bar dear, because I don't know myself. I couldn't tell you where it goes or what it does. I only know what I've been told. I don't even know how big the thing is."

" You're so terribly untechnical," her daughter grumbled, " and I don't believe that you're even curious about it all. It's thrilling—if it's what I think it is. As soon as I can leave my small Hugh I shall apply for a job in your factory, Mummy."

" If the damned war goes on much longer," Hugh Bland said, " I can see your son, Barbara, applying for a job there to work alongside his mother and grandmother ! "

Kitty liked her work, she enjoyed the sheer beauty and neatness of the mechanism on which she had to work. The work itself was easy, and needed only to be exact and perfectly adjusted. Carter brought her various instruments for testing the accuracy of her work, they were simple and easy to manipulate.

She said, " I shall like working with these things—they're attractive. I shall be able to keep my hands better, eh, Mr. Carter ? "

" Ay," he returned heavily, " Ah've not cared a lot abart watching you soil yer 'ands. Niver seems reit ter me as a laady should get 'er 'ands all mucked oop with oil and sic'like. These things—ay, they're bonnie, reit bonnie. Well "—with a heavy sigh as if he were making a great effort—" if they're bonnie, it's sumone bonnie as 'ul 'andle them, choose 'ow."

" Mr. Carter, if you say pretty things like that, you'll make me conceited."

He shook his head solemnly. " Ah doot as it 'ud tak' mor'n aut Ah could saay ter do that. Now, yer think as yer can manage ? If theer's aut as yer want ter knaw, cum an' find me, ondly, mind yer think on an' lock t'door."

That night, when she mounted her bicycle to ride home after work, she felt definitely content. She was doing work which was important, work which implied that the managers and owner trusted her and believed in her ability to do this job which held such important potentialities.

A few weeks later, when the sun shone brilliantly, and her little workshop felt hot and stuffy, Samson Leigh came knocking at the door.

She called as she had been warned to do, " Who is there ? "

His unmistakable deep voice answered, " Samson Leigh."

She opened the door and he entered, seeming, she thought, to fill the whole small space, not only with his actual bulk but with his personality.

" Whew," he said, " it's infernally hot here. What's Carter thinking about ? He ought to have put you in a fan. I'll speak to him about it." She watched him make a note on the paper which he carried pinned on to a small board. Never on his tours of inspection was Leigh seen without that board tucked under his arm.

" Otherwise," he asked, " you're comfortable here ? "

" Completely, thank you. Really enjoying my work."

" That's good hearing. Have you heard of our tremendous raid on Cologne ? The first of the ' thousand bomber ' raids. Some of your work was over Cologne last night, you know."

She shivered. " So, probably, was my son-in-law."

" Ah, yes, I forgot that you had a married daughter."

Kitty said, " I've not only got a grown-up daughter, I'm a grandmother."

" No ! Impossible ! D'you know, I can remember seeing you when I was home for the holidays. I used to see you drive down to your father's office. You had long yellow hair—well, you still have yellow hair. I used to like to watch you climbing down from your father's dog-cart."

Mechanically, he had taken out his cigarette-case and, taking one out, enquired, " May I smoke ? This is one of the few places in the works where one can smoke with impunity. Will you have one ? "

She shook her head. " I don't smoke until I go to the canteen for dinner. I'm so afraid of it making my hands less steady for this work."

" I don't think that the odd one would harm your nerves." He was leaning against the bench, watching her and smoking calmly. He showed no wish to hurry away, and Kitty glanced at the work which was waiting for her. Leigh intercepted the glance. " All right, Mrs. Hallam, very wrong of me. I'll go ! I shall begin to think that you are almost too conscientious."

Half an hour later Carter entered with an electrician to install the fan which Leigh had promised.

From that time he began to enter Kitty's workshop several times a week ; he never stayed very long, he usually smoked one cigarette, talked to her about the progress of the war and then left her. She came to look forward to his visits, to listen eagerly to the latest news which he brought her, news which was sometimes prefaced with the words, " I heard this in London yesterday—don't mention it to anyone else, at least not for the next few days, will you ? "

One morning he asked abruptly, " When are you going for your holiday ? "

Kitty said, " I wanted to speak to you about that. My son— my elder son—is going overseas again, and he wanted me to go down to Devon with him for his leave. I planned to take my holiday—I spoke to Mr. Carter about it. My leave begins on August the ninth. Can I work overtime so that I can get a stock of these things in hand, to tide you over while I'm away ? I can easily, you know."

He shook his head. " No, no, you work quite sufficiently hard. I've no doubt that already we have some in hand. I'll tell you what you might do, if you'll be so kind, leave your address. Then, if anything *should* need rushing through, we could send for you. I could probably arrange to fly you back from Devon. It's asking a good deal—we won't send unless it's imperative, I promise you."

Clifford was better, his skin was its normal colour again, and he and Kitty spent seven delicious days by the Devon sea. The weather was kind, and as she lay on the yellow sand, warmed by the sun, Kitty realized how, despite the fact that she liked her work, she missed the complete freedom to which she had been accustomed.

On the morning of the seventh day of their holiday, Clifford saw one of the porters coming towards them from the hotel.

" Gosh, he's got a telegram ! If it's to recall me, put your hands over your ears, for I warn you my utterances will not be fit for you to hear."

He shouted to the porter. " Who is it for ? Hallam ? Is that all ? "

Kitty said, " You open it and get it over, Cliff."

He read it, then looked up at her, smiling. " Hello, hello ! What's this, Mummy ?

" *May I send car to bring you and your son for dinner this evening ? Grand Torquay. Leigh.*

"Who is this mysterious Leigh ? Do we want to go or not ? He's enclosed a reply form."

Kitty said, " It's Samson Leigh, the owner of the factory where I work. My boss ! Shall we go ? "

" Why not ? " He scribbled the reply and gave it to the porter.

" Nice man ? " he asked.

" Quite nice I think. I don't really know him very well. He's always been very pleasant to me, particularly since I was given this special work."

Samson Leigh was waiting for them. Kitty had never seen him dressed formally, and the severe black-and-white seemed to make him look more broad-shouldered than ever.

He came to open the car door, saying, " This is really most extraordinarily kind of you both. My only opportunity, I'm going North in the morning."

CHAPTER III

I

WHEN they got home that evening Clifford slipped his arm through hers, and said in that confidential tone which never failed to please her, " Nice bloke that, eh ? Bit heavy in hand at first, but all right when he gets going."

She answered, " I've always found him very kind."

Later, she wondered if she had any right to feel so pleased because Clifford approved of Samson Leigh ? What could Clifford's approval matter to her ? Yet she was pleased, and she went to sleep that night content and happy. Not that their evening had been wildly exciting. It was evident that their host had been to some pains to order a dinner which was as good as wartime restrictions would permit, there were flowers on the table, and some wine which was excellent. The conversation had been sufficiently ordinary, there had been no great display of wit or conversational brilliance, but the memory left behind was of a pleasant interlude spent under pleasant circumstances.

Clifford had always been easy to talk to, Kitty reflected, during the two days which followed. He was ready to discuss anything and everything. True, he had not the depth of thought or feeling of his younger brother; in fact, he admitted to his mother that ' this idea of young Clive's, being a Catholic, seems to me to be a bit—well, I don't know—almost unhealthy. Introspective and all that, you know.'

She said eagerly that there was nothing unhealthy about Clive's attitude, and that though he might have given the matter a great deal of thought, he was most certainly not introspective.

Clifford said, " You know what I mean though, don't you ? To me it's a bit strange for young chaps to concern themselves about death, and after death. Particularly when they've been brought up to another religion. I'd rather that he was thinking about playing rugger, and reducing his handicap at golf. Get me, darling ? You see, I'm not like that. Maybe that's why it seems so strange to me."

" Doesn't religion touch you at all ? " Kitty asked.

" Oh, I don't know. I suppose that I do believe in certain things. I believe that ' those who were good will be happy ', and all that, but I don't know anything about the inner workings of religion." He raised his arms and yawned noisily. " Oh, damn it, to think that to-morrow all this comes to an end. How sickening. I'm getting sick of the damned war."

" Where are you going ? Have you any idea ? " she asked.

He shook his head. " I dunno. Might be almost anywhere. Funny things are going to happen soon. Exciting things, interesting things, dangerous things. You can't tell, and the High-ups don't tell you anything."

The two days passed, she returned to the North, and Clifford went to rejoin his regiment. During the long train journey home Kitty thought a great deal about her sons. Clive wrote happily enough from Canada, he loved his work, he liked the men with whom that work lay, he was young and keen. He had his faith. No, Clive did not present many problems.

Clifford was different. He had never been highly imaginative, though he had a good, sound brain. Since he had been in the Army Kitty felt that he had grown completely materialistic. Not that she blamed him; she had come to believe that many of these young men—flung into war, danger, and horror—had adopted a character more or less alien to their own, as a form of protection. Nothing mattered except to have a good time, and at the same time win the war. Politics did not interest them particularly. They were content to say, mechanically, ' Good old Churchill. He's the fellow,' or ' Trust Roosevelt. He and Churchill will cook up something to surprise the world.' After some pronouncement, their reaction was, ' What did I tell you ! They know what they're doing.'

She wondered if perhaps they didn't resent the war more than they would admit, They might ' damn ' the war and ' blast the Army ', but that meant nothing, they'd use the same phrases about their favourite dog. It didn't mean anything at all. But deep in their hearts, did they resent the years which were being taken from them, those years which might have been employed in making their way towards the goal of their ambitions. Was that why they resolutely shut their eyes and ears to everything except fighting, hot baths when they came out of the line, women, good food, and such music as was either completely sentimental or noisily metallic ?

They had developed a protective armour, they were content to feel nothing in particular rather than allow their feelings— either of hate or love—to master them. They refused to develop their consciousness. They firmly ejected from their vocabulary any words which were not devoid of sentimental meaning. This was ' pretty nice ', that was ' quite pleasant ', some man they admired wholeheartedly was ' quite a fellow ', even their enemies were merely ' unpleasant people ' or ' nasty blokes '.

Well, perhaps their attitude was the best one. If it saved them being shattered, if it saved them mental suffering, if they could wrap themselves in plate armour—so much the better. Only, she wondered, when it was all over, would they be able to think and feel and enjoy as they had once done ? She thought, ' There will be so much " crust " to chip away when they come back. I wonder if we shall be capable of doing it properly ? '

Clifford wrote a few days later,

When you get this I shall be on my way out to hold the gorgeous East in fee—whatever that means—again. Sand and too much sun, but always the thought of a couple of days in Alex when things get a bit further forward.

She went back to the factory, and knew that she was looking forward to seeing Samson's broad shoulders filling the doorway of her workshop, to hearing his deep, rather slow voice, and listening to his comments on the events of the war.

He came the first morning she was there, she heard his usual knock, and thought, suddenly and angrily, ' What is the matter with you, you idiot ? Feeling your heart beat more quickly, like some silly schoolgirl. You're a grandmother, and he's an elderly man.'

He said, " You look better for your holiday. That's a nice lad of yours. Has he gone yet ? "

She answered his question with a sense of pleasure because he thought Clifford ' a nice lad ', then automatically rebuked herself. Of course he was, she knew that without Samson Leigh telling her.

He said, " I don't know if you care for grouse. Probably you get more than you want, but I was shooting last Saturday—only rough shooting—and I'll send round a couple of brace if you'd like them."

Later he sent her pheasants, and then a salmon, always protesting that he couldn't eat half of what was sent to him. About the middle of September he asked if she would come and dine at his house.

" Not a big crowd, Margeson and his wife, and Vickers Mountain of Darlington. I hope that you'll say that you will. My cook isn't at all bad—as things are."

She went because she was curious to see in what kind of a house he lived. She had seen it through the trees which stood round it, but had never been inside. She was surprised at the beautiful things which the house contained; there was even definite if restrained luxury. His pictures were good, and when she praised them he spoke of them with knowledge and appreciation.

" My father collected most of them, but I've added a few myself."

Colonel Margeson and his wife were pleasant but dull; he boomed about the war, delving from time to time into technical details which conveyed nothing to Kitty, and little more, she felt, to Samson Leigh. Mountain was a thin, exquisite man in his early forties, kept out of the Army, he confided to Kitty, through continued ill-health.

Samson drove her home, in a small car which he used in going backwards and forwards to the works. He spoke very little, but when he left her at Marsh Hall he held her hand a moment longer than was necessary, and said how glad he was that she had been able to come, adding, " One day we might take a run somewhere— some Sunday, do you think ? It can't be really good for you to be stuck in that workshop all day and every day."

That winter she drove with him over the moors in the clear cold air ; together they saw the sea lashing itself into foam on the rocks near Robin Hood's Bay and Runswick, they saw the long expanse of grey water stretching away from Redcar to Saltburn, and the little churches which hid among tall trees in old-fashioned villages, where life seemed to have virtually stopped years ago.

He never attempted to grow sentimental, the whole world could have listened to their conversation, yet Kitty realized that this friendship was dangerous. She was coming to think too much of him, and it was obvious that he was happiest when she was with him. There was not the slightest question of being ' in love ', Oliver filled her heart completely, as he had always done, and yet Samson's heavy, rather bulky figure gave her a strange sense of excitement.

For weeks she would plead other engagements when he asked her to drive with him, then suddenly she longed to say, ' Yes ', and to go for miles, scarcely speaking, only conscious that she was near him, and knowing that he was content to have her with him.

II

The New Year came, and with it better news. Oliver believed that he might get home on leave, and in March he came. She was delighted to see him, to find that he seemed happier and less abstracted. She had asked Leigh if she could have a few days' leave from her work, adding, " My husband is coming home on leave, he wants to come up here, then to go and see his own people, after that we plan a few days in town together."

She saw his jaw harden, as if he clenched his teeth to steady it; she thought, ' Then he does mind ! Poor Samson ! I shall have to stop seeing him.'

He said, rather stiffly, she thought, " Of course, Mrs. Hallam. Just let Carter know when you want to go and when you'll be back." That morning he did not remain to talk, to smoke his cigarette, but gave her a curt " Good morning " and went away.

Oliver was delighted to be home, delighted with everything, and charmed with his grandson. He laughed, talked gaily, saying that the war ' was as good as over ', and that very soon they would all settle down again to ' win the peace '.

Hugh Bland said, " Ah, we lost that pretty conclusively last time."

" It will be different this time," Oliver assured him. " We possibly shan't be such nice, kindly victors where Germany is concerned, but we shall be considerably wiser."

Bland said, " I wonder—I wonder very much indeed."

" I don't . . ." Oliver boasted.

" Well, you're the man on the spot. You know more than I do."

Oliver laughed, a sound which seemed to Kitty to be as youthful as when Clifford laughed. " Believe me, we know far less than you do. Absolutely nothing but a little bit of our own particular line, not really much about that."

He told her very little concerning what he believed might be the course of the war; things were going very well in North Africa, soon the Allies would begin to really ' clean up '. Again that light boyish laugh. " Everything is under control, I promise you."

She said, " And Italy, Nollie. What about Italy ? I've always wanted to go there. Shall we go for a holiday when this is all over ? "

He stared at her, as if she had startled him. She fancied that some of the light died in his eyes, that his mouth looked harder.

" Italy ? " he repeated. " I don't know. They'll cave in, I expect. I was there in the last war, you know." He was speaking very slowly. " I was in the north, among the mountains, on the Adiege, and "—his words came still more slowly—" in Vicenza." He repeated, " In Vicenza."

" Darling," she cried impulsively, " I remember ! You lost your great friend there, didn't you ? The man who gave you that old ring. I'm sorry that I spoke of Italy. Don't look so sad, Nollie dear."

" No, no." His voice was normal again. " I hadn't thought of it—of him—for years. Have you still got that ring anywhere ? It might," he laughed, " it might be lucky for me to wear it."

He did not mention the ring again, but when they went to London, after calling at Croxton and having a tremendous welcome, not only from old Jabez and his wife, but from Mrs. Carter and children, Kitty took it with her. The morning before Oliver was going back she gave it to him, saying, " For luck, darling."

He stood twisting it round and round on his finger, frowning, then said, " I don't think that I'll wear it, after all. I've no right to wear another man's signet ring. And he was someone terrifically important—a count. No, I'll leave it with you."

She insisted. " I'd like you to wear it, I mean that."

" Very well—obedient as always."

Kitty went back to the North, she had been quite consciously happy with Oliver, there had been no clouds, no sudden moods of depression, he had been himself again—charming, tender—adorable.

In August Samson told her that the British had landed in Catania.

She said, " I'm not quite certain where it is. . . ."

" Sicily. This is important, this landing."

" Shall we go to Italy ? "

" Certain to." He lit his cigarette, offered her his case as he always did, accepted her refusal, and then said, " It's a long time since we had a Sunday drive together. Can you come on Sunday ? I've got to go to York to meet a man from town—I shan't be with him more than a very short time. Perhaps you could wander out and look at the Minster while we were busy." He watched her closely as he spoke, then said, " Do come, please. I've missed our drives."

" Yes," she said, " I should like to come."

He was as he had always been, rather given to long silences, but always attentive when she spoke. The day was beautiful, filled with sunshine; for miles they drove alongside roads which he chose in order to escape any possible troop traffic, until at last Kitty cried like a child, " Look—there—the Minster ! "

Samson turned and gave her one of his rare smiles, saying, " You greet it like an old friend. You've never given me such a warm greeting when I come into your workshop."

" Ah, but I see you every day, I haven't seen the Minster for months and months."

" I shall try to stay away for months and months, to find out what kind of a welcome you will give me," he said, adding in a lower tone, " If I were capable of staying away for so long."

She made no reply, but began to talk rather feverishly about the great old church, the walls, and the ancient city in general.

As they drove home in the cool quiet of the evening, Samson, without actually looking at Kitty, said, " I'm afraid I was rather foolish this morning. If I annoyed you—I'm sorry."

She wondered how to reply, he had said so little; if she replied that he must not speak in that way again—it sounded so prudish and formal. After all, they were good friends. If she dismissed it lightly—surely that was the better course to pursue.

She said, " Annoyed ! I thought it a very charming compliment ! "

When he came to see her the following morning he said, " Imagine what I was doing last night when I got home ? Reading the dictionary."

Kitty laughed. " Why the sudden search for knowledge ? "

" I wanted to satisfy myself as to the exact meaning of the word compliment. I find that it can be taken as ' delicate flattery ' or as a mark of respect or regard. In fact it appears to mean quite a number of things. I didn't mean any of these things—I merely doubted quite sincerely my strength of will to deny myself something which means a great deal to me."

Rather helplessly she said, " Oh, I see."

" Do you, I wonder ? You've known me for a long time now, you would say that I was a fairly serious person ? "

She laughed. " There are times when I think that you are almost desperately serious."

He leaned against the bench, as she had seen him do so often, and began to talk to her, slowly, gravely.

" I've always worked pretty hard," he said, " because my father believed in men working hard. I was put into the business, we made agricultural implements—you probably know that. My father died fifteen years ago, and begged me to keep on the business. I didn't want to. I've always longed to travel, see pictures—though I have no wish or ability to try to paint them— visit other countries. However, I did as he wished, and so far as material things go, I have reaped a very good harvest. But my— don't think this is too silly—my dreams had to go by the board. You can't run a factory like this and run off to the Continent whenever it pleases you." He smiled. " I've a too-well-developed sense of duty, I believe.

" Then you came here; the first time I saw you I was talking to Carter. I asked who you were. Hugh Bland's daughter. The little girl with hair like spun silk who I used to watch when I was a lanky schoolboy. I fell in love with you when you were about seven, my dear. . . ."

She said, " Oh, don't go on, please don't go on. You're going to make everything too difficult ! "

" No, I promise that I shan't make it difficult. Listen to me, just this once, afterwards—you shall do what you wish. I knew that you could do this work—and how right I was; you've been, you are—splendid—but I knew, too, that it would make it possible for me to come and talk to you sometimes. I *schemed* ! It sounds abominable, but it's quite true. I've fallen in love with you, Kitty— I've been a stolid, solid North countryman for nearly fifty years, and now I'm back where I was when I was sixteen and stood staring at you."

He made no attempt to touch her, but stood watching her with kindly eyes, even smiling slightly. Kitty met his eyes, made her small characteristic movement as she did when she was puzzled and said, " I don't know what to say—I wish that I did. Oh, I can't talk to you here. We've both got work to do, I've a new batch of stuff in this morning. Call for me to-night and take me for a drive. We're *friends* and I won't lose a friend—a friend like you— if I can help it."

" Very well—to-night, will nine o'clock be all right ? "

III

When she came out, Samson was waiting for her, he swung open the door of the car and she got in. " Where shall we go ? " he asked.

" Anywhere—not too far. I want to talk to you," she told him.

" Very well."

They drove through the lanes which he knew so well, where he told her he had rambled about as a boy, where he had ridden on his first bicycle, where later he had ridden his hunter, and later still driven his cars. He had said to her, and she remembered his words at that moment, " I'm Yorkshire through and through. I should have liked to have travelled everywhere, but I should always have come home to roost. That house of mine, it's not a thing of beauty, but it means a great deal to me, so do the gardens, and even the factory."

He stopped the car, they were near a tiny ford, where the water trickled over the smooth stones making music which reached Kitty's ears very soft and melodious.

" This do ? "

She nodded, and he leaned back in his corner and watched her.

" Let's get this all straight," she said, trying to keep her voice even and normal. " Did you really mean what you said this morning ? "

" You know that I did. I think that—in your heart—you've known the truth about me for a long time. Haven't you ? "

" I don't know—I was afraid. I didn't want this to happen."

He smiled. She saw his eyes crinkle at the corners as they always did when he was amused. " But you didn't do anything to stop it, did you ? "

She answered impatiently, " Oh, can't two people be good friends ? Here I am a grandmother ! Good heavens, I should have thought that I could have been friends with you, that we could have liked each other, that——"

" No, my dear. Women like you don't make *friends* with men easily. You're too attractive, too completely feminine. If you were a great-grandmother you'd still—quite unconsciously—be a ' honey pot '."

She remembered that she had found his friendship something which held an excitement, that she had waited for his light knock on the door of her workshop, and she wondered now if she ought not to have taken very definite steps to put an end to their meetings, conversations, and to his obvious desire to please her. It had been pleasant to drive about with Samson, he had never actually shown that he was in love with her, had never tried to force his attentions on her, never kissed her !

Then her innate honesty asserted itself, and she found her words coming rapidly and easily.

" I have been to blame," she admitted, " probably at least seventy-five per cent of this—situation—is due to my foolishness. I did like being with you, liked it all the more because you never wanted to flirt with me. Flirting is a thing I have always detested ! I suppose that I did know, perfectly well, what was happening, but I was able to satisfy myself—in the rather stupid, mean way one does—that everything was really all right. I'm not particularly proud of myself——"

Samson said, " Never mind, my pride in you is sufficient, I promise."

" Don't interrupt me ! I was lonely. Until this wretched war my husband and I have scarcely ever been separated. Then there were other things—I can't explain to you—that made his separation from me additionally difficult. You were so kind, there was a wonderful solidity about you, you became a sort of *rock*, and I took advantage of those things. I'm sorry, that's all I can say. Can you forgive me ? "

" Forgive you ! Good God, I find it difficult to imagine anything, any crime, for which I could not forgive you. But now—having realized, and admitted that you know that I'm in love with you; having admitted that you at least like me—what then ? "

" We must go on as we were—before," she said.

" But before—what exactly ? Before I fell in love with you ? Then we should have to put the clock back to the time when you were a small girl, as I have told you. I didn't plan to fall in love with you, and I can't fall out of love—to order. My dear, doesn't it ever strike you that your existence is pretty dull ? The factory, riding back home—I daren't offer to drive you back every night, with nearly five hundred pairs of eyes watching us—being tired,

going to bed, and beginning the same monotonous round in the
morning again."

" What is the alternative ? " Kitty asked.

For a moment her directness shook him, he began to speak,
then paused, and in the half light she could see his face—shadowy
and a little unreal-looking, puzzled and disturbed.

" The alternative—well, if——" he stammered.

She answered the question herself.   " The alternative is to
become your mistress.   To embark on a rather furtive—though
possibly quite pleasant—*liaison* with you.   Then, because I think
you forget this—when my husband comes home—what then ?   I
don't think that it's a very pretty picture.   I don't feel that such
an experience would reflect much credit on either of us, would it ? "

She waited for his reply, her brain racing ahead.   For a brief
time she had, almost unconsciously, felt the attraction of this big,
solid, kindly Yorkshireman.   Now she looked into the future.
Oliver returning, and once again she would have to face a confession to him.   It was unthinkable.   She had paid sufficiently
heavily for a folly commited before she even knew Oliver, when
she was young, inexperienced, when active pleasure meant a great
deal more to her than it did now.

Samson Leigh might have a certain attraction for her, she did
not deny that he had, but weighed in the balance against Oliver
Hallam—she could have laughed at the comparison.   Risk losing
Oliver, the man she loved, for the sake of having her life—
temporarily—made more amusing, more varied !

Leigh said heavily, " You really are devoted to your husband ? "

" I always have been."

" Then there is nothing more to be said.   I was foolish not to
discover that fact before. . . . I threw my caution, my restraint, to
the winds.   I see that—anything I might have hoped for would be
impossible.   Don't worry, I shan't ever mention it again—Kitty.
What a pretty name it is !   I should have liked saying it very
often."

The tension snapped, she was able to speak easily again.

" Say it whenever you wish," she said, " when we're not in the
works."

" Will you sometimes drive with me ? "

" If—this sounds so conceited—if it's not difficult for you,
yes."

Samson uttered a short laugh, like a bark, she thought.

" I have tremendous self-control—surely you've noticed that.
In the plan I had made for this evening—by this time I thought
you would be in my arms !   Shall I drive you home ? "

Ten days later he came into her workshop and said, " I've some
news for you.   I'm going to America ; the Government are good
enough to want my opinion on several matters connected with
airplanes.   You'll be all right with Carter and Willis and the rest
of the foremen.   They all have a great regard for you."

Kitty was surprised that her heart sank so at his announcement.
Since that evening when they had driven into the country together

their relationship had been kept friendly and nothing more. She didn't love him, she never would love him, but the thought of his going away disturbed and almost distressed her.

She thought angrily, ' What a weak illogical fool I am ! I want to run with the hare and hunt with the hounds—and I'm disappointed when I find it's impossible ! '

" Will you be away very long ? " she asked.

" Three months or so."

" The war may be over by then."

He smiled. " Don't you believe it, my dear—not in thirty months, let alone three. I'll see you before I go."

A week later he came in and told her that he was leaving the next day. " I'm flying. I've never flown in my life. Imagine it ! My life at the moment appears to be packed with new experiences. Good-bye, Kitty dear. Could you temper your scruples with generosity and let me kiss you ? "

" I hate it when you talk like that ! " she flashed.

" Then I won't talk at all," he said, and taking her in his arms kissed her; still holding her to him, he whispered, " That's one dream at least come true. Good-bye, darling Kitty."

CHAPTER IV

I

LIEUTENANT-COLONEL OLIVER HALLAM said, " Thanks, mine's an Alexander."

Major Patterson, who was seated at the same small table, said, " It's my fairm belief, sir, that these Alexanders arre the rankest poison. I shall have the same. Two Alexanders."

Oliver stretched out his legs and sighed with satisfaction. " Good to be in Rome at last. What a city ! Thank God we didn't knock it about; I don't think that I could have faced civilization easily if we had done so."

" And yet, looking it from a pairfectly sane and logical point of view," Patterson said, " Rome desairves no more consideration than any other city. The fact that Rome happens—the operative word is happens—to be the H.Q. of the Cartholic Chairch ought in reality to have no weight in a total war. In my opeenion——"

" In your opinion, my good chap, everything ought to be bombed to hell. In mine—Rome is not specifically Italian property, but the property and admiration of the world. We should not have robbed the Italians but the whole of civilization of part of its heritage." He drank his Alexander and breathed deeply. " That was good ! June in Rome demands the consumption of a good deal of liquid, I find. Have another ? " They were joined by a youngish man with bright curly red hair, his pleasant face was freckled, and his small eyes twinkled whenever he spoke, as if he found life both amusing and interesting.

Patterson said, " Behold Major Bladon ! The brightest and newest jewel in your crown, sir."

Bladon laughed. " I'm scarcely used to it yet ! "

Oliver said, " You soon will be, Races. What's yours ? "

Bladon sat down, his hands on his brown knees. " Oh, the Italian liaison officer has turned up, sir. Nice feller, quite young. About twenty-two or three. Good-looking bloke, speaks English as well as I do."

" Which after all," Patterson interpolated, " might not be the pink of pairfection, Races."

" Where does he hail from," Oliver asked, " and what's his name ? "

" I gather that he's a Roman, he seemed frightfully proud of it, too. He's a duke—you know, spelt D-U-C. Are they as lofty as our dukes over home, d'you think ? I mean would he be as big a chap as the Duke of Norfolk, for example ? "

" I canna speak with authority," Patterson replied, " so farr as Norfolk is concairned, but I imagine that the Duke of Argyll would most sairtainly be a more important pairson."

142

Oliver said, " Good Lord, a duke, eh ? We shall have to look to our manners. What's his name, Races ? "

" Gradisco, sir. He's got a string of Christian names and odd titles as well. But he's a modest chap, I promise you."

" Gradisco," Oliver repeated. " I once knew someone of that name years ago, during the last war."

" This chap would be far too young to be in the last war, sir."

Oliver finished his drink, then bidding the others ' Good night ' he walked back to the Grand Hotel where he was staying for a few days until the arrangements at the quarters taken for the regiment, out by the Via Appia Nuova, were in something like order. Rome was filled with troops, they were everywhere, the prices in the shops had soared to fantastic heights since their arrival, but that fact did not deter the men from spending money wildly.

Gradisco—Duc di Gradisco—a young man—about twenty or twenty-two. There couldn't be two Ducs of the same name, surely. The name rang in his head, despite all his efforts to fill his mind with other matters.

Young Bladon would do all right, good, energetic fellow, the men liked him ; liked him better than they did Patterson, whose dry Scottish humour they found disconcerting. Not that Patterson wasn't a capable officer, you couldn't wish for a better.

Gradisco—other titles as well—liaison officer.

Rome at last ! Their way there hadn't been a picnic. There had been some nasty, difficult patches ; far less smooth than they had been led to hope. The Italians were out of the war, they were to be regarded as co-belligerents, and were promised an ' honourable place among the peoples of the new Europe '. Poor devils, they had been badly let down by their damned Government. Even now they seemed to be torn in pieces between what was left of Fascism and the Badoglio Government.

Gradisco—Duc di Gradisco—young—a Roman.

Italy was going to suffer all the war. No mistake about that. The Hun wasn't going to give in so easily, he'd dig himself in pretty well. More than that—even when he was dislodged, he'd see that he left very little of any value behind him. Houses, schools, hospitals, even churches would all suffer at their hands when the retreat began. They had done plenty of damage already, and the hardest part was yet to come.

But Rome was saved. A few bombs dropped on railway and marshalling yards, and a church hit—possibly that was an understatement, but the whole thing wasn't too bad. Oliver frowned. How easily one talked and thought ! ' Not too bad ! ' It was all desperately bad for the unfortunates who were robbed of their homes, their goods—or their lives !

The fountains of Rome. Not playing as they must have done in peace-time, for the water position wasn't too good, but how beautiful many of them were ! No wonder Romans were proud of their fountains. He must go and see the Fountain of Trevi, where it was said if you threw money in the water you were certain to return to Rome. He must see everything possible of the city while they remained here. Find some knowledgeable Italian who would show him round.

Gradisco—' speaks English as well as I do '—liaison officer.

He frowned suddenly because that name kept coming back to him, no matter how hard he tried to turn his thoughts in other directions. As he entered the Grand, he paused for a moment, wondering if, for the sake of his own peace of mind, he could get in touch with this new liaison officer. In the little bar he saw one of his own officers, Captain Franks, and greeted him.

" I was waiting for Races, sir," Franks said; " he promised to come round here for a quick one. We're going on to the dell' Orso."

Oliver said, " You weren't by any chance with Bladon when this Italian liaison officer came, were you ? I rather wanted to have a word with him to-night. Give him the general lay-out."

" He's here, sir. You mean our Duke ? Yes, I saw him not five minutes ago in the entrance hall, talking to a couple of elderly men. Like me to find him for you ? Right, sir."

He went out, and Oliver, taking out his handkerchief, rubbed his damp palms. He ordered a cognac, adding, " Make it a double."

Gradisco—who was he ? A nephew of Yolanda's husband, a cousin—he stifled an exclamation of irritation.

' What is the use of pretending ? He's Yolanda's son ! '

Yolanda's son. He had known that he would hear of her, perhaps see her when he landed in Italy ; with each march leading nearer and nearer to Rome the conviction had grown, until now he told himself that he would have experienced surprise if this liaison officer had not been a member of Yolanda's family.

Where was she ? Would he meet her, talk to her again ? Had she changed a great deal ? he wondered. How lovely she had been, lovely and so dear. He still thought of that evening when she had told him that she was leaving for Rome, with pain. Not that he had thought of her often, Kitty had filled his mind and his heart, only at long intervals had some chance word brought it all back to him, vivid and painful. Now he recalled the sense of desolation that had swept over him as he walked back to his flat after seeing Yolanda for the last time ; not only had he felt desolate and abandoned, but he found it difficult to believe that it was true.

He drank his cognac and felt that spirit steady him. His mind was less confused. What would happen if he saw Yolanda again ? Was she still alive ; if this boy were the duc, did that mean her husband was dead ? And Kitty—Oliver's mind seemed to halt and stagger, as a man might before a heavy and unexpected blow.

Kitty, who had come to Devon to tell him of her affair with Cardingly ; that confession which had shaken him so terribly, and seemed to throw his whole mentality out of gear. Why had he never admitted his own love affair with Yolanda ?

' I ought to have done,' he thought, as he stood in the noisy little bar, leaning against the counter, his eyes turning always towards the door, searching for the first sight of the young man who was, he felt convinced, Yolanda's son. ' I ought to have told her—at first her story shook me so deeply, roused my jealously to such an extent that I could think of nothing else. Then later—I was, yes—*afraid*. We had both said, before we were married, that our lives before we met were no concern of anyone except our- selves—provided that we were completely free at that moment. I meant it then—honestly and sincerely. Then when Kitty told me about Cardingly I realized what the story did to me. I was afraid that if I told Kitty about Yolanda—she might react in the same way. Cowardly—unfair—mean—everything that is base, but true. Yes, it's dead true ! '

Again he wiped his forehead, it was wet and cold, as were his hands.

' God help me ! ' he thought. ' What a mess—what a beastly mess ! '

Franks was coming back. Oliver could see him walking across the hall and beside him a young man, tall and slim, wearing the uniform of an Italian officer. Oliver shivered, suddenly cold and desperately afraid.

Franks said, " I found him, sir. This is Capitain the Duc di Gradisco, sir."

A strange, harsh voice that Oliver scarcely recognized as his own said, " I am very much pleased to have you join us, Capitano."

The tall young man bowed. " It is an honour for me, sir. I am delighted that Captain Franks found me. Major Bladon told me to report in the morning to the camp on the Via Appia Nuova, where I went, as a matter of fact, this afternoon."

His English was perfect, his eyes steady and dark grey, his face rather long but well shaped, with a sensitive mouth and a good firm chin.

Oliver kept saying, " Yes—yes—oh quite—yes," while he tried to detect any likeness to Yolanda, or even to his dead friend Nino Chiot.

Franks said, " Will you have a small one, sir ? " Oliver nodded. " And what are we to call you ? " he asked Gradisco. " You'll probably be ' Duke ' to everyone in five minutes, won't he, sir ? "

Gradisco said, " Oh, please, just—by my name—Gradisco. It is a good thing that it is an easy name, some of our Italian names are quite difficult. In my family I am always called ' Nino ', my real name, of course, is Antonio. At least one of them ; I have a good many ! " He laughed, showing his beautifully white, even teeth.

Oliver thought, ' His name at home is—Nino ! ' But then many Italians were called by that diminutive ; that proved nothing. He said, " If you're not engaged I'd be glad if you could dine with me. It would be an opportunity for me to give you some informa- tion regarding your duties and so on. I am staying here."

Gradisco bowed again. " I shall be very happy. Would you allow me to telephone to my mother that I shall not be in to dinner ? It will only take a moment. Excuse me, please."

Franks said, as Gradisco went off to the hall, " He seems a

nice chap, don't you think, sir ? Pleasant feller." He laughed.
" I've never spoken to a real live duke before."

' He lives with his mother. Yolanda—it must be Yolanda.
What will happen if he says to her that he is dining with—Colonel
Hallam ? '

He said to ' Tip ' Franks, " Yes, pleasant enough lad."

Gradisco returned; his mother was charmed that he had met
his commanding officer, she would be delighted if, after dinner,
they would come up to her house. " It overlooks the Gardens,"
he explained, " and it is cool and quiet there in the evening, sir."

Oliver set down the glass which he held, his hands were shaking
and he was afraid that the two men might notice their unsteadiness.
His heart was hammering against his ribs, he wondered if its beats
showed through his drill tunic. To-night, within a couple of hours
—he could see Yolanda ! The last time—Vicenza in 1917, and
now it was mid-June, twenty-odd years later. He forgot to be
prudent, he forgot his fears, at that moment he forgot that Kitty
was his wife—and that he himself was the grandfather of a little
boy!

He said, " That would be delightful, if you are sure that it will
not inconvenience your mother, Gradisco."

" My mother will be charmed. May I return to tell her that we
shall arrive, sir ? "

II

During dinner Oliver had eaten very little, the food was good,
well cooked, but to him it seemed tasteless and unpalatable. He
forced himself to talk to Gradisco of his future duties, of his
brother officers, and felt a sense of pleasure that he could speak of
them all in terms of praise. They'd be decent to this pleasant
fellow.

He said, " If there is anything that puzzles you, worries you, if
you are in doubt or difficulty, come to me, or in my absence to
Major Patterson. He's a Scot and has a Scottish sense of humour,
but he's a good and efficient officer. I hope that you'll like the
work."

Abstractedly the young man answered, " I am sure of it, sir."
Then asked, " Might I take what is I am sure a great liberty ?
Please forgive me, but that ring you wear—might I look at it more
closely ? "

Mechanically Oliver took off the ring and handed it to him;
he noticed what fine hands Gradisco had, with long sensitive
fingers. He was examining the ring, frowning a little. Then he
looked up and said, " It is the counterpart of one which my uncle,
Count Chiot—well, really my great-uncle, for he was the brother
of my grandfather—gave to me. I can show you my ring when
we visit my mother this evening. This is very interesting. If I am
not presuming too much—or do you say too far, I forget for the
moment—might I ask where you found this, sir ? "

Oliver drew a deep breath, he must take the plunge, he must be cool and self-controlled.

" You say that it was given to you—your ring, I mean, by your great-uncle, Count Chiot. The ring which you are holding was given to me in either the winter of '16, or the very early months of '17, also by a Count Chiot, Nino Chiot, who was my friend and comrade. I was with him when he died. In the mountains, on the Sopra Adiege."

" My uncle! My mother's brother! "

" When you told me that your name was Nino I wondered, but, after all there are many young men called Nino." He was actually able to smile with comparative ease. " When you asked to see my ring, when I saw how intently you looked at the engraving, I felt that there must be some connection."

" And you were my uncle's comrade! How happy my mother will be! She has spoken of him to me so often, she loved him dearly. He was quite young——"

Oliver said, " We were all young—in those days."

Nino nodded. " Indeed, yes. Twenty-seven years ago. I was not even born then! Did you ever meet my mother, sir ? "

" I believe once—when I went to Vicenza with—the other— Nino. It must have been at the house of your grandfather. Your mother did not remember my name ? I mean when you spoke to her on the telephone."

" Sir, I was guilty of a great disrespect—I forgot to mention your name. I merely said my Colonel—as we do in Italy. How remiss of me! And," again he laughed, showing his teeth, " your English ' H ' is one of the few difficulties which your language presents to me. Perhaps I was a little nervous of trying to pronounce it."

Oliver nodded, then said gravely, " In case your mother does remember me, in case I should bring back too many memories—of your uncle— it might be well if you told her my name. It is— Hallam."

" I shall do so at once, sir. Please excuse."

He returned and said with smiling assurance that his mother would be most happy to see Colonel Hallam; she had added that Nino was to say that she ' remembered perfectly '.

As Oliver smoked a cigar, Gradisco told him something of his life before the war. His parents had a ' palazzo ' in Rome, ' where we are going this evening ', and also a house at Livorno. He was an only son, his father had died when he was twelve. He was now nearly twenty-seven years old, and had been intended for the diplomatic service.

" I have also the Chiot palazzo in Vicenza and some land near there. My mother's aunt, Contessa Elcano, left me another small palazzo in Venice. I have too many houses, I don't know what to do with them all. If I had had several brothers and sisters it would have been easy to divide them amongst us."

Watching and listening, looking back and obstinately refusing to look forward, Oliver let him continue to talk. He spoke of his mother with frank and obvious affection, he boasted that she was still the most lovely woman in Rome. " Did I say Rome ? I should have said—in Italy ! "

Together they drove through the crowded streets, where the sun's rays seemed to have grown mellow with the gentle coming of night; there were still soldiers everywhere, but as they turned into the Gardens Oliver was conscious of a sudden quietness. The air felt cooler, the noise of traffic was left behind.

Nino said, " Ah, how wonderful that Rome should be free again ! It has been a time of terrible suffering, dreadful fear—by day and night."

A huge house, with a courtyard inside the great gates which swung open to admit them. An elderly manservant said that the Duchessa was waiting for them in ' the small salon '.

" I am so excited, sir," Nino said, " to bring you to see your old friend, my mother."

Oliver nodded, the ability to speak had left him. For one brief instant he longed to plead that he was ill, that he had forgotten an important appointment, that he had pressing work which must be done immediately. They walked down a long corridor. Nino opened the door of a room, and standing back called, " *Mamina*— my Colonel."

Yolanda was facing them. Oliver saw that she had retained her wonderful, pale clear skin, the skin he used to say was like the petals of a magnolia. She took a few steps forward, and held out her hand, saying, " This is very kind of you, Colonel Hallam."

He laid his hand beneath hers and raising it, brushed it with his lips.

" It is kind of you to ask me to come to see you," he said.

" I remember you—so clearly," she said.

" And I remember you——"

Nino began to speak rapidly of the finding of the ring, and Yolanda listened, smiling a little, a small, very tender smile, Oliver thought.

She asked, " Have you always worn it, Colonel Hallam—ever since ? "

" No, Duchessa, only when I came overseas I put it on. But I have taken care of it." He thought, ' You're lying! Kitty put it away; Kitty asked you to wear it again ! But you don't wish to mention your wife ! '

Her voice had the same rather deep, full quality which he remembered, her movements were slow and graceful. Oliver felt that she had grown very self-reliant, probably she had carried the weight of the administration of her husband's property after his death. She spoke as if she chose her words very carefully, almost as if she weighed them.

She said to her son, " Nino *caro*, what liquors are you going to offer to Colonel Hallam ? Tomaso will bring the coffee, but you had better see to the liquors. He has never learnt to understand them."

They were left alone. Yolanda rose and went to the open window which gave on to a wide balcony. Oliver followed her.

" So you came back," she said. " How strange it all is.' I heard
that you were coming; I hear a great many things that Nino
knows nothing of. I—tried to arrange—that he should come to
you. Do you like him ? "

" He's delightful."

" Do you think that he is like me ? "

" Not in the least, so far as I can see."

For a second she touched his arm with the tips of her fingers,
so quickly did she remove them that he wondered if he had not
been mistaken."

" No, you're right," she said, " he is not like me." Then speaking very softly and rapidly she said, " Oliver, you must come and
see me. I must have time to talk to you. To-morrow ? Can you
come and take luncheon with me ? Please make a—great effort, I
beg you."

" I shall come to-morrow—will one o'clock suit you ? "

III

Oliver refused to be driven back to his hotel, he wanted to be
alone, to think and to try to order his thoughts. Nino protested
that it was too far, but Oliver remained adamant.

The night was warm, the stars brilliant, and the city seemed to
have gained in dignity and tranquillity. True there were still
soldiers, but the night seemed to have laid its hand on them, they
were less eager to rush about almost feverishly, attempting to see
everything, to buy, to chatter and shout.

Oliver felt curiously tired, the emotion which he had felt at
meeting Yolanda again seemed to have left him drained of energy;
he felt that he had been swimming against a strong current, and
that now he could do no more than drift along, barely keeping his
head above the water. She was still beautiful, he was still conscious of the fascination which she held for him, of the music of
her voice, and the grace of her movements—but he was no longer
in love with her. It was as if time had made a gulf between them
which it was impossible to bridge.

He thought, ' I shall always love her, she will always have a
place in my heart, but I am not—in love. I don't want to hold her
in my arms as I used to. How hungry I used to grow for her
caresses, her kisses, for the touch of her hands ! I want to talk to
her, to know what her mind is like—she's developed. She always
had dignity and self-possession, but she has something more
now. You feel that she is very finely tempered, like a beautiful
piece of steel.

' Our lives have been set in such different ways. She has lived
as the Duchessa di Gradisco, a woman with palaces and great
houses, land and properties; her life must have held a quality
which was almost feudal. I have lived in a comfortable English
house, as an ordinary business man, meeting people of my own
type and class. I have never travelled very far, I have never met

the great people of the world. Even if I wanted to—put the clock back—it would not be possible. She would find me terribly ordinary and limited. I should find her oppressively aristocratic and cultured.'

That night he lay awake, thinking, wondering. He must tell Kitty, he must confess to her that he had gone through that experience during the last war. How badly he had taken the story which she had told him, and how apprehensive he was as to how she would accept what he must tell her on his return.

Morning came, he felt shaken and disturbed; he drove out to the camp, immersed himself in documents, plans, and the general business of the day. Gradisco reported formally, his behaviour was charming but rigidly correct, and he made not the slightest reference to Oliver's visit to his mother's house. Oliver watched him narrowly, deciding that he liked the fellow, that he admired his modest dignity, and his readiness of comprehension. The lad had brains; more, he had an eagerness to grasp what was said to him quickly and with intelligence.

When he was leaving, Oliver held out his hand. " I'm glad that we have you with us. I'm sure you'll do very well."

Gradisco took the hand which was offered and said, " I am very proud, my Colonel. I shall try to "—he smiled—" give you every reason to remain ' glad '."

Later Oliver drove to the Palazzo Gradisco. He passed through the paved courtyard, ascended the great staircase with its carved banisters and glanced at the dark old paintings which hung on the walls. Along the wide corridor with its rich carpets and fine old furniture he went, the old manservant leading the way. He was shown into the room where they had sat on the previous night.

Yolanda came to meet him, she was wearing a dress of black and white, very simple; but even to Oliver's inexperienced eyes it was evidently beautifully made and exquisitely designed.

" I am so glad that you could come," she said. " I was afraid that at the last moment something might have prevented your doing so. Now, let me give you a cocktail. I mixed them myself. The quality is not so good as it used to be, but—I hope it will be palatable."

As he sipped his cocktail she talked easily, and at times amusingly, of the German occupation. Everything that was worth money had been hidden in the cellars. "They are very old, our cellars, and my servants built brick walls to hide my valuables. Before the walls we put barrels of wine, cases of bottles, and—the Germans never looked further! But it was a horrible time! You heard, perhaps, of the massacre—you must drive out to the place where those poor people are buried. Everyone ought to visit them! There is *proof*! That," she smiled, " is what logical people are always asking for, isn't it ? "

During luncheon she talked on. Oliver heard names which had been nothing more to him, attached to individualities so that, for the first time, they seemed real. This man whom he had always regarded as ' a bad fellow ' was dismissed as ' not really a bad man ', but, what is possibly more dangerous, ' a stupid one '; another whom he had visualized as being clever and energetic was stigmatized as ' a silly man of the world ', that is to say—' a man of his own very small and very cheap world ! '

Her remarks were crisp and to the point, she was often bitter, still more often hard and unforgiving; only when she mentioned the Holy Father did Oliver catch again the note which he remembered so well. The harshness died, the bitterness changed to tender regard, her whole face appeared to have softened, grown more gentle.

" Do you actually know the Pope ? " he asked. It had never occurred to him that people ' knew ' the Pope of Rome.

" But of course. I have met many great men, many wise men, but the Holy Father is the greatest and wisest of them all. He has only one fault—if fault it is !—he suffers too much, he shares too actively the sorrows of the people of the world. I shall try to arrange so that you may have an audience while you are in Rome."

" But I'm not a Catholic—I mean——"

Her smile deepened. " His Holiness does not only give audiences to Catholics," she said. " He has been blamed by some of your English bishops for that very thing. No, no, I am not going to embark on an argument. I think that the blessing of any good, sincere person is of value, don't you ? There, I am growing too serious, I must not bore you. The first British colonel who has come to my house ! And to bore him ! "

He said, " I'm only a half-colonel, not nearly so important as I sound."

She rose. " Let us have our coffee in my small room. I like it because it is not so vast as these. To sit in these big rooms is like trying to be intimate and confidential in the Colosseum. Come."

When their coffee was poured out she leaned back and watched him. Her face was inscrutable, not unkind but detached, almost impersonal.

" Let me give you another cognac," she said, " because I have a great deal to say to you, and it must be said quickly—or I shall lose my courage."

He smiled at her. " I don't believe you could ever lose that."

" My dear, I have lost it during these last years—very often. Since that day—June the tenth, 1940—when that blustering bully declared war. Even now, what is to happen to this unfortunate country ! She must—it is inevitable—become a battle-ground. But—I don't want to talk about that now. Tell me, Oliver, you married ? "

" Yes, in the early part of 1919. I married a girl I met when I was in hospital."

" You're happy ? I am sure that you are—you have children, no ? "

" Two boys and a girl; the girl is married and—I'm a grandfather."

" Imagine it ! And the boys—they are fighting. Ah, poor

Oliver ! What a misery it is. And this is—for us—the second war of our lives. It is wonderful that we can retain our sanity. How young we were, in those other days. My dear, I wonder if you ever thought of me, did you—or am I wrong to ask that ? "

He stared at her, seeing her as he had known her years ago. How lovely she was, even though time had laid its hand on her—but the hand, Oliver felt, had been laid lightly ; or was it that she knew how to lose her youth and gain the added beauty of complete maturity ? There was nothing provocative in her tone, no hint of sentimentality ; perhaps a trace of regret, or possibly nothing more than retrospection.

He said, " At first, I thought too much. Chiot's death hurt me terribly, I was very fond of him. I was more acutely unhappy—after you left me—than I have ever been in my life. But—well, one can't go on suffering in that way for ever. Life renews itself, you pick up the pieces and—go on."

" Yes, nature isn't as cruel as we often believe. I felt, at first, that nothing mattered, or could matter, any more to me. But it was the only way out, we couldn't have gone on. We both knew that. My husband was much older than I was, he was older than even his actual years warranted. It was a tedious life, full of small ceremonies, of dull social engagements, of long elaborate dinners and drawn-out functions. Oh, my husband was very kind to me, he was a person of great culture, tremendous artistic taste and knowledge, but—his personal dignity meant more to him, I believe, than anything in the world. I was young, you remember, I liked laughter, warmth, amusement—those things went almost completely after I married. I always had to remember who I was, what was right and proper for me as Duchessa di Gradisco—ah, how tired of it I used to get. In those days we kept both houses open all the year round. We had—it seemed to me—armies of servants, overseers, agents, and I was always getting them mixed, and forgetting their names ! "

She was talking very quickly ; it struck Oliver that she was pitching her voice a little higher than usual, and her cheeks were very faintly touched with colour. He thought, ' She's nervous, she's walking round and round what she really wants to say. She's lost some of her self-possession—she's more like the Yolanda I remember.'

She picked up a fan that lay on a little table beside her chair, and opening it began to fan herself rapidly, saying, " How hot it is ! How I wish that I could be near the sea at Livorno. I wonder if there will be anything left of our house there. Poor Livorno ! "

Oliver said quietly, " Go on with your story, my dear."

" Yes, I will." She continued more quietly, as if she had taken a decision not to allow her nerves to betray her. " Nino was born when I had been married—seven months. I was terribly ill, they thought that I was going to die." She laid down the fan and stretched out her hands towards Oliver, saying, " Oliver—did you never realize why I left you ? Why, after delays and delays, my marriage was suddenly hurried forward ? No one knew except my mother's sister Louise Elcano—she is dead now, six years ago. She knew—she was the one person to whom I could speak openly, she and my old Battista—you remember Battista, Oliver ? "

He held her hand tightly, staring, his face drawn and strained.

" Yolanda—what are you trying to tell me ? That Nino—that Nino is my son ? Explain—tell me—I can't understand it all."

" Dear Oliver," she spoke very gently, almost tenderly, " what is there to explain ? I was promised to Antonio Gradisco, it was considered a wonderful match for me. I wasn't in the least in love with him, but I was attracted by the idea of being a duchessa. He was kind, courteous, generous—and elderly. Then you came, and I managed to delay the wedding, not once but twice. Then—I began to be afraid. I told my aunt, she begged me not to make a scandal; I told her that you wanted to marry me, she persuaded me that it would never be a success, and that to throw over Antonio would cause a terrible disaster for my family, it might ruin the prospects of my brother—and you know how I loved him. So I went to Rome and as discreetly and diplomatically as possible the wedding was hurried forward. Fortunately it coincided with a visit Gradisco was paying to Rome on important business. That was the story, my dear."

Oliver repeated, " And Nino is my son."

" Dear, he's so like you, he always has been. Have you noticed his hands ? They're your hands, Oliver."

He spread his fingers on his knees and stared at them. He remembered that he had noticed Gradisco's hands last night, had thought how capable and unfaltering they looked. It had never occurred to him that they were like his own—no one really knew what they were like, not even their hands. He felt stunned, stupefied. His son—that tall young Italian, Antonio, Duc di Gradisco.

Oliver said, " He doesn't know anything of this, does he ? "

" No, no," eagerly. " There is no one alive now who has the slightest suspicion, not the slightest. Nino must never know—why should he ? You have two sons, you tell me; Nino is all I have in the world. He's good, honourable, he'll do his duty to his tenants, he'll improve his estates—we're robbing no one. The heir is the son of a second cousin of my husband's, he lives in New York. He's very wealthy, his father married a fabulously rich American girl. Apart from the fact that he might like the title—what would it mean to him ? Nothing ! Nino loves the land, the peasants worship him—he'll be one of the people who will help to rebuild Italy. Oliver—dear Oliver—you will never let him know, will you ? "

" No—I promise that, Yolanda."

" And you'll—well, I don't mean shield him, or protect him, but you will do what you can—reasonably, honourably, to send him back to me—safely." She suddenly covered her face with her hands; he heard her whisper, " My God, if anything happened to Nino ! "

He rose and stood at her side; leaning down, he took her hands and held them in his own; she turned and looked up at him. He saw the tears on her lashes. Stooping, he kissed her eyelids as he had done years ago in Vicenza.

"Darling, splendid Yolanda," he whispered, "I promise that I shall do everything that is in my power. My dear, if only everything had been different! You've made me regret so much—that might have been. I feel that I'm looking back on a dream, such a wonderful dream, which I once had. May I come and see you again?"

Her control had returned, he thought that mentally she had moved away from him once more, that she was accentuating the gulf which lay between them.

"Yes, but we must be wise. We must never talk of this again, or we shall begin to—lower our guards. Oh, I know how easy it would be to slip back into beautiful, sentimental recollections, to share memories, but—it isn't wise, it's foolish, foolish, foolish. We have this secret to keep, not only for our sakes but for Nino's, for your two sons, your daughter—and, my dear, your wife. We should begin by being so careful, so guarded, then we should grow careless, and one day would come a moment when we were not—watching, not being cautious, and—we should betray ourselves. Say that you understand, Oliver."

"I understand. I understand that you're being wise for us both. I will be obedient, I promise."

Once more he bent and kissed her, and felt her lips pressed against his cheek. Very gently she pushed him away, and whispered, "That must be the last time, dearest—the very last time. Now you must go. It is not considered—socially correct to spend too long alone with a British—or any other for that matter—colonel."

CHAPTER V

I

ROME was a pleasant enough place in the summer of 1944. There were times when the heat was oppressive, when the disorganization of the water supply made it difficult, but generally speaking it was gay and amusing. Oliver was working very hard, too hard to allow his private preoccupations to obtrude; he was forced to push them firmly into the background so that the work which lay before him might receive his full attention. Only when that work was over for the day dared he lean back and allow his mind to go over the various revelations which Yolanda had made to him. It was on those occasions, when Gradisco came to him with some question or demand for advice, that Oliver watched him closely, almost hungrily. This man was his own son, his eldest son. With every meeting he liked the young man more; he was energetic, he exercised tact in carrying out his duties, he was popular with the British officers. He never attempted to stress his importance, or to parade his obvious wealth; his attitude towards his superiors was always respectful, but never servile. Even Patterson admitted to Oliver, " Theer's something aboot that young chap that makes you feel a complete respect forr him."

Yet he had a sense of humour, for again and again Oliver heard him talking to his brother officers and listened to their laughter at Nino's remarks and replies. He had a firm and solid faith in the intentions of the British and Americans to set Italy on her feet again; indeed, Oliver had heard him express the wish, more than once, that for a term of years the Allies might take over Italy as a mandated territory.

" But surely the Italians would resent that—even if it were possible, which I doubt very much," Oliver said.

" My Colonel, Italy is a very puzzled and distraught nation," Gradisco answered. " She is torn between governments—Badoglio, the remains of the Fascists, and the authority of the Germans in the north. Italy at the end of this war will be ruined, much of her beauty destroyed; she will need a firm, strong, yet just hand to direct her. She would welcome, I believe, and I am a patriot, a government which was capable of giving her that direction. She has lived for so long in the dark, silent, restricted cellars of the Fascists that now, when she emerges into the strong light of day, she will be bewildered, even a little unsteady. You know how plants look when they have grown in the dark—white, debilitated, lacking sturdy strength."

Again and again, when Oliver watched him or listened to his eager speech, he felt that he was watching himself twenty-seven years before. Every day he noticed some trick of speech, some characteristic movement, which were exact replicas of his own. Vaguely he wondered why no one else noticed these things.

Gradisco was light-hearted enough, but there was a serious side to his character which showed itself immediately he became absorbed or deeply interested. He was surprisingly well read, and Bladon admitted to Oliver one evening after an argument, " It doesn't take our Duke long to get me well out of my depth. The chap's read everything—history, science, literature—and music ! By Jove, sir, he's just full of it. Do you suppose that all these Italian young feller-me-lads are educated like the Duke is ? "

He saw Yolanda very seldom; twice he dined there with Gradisco, when she gave rather formal dinner parties and appeared to Oliver to be the complete social hostess, and once when he visited her alone, when again they sat in her small room with the wide balcony.

He was not actually attracted by her; he was conscious of her beauty, of her undoubted charm and fascination, but he felt that her self-control was almost inhuman. Not that he wished for a reopening of their old relationship, but he would have welcomed a hint of regret, a trace of sentiment. He was lonely, he missed his wife and his children, his home and the work to which he was used ; he was disturbed deeply and sincerely whenever he thought of what he must tell Kitty when he returned, and he blamed himself without mercy for the deception which he had practised. He admitted his own cowardice, his weakness, and his grave injustice towards the woman who had shown so much more courage than he had done. He knew that he despised himself; not for his long past devotion to Yolanda, not for the fact that Gradisco was his son—these things had happened so long ago, and the existence of Nino neither added to nor detracted from his culpability.

When he had said that their lives—his and Kitty's—before they met concerned no one except themselves, he had been sincere; but he had spoken without knowledge of his own terrible jealousy. Kitty had been literally the mainspring of his life, he had given her complete love and devotion, he had—he admitted it now—idealized her. Her story had roused in him a jealousy so intense, a hatred of Cardingly so unrestrained, while it had fanned his imagination into a flame so fierce and consuming that everything which she had told him became enlarged, exaggerated, and hideously amplified. He had possibly suffered more acutely because he was by nature a quiet, even-tempered individual, and he had never realized what depths of passion and resentment existed in his character.

Towards the end of July he was told that they were to move out of Rome, to go forward towards the north, where the winter would undoubtedly see fighting which would be hard and terrible, but probably decisive. He went to tell Yolanda the moment the plans were completely formed.

She looked paler than usual, and lay on her wide sofa, not rising but stretching out her hand in greeting.

" Forgive me, this heat is terrible, Oliver. If only I could get away to the hills—to the sea. You look very tired, my dear. Ring for some wine, cold drinks—what you wish."

He rang, then came back and sat down near her. " I've got news for you," he said. " We've got our marching orders. We shall be off towards the end of next week. Viterbo, Orvieto, Chuisi and Perugia. After that—we shall see what happens. Perhaps Florence, I don't know."

Tomaso entered, she gave the order for wine and ice, then as the door closed, turned to Oliver. Her eyes were wide and startled, her lips parted; for a moment her self-control had deserted her. He could see that her hands were shaking.

" You're going—and Nino, he goes with you? Oh, what am I going to do? Every day will be torture, the uncertainty, the anxiety. If only he could be ill—not gravely ill, but sufficiently to make it necessary for him to stay here."

Oliver said, rather heavily, " And no one would resent such a thing happening more than Gradisco, believe me. He'd loathe hearing you express such a wish."

Her eyes flashed, he saw her chin tilt suddenly. " Don't you wish your—other—sons to be out of the war ! "

" No," he said, " I don't. I hate the thought of danger for them, but I'd hate it still more if I thought that they wanted to slide out of it. Clifford is in the Middle East, and Clive is ready to come back to England to be a pilot. That's not the safest job in the world."

Yolanda was calm again, the wine was brought and she motioned to Oliver to pour it out into the tall glasses. Then she said in a slow, rather drawling tone, " What curious names—Clifford and Clive ! "

" I don't think they're particularly curious ! " he retorted. Then, realizing that he had spoken sharply, he said, " Don't worry unduly, my dear. We all know that fighting's a nasty business, but I doubt if it's much more dangerous than walking about in the streets of Rome, with the traffic as it is at the moment. Don't dread the worst, hope and believe that the best will happen. The Hun may cave in—though it's not likely—we may break through suddenly —though frankly I don't think that's very likely either. But—it may not be as difficult as we feared. Come, Yolanda, where is that superb courage of yours ? "

She stared at him, miserable and apprehensive again. " It's gone, Oliver. It was like a bank account. I drew out too much and never replenished it. I'm bankrupt of my courage."

" I can't believe it. I don't believe it ! "

She asked abruptly, " Do you like Nino ? "

Oliver started. The question had come so unexpectedly, and with it had come, too, the realization of how much he did like Nino ; more—he knew that for days now he had been conscious of a definite sense of affection for him, that he had looked forward to his coming, and listened for the sound of his voice. Praise of him from Patterson, from ' Races ', from the rest of his officers, had been sweet in his ears.

He said, " I like him—very, very much."

" He adores you," she said softly. " You are his ideal."

" Not a very high ideal, I'm afraid, dear."

" I'm satisfied that you should be—our son's ideal. No, don't look so nervously round, no one can hear. I want you to promise me something. If—and God forbid that it should—anything terrible should happen to you or to Nino, would you—if you had time—tell him? I should like him to know. To know from your lips. I think it would make him very happy. He never knew his—he never knew my husband very well; he was a silent man, always absorbed in some important matter or other. He was proud of Nino, he was generous to him in everything, but he never tried to get to know or understand him. He must have seemed so *old* to Nino, as indeed he did to me. You're still young, Oliver; you've fired Nino's imagination——"

" I don't know why," Oliver said, a little confused. " I'm a very ordinary kind of fellow." But as he spoke he knew that his face had flushed with pleasure; knew, too, that Yolanda had noticed the added colour in his usually pale cheeks.

She smiled and said softly, " Ah, that pleases you then, my Oliver."

" I suppose that it does. Nino's a fine chap, he's made himself quite remarkably popular with everyone."

Still speaking very softly, she asked, " Will you promise to tell him, should—it be necessary ? "

Oliver's sense of confusion and pleasure had died. Her words, ' My Oliver ' disturbed him a little; was she trying to win him over by assuming this possessive expression?

He answered coldly and rather stiffly, " I shall—if circumstances made it possible. But this is all very foolish—nothing is going to happen. I refuse to continue talking in this stupid fashion; it's not good for either of us. My dear, I must go—I'm up to my eyes in work——"

" How strange you Englishmen are," Yolanda said. " That phrase—my dear, *can* be so unutterably sweet, and it can sound so dreadfully matter-of-fact and—what shall I say—middle class ! I have heard you say it when it was music—now you said it as some shopkeeper might say to the wife he had married thirty years ago. ' My dear, I must get back to business ! ' She mimicked his tone. " Shall I see you again ? "

" I don't think that I dare promise." He refused to show the slightest annoyance at her words. " I've so much to get through before we go."

" Very well. Please give my love to Nino when you see him. Will you let him come to see me before he moves ? "

How she changed ! A moment ago she had been imitating him, teasing him, now she was speaking simply and with such pathetic appeal that he longed to take her in his arms and whisper kind, consoling words to her.

" Nino ? Certainly he will come, as often and for as long as is humanly possible." He smiled, taking her hand in his and holding it firmly. " What do you imagine that I am ? Some kind of dreadful ogre ? "

She smiled back at him. " You have just told me that you must go, that you are horribly busy. How can I take up your time in telling you—what I imagine you to be ? Some other time. Good-bye, my Oliver."

" Good-bye, my dear, and try not to worry too much."

" That ' my dear ' was the one which holds music," she said.

II

Two days before they moved out of Rome, Nino came to Oliver's office.

He was smiling, and looked exceptionally handsome. Oliver leaned back in his chair, and heard himself speaking exactly as he might have done to Clifford or Clive.

" Now what is it ? You're looking remarkably set up with yourself.! "

" Sir, I have been lunching with my mother. She asked me to give you this letter. To-day is her birthday—she wants you to come to dine with her this evening, if you will."

" Her birthday, eh ? " He turned the heavily sealed envelope over in his fingers, then taking his paper-knife he slit the paper, and pulling out the sheet of thick notepaper read:

For my birthday present, will you come and have dinner with Nino and with me this evening ? Please try to come, I shall be grateful. It would be a pleasant memory to have seen you together again before you go. My love to you, Yolanda.

He refolded the sheet and slipped it into his inside pocket. Then looking up he met Gradisco's eyes watching him.

He said, " That's very kind of your mother. I shall be delighted. What a good thing I've cleared off my work, eh ! What time do we dine ? Half past eight. Good. Then by the time I've made myself respectable, do you think that you could drive me in and take me to some shop where I can find her a birthday present ? I can't go—empty-handed, you know."

" You are too kind, sir. My mother wouldn't wish you to disturb yourself."

" Nonsense. All women like presents, don't they—nice presents, and this one must be particularly nice. I rely upon you, Gradisco, to find something."

Gravely and with his ceremonious little bow, the young man said, " In this, as in everything, my Colonel, I hope that you can rely on me."

Oliver went to his room, conscious that he was excited, foolishly and unreasonably so. It wasn't really wise to go, particularly with Nino as one of the party. Yolanda might indulge in some of her dangerous sentiment, she'd be looking her best—and that best, Oliver reflected, was very, very attractive ! He ought to have refused, pleaded work. He frowned at his reflection in the mirror.

' Damn it, I don't want to refuse ! I want to see her, to take her an extravagant present, masses of extravagant flowers ! It's my last night but one in Rome, to-morrow I shall be dining in the mess. After that—who knows ! To-night—I'm going to " take the cash and let the credit go ! " And it will please the boy too.'

He wondered when he had first begun to think of Nino as ' the boy '.

As they drove into Rome Nino asked gravely what kind of a present he had in mind, and Oliver answered that he must know what kinds of things his mother liked, and that his only stipulation was that it must be something—' as nearly as possible worthy of her '.

Nino said, " Sir, a suggestion would help."

Oliver replied, " I'll make several. A bicycle—she wouldn't care for a bicycle ! Books—she probably has a library stocked with them. Rings—she appears to wear different ones each time I see her. Watches, bracelets, even a string of pearls—and scarcely the type of present for an elderly gentleman to give a charming woman, do you think ? "

Nino answered, his eyes dancing, " Roman society is very narrow ! I have it ! I remember where I saw it. Oh, what a good thought ! "

He was excited ; for the first time Oliver listened to him talking very rapidly and eagerly. He had seen a set of shagreen for a writing-desk. Only that morning when he had been to buy his own present for her. A shagreen photograph frame, rather a large one to hold a moderately large photograph. Could Oliver guess what the photograph was ? No ? Yet it was simple—of what was he so proud. Of being a liaison officer with the Army of Liberation !

" Now, my Colonel, you can guess, surely ! "

" I'm dull, Nino," Oliver said, scarcely noticing that he had called Gradisco by his Christian name. " Winston Churchill, perhaps—with a very large cigar in his mouth ? "

" Wrong, despite my admiration for this Churchill. Do you remember the photograph we had taken together ? Yes, the one which ' Tip ' Franks made with his beautiful new Leica. He kindly gave me the negative. I had it enlarged by the best photographer in Rome. It is splendid ! Now, my present and your magnificent one will stand on her desk together all the time we are away."

Oliver watched and listened to him in the shop. His eagerness had gone, and he was suddenly an aristocratic and dignified young Italian officer. A blotting-pad, an inkstand, everything that could be of use on a writing-desk, and all exquisitely made and beautifully shaped. From time to time, as a new article was brought forward, Gradisco glanced questioningly at Oliver, each time Oliver smiled and nodded, saying, " Yes, that too."

When they arrived, with armfuls of flowers, Oliver had insisted upon including magnolias, ' though they cannot stay in the room very long, their scent is too heavy '. They were told that the Duchessa was dressing. Nino rushed away to arrange her desk with their gifts. Oliver followed him slowly, wandering along the corridor, his thoughts absorbing and disturbing. This photograph—himself and Nino taken together. He remembered how Franks had boasted of its excellence, he had shown it round to everyone, but the print had been very small, and Oliver merely remembered two figures. Now—enlarged, would this likeness of which Yolanda had assured him be apparent? Probably not, these so-called likenesses were often almost non-existent.

He entered the little *salon*, and Nino cried, " Look ! Is it not very beautiful ? Oh, *mamina* will be delighted ! Look, sir ! "

Oliver let his eyes wander over the writing-table; the shagreen was very charming, its soft delicate green looked cool and pleasant; then he saw the big frame, which held the photograph of two men in uniform. For a second he started, the likeness was unmistakable. He might have been Nino Gradisco in thirty years' time; Nino might have been Oliver Hallam taken twenty-seven years ago. Both had the same tall, slim figure, the same easy fashion of standing, both their eyes were wide set and direct in their gaze, both mouths held the same sensitive quality and yet were not devoid of strength.

He licked his dry lips and said, " It's a very good picture; Franks certainly did very well."

He walked away, and stood on the balcony looking out over the gardens, his mind filled with doubts which were almost fears. Had the boy noticed the likeness, did it convey anything to him? The other officers—what had they seen? Probably, like himself, they had only been shown the small print. He called to Nino, who joined him.

" I want you to do me a favour," he said. " If you have the negative of that print, lend it to me. I should like some copies to send to England. Oh, you have it with you ? " as Nino pulled out his wallet. " Thank you, I'll take great care of it."

Yolanda entered and stood in the doorway for a moment like an actress ' holding her entrance ' on the stage. She was magnificently dressed in her usual black and white, but to-night the white predominated, and she wore a string of pearls, very long, which gleamed softly in the evening light.

She said, " I'm late. How nice to see you both." Then, " I can smell magnolias? What a lovely scent. Who brought them, Nino ? "

" My Colonel, *mamina*, he insisted on bringing them. But he says they must be banished to the balcony, they are too strong in a room. He brought a great many flowers, look—roses, all kinds of roses."

She touched the petals of a magnolia blossom lightly with the tips of her fingers. " How charming. Thank you," adding after a very brief, almost imperceptible, pause, " Colonel Hallam."

Nino took her hand and led her to the writing-table, saying, " Here are the birthday presents which Colonel Hallam and I have brought for you. We hope that you like them, and many happy returns of your birthday."

Oliver said, " May I offer my good wishes too, Duchessa ? "

She threw him her brilliant smile, then turned back to the writing-table. Oliver watched her closely, almost painfully intent.

She leaned forward, the smile still on her lips, then caught sight of the photograph. The smile died, her whole body was rigid, then she said sharply, " Who brought that ? " Turning again to Oliver, her voice still cold, she asked, " Did you ? "

Oliver answered. Speaking very evenly, his voice was almost suave. " No, Gradisco had that done especially for you. It was a complete surprise to me. It is excellent, don't you think ? I looked at it just now, and—don't tell me that I am foolish, will you ?—fancied that there is a faint likeness between your son and myself. I wonder if you can see it ? It may only be my imagination, for the other officers all saw the picture, eh, Gradisco ? None of them apparently saw any resemblance." He was talking to gain time, not for himself but for her, to give her an opportunity to relax, to lose that sharp, cold tone from her voice. He continued, as he moved nearer to Yolanda and pointed to the photograph, " Is it something in the way we both stand, or is it some likeness in the chin ? I can't make out."

She was mistress of herself again, smiling, and taking up the picture to examine it more closely.

" There is a likeness—no, not a likeness, of course, but a kind of *look* that is the same. It must be the result of my son's admiration for you, Colonel Hallam. Didn't you admit to that admiration the other day, Nino ? "

He replied firmly, and without embarrassment, " Indeed I did. Perhaps I have tried so hard to be like Colonel Hallam—in my work, in my manner towards people, that it has actually affected my physical appearance. I *can* see a faint resemblance, I believe."

" I am going to tell people that the picture is me taken with my Italian nephew. I have the negative," Oliver said, and watched the last hint of anxiety leave Yolanda's face. She began to thank him for his gift, to reprove him for his extravagance. When Nino moved away to mix the cocktails she whispered to him, " My dear, thank you. You were wonderful. That negative—you really have it ? "

In reply he tapped his breast pocket, and she smiled more easily.

Oliver thought that he had never seen her so gay as she was on this lovely evening ; she laughed at their stories of life in the camp, she told stories of herself, of certain members of what she called ' gone with the wind Fascist's ' Roman society, even growing slightly scandalous when she recounted the doings of the ' Ciano smart set '. Oliver felt happy and at ease, the years seemed to have slipped away, the gulf which had existed between himself and Yolanda, he thought, was bridged for this their last evening together. He could have imagined more than once that they were a small united family—a family in which the elderly father and the handsome son were leaving to go and fight, while their charming wife and mother determined not to allow their going to cloud the last evening together.

He leaned forward and said, " I think that you were wrong about the question of—bankruptcy."

Nino said, " Bankruptcy—you don't allow my mother to bore you with talking political business sir, surely ? Though I admit that she knows far more about political matters than I do. Once the war is over, I shall settle down to farm my land—on the *mezzadria* system—because I believe in it, for Italians at least. I don't believe that Italians will ever make completely successful industrialists. They want and need the changes which the rounds of the seasons bring to agricultural work. To work in a factory, to perform the same operations every day—for them is soul-destroying. Imagine an Italian being content to punch five holes in a piece of metal, each and every day. He would go mad, or go on strike—*sciópero* —just for some relief. They are individualists, as well as realists." His eyes were very bright, he looked from Oliver to his mother, intent on gaining their interest. " But I believe that there is a great and real Risorgimento coming once this war is over. The Allies have promised—they have admitted that Italy has done well to fling out Fascismo, which *she* did without waiting for the Allies to do it for her. It's a fine phrase, a phrase which fills one with hope—' Italy shall have a respected place in the New Europe as soon as the conflict is over '."

Yolanda said, " Fine phrases, Nino *mio*—do they always develop into fine actions ? "

He returned with increased eagerness, " *Mamina*, forgive me, but you must not speak in that way. No, these people are just people, they will keep their promises. I know it, thousands of Italians know it. That is why we want to be part, even if a humble part, of this great feat of high endeavour. They are not come here to extract payments, to destroy. General Eisenhower has said, and said publicly, ' The greatest obstacle which divided the Italian people from the United Nations has been removed by the Italians themselves'. You see, already we have won *recognition*. He added, ' We are coming as liberators '. No; so long as we continue to do our duty, to the best of our ability, our future is assured. The Allies will not forget! "

His eyes were shining, his cheeks a little flushed, his mouth curved into a smile. Oliver thought, ' My son. He's a fine fellow, filled with generosity and hope for the future. His tenants won't have much to fear from him, he'll do his duty by them.'

Scarcely knowing what he said, he spoke to Nino. " But for the sake of argument—for politics are strange things, unpleasant things, often unsavoury things—supposing that the Allies didn't remember those promises, supposing they—forgot. What then ? "

" Then," Nino answered, his voice low and touched by emotion, " then Italy would be ruined, but not ruined to such an extent as the people who betrayed her. She would have lost her material possessions—her colonies, her ships, her ability to trade; they would have lost something infinitely more precious. They would have to stand before the whole world as the army of *Giuda*—what do you say, *mama*, *Giuda* ?—ah, Judas. They would have sold their honour and sacrificed their friends. But," with sudden passion, " it is not possible! It could not happen! "

Yolanda shrugged her shoulders. " I have very little belief in these politicians, of any nation. I have seen too many of them,

listened to their fine words and seen their abominable actions.
Yesterday Stalin and his Russians were dogs, to-day they are
heroes; here in Italy Mussolini was a demi-god. Where is he
now? Chamberlain after Munich had saved his country, he was
hailed as Our Lord was greeted by the people of Jerusalem on
the first Palm Sunday. 'Hosanna!' 'Long live Chamberlain!' and
'Viva il Primo Ministero!' Then?" She shrugged her shoulders.
"Now your Churchill—he can do what he wishes, he can be wise,
dogmatic, determined, even something of a *buffone*, he is the
World's Pet. Where will he be to-morrow? Who knows. 'La
donna è mobile'—not only 'La donna' but the whole of
humanity!" She dipped her fingers into the cut-glass bowl at her
side, wiped them delicately on her fringed napkin, and said in a
tone which was at once critical and fastidious, "I dislike humanity.
I find my dogs much more faithful, more essentially decent in
every way. Shall we go into the *salon*?"

The two men followed her, Oliver absorbed in his thoughts.
Was Nino right in his determined faith, or was Yolanda wiser, if
more cynical? This was his last evening with her, he might never
see her again, for he had no false illusions about the dangers which
would attend the prosecution of the coming winter campaign. The
air felt tense, he fancied that Nino was hurt by what his mother had
said, even a little disturbed. His good-looking face, which had been
so filled with eagerness and hope, was clouded, he stood drumming
gently with his fingers on the piano-top, his eyes downcast.

Yolanda walked to the piano and opened it, saying, "I will
play to you."

How like her! Not asking if they wished her to play; simply
that statement, 'I will play to you'. Oliver was not particularly
knowledgeable about music, but it had always possessed the power
to lift him out of his fits of depression; now he wondered if
Yolanda had learned that it had the same effect on Nino. She
began to play without any preliminary of running her fingers
over the keys; she played softly, smoothly, and all the while
Oliver watched his son's face, and saw the cloud of melancholy
lift from it. Nino raised his head, and stood watching his mother
as she played. When she stopped, Oliver saw the quick smile
which passed between them.

"You like that, *mio filio*?" she asked.

Still smiling, he answered, "Have you ever known the time
when Chopin did not help me, *mamina*?"

"Ah, you're better! Now, listen!"

She played music which Oliver felt was essentially beautiful,
but which was decorated simply and without in any way detract-
ing from the original 'lines' of the melody. Mozart—Handel—
who had written it? She glanced up, her fingers still moving. "It
is English, Oliver."

He was too absorbed to see the little start which Gradisco
gave, or to notice the little puzzled frown between his fine eyebrows. He said, "Yes? What?"

"I shall try to sing it to you."

"I attempt from love's sickness to fly in vain,
        Since I am myself my own fever and pain . . ."

Her voice was not very strong, its quality was faintly husky, but it held a great deal of colour and her enunciation was clear and lovely.

The room was filled with the soft impelling sound. Oliver thought that he had never heard anything which moved him more deeply; the whole picture was arresting. The cool room, with its soft lights and exquisite furniture; the gleam of the wide polished piano-top, the beautiful woman in her dress of black and white, her pearls catching the lights and shimmering in indefinite colours. The young man in his uniform leaning against the piano, graceful and easy, listening with his lips a little parted. Outside the Gardens, where at long intervals the sound of a passing car reached them, or the cry of a bird saying good-night to the world.

The song ended. Yolanda rose and said, " It's nice, I think. I have an affection for the music of your Purcell. He is kindly and gentle, and yet reasonable and possessing a certain good sense. He over-decorates nothing; his music is like fine, craftsman-made furniture—it has line and form and the decorations are always subservient to those."

Oliver said, " Thank you—thank you sincerely." He glanced at his watch. " I must go, I had no idea that it was so late, and I must be at work early in the morning."

He saw her hand go up to her mouth, palm outwards, as if she tried to stifle a cry of protest; then she regained her control and turned to Nino.

" And you, too; must you go ? "

Oliver held up his hand. " Forgive me, I think that I can give Nino permission to stay here for the night, if that would please you? Only back in camp early, Gradisco ! "

The young man's face was alight, then he looked grave again.

" Sir, you have no car here, you remember that I drove you. I shall drive you back, naturally. It was more than kind of you to make that suggestion, I am very grateful."

Oliver, trying to adopt an attitude which should be at once light and yet sufficiently ' elderly ', replied, " Tut, tut ! Surely I can use my own car—if you will telephone for it. Say that I want it immediately, please."

" I shall do so, sir."

He rushed away, and his mother called after him. " Nino, bring a bottle of champagne, one of the few that we contrived to hide. We must have a stirrup cup ! Quickly, *filio mio* ! "

As the door closed she turned to Oliver. " You liked my song ? "

" Beautiful, my dear, beautiful."

" I sang it because I cannot say these things to you, Oliver."

Smiling faintly tolerant, he answered, " But you are not attempting to fly from—love's sickness ! "

" How do you know ? I scarcely know myself. I am most certainly my own fever and pain. I'm not really in love with you, but I could be so deeply in love—with love. I ought to have let you marry me, I ought to have kept you out here with me. To-night has unsettled me, it was so charming, so pleasantly—what shall I say?—intimate and domestic. It must be something very strong which exists between us, for it is difficult to make these huge rooms —intimate, or to bring to them a faint air of domesticity. How my friends would laugh if you told them that Yolanda Gradisco was—domestic! But then, they don't know me!"

Oliver said, "Do you know yourself, I wonder? How many of us know ourselves? Not many I fancy."

"Say good-bye to me now, my Oliver. I shan't see you to-morrow?"

"Impossible, I shall be hard at work all day, and probably half the night. Yolanda, I don't like saying—good-bye."

"But they have to be said, these farewells, darling."

He took her in his arms and kissed her gently, with deep affection but without passion; he heard her sigh contentedly as she lay in his embrace.

She whispered, "Oliver—that photograph. Have you any doubts now?"

He whispered back, his lips on her hair, "None, my dear, none at all."

"You'll take care of Nino—and of yourself?"

"As much as is possible—of him because I shall wish to; of myself—because you wish it."

"And my wishes still—weigh with you?"

Again he kissed her. "You mustn't ask me those questions, you know."

"But you have answered, just the same."

He laughed. "Only by implication. Don't worry, we shall both be back before very long."

"And then——?"

Taking her face between his hands he stared at her intently, then said, "God help me, I don't know! Good-bye, Yolanda, and be happy."

Reluctantly he let her go; she walked away and stood powdering her face in an old mirror with a great antique silver frame. Oliver's pulses were racing, he realized her beauty, the complete loveliness of her. He wanted her as he had never wanted any woman in his life; at that moment he would willingly have forgotten everything—duty, honour, self-respect—if he might have remained with her.

She did not turn to speak to him again until Nino came back with Tomaso in his wake, bearing a gold-necked bottle; then Yolanda joined them, smiling and watching Nino pour out the golden wine.

"Almost the last, eh?" she said.

"Enough left for we three to drink when we come back, *mamina*."

She raised her glass, and said, "Then—don't keep me waiting too long. I love Clicquot and I refuse to drink it alone or offer it to people for whom I have no affection. *Bon voyage*—good luck— and *andate con Dio*—both of you!"

A few moments later Oliver was driving out of the big court-yard; his last sight of Yolanda was as she stood, Nino's arm round her waist, waving to her son's father.

CHAPTER VI

I

'RACES' mopped his forehead and almost panted, " Gosh, did you ever know such heat ! How do you contrive to live in this country in summer, Duke ? "

Nino, so tanned that his face was almost the same colour as his belt and boots, smiled, his teeth looked fantastically white. " We know of places which are pleasantly cool. These hill towns are always baking in summer and freezing in winter."

They were moving slowly towards Perugia, the town had been captured and the Germans driven out three days previously; their advance had not been sensationally difficult. Oliver had been warned that ' your really tough time will be coming, Hallam. Don't get the idea—or let your people get it either—that it's all going to be easy going. The big tussle will come on the other side of Florence.'

Tip Franks grumbled, " What the devil did they build towns on the top of hills for ! I never knew such people, Duke. Can't you institute a new order of things, all towns to be built on the plains ? What's the good of being a blasted duke if you can't give a few orders ! "

Nino's face was grave when he answered, " There will be a great deal of rebuilding to be done. I can't bear to think of those lovely towns and villages being pounded to pieces."

Then he raised his hand and pointed to the distant town of Perugia, standing high up above the plain, beautiful and majestic.

" There is Perugia," he said, " not really so far away as it looks. This is the town of which it was said that ' more blood ran in the gutters of the town than ran in the veins of its citizens '. They were a fierce people those Perugians."

" More to the point at the moment," Tip said, " if water ran into the baths ! Whew, I feel that if I lay in a tubful of water my skin would just absorb the water—soak it into my system. I've never felt so hot, so dirty, or so dusty in my life, not even in the desert, and that's saying something ! "

Gradisco and Patterson drove on together; up the long steep hill the little car puffed and strained, but when they reached the top even the somewhat phlegmatic Scotsman stared open-mouthed at the vista which lay before them.

" Ma worrd ! " he breathed. " That is something ye might justly call a beautiful view."

The troops as they moved up in their trucks stared and pointed, and when Oliver descended from his car with Captain Moran he halted and called Nino to him.

" Where is Assisi, Gradisco ? "

Nino pointed in the direction. " There, my Colonel. If they leave us here for a few days I should like to show you the town of the ' Little Poor Man '; you would be interested—yes, and deeply touched, I think."

That evening they dined in the hotel, for no mess had been arranged for them; the town was full, and only accommodation had been found for the men in Italian barracks. Dinner over, Oliver wandered out on to the little parade which overlooked the plain, and with his arms folded on the balustrade let his eyes wander. The night was very still and hot, the great canopy of sky looked as if it would be soft to the touch. Not a sound could be heard, except that of men's footsteps, for the battle had moved on, and the word had been given that Assisi was not to be harmed in any way. After the rumble of the long convoy the quiet was grateful. Oliver thought that the noise wearied him more than the actual journey—the noise and the dust together sapped his energy. To-night he felt terribly tired. If only they were to be allowed to stay here for a few days. He thought how pleasant to drive into the country, to visit Assisi with Nino and listen to his explanations and stories of the place. He had called the town that of ' The Little Poor Man '—Saint Francis, Oliver supposed. The idea came to him that, of course, Nino was a Catholic. All these Italians were. Italy didn't run much to what the sergeants called ' fancy religions '—you were ' C. of E.' or ' R.C.'.

" Very kuris," one of his S.M.s had said; " reely quite a lot o' the chaps don't like being called ' R.C.' One o' them sed ter me the other day, wot was the idea. Quite respekful, but just wanted ter know what the idea was. I replied, ' Becos thet's wot ye're—R.C. meaning Roman Kartholic.' He said, ' 'Scuse me, S'Major, we're not, we're just C—C fer Kartholic.' I tried ter explain ter 'im, like 'ow the Pope lived in Rome, ceterer, ceterer, but 'e didn't seem ter see it. Kuris sir, don't you think ? "

Nino as a Catholic, what would be his reaction to the knowledge that Oliver was his father ? Would he be resentful, angry, hurt, or distressed ? Staring into the still night, Oliver frowned, and tried to dismiss the thought. He had only promised to tell Nino under—certain circumstances, and if those circumstances did not arise, then neither did the question of Nino's reaction.

It was Nino's voice which roused him from his thoughts. Nino, who was standing at his elbow, having come up without noise, and who said that he had discovered that he had relations in residence in Perugia.

" They are really second cousins of my mother's, sir. Guilia— the Contessa—was the sister of my mother's aunt, Contessa Elcano. They—the Riccis—have a villa here, a villa but really inside the town. If you cared to they will be honoured to offer you dinner to-morrow or, in fact, hospitality for so long as you remain here. I have been speaking to my cousin this evening."

Oliver laughed. " Good God, Nino, have you relations in every town in Italy ? "

The young man smiled. " I have none, sir, in either Venice or Milano."

" But all the rest, eh ? "

" Not really, sir, I was joking. Would it amuse you to dine, sir ? "

Suddenly Oliver had a picture of the photograph which Nino had given to his mother. Panic seized him. How could he go and visit these people, stand side by side with Nino, and run the risk of their noticing the likeness ?

He said, " It's more than kind of them, I appreciate that very sincerely, but I think that I must refuse. You see, I'm not here on a pleasure trip, not having a swan round, and heaven only knows what may crop up. I may be bidden to some dreadfully formal meeting. I think that I must decline, but it was most kind of your cousin. Please tell her so, Nino." He stopped and said, in reality trying to cover his dismay that he was using the young man's Christian name so often and so easily, " Funny the way I've slipped into calling you ' Nino '. It must be with hearing the other officers."

Quietly Nino returned, " They all call me ' Duke ' or ' Dukie ', sir."

" So they do. It must be that I've heard your mother say it then."

" I expect so, sir."

Oliver thought, ' Damn it, his voice is too even, too controlled. I believe that he's got some kind of—idea. Good Lord, that won't do ! I must go back to calling him by his surname ! ' He said, " Well, Gradisco, I shall turn in, I'm tired. It was heavy going in that heat to-day. I'm not so young as I once was. Good night."

II

On August the 22nd Florence was liberated, and they heard the next day that both Paris and Marseilles were in Allied hands. Everywhere men talked of the coming winter—of the passes which led to Bologna, the Futa and the Pistoia—of the tenacious way in which the Germans hung on to Bologna, and then back again to—the winter. Everywhere Oliver heard stories of courage in the face of danger and disaster; was told of women, both Italian and British, who had risked their lives to give assistance to escaped prisoners hiding in lonely farms, men who waited eagerly for the limited supplies of food which could be brought—at such fearful risks—to them. He wrote home, *The stories I hear are incredible, but every one on investigation bears the stamp of truth. The sheer bravery of these women—of whatever nation—fills you with pride and hope for the future.*

His life was very full, the work was heavy and there were many preparations to be made, plans to be discussed. He had little time to sit and think, and when he went to bed his mind was weary, and he sank almost immediately into a deep and heavy sleep. When he wrote home to Kitty he felt that he was a man writing from another world; true she could understand something of the conditions under which he lived, she even knew some of the men he met; but although he debated it long and earnestly, he never felt that it was possible to write of this strange meeting with the woman he had loved years ago. Of the fact that her son was also his—he was conscious that these things must one day be told, but that it was impossible for him to write them.

Kitty's letters to him came frequently and were filled with news of the children, Barbara's small son, and of the factory where she was still working. They were charming letters, gay, brave, and completely uncomplaining despite the fact that England was rationed and that feeding a family had become increasingly difficult. Yolanda did not write to him, though Nino frequently gave him messages which she had sent. The absence of letters from her was to Oliver a relief rather than a deprivation. He knew that had he remained longer in Rome he would have probably flung himself into an intrigue with Yolanda; his attraction for her and hers for him had been rapidly increasing, and he realized his own weaknesses. He had no wish to be unfaithful to Kitty, his love for her was as real and as true as it had always been; he had taken Yolanda in his arms, but he remembered with satisfaction that his kisses had never been either excited or passionate. He had always retained sufficient self-control to remember in time that he was—Kitty's husband.

Not that he flattered himself that he had behaved particularly well, but he had at least not behaved too badly, not given way to impulse or allowed his senses to master him.

The bright September sunshine began to lose some of its warmth; true it shone in the streets of Florence, touching the bright flowers which were for sale at the street corners, lighting up the lovely old buildings, and cruelly showing with devastating clarity how shabby were the clothes of many of the people; how their faces still bore the marks of the strain through which they had passed. Unless they were definitely questioned, Oliver found, neither British nor Italians made much reference to their hardships and experiences; still less did they boast of the dangers through which they had passed in their efforts to help their less fortunate friends.

He said as much to Patterson one evening, when they sat in the Grand Hotel together. " They don't tell you much, do they ? "

Patterson replied, " The British don't talk, the Italians talk a whole lot—neither o' them really gie away much—information."

" Perhaps they learnt the trick too well of keeping still tongues."

" That," agreed Patterson impressively, " Ah wad not doot in the least. A haird school wi' the cheerful Hun as a schoolmaster, an' ever ready wi' the tawse ! "

Oliver tried to see as little as possible of his liaison officer. He had realized how deeply attached to the fellow he was growing, and in his heart feared not only that he might betray himself by some chance word or look, but that Nino actually had some suspicion which might grow to be a conviction if they saw each other too often. He knew that Nino was popular, that his work was excellent and intelligent, and that he never attempted to spare himself in the least. Again and again Oliver found himself thinking and speculating about this son of his; how little he actually knew about him, of his tastes and opinions. True he had talked, in his mother's house, of his love for his country, of his hopes for the future, but Oliver longed to know the little apparently unimportant things in his life. Those small things which loom so large in the life of a family. He remembered that Clifford never touched cheese; that Clive always begged to be allowed to leave the table if rabbit in any form appeared, and that at the sight of boiled mutton Barbara groaned audibly and said, " Mummy, is there some cold meat that I could have ? " Clifford and Barbara loved to plunge into cold baths. Clive protested that if he attempted to do so he could never get really dry for the remainder of the day—a thousand things, silly, small likes and dislikes, came rushing back to Oliver, and with them a certain unreasonable resentment that he knew nothing of Nino's likes and dislikes.

The morning was cold and chilly when he heard that they were ' moving up '; it seemed that summer had died, and that autumn was bent upon making itself as assertive as possible. There were little whirls of dust and paper at every street corner, and small but bitter gusts of wind springing up unexpectedly. The flowers seemed to shrink a little, as if they felt unhappy at the loss of the sunshine. People's faces appeared to have an air of apprehension —coal would be unobtainable, wood difficult to buy and terribly expensive, food might be short, and prices prohibitive—clothes incredibly dear. Pockets were poorly lined, purses were lean. Oliver had never felt a greater admiration for women than he did upon that morning as he walked rapidly through the streets of Florence; their clothes were shabby, their shoes worn and old, their faces thin and often haggard, but they all bore themselves with an air of gay gallantry not untouched with defiance. It was as if they said, challenging the whole world which had been so nearly reduced to ruins around them, ' We have seen so much, been through so much—we can face anything ! '

One British woman he knew stopped to speak to him. She said, " I hear that you're moving out."

" To-morrow."

Quickly, and with a smile, she said, " Don't tell me where you're going, it must be one of two ways, and both will be unpleasant. Florence won't be particularly amusing either ! But," her smile widened, " we shall all come through. Good luck."

III

Late October, and they had advanced literally foot by foot; the Germans had look-out posts everywhere, and often long detours had to be made to avoid them. Through his glasses Oliver could see the snouts of their guns high up commanding the lower roads.

He said testily to Bladon, " Those damned look-outs ! They're the bane of our existence."

Bladon, grinning, replied, " I imagine not only the bane—but often the end of the existence of some of us."

Oliver, his eyes glued to his glasses, grunted, " Look at those bastards up there, sitting pretty ! They can sweep this road whenever they wish. Confound them ! "

Gradisco, standing near them, said, " Sir, excuse me, but have you ever seen that gun—in fact any of them at that particular post—fire ? "

Oliver snapped, " What the devil do you mean, Gradisco ? "

" In my opinion, sir, for what it is worth, they are dummies. If this is so it might argue several things—among others that the Germans have not quite so many guns as they could do with. You see what I mean ? "

" No, no." Oliver shook his head. " They'd never be such fools as to underrate our intelligence to that extent, Gradisco."

Nino made no reply, but he reflected that the average German was a moderately good psychologist, and knew that the average soldier believed that he would find what he expected to find in obvious places.

Later he took a risk. They were stationary, he had no particular work to do at the moment, he was an expert mountaineer; every winter he had spent a month or two in the mountains. He was completely surefooted, and though he liked actual danger no better than the next man, he told himself that ' risks were to be taken because they might not be risks of very serious quality after all '.

As the early winter night came on, he took with him his little Italian batman, one Pietro Marinoni, a small, intelligent creature to whom fear was completely unknown. He came from Gradisco's own estate near Livorno, and had begged with tears in his beautiful eyes to be allowed to accompany his master. Oliver had stared at the woebegone little man and had said to Nino, " But does he always cry so easily ? "

Nino, turning to the man, spoke in Italian, and gave the reply to Oliver.

" He says, sir, that he is not crying easily, that these tears are dripping from his heart. He says that really he is a very good comedian."

Together they crept upwards, towards the look-out post. Nino's ears were almost unnaturally sharp, and they squirmed and twisted upwards like two snakes, invisible in the darkness. Neither spoke, almost painfully they listened, there was silence round them, enveloping them like a cloak.

Nino reached the look-out post, and slowly raised himself to look over the parapet—the little platform was empty. With a quick movement of his hand he beckoned Pietro to follow him, and together they lay on the hard, frozen ground. Nino pointed to the ' guns '.

Three long, thin tree-trunks had been daubed with grey paint;

embedded in the earth, surrounded by sandbags, they showed not more than a foot of wood over the parapet. Gently Nino dug Pietro in the ribs.

" The guns," he whispered, " the German guns defending the pass ! "

Pietro whispered back, " No occasion to put them out of action—they have never been in it, Capitano ! "

They turned and wriggled and twisted back the way they had come. Once their ears caught the sound of heavy voices, and they lay still and scarcely daring to breathe flat on the hard ground. Nino laying his ear to the frozen earth heard footsteps, they halted, then moved away. Back in the British lines, Nino gave Pietro a slightly crumpled packet of cigarettes, bade him " Good night," and went quietly to his tent which he shared with Tip Franks.

Franks was crouching over a carefully shaded lamp. He looked up and exclaimed, " I say, Dukie, where the hell have you been ? The old man's in a devil of a sweat. You're to go to him immediately. By God, you're going to get a ruddy strip torn off you, my lad ! He's livid—abso-bloody-lutely livid ! "

Nino nodded, and turning made his way to the caravan where Oliver had his quarters. Mounting the steps, he knocked gently and heard a voice tell him, in no particularly gentle tone, to " Come in."

He entered, and Oliver looked up from the letter he was writing.

He stared, laid down his pen, and said coldly, " And may I ask where the hell you've been ? "

" Sir, if I did wrong I apologize sincerely." His manner could not have been more correct, but his eyes were alight and shining. " I went because I was consumed with curiosity—to the look-out post, sir."

Oliver sprang to his feet. " The devil you did ! "

" There are no guns there, sir. Camouflaged tree-trunks, nothing more."

" You saw this ? Were you alone ? "

" I took the liberty, sir, of taking my batman with me. We have been mountaineering together before. He is very good, silent, sure-footed."

" I don't doubt for a moment," Oliver said heavily, " the pair of you are blasted marvels, or that Everest would be child's play to both of you. But I happen to be in command here, and I will not have my officers creeping off into the night on these exploits ! It's unthinkable ! "

For the first time Nino Gradisco's eyes lost their brightness, he flushed under his tan, and again begged to be forgiven for his breach of discipline.

Then, almost ingenuously, he said, " I thought that the information would give you pleasure, sir."

" Pleasure ! I'm not out here for pleasure, Nino ! " His anxiety had robbed him of his caution. " Heavens, my lad, you might never have come back alive ! You're not to do these things. I will not have it. Now, understand that." He thought, ' I might be talking to Clifford ! '

" Yes, sir. I promise, and again I ask your forgiveness."

Oliver's anger had vanished, he laid his hand on Nino's shoulder. " That's all right, we'll say no more about it. Your batman got back safely ? Good. Sit down and tell me about it. Get yourself a drink out of that locker there. Now, let's hear all about it."

IV

They were all irked by the slow progress which was being made, their thoughts turned constantly towards Bologna, where the Germans still remained entrenched. Their progress might be slow, but they were fighting constantly and frequently against an enemy which held the higher and more advantageous ground.

Near Mount Gazzaro, where the snow lay deep and movement was made with added difficulty, ' Chalky ' White, young and showing great promise as a leader, was killed, and the next day Trench was so badly wounded that he died in the evening. Oliver sat in his caravan, with his head in his hands, reproaching himself for the thought which would keep recurring, ' What if it had been Nino ? What should I have done ? '

Santa Lucia and Covigliago were names which were always to remain with him as places of horror; the Americans were fighting like tigers on their left, they themselves were doggedly pushing on. The cold was bitter, the nights terrible. Captain Wilcox went down with frostbite in both feet.

The M.O., a kindly if not particularly brilliant man called Soames, assured him that once back in hospital they would put him right. Wilcox replied that they'd damned well got to, and be damned quick about it.

Patterson said later to Soames, " Ah, ye weer maist encouragin' tae the puir feller, but Ah doot he'll lose baith feet."

Soames said sharply, " What the devil do you know about it ? "

Lojano was badly battered, the sight filled Oliver with complete physical sickness; it was not merely wrecked houses, the ruined churches, the complete absence of life, but what it all implied to him. Homes gone, the patient building-up which had taken the best years of men's lives reduced to rubble, and again and again he shuddered as he wondered what poor broken creature might have died under those ruins.

Christmas came and went, parcels came from home, delayed and badly damaged; when it was possible they read the weeks-old papers which came to them. They were beginning to call themselves ' The little boys that Santa Claus forgot '; fighting in Italy seemed less important at home than it had done a few months previously.

Then at last they were over the passes and emerging through desolation and devastation on the road to Bologna. The winter was over, their hearts lightened, surely they were on the last lap. The earth was growing green again, among the ruins little spring flowers pushed their way. One morning Nino, smiling with delight, showed Oliver a celandine which he had found, and which he was going to send home to Yolanda.

Oliver looked at the bright, sturdy little flower, with its leaves as brilliantly yellow as if they had been enamelled, and said thoughtfully, " They'll be out in the English lanes by now."

The days were lengthening, and in spite of the marks of war the loveliness of the Italian spring was asserting itself. The last days of March saw them fighting on the outskirts of Bologna; on the twentieth of April they entered the town itself and rushed forward towards the Po.

" That's where he'll make a stand," Races said.

Oliver commented, " His last, please God."

Patterson said, " Awe this time they've been holding Bologna, Ah doot they've been daein' some varry haird diggin' on the river banks. Yon Po 'ul not be varry amusing, Ah doot—nae, Ah don't doot ! I *know*."

Races said, " I never knew the time when you didn't know, Pat, and always with dead, absolute certainty. I'd hate to have such vision ! "

They moved out of Bologna and took the road to Ferrara. Oliver's heart kept saying, ' Spring is in the sir. We shall be home by next winter ! '

Ferrara was full of Germans, hiding in cellars, in attics; the British soldiers hunted them out, good-humouredly and with laughter.

" Look at mine, Jake, I've got a fat 'un ! "

" Blimy, mine's a skinny little b—— ! Get a move on, Jerry ! "

" He's getting a move on orlright. Movin' like a lot o' perishin' hares, they are."

" Flamin' 'Uns ! Kep' us waitin' arbart in that b—— snow ! Wait while next winter, Jerry, we'll snowball yer in Berlin."

" Don't be flamin' funny, Bill—theer ain't no Berlin."

They were docile enough, these Germans; indeed, as Oliver said to Nino when they stood watching near the drawbridge of the great castello, they seemed dazed.

" They didn't believe that it could happen, sir."

" There have been times, Nino, when very few of us believed in our hearts that this particular victory could happen; there have been some desperate moments when *anything* might have happened."

The younger man smiled. " Perhaps because I didn't really know much about it, sir—I never had any doubt as to the ultimate outcome of it——"

Somewhere a rifle fired, the sound of a shot echoed against the grey walls of the castello. Oliver started, shouting, " What the devil——" when he saw Nino throw back his shoulders, watched his head jerk back and saw him, swaying, fall to the ground.

He cried, " God ! They've shot him ! Nino ! " He was kneeling beside him, trying to discover where he had been hit. He shouted with all his might. " Where's Major Soames ! You—find Major

Soames. Run for your damned life ! " Then kneeling beside his son he whispered, " Nino, speak to me. Where did he hit you ? Tell me——"

" Ugh ! " Nino grunted rather than groaned. " My back—I think."

Soames came running through the archway; he knelt beside Gradisco, his hands moving swiftly. Raising his head, he called to a little group of staring, whispering soldiers, " Come and carry him into that place there—gently now, easy does it." Nino's eyes were closed, his face stared white in the evening light.

Oliver said, " Bad, is it, Soames ? "

" Can't really tell until I have a look, sir. Hope for the best.",

A small, dark-eyed Italian soldier, who had been standing a few yards away when the shot was fired, hesitated for a moment, his face contorted with fury, then turned and ran swiftly into a tall house, up the stairs. He reached the topmost floor, tried the door of the room which faced the open square. It was locked. Raising his foot, he crashed his heel against the lock and burst into the attic.

A man turned from the window where he had been crouching; he was raising his gun when the Italian stooped, gathered every ounce of energy, and propelled himself through the air, clutching the German and bringing him down with a crash to the floor.

It was over in a few seconds; a few grunts—animal-like in their sound—a groan or two, a long-drawn sigh, and a moment later the little Italian walked composedly down the stairs, wiping a knife on the leg of his baggy trousers. As he reached the doorway he heard Bladon and Patterson shouting as they ran, " No reprisals. Colonel's orders."

The Italian smiled, and walked into the shabby little hotel where Nino lay.

In the big kitchen, where oil-lamps had been lit, Nino had been laid on the big table. Soames was working, feeling, trying to assess the actual damage. From time to time Pietro heard his whispered questions to the man who lay on the table; each time he heard the low reply which came with such difficulty he shivered like a frightened dog. The smile had left his lips, tears were pouring down his cheeks, he muttered prayers mechanically.

Once Nino coughed, and Pietro saw blood which ran down his chin and stained his shirt scarlet. An orderly wiped his lips, and laid a clean towel over the stain.

Soames moved to where Oliver Hallam stood, motionless in the shadow.

" Well ? "

Soames shook his head. " I'm desperately sorry—not a chance. It's hit the spine and entered the left lung. He isn't suffering a great deal, sir."

Oliver turned his head from side to side as if he were trying to escape a blow. He saw the little soldier crouching against the wall, and went over to him.

" A priest," he said, in his halting Italian, " get a priest—

quickly. For your captain. Run quickly, there is no time to waste."

Pietro rose to his feet, wiped his tears away with the back of his hand, and ran away into the street. Oliver went back to the long table. He spoke softly to Soames. " I know his mother—he may have some message for her. Move away where you can't hear, d'you mind, and the orderly as well. Thanks."

The two men moved off into the shadows, Oliver bent down and spoke to his son.

How ghastly he looked ! His face seemed pinched and old and very tired.

Oliver whispered, " Nino—Nino—can you hear me ? "

The heavy eyes opened, the lips smiled faintly. " *Yes, caro-papa.*"

" You *know* ! "

" I suspected, *caro-papa*—that photograph, my mother's use of your name, your kindness. I am very happy about it. Please tell her when you go to Rome."

" My beloved boy—Nino, I love you so dearly. Get better, try, Nino, try ! "

The smile flickered again. " I would do anything for my Colonel—anything, but some things are impossible, *papa.*"

The priest had entered; silently he came to the table, followed by the Italian soldier. Gravely he motioned them to stand aside, and bending over the wounded man began to speak rapidly and softly. Oliver could not catch the words, nor would he have understood them if he had done. It was over, more whispered words, a sign given, then the Italian coming nearer and assisting the priest.

The soldier knelt, he was participating in whatever rite this was which they were enacting. A wave of jealously swept over Oliver Hallam. This was his son, he was dying, and while a scruffy little Italian soldier might take part, he, the father, was shut out.

It was over, again those signs, again softly spoken words; the priest motioned Oliver to come back to the table.

Nino said, " It's been a wonderful adventure. I wish that we had more time to talk. There's not much time. I wish to speak to Pietro."

The soldier stood sobbing noisily. Nino said, " Pietro, soldiers don't cry. Courage ! God bless you, good soldier—good mountaineer. *Papa*—tell my mother—and—you won't fail us, will you ? The Allies—no ? God bless you, *caro, caro-papa.*"

He struggled to rise himself, and cried in a singularly clear voice " *Viva Italia !* "

Soames sprang forward and pushed Oliver away, a few moments later he came and touched him on the arm; Oliver lifted his head and stared at the doctor, dazed and broken.

" It's over, sir. He didn't have any pain."

Heavily, Oliver walked across the room and stood looking down at his son. The face was completely peaceful, his well-cut features composed and tranquil.

He said, " Soames, let me know what arrangements you make, please." Then to Pietro, " When you've done all that is possible for your master, come immediately to me."

He walked out, stiffly, like an old man, into the quiet square.

v

Races, said, " A stinking business. I wish the old man would have let us do something about it. Poor old Dukie. What a bloody shame it is."

Patterson nodded. " Ay, tae have got this farr. But *someone* did do something aboot it. Seargeant Parrker reported that a Gairman wi' a knife in his throat was found lying in the top room o' the hoose fra which he imagines the shot was fired. He'd got a rifle lying close beside him."

Bladon said eagerly, " No. Murdered, eh ? "

" Ah should say—murdered undootedly."

" By whom ? "

" Gawd only knows, and He's varry unlikely tae tell onny-body."

Bladon sniffed suddenly, then turned the noise into a cough. When the spasm was over, he said, " Damn cough. I've got cold, I think. Makes your eyes water. Well, I'm jolly glad—the swine ! And Dukie of all people ! Have another drink, Pat ? I want one badly."

CHAPTER VII

I

THEY were sitting in the semi-oriental splendour of Danielli's—Oliver Hallam, Bladon, and Patterson. There was a continual coming and going of uniformed men and women, people on leave; people who were contriving to ' do a spot of swanning '; people who came and went about their lawful occasions.

Oliver said, " I'm off in the morning. I shall be in U.K. in about a fortnight, with any luck."

Bladon, watching him, thought. ' How old he looks. Not the same chap we used to know. His hair's gone so grey, his face looks grey, too. He's never been the same since poor Dukie went. That was a bad business—shook the old man badly.'

Oliver continued. " And you're taking over, Patterson. I'm glad of that, you'll give the chaps a square deal, and they respect you."

" I have always done my utmaist tae eairn that respect, sir," Patterson said heavily. " Ah believe fairmly that Races here has gained a greater quota of—shall we say ?—affection, but candidly I have more respect paid tae me."

Oliver looked from one to the other; he'd known them both for a long time now, back in the desert, through Sicily, over the Straits, and on to Rome. That was when Bladon's majority had come through. He remembered they had been drinking Alexanders when Bladon came in to announce that Nino had reported for duty. Nino Gradisco—both these men had liked him, had been his friends. They'd been at his funeral, that quiet little funeral outside Ferrara, standing with heavy, wooden-looking faces in that silence broken only by the voice of the priest and the loud uncontrolled sobbing of Marinoni.

Soames had been very good; he had come to Oliver—puzzled and slightly embarrassed.

" Some slight difficulty concerning the flag, sir. Italian or the ' Jack ', sir, which do you think ? "

" Both," Oliver said, " he'd like that—yes, both, if you please."

" It's unusual, sir."

" Yes, it's unusual, but that's what I wish, Soames."

" Very good, sir."

Now he was released, going home, leaving the Army and the men with whom he had fought and worked, to become a civilian again. Mussolini was dead, and the last remnants of the German Army in Italy had surrendered. It was over—so far as Italy was concerned; now would come that time to which Nino had looked forward so eagerly, the time for which he hoped and in which he had wanted to do so much. Hitler was reported dead, Berlin had surrendered to the Russian troops, Hamburg—what was left of it, at least—was in British hands.

Bladon had said, " All over bar the shouting ! "

And Oliver Hallam was going home. First to Rome to see Yolanda, to tell her what he had not dared to write in those difficult, painful letters which he had sent to her. Her replies had been stilted, and he felt held a quality of hopelessness. Once his interview with her was over he would leave for Naples—and his work was over.

" It's queer," he said, " how one has looked forward to release, and now how reluctant I am to go. It's as if the curtain was being rung down. I don't believe that I shall enjoy being a civilian very much, Pat."

" Enjoy ? " the Scotsman repeated. " Maybe no, life is not precisely packed wi' enjoyment, sir."

Oliver said, " No, probably not. By the way, I'm taking Marinoni back to Rome with me. He was on one of Gradisco's farms." How queer that the old caution still persisted, and how strange to speak of Nino by his surname. " He wants to get back and begin work. Poor little beggar."

" There'll be a number o' Italians wantin' tae get back tae their work in these days," Patterson said. " My Gawd, they've got something tae do tae get their country running again, puir deevils."

The rest seemed to pass like a flash, young men standing before him and saying, " Good-bye, sir " and " All the best, sir," young men he had known under all kinds of circumstances—in danger, during long hours of intense boredom, during stretches of acute discomfort, he had ' torn strips off them ', he had given them tempered and restrained commendation, and now they were coming in to bid him ' Good-bye '.

Driving back to Rome, he said to his driver, " Don't take the Futa, go by the Pistoia, it's a better road, I think," because he dared not go over the old ground over which he had come with Nino. In Florence he walked about, meeting men he knew, and thinking all the time, ' I'm old—I'm right to get out. I couldn't have hung on much longer.' Watching Rome come nearer and nearer, straining his eyes to catch sight of the dome of Saint Peter's, then clenching his hands tightly because Rome meant Yolanda, and the necessity to talk of Nino.

The Albergo Eden, not the Grand—the Grand where he had first met him, talked to him, where Nino had noticed his ring and commented upon it. He didn't want to go back to the Grand, anyway ; they had told him that now it was strictly reserved for very exalted officers, and, after all, he was only a ' half colonel '.

Driving that evening to see Yolanda. The old courtyard, the quiet, the lovely scent of spring drifting in from the Gardens, and the familiar face of old Tomaso. " The Duchessa was waiting in the small *salon* to meet the Colonel," Tomaso said.

She rose as he entered ; the black clothes which she wore intensified the delicate pallor of her skin ; she held out her hands

and said, " My dear Oliver," then leaned forward and kissed him—
formally on either cheek.

He sat beside her on the wide sofa, as they had sat so often.
She held herself very erect, but her face was grave, there were
new lines at the corners of her mouth, her eyes looked heavy and
tired.

" You come back alone," she said, and sighed.

" Except that I brought back Pietro Marinoni, his batman."

She said, " Your letters told me so little. Can you bear to talk
to me, to tell me—everything ? "

" Yes, I think so. If I go slowly, forgive me. It," he smiled
unhappily, " hurts rather badly. As if there were a pain—here."
He touched his tunic above his heart.

" I understand, Oliver."

Very carefully, without imagination or chosen phrases, he
told her the whole story; using plain words and plain methods of
expression. He traced their advance step by step to Ferrara, and
came to the moment when the shot had rung out, and Nino had
fallen. He heard his voice shake, felt her hand laid on his firmly
and kindly, her voice said gently, " Wait a moment, my dear,
wait a moment."

He answered almost irritably, " I'm all right, let me go on,"
and ended his story.

Yolanda said, " And so he knew—it doesn't surprise me. He
was an intuitive person, our son. And now you go back to
England, eh ? "

Oliver nodded, " Yes, back to be a civilian."

She said, " I am going to Livorno. He loved those farms of his,
the people, there will be a great deal to be done. That was the work
he had planned to do, and I must go and do it for him since he is
not here to carry out all he wished to do. We shan't meet again,"
she continued, " it is all over and done with. Years ago, when
we were both young we found each other; again, when we were
older—perhaps wiser—we met again. We had—Nino. Now there
is no reason for us to meet again."

" But, Yolanda, I should like to know that you were well, that
you were happy, that . . ."

She smiled. " You're being conventional, my dear. In a year
I shall have begun to fade from your memory, in a few years I
shall be a vague memory. How often did you think of me in the
years which followed the last war—Nostra Guerra ? Not very
often, my dear—be honest. Good-bye, Oliver, and I thank you
for all you did, for your kindness and understanding. He never
failed in his letters to write of you with such admiration, and later
—although he never admitted anything—with deep love. You
must go. I am not able to talk very much, I am always so tired,
and if we talked, what should we have to say that was not bitterness and regret ? One war brought us together, the second did the
same—and parted us finally." Then, speaking in a level conventional voice, she asked, " Your sons ? They are safe ? "

" Yes, both of them—and my son-in-law."

" I'm glad." She was making a move to rise, he felt that he was dismissed.

" You'd like me to go ? " he asked.

When she answered, there was a note of appeal in her tone. " Oliver, it's so much better that you should. It's all over—over—over. Have all the happiness that you can find in this wretched, devastated world. God bless you, and keep you always."

He took her hand, as he had done the first time he met her in Rome, and raised it to his lips.

" Good-bye, and if you ever need me, I want you to send for me."

II

The train carried him to the Midlands. At Birmingham his father's car was waiting to take him back to ' Croxtons '. Kitty was home again, and waiting there for him. Oliver leaned back, and watched the landscape with eyes that saw nothing. He was terribly tired, he felt that the very weight of his clothes was too much for him to carry. He kept repeating, ' I'm old, too old. I ought to be buried there outside Ferrara.'

Not even the thought of Kitty, of seeing his children, his home, stirred him. Everything was removed and unreal; he was seeing everything through a kind of sad-coloured mist. He had no particular desire to go home, neither did he wish to find himself in any other place; what did it matter, places were mostly the same. Some were hotter or colder, cleaner or more dirty, more or less comfortable.

The car turned into the short drive, he told the chauffeur to stop, saying, " I'll walk up; take my baggage round to the back, will you ? Cook will give you tea. Thanks."

He opened the hall door, mechanically hung up his cap and slid his stick into the stand, then turned and entered the drawing-room. There were the same well-laundered but rather faded chintz-covered chairs, the water-colours in their narrow gilt frames. Kitty was reading; she turned and sprang to her feet, crying, " Oliver, Oliver, you're home ! "

She was in his arms, her hands stroking his hair, her blue eyes scanning his face, while she whispered, " My darling, what have they done to you ? Your grey hair—these lines—oh, Oliver, you never told me that——"

He said, " That I'd grown so old."

" No, no," she protested, " not old—tired, my poor one, you need rest and quiet. Come and sit down here. What shall it be ? Tea or a "—she smiled—" a ' man's drink ' ? Oh, I have some ready for you ! "

He sat down, and felt that he never wanted to move again; she brought him his drink, lit a cigarette for him, and all the time watched him with a kind of agonized intensity. Was this man with the grey hair, the brown face which still contrived to look grey, with the deep lines graven at each side of his mouth and his heavy, miserable-looking eyes, really her husband? Even his voice—the voice she had loved so dearly—had become harsh and constrained; he spoke in short, clipped sentences as if he wished to say all that he had to say as quickly as possible.

" Are the children at home? "

" Clive is stationed near Maidstone; Clifford's in India—I told you—and Barbara's with her husband and the baby near Edinburgh. I'm all alone at the moment." She laughed. " I've much to tell you, I scarcely know where or how to begin ! "

He said, " If you can bear to listen, I want to talk to you. It won't be easy. The sooner I get it over the better. May I have another drink, or is it too short? "

" Too short? I've been hoarding it ever since I knew that you were coming home—and your father has been very generous, too. There ! Now, what is it, darling? You're sure that you're not too tired? "

" I *am* tired. That's got nothing to do with it. I want to talk to you. First, I've got to go back over—what's over and done with. You remember when you came to see me in Devon, and what you told me? I behaved badly, Kitty, and I know it. I didn't realize that I could have such a flaming devil of jealousy in me. That jealousy blotted out everything else. My sense of justice, of right, of ordinary decency. I ask your pardon, ask it very humbly and sincerely. Please forgive me."

" I have, Oliver, years ago."

" Now, this is the story I want to tell you. During the last war . . ." His tired voice, enunciating those short, clipped sentences, continued. He told his story without regret, without tenderness, without beauty. It was an unvarnished, plain story which he told her, neither offering excuses nor asking for sympathy.

Kitty Hallam sat very still, listening gravely; he never asked for comment, and she did not attempt to make any. He went on to tell her of his meeting in Rome with Gradisco—and Yolanda.

Then she said, speaking scarcely above a whisper, " And he is your son? "

Oliver's heavy eyes met hers. " He *was* my son," he said. " He's dead." The story continued. How much he remembered. Small trivial things, all concerning Nino—never did Oliver use superlatives, rather it seemed that he purposely chose the most ordinary, matter-of-fact words and expressions. He ended with the story of what happened at Ferrara, and of his last meeting with Yolanda. Then, for the first time, he quoted the words which had been spoken between them, told the story of their good-bye.

He ended and sat with his hands hanging listlessly between his knees. " That's all," he said, " that's the story."

She got up and came over to him, then dropped on her knees beside his chair, and taking his hands, held them gently.

" My poor Oliver," she said softly, " oh, my dear. I wish that I could help you."

He turned his haggard face and stared at her. " You mean that you can—forgive me, Kitty? "

" Forgive you ! Oliver, perhaps it is easier for a woman to forgive. I don't know ! We've talked of this so often, but I've always meant it—before you ever knew me, before you dreamed that I existed—how can I blame you for what happened then ? I can't. I don't want to. Never talk to me about *forgiving* you, only let me help if I can. Your tired face, your eyes—they cut me to the heart, darling.

" And that poor boy—you mustn't try to forget him, to shut him out. Perhaps one day you will be able to talk to me about him, to tell me little details so that we can both make a lasting, enduring picture of him. That's only fair to him. He talked to you about—rebuilding, making everything grow, giving the new world a good start. We've got our own worlds, my dear—you and I have a small and very precious one of our own, we've got to rebuild, to plan and work. Are you sufficiently strong to work, Oliver dear—with me ? Sufficiently strong and determined to not look back but resolutely to look forward ? "

He brushed his hand across his eyes, when he spoke his voice was husky, but some of the harshness had gone from it.

" I'm not very proud of myself, Kitty. There were moments when I felt that I could have so easily fallen in love with her again. . . ."

She smiled. " Dearest, for about ten minutes I imagined that I might conceivably fall in love with a very kindly, stout Yorkshire-man! "

" What's happened to him ? " Oliver asked quickly.

She replied with overdone gravity, " He is going to be married next month to a young—well, not so very young—woman called Gwendoline Mary Hunter Price who breeds Angora rabbits and plans rock gardens."

He sighed. " You think that we can get everything all right, Kitty ? "

She answered firmly, " Darling, everything *is* all right—so far as we are concerned. Oliver, the past was dreadful, nightmarish, the present isn't very bright, but—the future can be something very good. That is *ours*. Let's rebuild—on a wonderful foundation, build something very good, sound, lasting—and real."

His smile did not hold any mirth. " You sound so hopeful, my dear."

" Hopeful ! " She threw scorn into her voice. " Hopeful ! No, rather say confident ! Smile, Oliver—not that sad, twisted smile. Darling, you're ten years younger than when you came into this room. Yes, you shall even have a third—yes, a *third*—whisky-and-soda. This is a celebration. The laying of the foundation of our small piece of the New World. Drink a toast ! "

He raised his glass and, smiling at her, said, " To the New World—everywhere."

THE END

Sirmione,
  Prov. d. Brescia, Italia.
April 1947.